and it will be a beautiful life

and it will be a beautiful life

CRAIG LANCASTER

THE
STORY
PLANT

The Story Plant
Studio Digital CT, LLC
P.O. Box 4331
Stamford, CT 06907

Story Plant hardcover ISBN-13: 978-1-61188-299-5
Fiction Studio Books e-book ISBN-13: 978-1-945839-50-4

Visit our website at www.TheStoryPlant.com

First Story Plant Printing: May 2021

Printed in the United States of America

0 9 8 7 6 5 4 3 2 1

For Bob Kimpton

THE PRINCIPLE OF CONSERVATION OF LINEAR MOMENTUM

The linear momentum of a system has constant magnitude and direction if the system is subjected to no external force.

On the other hand...

MINNEAPOLIS/ST. PAUL INTERNATIONAL AIRPORT

Thursday, March 7, 2019 | 8:17 p.m.
748 miles from home

In a practiced motion he slipped halfway into his coat, then slid the backpack strap onto his right shoulder behind it. He wrenched himself and dangled his left hand back, trying to catch the loose sleeve, and he clipped the head of the man from 6B, who was sitting in his seat and placidly awaiting the jumbled exit.

"Sorry," Max said.

Pursed lips and no reply from 6B. Max set his backpack down in his own seat, 6C, across the aisle, shed the coat, and tried again, this time with more precision and control. He hooked the left sleeve and finally shimmied the coat fully onto his shoulders, then he brought the backpack up again.

"I never understand the hurry," 6B side-mouthed to 6A. "We're all going to get off in due time."

6A, a woman about 6B's age, Max figured, similarly neat in dress and taciturn in manner, gripped his hand without a look up.

"There's no need to race everyone," 6B groused on.

"Some people like to stand," 6A said. She glanced at Max and offered a fractional smile, one he couldn't quite interpret. *Don't mind my grumpy husband*, maybe? Or, *you clumsy oaf*. That was the greater possibility.

Max swallowed hard. "It's just that I have a tight connection."

6B looked at him with merciless erosion. "I wasn't speaking to you." The final syllable drew out, mocking and disdainful.

"OK," Max said. Another quarter-way smile from 6A, then forward movement began up ahead, followed by the murmur of insincere goodbyes from the flight crew.

Max took half a step back, crowding 7C and clearing the space between the seats. "After you," he said to 6B and 6A. They shuffled into the aisle, collected their things from the floor and the overhead bin, and walked toward the door. Max hung back a couple of steps.

"Thanks for the lift," he said to the captain as he exited, the same words, the same flat delivery as several hundred times before. The flight attendant smiled, the same as ever. Max hucked the backpack higher on his shoulders, ducked his head, and stepped into the jet bridge.

He merged with the stampeding humanity of the F concourse at 8:23 by his atomically precise watch, and though he dutifully put one foot in front of the other, dropping heavy steps toward the gate at the end of C, he knew there was little point to it all. The words he hadn't wanted to see—"on time"—had stared back at him from the departure board, and he knew there was no way to bridge the distance before Flight 859, the last plane home for the night, pushed back from the gate and headed for Billings without him.

Still, he trudged on, past gift shops and fast-food offerings, past mothers pushing strollers holding conked-out children, against the flow of business travelers and students, to the end of the F concourse, left turn, under the mezzanine, a veer away from the signs pointing to baggage claim, a right turn at the C concourse, all the way down, past the art gallery, onward, ever onward.

On the people mover, he thought of a treadmill, then ricocheted off to a memory of his seventeenth year, Billings Senior High, the quarter-miles he could toss off when he was a young man of remarkable want-to if not quite elite speed. In those days, he could cover the distance in 50.12 seconds. Assuming constant speed—a faulty assumption—that's a three-minute, twenty-second mile. In an hour, 17.96 miles. In twenty-four hours, 431.04 miles. It can't be done, of course. Not by the human machine. Even if it could, he would be left well short of Billings.

Gate C27, now emptied out, came into view. If he were suddenly in possession of his youthful gait, could he have made it by dashing through the nighttime terminal like the Hertz commercial O.J. Simpson of his memories, before the Juice became known for other ways of running? Probably not. He knew the speed but not the distance or the time of flow. Would have been fun to try, though, in another life.

"It's gone, I guess," Max said to the gate agent.

"About to be." The agent, maybe Alexandra's age, tilted her head toward the window. The jet bridge was pulling back from the plane.

"No chance you'd..."

"I'm sorry," she said.

"Yeah."

"They'll be happy to rebook you at customer service."

"I know the drill. Thanks."

"I'm sorry for the inconvenience, sir."

"Me, too."

Sorry didn't begin to cover the half of it. The whole thing, right down the line, had been a series of misses that had taken Max increasingly afield from the promises he had made. First had been the standby day in Wisconsin while the eggheads back in Germany scrutinized the tool data remotely. He had pushed his come-home flight back a day when that happened, a two-hundred-dollar charge that wouldn't cause even a blink in accounting when his expense report went in. Then the hour-long shutdown in Indiana, six miles from the end of the run. That had wiped out his margin of error. The hour and fifteen minutes on the tarmac at Midway as the airline mechanics replaced a cockpit panel. That was the setback that had pushed him into the red. The distance between the gates in Minneapolis had finally torn his plans for good.

On the other end of the call, Janine wanted none of it.

"I knew," she said. "Of course you wouldn't be back."

"I couldn't do anything about it."

A sigh across the miles. "You never can."

"It was just bad luck."

"I said, 'You going to be home Thursday?' You said, 'Oh, yeah, no problem.'"

"I didn't know this—"

"Just stop."

He stopped. Silence wedged between them, wiping clear the rest of what he might have said in his own defense.

"This is important to me," she said, emotion edging into her voice.

"To me, too."

"No."

"It is."

"It's not, or you'd be here."

"I couldn't."

"And there you are. You just had to take the late plane, and now—"

"I didn't have a choice."

"Yes, you did. And you made it."

"I'll be there by lunch," he said brightly, as if some cheerfulness he pulled out of the ether or some other nether region could right this skidding thing. "Maybe we could—"

"Alexandra and I are going to brunch after the thing. To celebrate."

"I should be there."

"*Alex* and I are going to brunch."

"OK. I'll wait at home."

Max lingered in front of the vending machines, considering his options. The airline rep had come by with an overnight kit—a floor mat, a blanket, a tube of toothpaste and a miniature brush, some wet wipes. "Thanks for flying Delta," he had said. Max had built himself a bivouac at Gate G5—another long walk after the rebooking and before the *contretemps* with Janine—and was now procuring the provisions that would carry him to the other side of the night.

A swipe of the card, buttons punched, and a bag of cookies preserved into crispy permanence dropped from their perch. Max pushed back the door and collected them.

He moved one machine to his left, swiped again, and punched in the code for a Diet Coke. A mechanical arm with a big receptacle moved up and over, collected the bottle, and deposited it in the holding chute. A cylindrical door opened, and Max grabbed the drink.

"That stuff will kill you."

Max turned around. Jogging Suit Man, who had also made camp at G5, smiled and pointed at the soda. "Chemicals. So-called essential oils. Artificial sweeteners. Caffeine."

Max shrugged. "Not going to be able to sleep anyway. I'm not worried about the caffeine."

"I used to drink that stuff. A two-liter bottle a day, at least."

"Yeah?"

"Now, straight-up water. At least a hundred and twenty ounces daily. Usually more."

Max thought of Niagara Falls. And then he thought of urinals into infinity. And then he thought of the sublime freedom of peeing outdoors, perhaps discreetly covered by an open door on his rental car but otherwise whizzing into the weeds, as nature intended.

"Interesting," Max said.

"I started running," Jogging Suit Man said. "Sixty-nine years old, can do a nine-minute mile. Running and a morning swim in the ocean. Can't beat it."

"I can run faster than that."

"Oh?"

Max's hands went to his ample midsection to cover the lie. "Could."

"Ah."

Jogging Suit Man, like Seat 6A, regarded him with a smile that couldn't be deciphered.

"OK, then," Max said.

"OK," Jogging Suit Man said. "But that stuff will kill you."

Max looked at the bottle in his hand, then back at Jogging Suit Man. "When?" he asked.

MINNEAPOLIS/ST. PAUL INTERNATIONAL AIRPORT

Friday, March 8 | 4:03 a.m.
Six hours and fifty-nine minutes from home

Jogging Suit Man, ruddy of cheek and wet of hair, settled into his makeshift camp next to Max's. He had come from the men's restroom across the concourse, so Max couldn't be sure whether the drenching was from the faucet there or from the laps he had run through the quiet airport. Max had logged seven of those once he realized they were happening. The times had been a scattershot across the clock; on one lap, Jogging Suit Man would be unseen for eight minutes and twenty-nine seconds, on the next for four minutes and three seconds, and so on. The inconsistency had gnawed at Max.

"Now I won't have to work out once we get to Billings," Jogging Suit Man said after he sat down and gently blotted the excess water from his head. "Fortuitous."

Max, sitting on his own mat, looked around at the clumps of stranded travelers, all either snoozing (*how?*) or otherwise uninterested in him and his impromptu bunkmate.

"I timed you," Max said, surprising himself with the revelation.

"Oh?"

"Nine-minute mile," Max scrambled. "Was trying to figure out how far you went, that's all. A hobby of mine."

"Timing people, or math?" Jogging Suit Man's smile left no room for interpretation. Bemused.

"Math." Max looked down, fixating on the carpet.

"I definitely wasn't on that kind of pace. Just needed to move," Jogging Suit Man said. With precise hands, he folded the thin airline blanket into a perfect square and set it down.

"I figured. The lap times were all jumbled."

"Well, I stopped a couple of times and looked at the art. There are some fine Cuban works over there, in an airport of all places. Do you like art?"

"It's OK," Max said.

"That's precisely what Baudelaire said."

Max went flush at the gentle mockery and hoped it didn't show. He couldn't rightly say whether he liked this guy—he suspected he probably didn't—but he was fascinated nonetheless.

"I read," Max said, patting the Craig Johnson paperback at his knee. *Seventy-six books last year, Baudelaire.*

"Reading's fine, yes, indeed," Jogging Suit Man said. "You can't get far in this life without reading. But you know what they say about a picture."

"Sure."

"What I mean is, I look at a painting—let's say *Saco Bay*, by Homer—and—"

"I'm not familiar."

"You really must rectify that. But the point I'm making is, here's this painting of two women, sunset, silhouette, the sky this color that's all at once familiar and unlike anything I've ever seen on this earth, and I feel like if I could just step close enough—"

"You could be in there with them?"

Jogging Suit Man, for the first time, looked as if he had been knocked conversationally off his stride. "Yes," he said. "Yes, that's it."

"I understand," Max said.

"There's an aliveness in it. Being moved by art tells you that you are alive."

"I guess."

Jogging Suit Man held Max in gaze for a few uncomfortable moments, grinning as if Max were a lifelong knucklehead buddy. Max shrugged and then fortified his response. "I get what you're saying. I just don't look at a lot of art, I guess."

Jogging Suit man nodded and continued prepping his staked-out area. "I'm from that country," he said.

"What country?" Max asked.

"Maine. Saco Bay. Biddeford, really, but it's close enough."

"I've never been."

Behind them, on the other side of the row of low-slung seats, a sleeping traveler farted, grumbled, flopped over, and returned to slumber. The uninvited cloud wafted into their space. Max and Jogging Suit Man covered their noses and mouths with upheld hands, and Jogging Suit Man began coughing, a little at first and then rapidly, until at last he smothered it. He looked at Max and shrugged, and they both giggled.

"You OK?" Max asked.

"Just gassed. Literally and...well, literally."

Jogging Suit Man uncovered, venturing a test of the air quality. With both hands, he swept back his silver hair. "That man ought to change his diet," he said.

Max felt around on his right side, opposite Jogging Suit Man, and pushed his half-eaten bag of cookies into the recesses of his campsite. "Yeah."

"Maine is the best place on earth," Jogging Suit Man said.

"I've heard good things. I like Montana."

"What's not to like?"

Max thought the question rhetorical, so he clamped down on a powerful urge to answer, which, he feared, could turn into a ceaseless ramble through the many things and people and situations in Montana that weren't to like but that, yeah, the place itself was just dandy.

"It'll be good to get home," Max said now, a lie tangential to the discussion at hand.

"Were you on a work trip?" Jogging Suit Man said.

"Yeah."

"Best left to young fellows like you. What do you do?"

"Pipeline inspection," Max said, surprised that a simplified version of the truth had popped out of his mouth. These past few years, to amuse himself during inevitable conversations initiated by fellow travelers, he had been fudging the details of his employment, passing himself off as a plumber or an electrician or a basketball coach—anything, really, where he had a bit of operational knowledge and at least a mild interest. The one time he had gone too far, co-opting Alexandra's job as the president of the Montana Regional Multiple Listing Service, he had stupidly ignored two things. First, that there's in-flight WiFi and such declarations can be verified, and second, that there was a chance (one hundred percent, in that case) that his seatmate would be a real estate agent. It had been a long flight.

Jogging Suit Man's interest seemed piqued. "Petroleum or natural gas?" he asked.

"Petroleum, mostly."

"Are you actually inspecting the welds as they put the pipe in, or does your work concern right-of-way issues, or—"

"No, nothing like that. I track tools through the line."

"Pigs," Jogging Suit Man said knowingly.

"That's what they call them, yeah." Max usually had to explain the term, which is why he defaulted to the more accessible nomenclature with people outside the business. P-I-G—pipeline inspection gauge. Also, the damn things often squealed going down the line. *Pig tracker or pipeline inspector, which job title would you put on a business card?*

"That certainly explains the interest in my rate of speed. I'd say it's a bit more than a hobby, wouldn't you?" Jogging Suit Man didn't wait for Max to answer. "What were you running, a cleaner?"

"Not this time. Diagnostic."

"A crack tool?" The well-informed staccato call and response Jogging Suit Man was engaging in caused Max to wonder if he was dealing here with an oil man. He had heard that some of them tended to retire to Maine for the coastal lifestyle and the open space.

"Yeah, a crack tool," Max said. "You in the business?"

Jogging Suit Man laughed, big and hearty.

"No. It's just that I read, too."

"About fluid dynamics?"

"About whatever."

Jogging Suit Man set his folded blanket upon an airline pillow that Max surmised had been swiped from first class. He stretched out on his side and set his head down, then sat up again. He offered a right hand across the distance to Max.

"Charles Foster Danforth, retired pediatrician."

Max clasped the hand with a well-exercised grip. "Max Wendt, pig tracker."

PARKHILL DRIVE, BILLINGS, MONTANA

Friday, March 8
748 air miles | One hour, forty-seven minutes | 419.439 mph average
3.8 road miles | Nine minutes, twenty-eight seconds | 23.668 mph

Max noticed two things after breaching the front door. First, Janine's Billings Realtor of the Year Award—the flashpoint of her justified anger and perhaps even injury at his tardiness—sat on the entryway table, turned toward the door. Second, its presence confirmed that Janine, and maybe Alexandra, had come to the house after the award was given, placed the plaque there in all its accusatory glory, and left for a brunch where he wouldn't be welcome.

He found himself again swimming through a lack of clarity about Janine's attitude and intentions toward him. She usually wasn't unpleasant. She rarely was unkind. In fact, Max often thought her responses to stimuli were almost too perfectly in proportion. If he kissed her, she kissed him back. If he spoke to her, she partook of the conversation. If he retreated into silence, she left him alone until he was ready to speak again. He knew he had no room to complain about any of it, but that knowledge didn't leaven his sense that she regarded him essentially as just another accumulation of a long marriage. Furniture, in other words, although Max quickly reminded himself that the living-room sectional had never been so unreliable as to get on a plane and disappear for a week.

Max rolled his two clamshell suitcases, one filled with his gear and the other with his soiled clothes, through the narrow entryway and into the living room proper. He then knelt gingerly, careful to keep his bad left knee airborne and his good right one planted, leaning into the hall table for balance, and he examined the plaque. It was the standard bauble, equally suitable for volunteer appreciation awards and youth sports participation trophies, with *faux* dark wood backing and a handsomely engraved silver plate:

2019 Billings Realtor of the Year
Janine Garwood

Max would have liked to say he had long since assimilated Janine's decision to use her maiden name out in the professional world, that he could understand her desire to use her own credentials as she built, with Alexandra's help, a formidable realty and property management business. Max would also have liked to say he had been homecoming king back in '81, but that wasn't true, either.

So, he now wondered, had Janine come home with the dark intent of setting this award precisely where he would see it before he saw anything else, so any sense of guilt he might harbor about his absence that morning could be inflamed before he even unpacked? He hadn't known her to be that cunning. He shook his head. *It's not fair to put that on her. She came home and set it here, a place of honor. That's it.*

At the entry to the living room, he escorted his suitcases to the left, down the main hallway, to the second door on the right, and into what he had staked out as his office. It wasn't much. A couple of standup particle-board bookshelves from Target, filled with the contemporary western-set novels he loved, by Johnson and Box and Burke and McCafferty and Florio and Wheeler and Harrison (Jamie, the daughter; he had always found the old man inscrutable), a small closet filled with seasonal-appropriate fire-resistant clothing, boots, and other gear, a corner desk holding an ancient MacBook and a scattering of mail Janine had dropped there in his absence. Finally, there was the undressed queen mattress and box springs atop a cheapo bedframe from Costco, where his suitcases lived when they weren't in transit, always open, either waiting to be filled or in the process of being emptied.

Max set the suitcases parallel on the bed, unzipped each and flipped the top compartments open simultaneously. Always, he worked from left to right, taking inventory of the equipment first, as he would have to scramble if anything had been left behind or gone missing, then finishing with the pile of clothes.

First, he pulled his wallet from his right front jeans pocket and from that extracted a laminated yellow card. One by one, he checked the list he had printed there against the items organized in the suitcase:

- Wireless receiver and Bluetooth antenna
- Cab sound control unit and cables
- Wireless geophone
- Headphones
- Pipe locator
- Seasonal work gloves
- Collapsible traffic cones (2)
- Plug-in GPS drive
- Three-way power converter
- Car-top strobe
- First-aid kit
- Duct tape
- Batteries (Cs, AAs, and AAAs)
- Cellphone signal booster
- Safety glasses
- Hearing protection
- Small sledgehammer
- Strap-on headlamp
- Tape measure
- Gas monitor and charger

- Rubber gloves
- Gallon-size freezer bags
- Assorted screwdrivers and wrenches
- Hard hat
- Binoculars
- Heavy-duty absorbent cloths

The common hand tools and the batteries tended to be the most frequent casualties of Max's travels, being instantly recognizable and of interest to light-fingered baggage inspectors. The pricier equipment got left alone, because (a) it wasn't explosive (the suspicion of which, on X-ray, was the reason his stuff always got opened) and (b) most people didn't know what the hell it was for. Max thought it vulgar that these unseen people between his check-in and the loading of the plane could both let him know they'd been through his goods—there was always a tell-tale TSA we-examined-your-things flyer in his case when he reached his destination—and blithely steal from him. His frequent letters to the feds had, as yet, prompted neither a response nor recompense. For that reason, he was pleased to see that everything he took to Chicago had also made it home. He tucked his checklist back where it belonged. He left the suitcase open, as he would repeat the inventory before leaving again.

Max now sidestepped to his right and started in on the clothes. He had learned long ago to pack two more of everything than he would need by the schedule, because days out on the line tended to slide in unexpected ways—a perfect example being the lost day in Wisconsin while the engineers fiddled with the tool and Max relaxed—that is, intermittently jacked off and slept—back at the hotel.

First, he removed and folded the unused extra clothing—a pair of Carhartt fire-resistant jeans, green-and-blue plaid boxers, heavy-duty Smartwool socks, and a black, long-sleeve, moisture-wicking fire-resistant shirt. Everything except the boxers would go in his office closet.

Next, he made three piles of dirty laundry on the floor: underwear and socks, off-duty jeans and shirts, on-duty fire-resistant clothing. These, he would carry to the basement and begin cycling through the wash. There had been a time, when Alexandra was a little girl, that

Janine had quietly herded his laundry after a work trip, not out of a fealty to traditional gender roles but because she found it easier to integrate him into her own household system than to expect him to figure out how it worked. That time was far in the past, like so many others that existed only as scar tissue. For all he knew now, Janine sent her laundry out, or had her assistant do it. And it had been years earlier that Alexandra's had moved off with her to college and then to her waiting, larger life, never to return.

Max stuffed each of the piles into its own drawstring bag, pulled the openings tight, and toted the bags back down the hall, through the living room, into the kitchen, and down into the basement. At the foot of the stairs, he flipped a switch, casting the territory Janine had annexed for *her* office in a soft light.

Max had always loved the walkout basement, considering it one of the prime features when they'd bought the house in '86, not quite a year into their marriage. Pull the blinds back from the double sliding glass doors and there was a view to the in-ground pool they'd installed in '97, making theirs the cool house for Alexandra and her friends. That had pretty much been the decisive factor in getting it, the desire to keep their girl close throughout her adolescence. That it didn't work was beside the point; not many things do. The pool didn't get much use anymore—and certainly not now, in early March—but every summer day that Max did the mowing and then soaked himself redeemed the effort and expense of maintaining it. And it gave Janine a nice view when she was down here plotting her block-by-block takeover of the Billings real estate market.

Her ascendant middle-age career, in fact, had been the wedge that had turned the basement from a TV-and-billiards room into a well-appointed office with leather furniture, a huge oak desk, and classical prints where family photo collages used to hang.

"I need a place where I can spread out," Janine had said. "You know, a place where I can occasionally bring clients or host staff parties."

"What about me watching games with the guys?" Max had countered.

"When was the last time you did that?"

He couldn't conjure an answer. And thus ended another negotiation in her favor.

In the laundry room, Max shook the contents of the socks-and-underwear bag into the washer, put in a color catcher, measured the detergent, and keyed the permanent-press setting into the machine. As the tub filled and began churning, he realized that he was in second-day clothes that were well past the point of ripeness. Standing there on the cold concrete floor, he stripped, button-front shirt off, khakis off, white tube socks off, paisley boxers off. He then felt through the pockets of his doffed pants to intercept any forgotten items, wishing to avoid his twice-annual wallet washing.

From the left front pocket, he pulled the business card Jogging Suit Man—Charles *Foster* Danforth—had given him at the baggage claim that morning. He had already forgotten.

"I'm here doing a CPR class for the American Heart Association," Danforth had said. "My little post-retirement contribution to the betterment of the world."

"Two-inch-deep compressions," Max had replied.

"You're familiar, then?"

"Have to renew my certification next year."

"Maybe I'll be back for that next year and teach you a thing or two."

"Maybe."

"Max," Danforth had said, "I'll be done around seven tonight, if you want to get together for a beer."

Max hadn't known what to make of the proposition. He had figured Danforth for someone unrestrained around others, overly talkative, maybe even a bit lonely. He had watched, amused, on the Minneapolis-to-Billings flight as Danforth, up in 2B, had talked himself blue to 2A while Max dealt with a case of the jimmylegs in 7C. Was this a come-on? Max hadn't gotten that vibe, but he also had never been particularly good at recognizing one, conventional or otherwise.

"I can't."

"Well," Danforth had said, "take my card anyway. I'd like to hear from you from time to time, Max Wendt. I want to hear about your travels and adventures chasing that underground porcine temptress."

Flummoxed, Max had accepted the offering, if not the further invitation. "What for?"

"Call it geriatric inquisitiveness."

"Huh?"

"I'm old and I'm curious about things."

"OK."

"Funny old fella," Max said now, popping the card twice across his left palm.

The washing machine was going full-bore, gurgling and thumping as it tossed his goods in the froth. Max took note of the time remaining, then looked at his atomic watch, precise to the hundredth of a second, the only article left on his body, and he calculated his return to push the next load.

Up the stairs he went, carrying Danforth's card in his right hand in the absence of a pocket. Unexpectedly, he felt good, even playful. It was joy, as if a dose of sugar had hitched a ride on his blood. He opened the door separating the basement stairs from the kitchen, stepped onto the landing, pivoted, and attempted a Michael Jackson moonwalk across the laminate floor.

"Max!"

He spun a quarter-turn to his right, his dingus following through like a flattened-out golf swing. There, in the living room, dropped the jaws of his wife, her twenty-four-year-old assistant Kara, and his beloved daughter, the light of his life and the holder of his heart.

"Oh, Dad," Alexandra said. "Really? Come on."

PARKHILL DRIVE, BILLINGS, MONTANA

Friday, March 8 | 9:57 p.m.

*According to a researcher at Cal Tech, ejaculate, upon launch, travels
at an average rate of 27.96 mph (over an exceedingly short distance).*
· *In three minutes and forty-four seconds of diligent effort, Max Wendt
was unable to produce a specimen that could confirm this.*

Janine lay on her back, propped up by pillows, a stack of marketing
materials at the ready. She reached out for Max's hand, found it, and
gave it a quick squeeze and a quicker release. When he had rolled off
her, whispering "I'm sorry," she had wordlessly left the bed, dressed
herself, gathered her nightly market studies and new listings and
returned.

"I'm sorry," he said.

"Stop apologizing."

"I'm sorry." A sigh now from Janine, light enough to be neutral and heavy enough to let Max know her patience was a perishable commodity.

"It's just—" he started, then stopped.

"Mmm hmm." Janine plucked a paper from her stack.

"It's just that I thought of, you know, today."

"Today in the kitchen, you mean?"

"Well, yeah."

"Well," Janine said, a chuckle scratching at her throat, "that'd do it."

"I'm sorry."

"Max."

"And, again, I'm really sorry about missing the thing this morning."

"I know. Let's leave it be."

"No, it's not OK." He sat up, voice elevated, and set a hand on her shoulder. "It's a big thing for you, and I missed it. I need to do better, maybe even not take a job that might conflict with something big like that."

That rang some sort of bell for Janine, who set her work down and made a quarter-turn in bed to face him. "Really? Skip a job? You'd do that?" She had been pressing this issue for at least a year, once it had become obvious that, between her growing real estate business and the rentals she and Alexandra were buying and managing, there was more than enough income for Max to come off the road for good. *But what then*, he wondered. *Golf? Pinochle, whatever that was?*

"Well, no, probably not, but—"

"Max, leave me alone."

"I'm really, really sorry, OK? I wanted to be there. If the damn job had gone the way it was scheduled, I would have been."

"Oh, Max." The exasperation nearly got to her. She clammed up, let the wave pass her by, and approached him now with the calm dispassion that almost always left him feeling worse than he would if she just hauled off and blasted him. "Look, it's not the award, OK? These things aren't a meritocracy. I didn't get it because I'm the best or the brightest. I got it because somebody realized I hadn't gotten it before, and next year, regardless of how many houses I sell, somebody else will get it. It's just that the whole thing was validation from people I respect, people who are striving for the same thing I'm striving for, and it would have been nice to have my husband there." Max couldn't be sure, because she was looking at her hands and not at him, but he thought maybe Janine was trying to keep her eyes from spilling. His heart rumbaed.

"I'm sorry."

"Stop saying that."

"I'm sorry."

Janine scooped up her things and left the bed again. "I'm going downstairs to work."

Max checked his watch. "It's almost 10:30."

"You're probably tired, then," Janine said.

"Aren't you?"

"Not really," she said. "A lot to do. Sleep tight."

In the darkened bedroom, Max replayed the day through the lens of recall. There hadn't been much to say about his impromptu floor show; upon being discovered, he had crouched low behind the kitchen island while Janine kept saying "Max!" and Alexandra had come apart giggling and Kara, her face flushed from pink to vermillion, had turned away.

"Turn around and let me get past you," he had said, and despite Janine's repeated "Max!" and "Oh, my god," the three of them had finally faced the wall, quivering, giggling, and Max had dashed through, up the stairs, his fat ass bouncing, and into the closed-off sanctuary of the bedroom. While he had dressed, preparing to come down and apologize shamefully, Janine had called up to say they were leaving again, and Alexandra had preceded the closing of the front door with "See you later, Flashdance."

Janine hadn't come back until well past the time Max had given in to the rumbles from his gut and baked up a pan of Bagel Bites. He had made some halting attempts at apologizing for all of it, the absence and especially the naked presence, but Janine hadn't been especially receptive. Not in a hostile way; that really wasn't her *modus*. She had been preoccupied with her own cares, leaving no way in for Max's garbled attempts at domestic placation.

It had come as some surprise, then, that once they had retired to bed, she had been receptive to his sexual overtures. He had been pulling out every stop he could think of to find some footing with her, and damned if silly bedroom humor hadn't been the winner.

"I'm Chesty the Bear," he had said with an exaggerated snarl, and he had uttered a guttural "grrrrar" as he reached over and cupped her breast. Janine had laughed, real and fulsome, a sound that infused Max with a rising euphoria.

"Get a better grip there, Chesty," she had said, dropping the neckline of her gown and revealing the breast in full, and so it had begun.

Thirty-four-plus years of marriage and sex, by nature, tended to make things a bit rote. "It's a long time to eat the same brand of cereal," Max's old boss, Mark Bonk, had said once in explaining why he was scrapping Marriage No. 1. A requisite amount of kissing, of sucking, of finding and touching, and then sometimes it was Janine on top and sometimes, including tonight, Max on top. A little bounce, a little breath, some moaning for good measure, and there you are.

Except Max couldn't get there.

He kicked the sheet and comforter now and swung his legs out of bed, to the floor, and stood up. He walked into the hallway and down the stairs, making a left U-turn into the main-level hallway and following it down to his office. He stepped heavily, unburdened by any worries that Janine might hear his migrations. One of the things she had done when she claimed the basement as her own was have it refurbished, with extra insulation in the ceiling. You could operate a recording studio down there, isolated as it was from the sounds of the rest of the house.

He latched the suitcases and removed them from the bed, arranging them in a line on the floor, and he climbed atop the mattress and lay on his back. He hooked his thumbs in the elastic of his underwear and lowered it. He touched himself and detected response, and he took hold and tilted his toes hard toward the opposite wall, and inside his head the movie unfolded—sometimes featuring Janine, sometimes some long-ago girlfriend, sometimes a memory of some porno he had played on his phone in some Comfort Inn somewhere—and he gave himself the action only the best lover he'd ever had could conjure.

When it was done, he cleaned up, hid the evidence away in the bottom of the trash can in the hallway bathroom, set the suitcases back where they belonged and opened them up, then headed across the house so he could go downstairs and say a proper good night.

"You going to be done soon?" Max asked.

"Soon."

"OK. I just wanted to say good night."

"Good night."

He moved in. She tilted her cheek for his offering. He took what she yielded and then withdrew.

"Please tell Kara I'm sorry."

Janine broke into a smirk, ever so slight. "I think the better play with Kara is just to pretend it never happened and hope she forgets."

"OK."

"Good night, Max."

He pulled back farther and started up the stairs. A few steps up, he stopped.

"Calendar is clear next week," he said.

"Yeah?"

"Maybe we should go to Chico Hot Springs. Next weekend, just you and me."

"Weekends are tough," Janine said. "Open houses. But maybe Tuesday-Wednesday? I could swing that."

"Sure. Whatever works."

"That would be nice."

"I'll make the arrangements, then."

"Sounds good."

"OK," he said, rapping the stairway rail twice with his open palm. "I'll get on that tomorrow, sweetheart." He started upstairs again.

"Oh, and Max?"

He stopped.

"Yeah?"

"Call your daughter tomorrow. She misses you."

"Roger that."

"Good night, Max."

"Good night."

FANCY SUSHI RESTAURANT, BILLINGS, MONTANA

Sunday, March 10
Eight minutes, twelve seconds after lunch was ordered

"Dad, listen to me." Alexandra gripped her water glass with both hands and pushed it to the middle of the table, so Max knew she was serious.

"I'm listening."

"Tyler says you have to lose some weight. Now that you're fifty-six—"

"I'm fifty-five."

"Whatever. He says it's crunch time now, time to make the change, or...you know." '

Her hands left the glass and reached up to her own throat, *faux-*strangling herself.

"He's going to kill me?"

"*You're* going to kill you. And that would hurt me so bad that *I'd* have to kill you."

"So I'm dead no matter what? Cool. Let's get some cocaine after we're done here."

"*Dad.*"

"I'm fine, sweetie. I am."

"I saw you limping on your way in."

Max imagined that his face got as knotted up as his gut. *Dammit.* This had all started well enough, with a kiss on the cheek from his daughter, a long hug, shared *I've-missed-yous* and funny little rips about the restaurant décor ("postmodern glitter bomb," Alexandra had called it), some good-natured busting of his balls by his daughter ("Well, Dad, it's an intimate lunch—nobody eats at 2:45 p.m. but you"), but ever since they had ordered, it had been a high-pressure medical lecture from Tyler-by-proxy.

"It's my trick knee," Max said. "It always gets a little gimpy when it rains."

"Dad, seriously, Tyler says you'd move a lot better if you just lost some weight."

"Oh, let's give Tyler a rest." *Too loud,* Max thought. *Inside voice, Max.* "Tell him I'll try to do better." Softer now. "I'm here to talk about you."

Alexandra sat back and regarded him with the faintest of smiles, so that was good, he guessed. And it's not as if he had a particular problem with his son-in-law. No problem at all, really. Any father would be proud to have his daughter meet and marry the likes of Dr. Tyler Keisling. Bachelor's of science in biology from the University of Washington, master's in integrated biomedical sciences from Notre Dame, Ph.D. from the Johns Hopkins School of Medicine. Three years ago, he had arrived and taken over the emergency department at Billings Clinic. Alexandra had been his real estate agent (a three percent commission on a $590,000 house—every time Max thought of it, he knew he had gone into the wrong business). A month later, Alexandra moved in with Tyler. No problem. No problem at all. And yet...

Something about Tyler rubbed Max a little raw, something beyond his good looks and better graces and undeniable charm (oh, did *Janine* ever swoon when he showed up). It was also something so indistinct that Max would have looked like a fool grousing about it to Janine, and while he had never much shied away from playing that particular role, in this case he had held tight to his feelings. There was an earnestness about Tyler that sometimes landed at loggerheads with Max's moments of whimsy. Max was thinking now of just a few months ago, Thanksgiving, when he had inadvertently released some flatulence at the table, looked around innocently and asked, "Did somebody deflate a football?" and Tyler had said, "No, somebody isn't getting enough roughage." That kind of riposte could take the starch out of a guy.

"So," Alexandra said, "talk."

Max cut short a sip from his iced tea. "How's business?"

"Business is good. Closed on two new rental places on the West End last week, free and clear."

"How many now?"

"Sixty-three," she said.

"All paid for?"

"Every last one. Revenue's up eighteen percent year over year."

Max whistled appreciation. He didn't have the baseline, so the eighteen percent bit hung out there out of context, but he knew which way the fever chart was running.

"You know," he said, "when you were a little girl and I was doing all that math with you, I sort of figured you'd, I don't know, go into physics or something."

"I prefer compounding interest," she said.

"Yeah."

"Make nine percent interest annually and you double your money every eight years. That's the sweetest equation I know."

"I guess so."

"And I make a lot more than nine percent."

When had she become such a killer? Max remembered a long-ago summer—had to have been '91, because that's the year Janine's grandmother was dying and she was always flying out to Seattle with little warning—when he had brought Alexandra on a couple of pipeline runs, Kansas and Missouri, hot as all hell and out in the boonies where he could let her wander the cornfields within his range of vision while he waited out the pig. She had been five years old, all sunshine and endless questions, and then the pig would come and he would gather up his equipment and he would whistle for her—"Let's go, princess"—and here she would come bounding back to the car, mirthful leaps punctuating her steps, corn silk in her hair.

And he would show her, even then, when he had to do the math by hand. *Here are the numbers we care about: time, speed, distance. Any two of those, and you can find the third. If we have the rate of flow and the distance, which we do, we can figure out the time to the next checkpoint. If we know the distance and the time, we can figure out the rate. If we know the rate and the time, we can figure out the distance.* He would do the math, and she would pretend to follow along in a little notebook he gave her. And it was pretend when she was five. Not so much just a few years later. She could do the real calculations faster than he could.

That girl was gone, mostly. But sometimes, he would think he caught a glimpse, a nod or a smile, something deep inside her that would always be a part of who she was. Sometimes...

"Who was your fourth-grade teacher?" he asked her now, a whipsaw of a question if there ever was one. Alexandra looked confused, then bemused, then amused, all in the space of a moment.

"Mrs. Spurgeon," she said, a smile lifting the corners of her mouth. "Why?"

"I was just remembering something," he said.

"Tell me."

Max settled into his chair, his arms limbering for the gesticulation his tale would require. "We deposited you in that class, and not a week later, she comes to us and says, 'You've already taught her algebra. What am I supposed to do with her? That's seventh grade.'"

"She said that?"

"Sure did. And your mother and I were, like, 'Hey, that's your problem.'" Max giggled, springing a quizzical look from his daughter. "Math joke," he clarified.

"Well," Alexandra said, "I'm still doing multiplication and division and finding for X. Maybe just not in the way you imagined. Sorry to ruin the dream."

"You're very talented," he said.

"I'm a *hustler*," she said. "To slough it off to talent is to discount how hard I work."

He held up his hands, surrendering. "I meant no disrespect."

The food arrived. Max checked his watch and ran the math. Eleven-minute-and-seventeen-second ticket time. Not bad. A single spicy tuna roll for Alexandra, a bowl of Tom Yum soup and a side of teriyaki chicken for him, no rice, no sauce, daughter's orders.

"Sweetheart," he said, "you know I'm buying lunch. Why aren't we having a steak?"

"Tyler says—"

"Here we go."

"No, Dad, listen," Alexandra said. "High protein, low carb. That's the path, OK?"

"Steak's protein."

"The loaded baked potato and the chocolate cake for dessert aren't. Listen, broccoli and cauliflower—"

"I hate cauliflower."

"—eggs, avocado. A little fresh fruit. Not that shit you eat, OK? If you'll do that and maybe get just a little exercise—"

"I know. I know."

"Being on the road is no excuse," she said. "I mean, there's not a hotel in the country that doesn't have a workout room these days."

"I know. I've seen them on my way to get free cookies in the lobby."

"*Dad.*"

"I'm kidding."

"Well," she said, "I'm serious."

Max's phone vibrated, doing a modern dance across the table toward him. He flipped it over.

"Who is it?" Alexandra asked.

"Dex."

"Put it on speaker. I'll say hello."

"Honey—"

"Oh, come on. There's nobody else here."

Max punched up the call on speakerphone. "Hey, Dex."

Here came Dex, his cadence always half again as fast as everyone else's. "You busy?"

Alexandra leaned in. "Hi, Dexter."

"Who's this?"

"Blondie. Remember me?"

"Alexandra! Hey, girly, how are you?"

For Max's benefit, she gave an exaggerated eyeroll at the loving condescension. "Just having lunch with my pop. I guess you're here to take him away from me again."

"Oh, shit, I'm sorry. I'll call back."

"No, go ahead," Max said. A nose scrunch from Alexandra.

Dex walked through the door that had been opened. "Listen, Mantooth wants to do a cleaner run in Buffalo next week. Just came up yesterday, so I'm scrambling. Western New York in winter. Your favorite, baby."

"What days?" She was in a full-on frown now.

"Tuesday through Thursday. You know the drill. In, out, bing, bong."

"That's two days from now."

"Yep."

"Jesus."

"Yep," Dex said again.

"I might have a conflict. Can't Hanley do it?"

"I fired Hanley's ass. Chicago was the last straw."

Max couldn't hide the surprise. On the merits, it had to happen. Only the timeline took him aback. "Well, good. Macartney? Smithlin? There's gotta be somebody else."

"Nope," Dex said. "I need you. And I need an answer fast so I can get this thing rolling. You in?"

Max looked to Alexandra, who volleyed the look back in a way that fully enunciated *look, we all know what you're going to do, so just go ahead and do it.*

"Yeah, I'm in."

"Great," Dex said. "Now, let me tell you the issue."

"Hold on," Max said. "Let me take you off speaker."

Alexandra, idly picking at her lunch as his went largely untouched, attenuated to things again, pouting at being cut out of the loop. Max puckered a kiss. She wasn't having it.

"OK, go."

"I need you to train Hanley's replacement," Dex said. "Buffalo, that little dinky five-mile run, is a good place for it."

"Aw, man, why can't Bonk handle that?"

Alexandra, divested of Dex's half of the phone call, took full interest in the scraps that were coming from across the table.

"There's a very good reason," Dex said, "and I'm gonna get to that in a second, although when I tell you this new employee's name, I probably won't have to."

Well, Max thought, *this is intriguing. What'd Dex do, go off and hire Kornbrock from Qwest?* Little Bonk (aka, Mark Bonk Jr., aka, meet the new crew leader, same as the old crew leader, just younger and angrier) hated Kornbrock more than he hated Tom Brady, and he hated Tom Brady enough that the great quarterback had blocked him on Twitter, after first calling him "a titanic asshole," which may well have been the truest dart Brady had ever thrown.

"OK, let's have it," Max said.

"You're going to be meeting Alicia Hammond when you get to the hotel in Buffalo. She's the new hire."

"Come again?"

"*Uh-lee-shuh Ham-und,*" Dex enunciated.

"A girl?"

Max could have said, "Hey, look, the mayor is walking naked down Grand Avenue" and not gotten more of Alexandra's laser focus.

"A *woman,*" Dex corrected. "Jesus, man, what's wrong with you? I didn't think this would faze you even a little bit. But you see the problem I have, right?"

"Bonk."

"Precisely."

Left unsaid, but as certain as the spin of the Earth, was that Little Bonk would try to screw this woman if he found her attractive or bury her under waves of belittlement if he didn't. The belittlement might come no matter what. There wasn't much time on a pipeline crew for anything other than work, sleep, and ball-busting, and Max had to wonder how a set of ovaries would fit into that mix. He also figured she could navigate the likes of Bonk if he showed her the way, which is why Dex's problem was now his.

"You sure about this?" Max asked. Alexandra flipped her hands apart, facing each other, incredulity on her face.

"She's fully qualified. Aced the diagnostics. And, come on, man, you've seen women in the field."

"Right," Max said. "I've seen 'em as safety coordinators and right-of-way negotiators. But it's been damn near thirty-five years out there, and I've never run the line with a woman, night after night, day after day, alone in the middle of nowhere, sleep-deprived. And I've damn sure never had to put myself between Little Bonk and his appetites, you know what I mean?"

"Oh, this is such bullshit," Alexandra said.

Dex motored on, a little more softly. "Listen. She's the kid sister of my brother's wife. Good person. Intelligent. Needs a break. This could be good, for her and for us."

"Kid sister? How old?"

"Thirty-three, I think." *Alexandra is thirty-two. Jesus.* "She's had a rough go—"

"Rough go how?"

"That's her story to tell. But she's fully qualified for the work. I think she'll be a good add, but she needs somebody who knows the terrain to get her going. And that's you."

It was very much what Max had hoped he would never hear. He had a good thing going. Jobs came up, he showed up, he tracked the tool, he finished the run, he went home. Let Little Bonk handle the paperwork and the client updates and the field supervision. Let Dex handle the home office and the scheduling and the drumming up of new work. All Max wanted to do—all he ever wanted to do—was track the pig. He liked the travel. He liked the monotony. He liked the time inside his own head. Where other guys—Big Bonk first, and Dex after Big Bonk had retired—had grown weary of the airports and the restaurants and the hotels and had willingly left the field for the comforts of the office, Max couldn't wait to get out there again. Alone. Not as the spiritual guide and bodyguard to some newbie.

"You going to tell Little Bonk what's what?" Max asked. "I don't want to have to do this and deal with his nonsense." Wild, unbelieving arm waves from Alexandra. Max made like a lowering elevator with his free hand. *Settle down. I've got this.*

"He's in charge of the job logistics," Dex said. "You're in charge of the training. He won't mess with you. The boundary lines have been made clear. Just...you know..."

"Make sure he doesn't touch her."

Alexandra's fork hit the table, dropped from a height, a clattering in the mostly empty dining room.

"That's it."

"Unreal," Max said. "I'm serious about this, Dex. Keep that guy out of my part of it, or I'll walk away."

A chuckle came back at him. "Max, you've threatened to walk a thousand times since I've known you, and here you are."

"Just because it hasn't happened yet..."

"Yeah, yeah. I know. I appreciate you."

Max looked again at Alexandra. Her arms crossed on her chest, and her lunch was finished. He smiled weakly.

"You know, Max," Dex said now. "You could have had this sweet office job and I'd be the one out there doing it, but you didn't want that. So this is what you've got. Feel lucky I'm not pushing you toward the door, old-timer."

"Ouch. You're as old as I am. Older, in fact."

"But you're an old tracker," Dex said. "I'm in my prime as an executive."

"Ouch again."

"I'm just kidding with you, man. You can track till you keel over. Just make sure Alicia is trained before you do so she can take your place."

"Inspirational."

"Enjoy Buffalo."

Alexandra stood as Max blinked out his phone. "Duty calls, I guess," she said.

"Where are you going?"

"I'm done."

"Sit down." He said it more harshly by half than he had intended, but she sat. Softer now, he said, "I hustle, too, you know."

"Oh, I know," she said. "With pretty young things, apparently, who are just dying to learn from you. I never knew your work was so exciting, rock star."

"Don't start."

"No wonder you were gone all the time."

"Are you even serious right now?" Max felt the anger flaring from his insides, flying toward every exit. "Don't start with me, Alex. I wasn't gone that much."

"Right, Dad. The dog didn't even know what you smelled like."

"We had a dog?"

Alexandra looked stricken. "*Dad.*"

"I'm kidding." Barney the Beagle. An unrepentant pooper in Janine's tulips. Max remembered.

Alexandra came to him, arms around his neck, a kiss on his cheek. "I'm sorry for roughing you up," she said. "Sounds like they need you. You should definitely go."

"I guess."

She stood, straight and businesslike, the little-girl kisses ceded once more to who she was now. "If you had an HR department that was worth a damn, you wouldn't have to tell a guy he can't fuck his pipeline workers. So this Bonk, he's some swinging dick, huh?"

Max winced at the profanity. "Don't say *fuck*, honey."

"Oh, OK. But *dick*'s fine, I guess."

"In this case, *dick* is accurate, at least. Just spare me *fuck*, OK? It's not fucking ladylike."

"OK, Dad. Call me when you're fucking back."

Max considered his food and the two bites, if that, gone from it. *No way that's happening now.*

"You're leaving? Already?"

"Work beckons," she said. "You know how that goes."

She leaned down and kissed him again. "You better figure out how to break this to Mom," she said. "She's going to be pissed." And before Max could even catch up to himself and the promises he had made to Dex so blithely, simultaneously just as blithely breaking an extant promise to Janine, Alexandra was out the door, leaving him to consider the tabletop.

It's a hell of a thing, Max thought, *to wrestle with what you ought to do and what you're going to do.* Janine and the getaway plan they had haltingly spoken into the universe, neither had crossed his mind. Dex had dangled an offer, and Max had scooped it up, tainted as it was by uncertainty and, now that he considered it more deeply, peril. Why? He knew why, of course. Because it was there. Buffalo—three flights away, a day of work, three flights home—was preferable to any here that could be put in front of him.

Further, Alexandra knew it. She had always known it. And she had blossomed despite it.

At once, Max felt naked, stripped away, exposed.

The server, having sidled up, punctured the moment. "Was your meal not satisfactory?"

Max pushed his plate and bowl toward the table edge. "It was fine," he said. "I assume. Not hungry, I guess."

"I can box it up."

"No need. Just the check, please."

Alexandra. She had apologized on the way out. "Sorry for roughing you up." Those had been the words. Max now thought that they hadn't quite been on target. The way she had said the things that wounded him, that hadn't been accidental. He had been carved by a tongue unsheathed by opportunity. What she was sorry for, if indeed she was sorry at all, was the attendant pain of the message. But the message itself, that was on point.

"Holy shit."

Max looked around the dining room, catching the attention of the server as she stood at the point-of-sale machine. He beckoned her over.

"Sir?"

"You have hamburgers or something?" Max asked.

"I don't understand."

"You know. Meat. Bun. Cheese. Standard items."

"This is an Asian restaurant, sir."

"On a children's menu, maybe?" Max pressed. "Something for the kids?"

The woman was all but agape at the dichotomy. Hadn't she just taken his mostly uneaten lunch away? Hadn't he said he wasn't hungry? He couldn't blame her for the confusion.

"We have chicken fingers and fries."

"That'll do," he said. "Pretty small portions?"

"Well, you know, for kids."

"Yeah. Better make it two. What about dessert?"

Another *what's-with-this-dude* look. "We have tiramisu."

"Ah, yes, a classic Asian delight."

She tilted her weight, one foot to the other and then back again. "Do you want it?" Nobody, it seemed, was in a mood for his bullshit today.

"Two, please."

"Two chicken fingers and fries, two tiramisus to go."

"For here."

"For here?"

"For here," he confirmed.

"But—"

"I'm unpredictable," he said.

"I guess."

She went back to the point-of-sale terminal for the adjunct to his bill. Max fashioned his right hand into a road grader and swept the leavings of lunch onto the floor. He tilted his eyes toward the ceiling, to a mirror ball turning languidly, reflecting his hatted head in its many pixels.

"What the hell," he said.

To: Wendt, Max; Hammond, Alicia
From: Bonk Jr., Mark
Subject: Cleaner-inhibitor run, Grand Island line, Tonawanda, N.Y., 3/12/19

All: This is your invitation to join the above project. We will mobilize into the Buffalo, N.Y., area on Tuesday, March 12th. On 3/13, we will track two cleaners for Mantooth Energy Co. across Grand Island, with an inhibitor injection in between. If all goes as planned, we will de-mobilize on Thursday, 3/14.

We will have our pre-job meeting the evening of the 12th at the Sleep Inn in Amherst. Stay where you wish, but it's a good hotel with a Mantooth rate (which you should ask for if staying there or anywhere else). I'll let you know the meeting time once you've responded to this email with your ETA.

Please buy round-trip airline tickets, secure your hotel, and arrange for the rental of an intermediate SUV with four-wheel drive. It's the snowy season in the Buffalo area. Bring all of your tracking equipment and your cold-weather gear. This is a run we've done many times (a good starter for Alicia), and I anticipate no problems.

I'll be bringing transmitters for the front cleaning pig and the back brush tool. This is also a single-site run, so make your hotel reservations for two nights.

Attached are the map and info sheet on the line. We're scheduled to run 160 cubic meters an hour, or 1.42 miles per hour. If all goes well, we'll finish the run by mid-afternoon Wednesday.

On mobilization day, please text me when you're on your way to Buffalo, so I know you're in transit. If you have any questions in the meantime, reach out. See you soon.

MB2

To: Hammond, Alicia
From: Wendt, Max
Re: Fwd: Cleaner-inhibitor run, Grand Island line, Tonawanda, N.Y., 3/12/20

Hi, Alicia...

Glad we'll be working together. I'll explain all of this stuff when we're on site. In the meantime, if you have any questions, just holler, OK? And take it from me, just go ahead and book the Sleep Inn. No sense in complicating things. I'm not sure why he always tells us we can stay where we want when the best option is the place where he's calling the meeting, but he does, as you'll find out soon enough.

To: Wendt, Max
From: Hammond, Alicia
Re: Re : Fwd: Cleaner-inhibitor run, Grand Island line, Tonawanda, N.Y., 3/12/20

Too bad. I was going to stay at the football stadium. Go Bills!

To: Hammond, Alicia
From: Wendt, Max
Re: Re: Re : Fwd: Cleaner-inhibitor run, Grand Island line, Tonawanda, N.Y., 3/12/20

You enjoy disappointment, huh? Well, welcome to pig tracking!

BILLINGS LOGAN INTERNATIONAL AIRPORT

Tuesday, March 12 | 4:43 a.m.
BIL>MSP: 748 air miles
MSP>DTW: 528 air miles
DTW>BUF: 241 air miles

Max made his usual notifications by way of text message. First, to Little Bonk: *At the gate in Billings. See you this afternoon.* Then, to Janine: *Safely at the airport. Love you.* It occurred to him after the second text left his fingers that he could delightfully mess with both of their worlds just by flip-flopping the order. Little Bonk would be endlessly befuddled, and more than a little skeezed out, if he received a *love you* message from Max. And Janine, who even after all these years knew little of the inner workings of his job, might begin to wonder if ol' Max had someone on the side waiting in Buffalo, what with the whole *see you this afternoon.* Maybe he would do it on the next job, just to keep both of them guessing.

His phone pinged back, a reply from Little Bonk: *Sweet. Safe travels.* Little Bonk would be making his way to the Denver airport now, the first leg of getting himself to Buffalo. There was a chance, Max had figured, that the three of them might end up at the same gate in Detroit, since Alicia lived out in Saginaw and would presumably be driving over to catch her own flight. The thought had given Max an abstract queasiness that he wouldn't have been able to describe to anyone; given the vagaries of flight schedules and hub airports, it happened sometimes, several pig trackers all jammed up in one airplane. Max always vastly preferred the pleasure of his own company, which was impossible when another guy (or woman, now) in your line of work wants to engage in cock-and-bull about the job. More likely, though, was that Little Bonk would be going Denver-Atlanta-Buffalo, and since Max wouldn't know Alicia on sight anyway, he would be on his own today. His gut unclenched at the realization.

Max wouldn't get a response from Janine. He could be sure of that. What had Alexandra said? *She's gonna be pissed.* A fair assessment, but also one that misfired by more than a smidge. Janine hadn't taken well the news of another job so soon after the last, the cancellation of the Chico reservation not a day after it had been made, the rearranging of the schedule that seemed to be in full churn through weeks, months, and years. But pissed? No. Max might have been less spooked had she initiated a tirade. Instead, Janine had said, "Well, OK, then," and Max's claim on her for an entire Tuesday and Wednesday had been revoked and redistributed before he even got the first "I'm sorry" out of his mouth. What followed was stasis, Janine in her world and Max in his, with cordial biddings of good night and no more nookie whatsoever.

Max dug around in his pants pocket for his car keys, which he intended to transfer to his backpack for safe holding until he came back Thursday (he hoped; despite it all, he still had designs on pulling the whole thing out of the smoldering fire of marital strife). He fished the keys out, opened the zipper pocket on his backpack, tossed them in, then looked again and found the card the Danforth guy had given him.

Charles Foster Danforth
Pediatrician, retired

Man of the world, always
DocCFDanforth@gmail.com

Funny old guy. Amid the swirl of discordant domesticity, Max had tossed the card in and promptly forgotten it. Now, he zipped open the top of the backpack and removed his work-issued laptop, the size and weight of cannon ordnance, all the better for riding out the pounding of dirt roads and barrow pits. He tapped into the WiFi provided by the Billings airport, launched his email program, and began punching out a note:

> *Charles:*
> *Remember me, Max Wendt? We met at the Minneapolis airport last week. You asked me to stay in touch, so...*
> *In fact, in a couple of hours I'll be back at MSP. I'm heading out to do a run near Buffalo. Not a run like you do. (See? I remember. Nine-minute mile. Very impressive.) A pipeline run. You asked about a cleaner, and yep, that's what we're doing this time.*
> *I like Buffalo. I'm there maybe three or four times a year. Good clams casino at this place in North Tonawanda. A Ted's Hot Dogs right down the street from my hotel. What more do you need?*
> *Anyway, write back if you want. I don't really know what you want to know (you're the old guy, so you're going to have define "geriatric inquisitiveness" for yourself), but I'll write back, if that floats your boat.*
> *Hope all's well in Saco Bay.*

He sent the message on its way just as the gate agent began breaking it down for the gathered, grumbly early-morning herd. Those needing help go first. Then active-duty military. Premium cabin. Sky Priority. Then the zones. You were nobody in the world of air travel if you had only a zone number, Max often noted with a satisfaction too smug by half. What had he done to earn status, outside of piling what was, ultimately, somebody else's money on a Delta SkyMiles gold card, to the tune of about sixty grand a year?

When Sky Priority was called, Max stepped forward and lay his phone, with electronic boarding pass, on the reader eye. It beeped acceptance, then the printer kicked something out.

"Looks like you're in 1A this morning," the gate agent said, handing him the paper.

Was anything in life sweeter than a first-class upgrade? Max thought not. He fairly danced down the jet bridge, gave the welcoming flight attendant his warmest hello, and said, yes, he would absolutely *adore* a cup of coffee before takeoff, thank you very much.

SLEEP INN, AMHERST, NEW YORK

Tuesday, March 12 | 6:22 p.m.
Fifteen hours and thirty-eight minutes before the start of the run

One thing was certain: Dex had understood the magnitude of the problem when he had hired Alicia, and he had done well to get out in front of it by dropping it onto Max's plate. The young woman who came off the elevator and joined Max and Little Bonk in the otherwise empty breakfast nook...well, that was just it, Max noticed. She wasn't *young*—in fact, she had probably four, five years on Little Bonk—but she was undeniably attention-getting. Max looked at her and saw Alexandra, and not for any reason that could be summed up in the physical. Where Alexandra was tall and slender, like Janine, this woman was shorter and sturdier, and maybe just a little overweight, although who the hell was Max to judge something like that? Where Alexandra had blond hair, styled and worn short, Alicia's was black as a winter night, pulled back in a long ponytail. Max saw his daughter on the peripheries of this woman, in her age and in her bearing, in the easy manner of her smile and her wave, like maybe the world hadn't yet beaten down on her too hard, just as it hadn't with Alexandra. (But *she's had a rough go*, Dex had said, so maybe she just skillfully covered the wounds.) And despite himself, Max saw someone he would have to protect in a subtle and crafty way that didn't put him at loggerheads with Little Bonk or, frankly, with Alicia. What right did he have to assume protection of her, or to assume she required it? That question is where she and Alexandra diverged. With Max's own daughter, it had been a job inseparable from everything else he tried to be to her. He had seen her first breaths. His had been her first hand to hold. If anyone hurt her, vengeance would be his. But this woman was someone else's daughter, someone else's beating heart, and her own sovereign person. Right there, he told himself to remember that.

Max beat Little Bonk to a standing position, no easy thing. "Alicia?" he asked.

"Yes, sir," she said, thrusting her right hand to him, which he accepted.

"No sirs around here," Little Bonk said now, catching up to the action and rising from his own chair. "Just co-workers. Welcome to the crew." After a handshake, he invited her to sit.

"So," Little Bonk began, "I'm going to go over this job, and Alicia, if you have any questions at all—"

Max choked down a bit of phlegm that had risen up in him. "Actually, Bonk, if you don't mind, just go over it as you normally would, and I'll follow up with her after. Dex wants to do this by immersion." He glanced to Alicia, who stared back at him earnestly. "I mean, if that's cool with you."

"Let's go," she said.

"OK, all right," Bonk said, effecting a blithe shake-off of the slight correction. "Let's get to it."

Little Bonk rattled off the particulars, a several-minutes spiel that mostly focused on the scope of work, with an emphasis on staying out of traffic what with the profound snowfall on the ground. He told them to be at the station in Tonawanda, four miles away, for the pre-job meeting at seven-thirty local the next morning. First pig was due into the line at ten a.m. local. Biocide injection after that, then the second pig. Receive them both on the other end of the island, call it a job well done. He passed around the paperwork and got their signatures, and that was it.

"Clear?" Little Bonk asked, mostly for Alicia's benefit.

"I guess," she said.

"It will be," Max said. "Seeing it happen takes it from the theoretical—"

"—to the hot-damn-we-did-it," Little Bonk finished.

"Right," Max said.

"OK," Alicia said. "Sounds good."

"I'm gonna go get me a steak," Little Bonk said, standing up. "You guys want to come?"

"Not tonight," Max said.

"Alicia?"

"Not tonight," Max said again. Little Bonk gave him a look of *oh, OK, Max, I guess you want her, you old horndog,* and Max burned. "Follow-up, remember?" Max tacked on, irritated. "Don't worry. I'll make sure she has some dinner."

In the second or two that followed, Max could see in the incremental shifts of Little Bonk's facial expression that he had run the calculus and come to a decision. Had he found a clear lane for taking a run at Alicia, he would have taken it. Max had put up a detour. Little Bonk could counter it, take his chances, try to find another way, or he could simply call up the woman he surely knew here in Buffalo—he knew at least one in every town on every line—and have a no-fuss good time tonight. Given the options and the odds, Bonk took the path of least resistance. Max counted on that. Max knew he would also pay for his interference later, not in any sort of punitive way but in the ball-busting that seemed to light Little Bonk's fuse almost as much as the touch of women who weren't his wife. The gibes would surely get unloaded tomorrow, cutting remarks only he could hear or text messages only he could read: *I didn't know you had it in you, Max. Did she know you had it in her?*

"All right, then," Little Bonk said, tumbling toward the lobby and his waiting indulgences. "See you both in the morning."

Down Niagara Falls Boulevard at Ted's—a footlong chili dog and an Italian sausage for him, a regular dog with mustard for her—Max reconstructed the meeting for Alicia and funneled everything into practical terms: what would happen at the pre-job tomorrow, the difference between local time and pipeline time (Mountain Standard; always Mountain Standard), the drive over the bridge to Grand Island, the standing and the waiting while the Mantooth crew drained down the trap, prepped the pigs for entry, loaded them, pressured up the line and opened the valve, releasing the tools into the flow of product. He explained that while a lot of trackers called it "chasing the pig," the point really was "staying ahead of the pig." Their job, simply put, was to make sure the tool kept moving by compiling verifiable evidence that it passed certain points along the journey from launch valve to receive valve. The job tomorrow, he told her, would be the easiest one they do. Launch, one crossing to record, receive. Repeat it. Go home.

The information—and it was a lot, for anybody—seemed to stick with Alicia, at least in the telling. The doing tended to expose newbies, until they saw it a few times and could anticipate rather than react. Those who never could make that adjustment didn't last long.

"Until Mr. Strongley called me, I had no idea this sort of thing was even done," Alicia said.

"Nobody knows, unless, you know, they know." *It is what it is. It ain't over till it's over. Jesus, Max.* "And it's Dex, by the way. You're kin, right?"

"Sort of, I guess. I don't know him that well."

"Anyway, what I mean is, it's a quiet kind of job," he said. "Nobody really knows we're out there, especially if we're working at night, and nobody really knows what we're doing. It only becomes a big deal if there's a leak or a breach or something, which, unfortunately, does happen."

"Yeah," Alicia said. "My dad wasn't very happy about it. He has a No Pipelines sticker on his car."

"Too late for that." If he remembered, Max thought now, he would show her a pipeline map of the United States. It looked like spider veins on an old lady's leg. He had taken the practical position that if we already have pipelines—and we do—somebody ought to be responsible for making sure they remained unplugged and uncorroded. That's where the job came in.

"But eventually there's no more oil, right?" she asked.

"Maybe. I'm sure I'll be dead and gone." Max downshifted. The future efficacy of his line of work wasn't among his preferred topics. "So why do this?" he asked her, and then he scrambled when the blunt force of his question occurred to him. "If you don't mind my asking."

"Needed a job."

Max popped the last bite of his dog into his mouth and spoke through the chew. "I heard that."

"What I mean is—" She stalled out.

"What?"

"Nothing."

"OK."

She put her elbows on the table and pressed her face into her hands, then dropped them. "We're going to be working together, right? Not just this job, but in the future?"

"For a while, yeah," Max said. "Eventually, you'll be trained and we'll get divvied up, especially if we've got two jobs in the same week. The way it goes sometimes."

"I understand," she said. "But I'm going to be working with you, right? I don't want to be all secretive and stuff, but I get the feeling maybe I ought to hold my cards around some people."

"Bonk?"

Downcast eyes. "Yeah. I don't mean anything by it, I just—"

Good instincts, Max thought. *That'll help.*

"I get it. You'll be working with me. I'll tell Little Bonk and Dex how you're doing. Anything else, it stays in here." He rapped his chest twice.

"Little Bonk?"

"Long story. We'll get there."

Alicia looked up, brightened. "The thing is, I have a kid," she said.

"Me, too."

"Mine's eight. Rexford is his name. For real. Rexford. A family name," she said. "Not my family."

"Mine's..." He stopped, considering. He tossed her a smile to soften the ground. "How old are you?"

"Thirty-two."

"When were you born? What month?"

"October."

"Mine's a few months older than you," he said.

That did it, as he hoped it would. In Max's experience, advancing age was mostly a pain in the ass—not to mention other bodily precincts—but it also had one delightful quality: It was easy enough, with a younger person, to make the "trust me, I'm older than the hills" play and get them to start talking. On the flip side, it was sometimes difficult to get them to shut up again, but that challenge had a way of crossing all age ranges.

"He's my world," she said, and as if a toggle switch had been engaged, Alexandra lit up the corners of his mind. "I'm on a parenting plan with his dad, and one of the requirements is that I'm working. So here I am."

Here she was. In a place where, when the working day ended, she was still hundreds of miles from home. That wasn't easy, especially with a kid, as he well knew. For years, the absences had been an intense focus of Janine's number-crunching. *Yeah, sure, you get paid for twelve hours, but you give them the other twelve for free, because you're not here.*

"So his dad has custody?"

"Full. I get visitation. Supervised."

She's had a rough go. There was something more to that story. He didn't ask. She didn't tell.

As if it were on a jailbreak, a tear slipped down her cheek. She swiped it clean. "I'm sorry."

"It's OK," he said.

"I just really need this job to work out."

"It will. It's not particularly high-concept or even high-difficulty. Some guys can't handle the punctuality. Some can't handle the solitude. But if you can, it's a decent enough way to make a buck." Only in the mental echo did he realize he had said *guys*, not *people*. Old habit. His cheeks burned. She seemed not to notice or care.

"I think I can handle that," she said.

"Good. So don't worry too much, OK?"

"OK."

The pain, almost undetectable if all she was given was a glance and yet also roiling beneath her surface now that Max had a clue, took him aback. He swore to himself he wouldn't press, wouldn't dig, wouldn't do anything except let her say what she wanted to say when she wanted to say it. On the drive over, he had almost apologized to her for the way he and Little Bonk had minimized her back at the hotel, talking about the basic act of her eating dinner as if it were their dominion. He had wanted to tell her that she should never give more of herself or her time to the job than it had coming, that when the hours went from work time to downtime, she could do whatever she damn well pleased. The opening to say it hadn't come during the small talk, and saying it now would have lacked both context and the affirmational quality he intended. He would have to wait for another opportunity.

They rode back to the hotel in silence—not the strangling kind, but rather the variety that comes on when two people, after some time together, have become more than strangers and less than friends. In the parking lot, Max asked her to point out her rental. He suggested they meet at six-thirty, after breakfast, to set up her equipment in her car, and then drive to the station in a mini-convoy. She said that would work.

More silence on the elevator ride. She got off on the second floor. They murmured their good nights. He rode up to the fourth.

Once in his room, Max followed his well-honed checklist. The next day's clothes folded neatly on the chair. His gas monitor and wireless geophone charging on the desk. Boots at the ready. Thermal socks, too. Hard hat and safety glasses and everything else he would need already down in the car.

Stripped to his underwear, he eased into the sheets. He found the Lakers and the Spurs on the TV.

He looked at his phone. No texts. A few Facebook notifications. He tossed a text Alexandra's way: *Remember when I used to call you Pookie Nose? Love you.*

By the time she answered—*Yes, you goof*—he was already unmoored in the sea of his subconscious.

To: Wendt, Max
From: Charles Foster Danforth
Subject: Re: it's me

Hello, Max. So good to hear from you. I didn't think I would. You've surprised me. I like surprises.

At the risk of coming across as a repulsive old scold, I must say that clams casino and hot dogs, while they have their undeniable charms, do not reflect a classical appreciation of the fine American city you're in, nor do they do your overall health any good. If you perceive that as unnecessarily direct or intrusive, please remember that I am an old man steadily getting older, and also a man who sank a good deal of his time and money into being learned about the ways of the human body. My clinical advice, offered for free and with no expectation that you'll follow it, is to rein in the abuse of your digestive system and to absorb more of the culture that's around you. It's a wonderful gift, this world.

Do you realize where you are? In architectural terms alone, you're in a place that changed the game, particularly with the buildings that *went up between the Civil War and what my grandfather, Preston Foster Danforth, the old scamp, called the Great War, even if that moniker was eventually usurped by a greater war that came along. (This, Max, is the folly of our human condition. We are terrific at war. We are less terrific at things that would be better for the collective us. But I digress.)*

I wish I had the time to go back there. It would be charming to see you, of course, but I think I would leave you to the pig and go walk those radiating boulevards downtown (I bet you never thought of Buffalo and Paris as comparable, but there you go). I'd see the buildings of Wright, of Richardson, of Sullivan, of Mori, and my day would be spent before I even got to the art galleries or the wine—yes, my friend, the wine; you take the chicken wing, I'll take the pinot.

You asked what I wish to know. It's your dime, friend, so you can choose any topic you wish, and I will absorb and respond. But if you need a prompt, here are two:

1. Where do you go next? And what do you plan to do with your time there, pipeline duties notwithstanding?

2. What ignites you, Max? What sets your toes to tapping, your heart to laying down percussion, your soul to elevate? If you didn't, or couldn't, grip another man's hand and say "Max Wendt, pig tracker," what would you say?

Max Wendt. Max Wendt where?

I'm sorry, chum. I'm a sucker for bad wordplay. It is my one true vice.

CFD

TEXAS ROADHOUSE, TONAWANDA, NEW YORK

Wednesday, March 13 | 7:07 p.m.
Three hours and eleven minutes after the run
Ten hours and fifty-eight minutes before the first of three flights home

By the end of the workday, Max wanted a steak every bit as much as Little Bonk did, which was saying something, what with steak being a pillar in Mark Bonk Junior's Trinity of Unclean Living: steak, surliness, sex. In no particular order.

They had much to celebrate, the whole abbreviated crew. It had been a clean run, entirely expected but also entirely a relief when all was done.

Every run started with an optimal visualization. Start here at this time, finish there at another time, a steady flow in between, verifiable passes at every designated milepost. A smaller number went that way. A smaller number still went completely sideways. Max was grateful, every time, for achieving the expected. The ordinary, in the general unfolding of life, tended to get stale. In pipeline work, it was the highest aspiration.

More important, on this particular project, was that Alicia had gotten it. How a newbie would take to the work was a galaxy of unpredictability—beyond the physics and the dynamics of flow, could an initiate into the world of petroleum delivery *visualize* the shape of a job, could she understand that the mathematics behind it all would never lie to her, could she trust her training and her equipment and record clean passages out in the field, could she learn to wait for a transmitter fastened to the pig some number of feet underground as it sent electronic and audio signals to her while zipping by?

Many new hires—people possessed of good enough brains and an ability to haul themselves from place to place—simply could not. They couldn't show up on time. Or they went off tracking a ghost pig, when the real one was either behind them or hopelessly ahead. Max had seen those employees arrive and then disappear just as quickly once their deficiencies became clear. Dex, and to a lesser extent Little Bonk, had developed a bloodless way of dispatching them into unemployment, because it simply wasn't worth the effort to carry someone who couldn't or wouldn't shoulder the work. It was another reason Max had stayed in the field, stoically resisting any responsibility for hiring and firing. Every termination would have eaten away at his insides. The only co-worker whose firing he had ever sought was Hanley, and that's because Hanley's fuck-ups—sleeping while on the line, lying about where he was, fudging his passage data—had landed too close to Max.

He no longer worried about Alicia. She got it. All of it. She understood the principles and the practicalities. At the receive valve, after the second pig had arrived and snuggled up to the first, Max had shown her how to dial down the gain on her receiver and sweep the above-ground trap to pinpoint the location of the tool inside the pipe.

"Find it," he had said, and then he had fallen back with Little Bonk, the two of them leaning against the Mantooth truck and watching as she slowly stepped, foot over foot, parallel to the flow of the line. She worked her way to the end, then came back again, zeroing in.

"She knows her way around a tool," Little Bonk had said, side-mouthed.

"Oh, stop."

"Like you weren't thinking it."

"This may blow your mind, kid, but—"

"It's here, I think," Alicia had said, her hand against the steel as if bisecting it, marking the spot.

"It blows something," Little Bonk had said, more under his breath now that she was peering back at them.

"Oh, shut up," Max said.

Max ambled over and took the receiver from her. "Keep your hand there," he said, and he cringed at the setup line that Little Bonk, thankfully, didn't take.

Max had swept the trap, nimbler, more sure of his steps, but he ended up in the same place as Alicia.

"That's it," he had said. "Good job."

"Hot damn," Little Bonk had said, clapping his hands. "We've got us a full crew again."

Alicia's great reward, beyond the company she kept, was the revelation Little Bonk made while they dug into dinner. Another job loomed, ten days out.

"Cushing line," Little Bonk said.

"This'll be fun," Max tossed in.

Alicia dabbed her mouth with a napkin. "Fun, why?"

"Three hundred miles of line," Max said.

"The flow going, tops, three miles an hour," Little Bonk finished.

"That's—" Max started.

Alicia closed the loop. "One hundred hours." *Impressive*, Max thought. On one hand, it was easy math, cleanly divisible. On another, he had seen more than one would-be pig tracker thrown off-course by the easiest of equations.

Her expression crinkled. "Just you and me?" she asked Max.

"Hell, no," Little Bonk busted in. "You'll meet the rest of the gang on this one. Two crews, two men each, day and night, twenty-four hours of coverage. Sorry, two *people* each."

Alicia waved off the minor misogyny.

"You and I will be on nights," Max said. "This run will be leisurely enough that I'll be able to hang out with you at first, make sure you're getting set up right and getting the passes, and then once you're ready, we'll leapfrog down the line."

"What does nights entail?" she asked.

"We're on the line midnight to noon, local time—Central time, that is. Start in Missouri, finish in Oklahoma."

"It just rolls along," Little Bonk said. "Track, drive, sleep, drive, track, drive, sleep—"

"You get the picture," Max said.

"OK," she said.

Max sensed hesitation. "It's a lot to take in," he said. "You'll get it."

"Today," she said. "I thought today was hard. Five miles."

"It didn't look too hard for you."

"You fuckin' rocked," Little Bonk said.

"Thank you," she said.

"It's like anything else," Max said. "You learn by doing. It makes no sense. Then it makes some sense. Then it makes total sense. It's going to be fine. Promise."

"OK," she said again, smiling.

"Goddamn," Little Bonk said. "I feel great. I'm gonna go get laid."

Max looked with alarm toward Alicia, who snorted laughter into her water glass. If she could take Little Bonk's regular forays into his inner juvenile, she would truly be one of them. Max still wrestled with all that came with being under the supervisory thumb of a twenty-eight-year-old who was undeniably good at the work—with a dad like Big Bonk, how could he be anything else?—and yet didn't seem to have any interests that lay beyond petroleum products and soft feminine bodies into which he could sink balls deep.

"That's great, Bonk," he said. "How about paying the check first?"

Max waited for sleep, giving half his attention to some home renovation show on HGTV. He had lived long enough to see a world where replacing a sink rated as compelling television, so there was that. Janine, not surprisingly, loved these shows, all of them. If you had a show where you bought and renovated hovels, employed exasperated electricians, and somehow ended up with a hundred grand after flipping it in resale, you had Janine's eyeballs, not to mention her calculations on her own financial future. Max watched, considering the star of the program. He had never seen a construction guy who looked like that, or one who wore jeans that tight.

A text message came over the transom.

Thanks for all your help today.

Max thumbed a reply. *Not a problem.*

Three dots in a bubble, a harbinger of a message. *UR a good teacher.*

I'm not. Had a good student.

To-may-to, to-mah-to.

Max had to laugh. *Thanks for saying so.*

See you in 10 days.

I'll be there.

Max's final message was an echo rhyme, a word-for-word repetition of how he had left things with Janine on the phone not an hour earlier.

"I'll be there tomorrow," he had said. "Let's go on a date Friday night, like old times."

"Oh, Max. I've got so much to do."

"Easy peasy," he had said, a bit too pleading. "Dinner and a movie. You pick the show. I'll buy the popcorn." If she caught the invocation of what he had so often said to her back when they were dating—"I'll buy the popcorn"—she didn't register recognition, and thus Max wished he hadn't said it.

"OK. But, Max, look, if there's any chance at all—"

"I'll be there. Job's done. I'm coming home tomorrow, a day to spare. Nothing to worry about."

"OK."

"I'll be there."

Had he never not been there when the schedule cooperated? He couldn't control uncooperative tools or recalcitrant engineers or unexpected line shutdowns—he could be apologetic, he could be angry, he could be conciliatory when he called Janine, hat in hand, but he couldn't control those things. The field was now clear of those concerns. He had to get himself onto three flights. He could do that. He *would* do that.

He would be there.

To: *Charles Foster Danforth*
From: *Wendt, Max*
Subject: *Re: Re: it's me*

I don't know if you appreciate what's involved with my work. It would be cool to see museums and sip wine and stuff, but I'm where I am to work, and when I'm not working, I'm asleep. I don't have time for anything else.

I like your questions, though. It's cool. I'll play.

Next, I'm doing the longest line we pig. Over 300 miles from up around Moberly, Missouri, down to Cushing, Oklahoma. Five days and nights in the field. And I'll be on nights (midnight-noon), so my sleep will be pretty worthless.

As for what "ignites" me, man, I don't know. I'm stuck in this hotel in Minneapolis—remember that flight we both missed? Well, I didn't just miss it. The damn thing didn't happen. Engine trouble. I couldn't take another night on the floor, so I'm at a Holiday Inn Express. Maybe I'll wake up an architect or something.

Anyway, I'm stuck in this hotel, my wife is pissed off because I promised her I'd be home, and all I'm thinking about is when I get to leave again. It doesn't matter that I'm going to Bumfuck, Missouri. It's that wherever I'm going isn't where I'm supposed to be right now. Unwind that.

The thing is, I'd made some plans with Janine—that's my wife. I had time. I had a day to spare. And now, everything's so overbooked with this flight cancellation, I'm going to get home—if I get home, because who knows what happens with the flight tomorrow—a few hours before the thing I promised I'd be there for. Being late, not being there—if you knew my work, and maybe you do, you're a pretty smart guy, you'd know how uncomfortable that is.

Anyway, I haven't answered your question. My daughter. Alexandra. She's the north star. Everything else is what it is. I'm 55 years old (so, listen, enough with the old-man stuff—you're not that much older than me, and I bet you've got more tread on the tires). I don't know what Janine and I have going, except that it's been 34 years and we're still in, so that's something. But Alexandra still has it all in front of her, whatever her heart desires. I want to be around long enough to see her pluck those stars out of the sky.

Tag. You're it.

Max Wendt

Max Wendt Everywhere, Man

Max Done Wendt to Sleep

JAKE'S RESTAURANT, DOWNTOWN BILLINGS

Friday, March 15 | 6:18 p.m.
Three hours, thirty-four minutes after the last flight
Eighteen minutes into the dinner reservation

Max sat at a table for two in the back of the room, and he watched the flickering shadows on the wall near the hostess's stand, each holding the promise of materializing into Janine, and each, so far, morphing into the disappointment of being someone else.

He had broken airline protocol by texting her as the plane taxied to takeoff at MSP, so he was sure he would actually be on his way this time. *I'll be there.* No response.

He had texted again after wheels down, a fresh coating of snow in Billings, frigid and gray.

I'm here. No response.

He had gone home. She wasn't there. He had waited. She hadn't shown. He had napped on the couch, *Mary Tyler Moore* beaming out from the nostalgia channel. He had awoken to *Hazel*, a show hopelessly dumb and constellations less funny.

He had dressed. He had texted. No answer. He had arrived at the restaurant. No Janine. No dice. He had sat down. He had waited.

He waited still.

It was only when he about gave up on shadows and light and began looking for the server, so he could pay for his beer and pass on his regrets, that she sauntered toward him, still in her coat over the smart business suit—*power red*, she called it—she had surely worn to work that morning. He jostled the table while standing up.

"You're here," he said.

"I am."

"I'm glad."

"Good."

They sat. Max could feel the astonishment still etched into his face. Janine, a perfect contrast, wore a mask of nothingness.

"Take off your coat," he said.

"No."

"I'm sorry about—" he started.

"Please, no apologies."

"You're angry."

"I'm not," she said.

"You have every right."

"I haven't been angry in a long time."

The incongruity of her words with the situation and the daylong silence, and with Max's surety of Janine's attitude every time he called to change the schedule on her, every time he left, every time he arrived—none of it computed. And before it happened, Max knew what the evening held for them. Here, in this public place, amid the happy chatter of nearby lovers, they would douse the light. She had worked up her gumption—when, he didn't know—and had decided to do it here. No chance of an ugly fight, no opportunity to dig in their heels, arrest the slide, and walk things back. No way to cite the years gone in a compelling argument for holding close those yet to come.

"We've had a good run," Janine said. "I'd like to be thankful for that and let the rest go."

"Divorce?"

If ever there were a word with a built-in detonator, that was the one. Janine's eyes filled. They didn't spill. "Yes."

"Why?"

"You know why. We both do. This didn't happen tonight. It's been happening for a long time. I just want to acknowledge it. That's long overdue, and I'm tired of not facing it."

She was wrong. If it didn't happen tonight, why was tonight—right now, here—when his memory banks dumped their contents, a fast-unfolding reel-to-reel of the lives they had given over to each other? First date, second date, first kiss, the faithful early gropes in her parents' den, the two of them always together at the beginning, inseparable, the church wedding and the mortgage and the tree at Christmastime and Alexandra, *oh, god, Alexandra*, the first time he ever knew true meaning in his life, and how he had tried to hold tight to her even as the world came calling...

"Max?"

"Hmm."

"This doesn't need to be contentious. We can be fair with each other. We can be kind."

Don't mind our mess.

"I know," he said.

"You can stay at the house while we sort things out."

"That's kind."

"Max—"

"No, really, that's kind."

"Do you want the house?" Now, for the first time, she betrayed distress. "I figured I'd buy you out, but if you want to buy—"

"Janine," he said, "you'll have to forgive me. You're way out in front of me here. I need time to catch up before I'm ready to talk about all that."

"Of course." She stood. *Here's your purse, what's your hurry?*

"So, no dinner, then?" he asked.

"You're being sarcastic."

"I am?"

"You are. But it's OK." She smoothed her coat. "I think we should tell Alex and Tyler. We could go tonight. If you want."

"No."

"It's just that...well, it's out now, and I don't want to hide from it, and—"

"I'm not hiding. I'm, like, literally just finding...I mean, Jesus, Janine."

Her words came through bound teeth now, low, lest someone at some adjacent table catch a hint of what was happening. "I said I don't want to hide. I suspect Alex knows. She's always had that way with things."

"She has."

"You don't want to come?"

Max could picture it, being in the same room with Janine and Alexandra and Tyler, a breezy hello and, *hey, it's been a good run, but now it's over. How do those second-quarter projections look?* Tyler, no doubt, would tell him how to safeguard his health in the midst of a divorce. *Sure, Tyler, send your recommendations to me at the South Side flop house I'll be renting, you unctuous motherfucker.* Alexandra, ever the good daughter, would be a fair emotional broker—she would probably even cry for some of the same things Max wanted to cry about now—but when practicality was needed, she would be on the side of what was hers. She wasn't in business with her old man.

"No, I don't want to come. Tell Alexandra I'll call her tomorrow."

"OK, Max. Maybe we can talk some more."

"That would be kind."

That swipe—and that's what it was, what Max fully intended, a tennis ball returned right between the eyes—gave Janine her release to turn and recede into the shadows on the restaurant wall. Max sat alone, watching the sweat roll down his beer glass, the savory smells of the steakhouse running headlong into his battered senses. He had imagined what this might be—you couldn't have the kind of sprawling impasses he and Janine had shakily bridged these past several years without at least imagining how everything might fail and fall. He had sometimes even followed those thoughts to the occasional off-ramp where maybe he would be happier, maybe he would have more fun, maybe he would do some of those things that he once assumed were his for the taking and instead had been tossed to the wind, one by one.

Maybe, in this new iteration, he would be more fulfilled. Maybe he would yet be a better man.

Then again, maybe not.

Max went home, a frosty drive through streets whose familiarity to him had unexpectedly shifted with the news of the day. He had been born here, up the hill at St. Vincent's, on the hottest day of July in '63. Grew up, from days old to high school graduation and beyond, in a little box house on Wyoming Avenue. School straight through, then on to Eastern Montana College, right here, a walk-on to the track team (where he excelled) but adrift in what he ought to study in the classroom (where he crashed in flames). College hadn't taken. Nothing much had, until Mark Bonk, his parents' next-door neighbor, had said, "Better to come out to the pipeline with me than to sit around pulling your pud here." It was the kind of logic that had broken through the veneer of Max's aimless youth. Later, with Janine, came some stability, once. With Alexandra, responsibility, in rhythm with his father's passing. Talk about parallels. He had grown, and the place had grown with him and around him, and now, just tonight, it was something else entirely, a place where he would have to learn to live with himself.

Now that the prospect had gone from theoretical to stand-here-and-deal-with-it, Max felt a faltering. He wasn't sure he could.

The home they had made together sat full of similarly disconcerting perspective shifts. The hallway real estate trophy, still there to greet him, to whisper to him that this had been the start of the finish, Janine's stretching out for ambitions that lay beyond the horizons they had once set together. When Alexandra had been a girl, he had traveled—and worked—even more than he had done in the years since she had grown up. He and Janine had an agreement. He would pull in the living and she would manage the home, and they had both upheld their ends of that bargain for a long time. Janine, of her own volition, had changed the compact. He had given supportive words to her decision because he thought he should. He didn't understand it, and at some point, as she ascended a career that far exceeded his, she had decided that she didn't owe him an explanation. *Had that been fair?*

Now, he looked around and no longer saw the accumulations of a life together. He saw her things and his, with hers winning the tug-of-war. Of course it was her house, and would be her house. He would need more than the small apartment he had fancied on the drive home, in that sliver of a moment when he saw opportunity rather than destruction. It hadn't lasted, the sliver or the optimistic thought. He would need a storage unit. A moving truck. A bed. Good god. He would need the makings of a life. *Where? How?*

His phone buzzed in his shirt pocket. He withdrew it. Alexandra. He couldn't not pick up, and yet he also felt a powerful compulsion to carry the phone over to the freezer and drop it into the ice bin.

"Hi, sweetie."

"Dad, are you OK?"

"Never better."

A sniffle, then a cough, then the sputter of a half-committed laugh. "Oh, Jesus," she said.

"I'm fine."

"You should come over and talk. We want you to." Pulled back from the phone, she said, presumably to Tyler and maybe to Janine, "Don't we?"

"I don't think so," Max said. "Let's talk tomorrow."

"Dad—"

"Tomorrow, sweetheart. It'll be better to do it tomorrow."

"Let's have breakfast," she suggested, as if having breakfast would ever be the same thing again.

"Yeah, OK."

"Mom's going to stay over here tonight, OK? She thought that would be best."

"Whatever you all want to do."

"OK, Dad. Tomorrow at eight? I'll meet you at Stella's."

"Sounds good, Pookie Nose."

That broke her. When she found the words, they came out like they had been shredded on the journey between her diaphragm and her tongue. "Good night, Dad."

"Good night."

Max closed out the call. He followed the well-worn path from the living room down to his office, where his clamshell suitcases sat upright, unopened, their contents unverified and unsorted. In his haste to get ready to meet Janine downtown—his useless hope that he could manage to turn everything around even as Janine made her own plans to blow it apart—he had departed from his routine. Fifty percent of him pressed to make it right now, get those suitcases on the bed and broken down so one job could be officially closed and the clock could begin winding down to the next one. Forty-nine percent of him thought it could wait until morning, when he would be of a better mind to come down here and do ordinary things again.

Later, he would tell himself he should have known that, in America, the one percent always wins. He grasped the suitcase handles and wrestled them out of the room, down the hall, out the front door, into the truck.

And then he was gone, gone, gone.

WYOMING AVENUE, BILLINGS

Friday, March 15 | 7:57 p.m.
Seventeen years, twenty-one days since Max's last visit

Every light in Mark Bonk Senior's home shone into the night, which gave Max a view to the house to its left, his childhood home, his erstwhile bedroom window not a dozen feet from Big Bonk's living room. On the drive over, Max had thought himself in for a cavalcade of memory, but it hadn't been that at all. He felt almost detached, as if whatever once connected him here had been severed and the blood drained out. He knew the sidewalk cracks and the frozen lawns and the streetlamps at either end of the block, certainly. But those things had belonged to another boy.

Big Bonk, apparently having heard the truck's engine cut off and the driver's-side door slam, brought himself onto the screened-in porch. Backlit by his own insatiable appetite for electricity, Big Bonk looked...well, less big. Scrawnier for sure in the arms and the legs than he had been, what, a year and a half ago, when Max had last seen him. It had been at Big Bonk's retirement party out at the Windmill. Another moment, seemingly isolated when it happened but now illuminated by context, snapped into place in Max's understanding. Janine had been pissed when Big Bonk retired from the home office and Max didn't step into the job, as was his right. It would have meant leaving the line, aside from the occasional one-off job, and being home every night. Max couldn't contemplate that, so Dex had come in out of the cold, Little Bonk had moved up to field lead—another role Max had no interest in—and the great world had spun on.

"Who's that?" Big Bonk called out in a chainsaw voice.

"Wendt."

"Max?"

"Do you know any other Wendt?"

"Well, hot damn. Not anymore."

Big Bonk, looking more like a rolling pile of odd parts than a human being, got himself to the screen door and pushed it open. Max clambered up the stairs, into a man hug infused with Old Milwaukee.

"What brings you out?" Big Bonk asked, his massive left hand still holding a chunk of Max's neck, as if he might lift the younger man like a mama cat moving her kittens.

"Just thought I'd come by."

"In this fuckin' freeze?" Their breath hung between them. "What are you, nuts? You gone plumb loco?"

Max fumbled his answer. *Where to start? Yeah, probably. Maybe.*

"Well, it don't matter none," Big Bonk said, grabbing him again. "Come on in. We'll get drunk, maybe play some grab-ass. I ain't too choosy anymore."

Once Max was seated inside, a can of beer in hand, he made a better accounting of the situation. Rather than a blow-by-blow, he told Big Bonk a straight-ahead version where Janine had said she wanted a divorce and he had been blindsided. The latter wasn't really the truth—with even a small passage of time, he saw in retrospect that it had been coming awhile—but it made the story digestible for Big Bonk, a man not ordinarily given to nuance.

"Marriage don't make no damn sense to anybody, even the folks who seem to know what they're doing," Big Bonk said in what Max considered a moment of near profundity. "I've been through three of them. Been convinced for a while now that they're meant to go kaput. They're like spark plugs."

"It's an interesting theory."

Big Bonk drained the remainder of his beer, then crushed the can on the coffee table between them. "You want another?" he asked, getting up.

Max sloshed his in the can. "No. I'm good."

"I mean, I ain't more than acquainted with your wife," Big Bonk called in from the kitchen, describing a woman he'd known since 1984. "I see her picture on the bus stop benches downtown, but her and me, we don't travel in the same social circles, you know what I mean?"

"Sure."

Big Bonk strode back in, popping the top on his can. The crushed empties littered the room, three on the coffee table, maybe another half-dozen on the dining room table, a few on the bookshelf behind him. He sat down.

"I do remember when you said you were gettin' hitched," Big Bonk said now. "You were standing right in that yard next door. You said, 'Hey, Bonk, we're getting married.' You remember that?"

"Sure do," Max said. He didn't.

"And I said, 'Well, hot damn,' because that's what I say. And I meant it. God bless, man. I had only the best wishes for you."

"I appreciate that, Bonk."

"Same thing now. You're getting divorced? Well, hot damn. It's a change either way, ain't it, coming into a marriage or going out? Change can be good."

It had a certain undeniable symmetrical logic, but Max found it wanting compared with how untethered he now felt.

"I'm just struggling a little, you know?" Max said. "Even if it's been coming a long time, like Janine said, I didn't see it until it landed between my eyes."

"Well, hell, no," Big Bonk said behind a hoppy belch whose bubble burst between them. "You've been on the line all these years. She's been here, doing her thing, building herself something. Those pictures on the bus benches. Ain't a nobody who gets on those things, you see what I'm saying?"

"Of course."

"You know, she has a smile that says she could sell pig shit to the Queen of England. She good at that real estate stuff?"

"Unbelievably so."

Big Bonk slapped his knee as if he had just unified the chaos theory. "Well, see, there you go. She's got her own shit. You've got your own shit. And she doesn't much want her shit mingling with yours anymore."

Shit.

"It happens, man," Big Bonk said. "That's the way it went with the third missus. She come to me one day and said, 'I want something else for my life.' So I say to her, I say, 'Well, that just suits me fine. Leave the key, because it's my house, and don't take my goddamn saw horses, because I just bought those. Otherwise, it's a free world, honey.'"

Big Bonk, bewildered by his own monologue, stared at Max, only it wasn't directed at him, or at the wall behind him, or at the room behind that, or at the backyard, or at any other fixed point in all of Billings, Montana.

"Thanks for talking with me, Bonk."

"Ain't no trouble a'tall." Big Bonk found his bearings. "You got a place to stay?"

"I was hoping here, at least tonight. I'll find something tomorrow."

"Damn right," Big Bonk said. "You can't be out drivin' after the way I've been drinkin'."

"Exactly. I'll go get my stuff."

"I'll go get us some more beers."

They talked on into the night, skimming their shared adventures and making them funnier and more interesting in the remembrance, until at last the able brewers of Milwaukee found the quantity that would arrest Big Bonk's tongue. As he lay on his back on the floor, managing to push out and draw back in phlegmatic breaths, Max watched him from his seat on the couch. Only eleven years separated them, but Big Bonk had always seemed so far beyond him in age, in world-weariness, in native wisdom (if not traditional book smarts), in everything. He and his first wife, Rebecca, had moved into this house in '78, and Max had found that he could sometimes run away from matters at home by going just a door down, where young Mark Bonk and his lovely wife treated him like the man he would someday be, slipping him the occasional beer and a pack of smokes, and letting him wear out Frampton on their record player.

How had the years gone so fast? And how much progress could they have possibly made if they were both still here, on the same patch of earth where their friendship had taken root? Forty-one years, call it twelve feet from his old house to where he sat now. Even with his head full of suds, Max could cut the math down to size: Twelve feet, give or take, covered in 360,000 hours, take or give. That's going nowhere, and nowhere slow.

Before Big Bonk dropped off, he had asked about the work, their truest bond and most common language.

"Dex hired a woman," Max had said.

"Hot damn. I heard that."

"She's gonna be good. She gets it."

"She going to be able to deal with all those guys?"

"As long as I keep her away from your son," Max had said, and that brought out the big honker of a Big Bonk laugh.

"Yeah, I keep telling that kid, I say, 'Boy, your alligator mouth is gonna overload your tadpole ass if you don't watch it.'"

"It's not his mouth I'm worried about."

Another honk from the double-B. "He's my boy, all right. Every time you think he's sowed that last wild oat, here comes another helping." His voice dropped, gravity settling into it. "He's doing all right, though? Kid was damn near born on the line, but that's a big lift, at any age."

"He's great," Max reassured him. "You raised a good one."

Amid all the bullshittery and shaded meanings, this was the unvarnished truth. Whatever his peccadilloes, Little Bonk could wrangle a job and was, at his core, a decent and helping human being. Max had known the kid all his life and would stand up for him all day long. While he wasn't prepared to cop to the cliché of being proud to have his daughter date Little Bonk—honestly, he wasn't sure who would eat up and spit out whom in that theoretical pairing—he would go to the wall for the boy Little Bonk once was and the man he had become.

"It was his mother what done it," Big Bonk said, fading. "Good lady. I couldn't get out of my first marriage fast enough. Third one, I just didn't want any bullshit. But the kid's mom, I should have hung in there. I should have done better. She deserved better."

"Yeah."

He pushed himself up on his elbows, a last rally. "So it's over then, huh? No doubt?"

"It's over," Max said.

"Well, hot damn."

STELLA'S KITCHEN & BAKERY, DOWNTOWN BILLINGS

Saturday, March 16 | 8:18 a.m.
Two hours, ten minutes after Max fell asleep
Forty-eight minutes after his alarm went off

Alexandra came to breakfast carrying optimism and a plan for Max's post-divorce life, because of course she did. (When she actually used that phrase—*post-divorce life*—Max wondered wordlessly what to call the life he already had. Preamble life? Fake life? Your-time-hasn't-been-your-own life? Pre-divorce life? You'll-miss-it-when-it's-gone life? He didn't know. Maybe Alexandra did.)

He ordered the pancake-as-big-as-your-face, and when Alexandra started in again on his diet, he said, "Alexandra, my darling, I swear to god, if you say one word about my cholesterol, I'm going to order three of them and jam them in my motherfucking mouth, and I'm going to make you watch."

That had clammed her up good. And Max had to concede that it was a lot more satisfying than when he had paid her a quarter a minute for her silence when she was a little girl and some solemn occasion—a Christmas church service, say—needed to be observed. As a general guideline, he didn't endorse payoffs, and especially not those that quelled his daughter's delightfully high spirits, but inherent in any guideline is the understanding that it occasionally must be violated for the greater good.

"OK, fine," Alexandra said. "Aren't you just a joy this morning?"

"I haven't slept."

"I shouldn't wonder. I'm sorry, Dad, I really am. But I also understand where Mom's coming from on this. Is that wrong?"

"Of course it's not wrong. I understand it, too."

"Do you?"

From Janine's point of view? Certainly, he did. Gustav and Belle Wendt hadn't raised a boy who couldn't see beyond himself. The part he didn't understand was how he had let this stasis with Janine stretch out so long without giving due consideration to the notion that it all might go this way. He couldn't grasp the finality of it, how there wasn't a strobe light and a blaring horn and a road sign that said THIS IS IT—LAST CHANCE, something that might have warned him away from the peril he was in. That's what he had contemplated while sitting on Big Bonk's couch, rolling it over and over in his head until at last exhaustion had its way with him. What he had decided, to the extent that he had decided anything, was that the warnings were supposed to come from inside him, and those systems had failed spectacularly, and here he was, threatening to jam three hotcakes down his throat to punish his daughter for giving a damn about whether he lived or died. Some plan.

"I understand it," he said. "I just don't know what to do with it."

"Day by day," Alexandra offered with a sunniness that suggested she had come up with that herself. "I'd like to do something for you and your post-divorce life. If you don't mind."

"What?"

"I've got a rental that's available—a cute little two-bedroom over by the college. It's got a garage. A sweet little yard that gets mowed as part of the rent. You can have it."

"Sweetheart, I can afford to get a place. You don't have to put me up."

"I want to. I don't expect you'll want to stay there forever—I didn't—but for now."

"Wait a minute. It's not that little place over—"

"The very one."

Well, if that's not a kick in the hippocampus. Seventeen-year-old Alexandra, busting out the hammer on her piggybank and carrying the paper on her passbook savings, announces to Max and Janine that she has $13,672 in the bank—a short lifetime's accumulation of allowances and tooth fairy payouts and birthday card cash and quarters for silence and summer job paychecks—and that she would like to put it all toward a house. Not school, because she's already sewn that up with scholarships. Not a car, because what does she need a car for when she has Boyfriend Whose Name Has Been Lost to the Passage of Time, and anyway, cars don't appreciate in value. Houses do. She knows this at seventeen. She also knows that she probably can't qualify for an FHA loan—not because she lacks the down, but because she lacks the ongoing income—and so could Max and Janine, pretty please, co-sign the loan, *please, please, please*, they know she's good for it, and the first moment she's able, she'll refinance in her own name.

That was sixteen years and upward of sixty home buys ago, which Alexandra steadily parlayed into a tidy little bundle of equity and monthly rental fees. She lived in that little house all through college, and by twenty-four, she had it paid off. In recent years, Janine had joined the venture, adding another fifteen rental properties to their empire.

"I can't believe you still have it," Max said.

"It's my first dollar bill on the wall."

"I don't know what to say."

"Say yes. It's the best deal you're ever going to get."

He gave it a moment, considering. "Yes."

"Wonderful," Alexandra said. "You're doing the right thing."

"On one condition," he said.

"And that is?"

"The house still costs you something, right? Landscaping, property taxes, utilities, whatever. Let me pay that."

"Deal," she said.

"This is your idea, right?" Max asked. "It's not your mother's doing? Because she and I still have some things to sort out, and I don't want to...I don't want to complicate it like this."

Alexandra whittled off the corner of her egg-white omelet.

"She sees the books, same as me," she said. "But this is all me. Our partnership pays out in proportion. She takes the earnings from her houses. I take the earnings from mine."

"I see."

"Or, lack of earnings, in this case," she said, and then she caught him frowning at that. He couldn't help it. Flagrant money talk tended to sit with him like taco-night indigestion. Ironic, considering he worked in an environment where black money flowed ceaselessly downstream. "Don't worry," she added with a cheerful bent. "Take your time. Stay as long as you want. I want to do this for you."

Max gave his daughter a smile, bottom lip pulled tight over the top. "OK, honey. Thank you."

After he and Alexandra said their goodbyes, Max found Big Bonk in his front yard on Wyoming, putting holes into empties with a pellet gun, squatting low and using his porch as a turret.

"A better activity for the backyard, isn't it?" Max said.

"Probably. But this lets the neighborhood ne'er-do-wells know that I'm on to their crap."

"Right. Well, listen, just came to pick up my stuff."

Big Bonk boosted himself, his Daisy air gun as a crutch. "Gotter done, huh? You sure you don't need to stay awhile longer?"

"No, I'm good. I appreciate the hospitality."

"Want to have a beer before you go?"

"It's a little early."

"For what?"

"Good point."

Max chugged his beer and cursed the name, whatever it was, of whoever had come up with the hair of the dog. The morning chaser was just making everything he felt even worse—the headache from the Old Milwaukee overload the night before, the bleariness from a lack of sleep, the bewilderment that his daughter would now be his landlord, the sheer emotional and physical heft of the coming move. That last part he now wanted over with lickety-split. If a man's leg needs amputating, better to cut it off right then and burn the stump. That's how he had come to feel about the house on Parkhill Drive and his stuff within. Get it out of there. Disengage. Move on.

"I gotta go." Max slapped the empty can on the table. "Thanks for everything, Bonk."

Max received a full-can salute. "Go forth, young man. It's a new world now."

"It's a shit world."

"Can't argue," Big Bonk said.

"All right, then."

Shot through with the liquid gumption to do what was necessary, Max didn't tarry. He got up and wrangled his clamshells toward the door, down the steps, to his waiting truck, into the bed, his movements in reverse of what they had been just more than twelve hours before.

Big Bonk followed him onto the porch. "When do you go out again?"

"A week."

"Be good to be out there, considering."

"Always good to be out there." Max gave a wave and then climbed into the cab. One week to move, one week to at least plant himself into some different dirt, one week to get used to a new route to the store, to the airport, to everywhere. One week until Missouri, which Max never much figured as a place that could soothe his troubles. Now, though, he would take anyplace that didn't strangle him the way Billings threatened to.

With the fifteen-foot U-Haul truck backed into the driveway, Max made quick work of his share of the Parkhill house. Wasn't much to do, when he got right down to it. The bookshelves had come apart as easily as they had gone together in happier times. He stacked them nicely into the cargo bay. He had managed, alone, to cajole the armchair up the ramp, having engaged in the necessary gymnastics to work it out the front door. The sectional, Janine could keep that. The

TV was coming with him; she never watched it anyway.

His books. His bathroom accoutrements. His clothes and hangers and office desk and chair. He would buy cookware, or he would live at McDonald's. Either option would do. The more he went through the stuff, the more he realized that there wasn't much use in fighting over it. Most items were plainly his or plainly hers, and the ones that were debatable, well, they were hers.

Toward the end, Alexandra came by with the key and a call sheet for the electric company and the gas people and the cable provider. "Just let them know to transfer it into your name," she said.

"OK, will do."

"Dad, why don't you wait until tonight? Tyler can come help you."

"Hell, no."

"OK. Well, I'm glad."

Max scooped up the clock radio. *His.*

"Are you?" He wheeled on her, a rising hostility that took him by surprise.

It surprised her, too. "Not that you're divorcing."

"Oh." He was almost disappointed by the walkback. He had felt alive, just for a second there.

"I'm glad you're getting on with it," she said. "It's healthy."

"It's something."

"Dad—"

"No, listen, I'm almost done. Let me just do this, OK?"

"OK." She tiptoed up to him, gave him a kiss on the cheek. He leaned into it. She turned away and left. He followed her out to see her off, silently turning down Janine's new trophy as they passed the hall table.

Back inside, he looked around, bewildered, as if he had lost his place. And he laughed because he *had* lost his place. He carried the clock radio outside and found a place for it in a box still open. *Should have gotten the ten-footer*, he thought, as he looked at the gaping caverns amid his smattering of boxes.

Back inside again, he scoured the hallway closet and found a couple of old winter coats that he could wear again if he would deign to take Dr. Tyler Keisling's advice about trimming down. He left them in place.

At the bottom of the closet, on the floor, two pleather bags, one slightly larger than the other, sitting upright. Max unzipped them and peeled back the skin. A red bowling ball, scripted *Janine*. A blue one, *Max*. Artifacts of their twenties and an active social circle, a decade and relationships long since blown out to sea. Max crouched, got one hand under *Janine*, the other under *Max*, and he stood, knees and hips straining, and he rolled the balls toward his fleshy chest for a better hold. His butt against the railing for balance, he walked them downstairs into Janine's office. Breath heavy, he used his elbow to toggle on the lights. He crouched again and set *Janine* down. "Stay there," he said.

He stood up straight now, with the larger bowling ball in both hands, and he caressed it, feeling its weight. When he was ready, he slipped it to his right hand, reared back, and sent it through the sliding glass door with a terrific crash, the curtains left whipping in the wind that poured in from outside.

Quivering, he knelt for *Janine*. Gave her a few spins in the palm of his hand. He couldn't believe he had done it. Then, before he could make another choice, he rocketed the second ball through the other pane of glass, picking up the spare.

To: Wendt, Max; Hammond, Alicia; Smithlin, Thomas; Macartney,
Stephen
From: Bonk Jr., Mark
Subject: Crack tool run, Cushing line, Moberly, Mo. 3/24/19

*You're invited to join the above project on the above date. We will mobilize
into Moberly, Missouri, on Sunday, March 24th, with a planned launch
of the tool the morning of March 25th.*

*This run is 330 miles from the Moberly station to the receiving station
in Cushing, Oklahoma. At the planned rate of 3 mph, this will be a 110-
hour run. Assuming an on-time launch on the 25th, we will receive the
tool in Cushing in the early-morning hours of March 29th, on the night
shift.*

*At this time, there are no planned shutdowns of the line, but as you
know, that can change. Please secure a one-way ticket into Kansas City,
Missouri (except for Macartney, who will be driving up from his home
in Pig Nostril, Missouri, or wherever it is he lives) for March 24th. From
there, you will receive your rental car and drive to Moberly. Once we're*

about 24 hours from trapping the tool, I will let you know when you can buy your return flight.

We will have our pre-job meeting the evening of the 24th at the Comfort Inn in Moberly. Stay where you wish, but it's a good hotel with a Mantooth rate (which you should ask for if staying there). I'll let you know the meeting time once you've responded to this email with your ETA. So go ahead and get those flight reservations, rental reservations and first night's hotel, and get back to me with your travel particulars, please.

This is a moving run (that is, we'll be staying in a different town each night—the where of it depending on your shift and where we are in the run). You guys know the drill. Alicia, you'll know it by the time the week is out.

We usually do crew assignments at the pre-job meeting, but since Alicia's still settling in after a BIG-TIME AWESOME debut in Buffalo, let's do them now: Max and Alicia on nights, Tommy and Steve on days. Remember, our shifts are local time (noon-midnight days, midnight-noon nights) but pipeline time is MST. Let's keep it straight.

Lots of intermediate pumping stations on this one, gang, and we'll be traveling in three states. Some hostile-landowner issues, too, so let's remember to be safe and look out for each other. I have a list of properties we avoid because the landowners don't like us (or, to be truthful, don't like Mantooth). We've done this line many times, and I anticipate no problems.

I've attached a line map and an info sheet. You'll get tracking spreadsheets on launch day, after I build them. Bring your gear, bring yourselves, and bring your A-game. Any questions, let me know. On mobilization day, please text me when you're on your way to Kansas City, so I know you're in transit. See you in the Show-Me State.

MB2

To: Wendt, Max
From: Hammond, Alicia
Fwd: Re: Crack tool run, Cushing line, Moberly, Mo. 3/24/19

Hostile landowners?

To: Hammond, Alicia
From: Wendt, Max
Re: Fwd: Re: Crack tool run, Cushing line, Moberly, Mo. 3/24/19

Big morons with small...trucks. Yeah, trucks.

To: Wendt, Max
From: Hammond, Alicia
Re: Re: Fwd: Re: Crack tool run, Cushing line, Moberly, Mo. 3/24/19

That made me laugh!

To: Hammond, Alicia
From: Wendt, Max
Re: Re: Re: Fwd: Re: Crack tool run, Cushing line, Moberly, Mo. 3/24/19

Curtsy

BILLINGS LOGAN INTERNATIONAL AIRPORT

Sunday, March 24 | 4:03 a.m.
BIL>SLC: 387 air miles
SLC>MCI: 920 air miles
Kansas City>Moberly: 141 road miles

The new place was three minutes closer to the airport, so that was something. Max finger-drummed the edge of his seat. All airport gate chairs were uniformly uncomfortable in his experience, designed by the same people who did the aircraft chairs, no doubt. He considered his surroundings and the early-morning bleariness that radiated off damn near everybody who had made it up from security. He didn't often sit on this end of the single Billings terminal, as his flights tended to go east toward Minneapolis and on from there.

Counterintuitively, the quickest way for him to get to Kansas City was to go south and west to Utah, then shoot through the gut of the country like a right cross to a fat boy's midsection. *Bam.* He would be there for lunch, with only the two-hour drive to Moberly to be covered after that.

He shrugged, rotating his head counterclockwise to work out the kinks. The week behind him had been, in the imprecise ways of the common vernacular, endless. Strange enough had been the sensation he had picked up after walking into Alexandra's rental house again sixteen years after being a party to its purchase. It wasn't the same place—on the same spot of terra firma, yes, but different in every other way, in its colors and its finishes, and certainly in his juxtaposition to his daughter now when he stood inside it. Regardless of any other long-established dynamics that existed between them, here he was a tenant, and he was so disconnected from any such status, to anyone, that he had been going through his days continually wrong-footed.

Alexandra and Tyler had swung by the third night he was there with some glasses and plates and flatware, the remnants of Tyler's bachelor days, and though *you're the bachelor now* had been implicit in the offering, Max was truly grateful for the gift and only half-serious when he said he would find something high in fat and sugar to place upon his new-to-him finery. Those items, combined with the familiar ones plucked from the Parkhill house, along with a few odds and ends he had snared at a used-furniture store, had given the place a patina of home.

"Good ol' Max," Tyler had said, clapping him on the shoulder.

"Can't keep a fat man down," Max had said in return. Self-deprecation, he figured, would be a reliable cloaking device against what he already knew: that the days were hard and strange enough, his being transplanted here with only a nominal say in the matter, but that the nights drew out intractably. Max had given not nearly enough consideration to how much Janine's snoozing lump had become inseparable from his own on those nights when they lay together. He hadn't anticipated the crush of silence when there were no more words coming at him, even cursory ones. The loneliness, abject and cruel, leaned on him until sometimes he couldn't breathe.

When mobilization day came, he fairly bounded out the door, hungry for normalcy. Every pipeline run carried some flavor of anticipation, but this one, he realized, meant something beyond the ordinary. He was being released back into his desired habitat. Billings, his home since birth, had quite abruptly become foreign territory.

Max withdrew his laptop computer and set it across his knees, gunned it up and found the WiFi lifeline. One by one, his email stash populated. The first was from Janine, presumably the item she had promised him before he left: her proposal for how to disentangle the circulatory system of a thirty-four-year marriage and make a fair accounting for all concerned. She had kept their scant communications on a maddeningly perfunctory level since he had left the house. Her only nod to the destruction he had left behind had been a text message: *Do you feel better now?* To which he had replied: *A little bit, but my only regret is that I didn't have more glass to destroy and more bowling balls to do it with.* She had said nothing else after that and had migrated all communication to email—with Alexandra CC'd, the better to keep either of them (but especially Max) from saying something stupid.

He bypassed Janine's message—it would make better reading in the air—and moved on to some batch projections Little Bonk had sent him. The kid didn't have to do it, but Max appreciated the gesture, which essentially amounted to recognition that Max knew the job better than he did. Little Bonk had adopted a policy of over-sharing with Max, because every now and again—not often—he would miss a detail that Max would catch and flag to his attention. For his part, Max had mastered the art of "Hey, I'm sure you're on top of this, but..." It kept Little Bonk's considerable self-regard propped up and avoided the dumb turf battles Max had seen in other crews from finding purchase on this one.

The third item was the one that caught his full attention.

> *To: Wendt, Max*
> *From: Charles Foster Danforth*
> *Subject: Let us start anew*
>
> *Max, as much fun as I was having on our previous email string, I couldn't disengage myself from your subject line: It's me. I know I'm just an uppity old man—an uppity old man with an expensive education and classical tastes, and I shan't apologize for either*

at this late stage—but it should be It is I. *Subjective pronoun case after a passive verb. I know I'm horrible to harp on this, but one can't just set aside decades of being pedantic, can one? I think not.*

Daughters are wondrous, indeed, or so I am told; I have sons. That is to say I had sons, two of them, but now I have one: Remington Preston Danforth, or Remmy, as he's been known almost from the time he revealed himself from the cosmos. His older brother, Charles Jr., died when the World Trade Center collapsed on 9/11. I do hope it's not jarring for you to read that put so plainly. It's jarring to me to write it, even after all of these years, but I've found that a simple declarative sentence allows me to communicate the horror of that loss without too much trouble. It's just that a simple declarative sentence doesn't begin to capture the light and the color and the spirit of Chas. He was a remarkable man. Should you and I ever have occasion to enjoy that beer we once talked about, I should be well pleased to tell you about him.

But first: Tell me your favorite thing about Alexandra. Make her live and breathe in your reply, please. To the best of my ability, I would like to "see" her as you see her.

And if you'll allow me to overplay my hand, another request, this one for the next time you're in the field: Wherever you stay each day or night, I want you to ask one person the following question and report the answers back to me. What do you like best about where you live? *Don't give me that folderol about having no time for anything but sleep, Max. You eat (clearly— sorry, old boy, but you ARE a bit heavy). You put fuel in your vehicle. Surely you can find time for this.*

Be of good cheer. The whole world is opening up to you.

Your friend,
CFD

Something broke inside Max, something distinct and yet inseparable from his larger emotional system—a cracking that reminded him, almost instantly, of when he was a boy and he would grab a hanging icicle after a freeze and his hard-target tug would bring a wall of ice crashing down from the roof. He'd be damned if he knew what, exactly, had done it now, whether it was the question about Alexandra or the controlled spill of Charles's heart when he talked about his son or even those last couple of words—*your friend*. It could have been any of them. It could have been all of them. However Max had managed to fold himself neatly into a box and get through the preceding week, it was all undone now. He pulled at the bill of his hat, sliding the cap downward until it hung on his face, covering him from nose to chin, and he wept into it, two years' worth of his sweaty leavings—the saltiness and the sickly sweetness—entering his nostrils and exiting again by way of his mouth, then repeating, again and again, with each heave and drawn breath. When he feared he was being watched, he closed the laptop and set it aside, and he hunched himself over, his shoulders balled up and his head down, and he let himself go in fits and starts and sniffles and snorts.

When it was done—when his interior voice had finally, silently urged him to consider where he was and what a fool he must have appeared to be—he looked up and realized things in the airport had spun on without regard for his momentary breakdown. His fellow passengers were a larger throng now, more restless and triggered by anticipation, and they were apparently not inclined to look beyond their own cares and see his. He felt ashamed and...*cleansed*, as if those two things could live inside the same space. Something had been bound up inside him, and it was out now.

Max checked his watch. He had enough time. He gathered his things and cruised down the terminal toward the snack bar, to a row of seats out of the scrum of waiting travelers. There, he set up his laptop again, a compulsion to get an answer out while the words were still arranged in his head the way he wanted them.

To: Charles Foster Danforth
From: Wendt, Max
Subject: Re: Let us start anew

Chuck:

Has anyone ever called you Chuck? I bet they haven't. I bet you'd turn beet red if I ever called you that to your face. Maybe you're beet red now. I hope so. Listen, Chuck, you couldn't get away with any other name if you hung out with the people who hang out with me, so let me also say that my crowd would kick your skinny ass if you called them fat. And they are fat, every single one of them. I've never seen a guy get skinny on the line. I've seen all of them blimp out.

So, yeah, I'm fat. I'm a peaceful guy, so let's leave it at this: I know I'm heavy. I wake up with me every day. It's none of your damn business, so I'd appreciate it if you just wouldn't say anything if you're inclined to say that.

How about them apples? Apples are also red. Like your face right now. Chuck.

I'm only saying this because I really do like you. You amuse me. Lots of people do that. You also make me think, and not nearly enough get to me like that anymore, maybe because I don't let them.

I've decided I'll let you.

I could tell you so much about Alexandra—about how she never disappointed us outside of the occasional dumb kid thing (there was a period, when she was about 13, when everything out of her mouth was the brattiest thing I'd ever heard, until the next one, and then, about a year later, it just stopped and she was lovely). I could tell you about how she was and is self-motivated almost to a ridiculous degree, about how Janine and I would sometimes look at each other like, holy cow, this kid— but maybe the thing I could tell you is that she's had a plan for herself ever since she could, you know, say "I've got a plan for myself." It's detailed, it's precise, and she's damn near reached it.

Here's the plan:

Alexandra, she's 32 now, has been aggressively saving

most of what she makes since she was a little girl. She knew about compounding interest before I did, and that's no lie. I have always sort of lived by the idea that the money's here to spend and more will show up when I need it. Not Alexandra. Since she graduated from college, she's been selling real estate and investing in rental properties, and she has this sort of self-sustaining, increasing bundle of money—I've never asked, but it has to be large—and when it gets big enough, she's going to disengage from it all and have her family. Every time I think she's stretched herself too far out or has gotten too fixated on dollars, I remember what she's in it for. She and her husband—Dr. Tyler Keisling; you'd like him, because he's a self-important guy who gets red in the face if you call him Ty—have held off starting a family because they want to be 100 percent about the kids once they do. And they're close. They talk about it. This thing is about to happen.

Now...

You know what I do. I've tried not to wonder too much if this plan of Alexandra's is directly related to how often I was gone when she was little. Not that it seemed to throw her off-stride. I was there for a lot of the important stuff, and more than that, I was aware of everything, even if I wasn't there, but still—is she thinking about me, reacting to me, when she talks about always being there for her own kids? I don't know. Maybe. Maybe even probably.

What I do know is lots of people talk about what they're going to do, and many fewer of them actually do it. I know a lot of people make plans. Fewer follow through. Lots of people talk a big game. Fewer play it.

Alexandra is in the select few, and that makes me so unbelievably proud of her, and it makes me hope that maybe Janine and I did something right in raising her, even though I often think we didn't bless her with anything, that all of the blessings have come our way just because of who she is. I recognize just how special she is not because she's my daughter, but because I'm in the group that jabbers about doing and plans on doing and talks a big game. And yet, here I am in an airport, waiting to fly to Kansas City. Again.

I hope we have that beer, Chuck. I'd like to see you again sometime. (Why, I have no idea, you pompous bastard.) I think we have things to talk about. I'd like to hear about your sons. I'm so awfully sorry about Chas. I was on a job that day, in Michigan. We finished up and cooled our heels for five days in Detroit before I could get a flight home. Even then, only time in my life, I flew nervously. It was a horrible time. I'm sorry.

Me gotta go now or the plane will leave without I.
Max Wendt Nuts

P.S. Are you for real about interviewing people? I'll think about it. I have this suspicion that you're yanking my chain.

The intercom blared a warning that Delta Flight 1796 to Salt Lake City was in the final stages of boarding. Max closed up his things and stood, the ache pulsating out to his hips, and he jogged, bad knee and all, up the ramp, and presented his phone to the electronic eye.

"You're in 7C, Mr. Wendt. Have a good flight."

To: Wendt, Max
CC: Alexandra Wendt-Keisling
From: Janine Garwood, Garwood and Associates
Subject: The plan

Max:

What follows is my proposal for how we make an equitable division of what we've accumulated during our marriage. I have made this proposal after deep contemplation, trying my best to be fair to both of us. I don't pretend it's a perfect proposal, and if there's any counter-proposal you wish to make, I would welcome it. If we can come to an accord between ourselves, we can proceed with a no-contest divorce. Any lawyer can draw up the agreement we've set forth here, we can go before a judge, and it can be done. When we got married, we did so with open hearts. If we can conclude our marriage in the same way, I would be pleased. I hope you would be, too.

I am satisfied with the division of the household goods that you made unilaterally. There's nothing that you took that I wish to have back. If there's anything you left that you'd now like, let me know.

Otherwise, I think we're in a good place with regard to that.

To be honest, we're down to a house and a business. The first, we purchased and improved and lived in together. The second, I built primarily by myself, with my own vision and my own determination to make it happen. Yes, you were the family breadwinner for the first two-thirds of our marriage, which includes some overlap with my early years as a businesswoman, when I was just getting going. You should be fairly compensated for that. But, and I hate that this sounds like a warning, but I guess it is: If you have any designs on getting half my business (that is, community property), you may as well say so now and get yourself a lawyer, because there will be a fight. I hate that I even have to take this stance, but I want you to know the stakes. The bowling balls through the basement slider were not reassuring to me in my assessment of your attitude toward this.

If you're inclined to hear out my offer with regard to the house and the business, here it is:

We will get a professional appraisal of the house—you can choose the appraiser, if you wish—and I will give you, in cash, 90 percent of its value in exchange for having my name solely on the deed. I shouldn't have to tell you that's 40 percentage points more than you'd get in a split-it-all-down-the-middle divorce, thus reflecting both your interest in the house and some recompense for your financial assistance during the early years of my business. And it allows us to end our marriage without liquidating everything. I love that house; it is my home. In the years we lived together there, I spent countless more nights in it than you did. That sounds like blame, but I don't mean it that way. It's a fact.

The rest of it is easy: You continue with your job, your medical and life insurance, your 401(k). And I continue with mine. What you make is yours. What I make is mine. We will get off each other's paperwork, in other words.

Does this sound amenable to you, Max? Is there anything you'd like to change or add?

In closing, I want to say one thing: I know you're emotional about this now. I can even appreciate how it must have caught you off-guard in the moment, although surely by now you've had a chance to think about it *and see that it shouldn't have been a surprise. I think you should reflect on this, read it again, reflect some more, then let me know your disposition. Work to get beyond the emotion and make a rational decision.*

I've been emotional about it, too. But I cried myself out long ago. Now, I just want to be done.

Have a good trip.

– J

To: Wendt, Max
From: Alexandra Wendt-Keisling
Re: the plan

Dad, this sounds pretty good. I'm telling you the same thing I told Mom: I love you both, I will always love you both, be good to each other, even in parting. Plus, what did you buy that house for, $50,000? It has to be worth $325K. That's $292K in your pocket. Or in your IRA. I can hook you up with a tax guy so you can take maximum advantage of that.

Love you,
Alex

ALONG A FENCELINE IN NORTH-CENTRAL MISSOURI

Monday, March 25 | 10:01 a.m.
One minute after the scheduled start of the run

Max walked down into the barrow pit with Alicia, their boots crunching the brown, shock-frozen weeds beneath their feet. He stood, holding two squat, gray boxes in his arms, and he nodded toward her, asking her to demonstrate how to find the buried pipeline, as he had taught her to do in New York.

From the front pocket of her high-visibility vest, she withdrew a black plastic stick, about the circumference of a broom handle, tugged on a silver crown at the top of it, and pulled the pipe finder out to full length, like a retractable antenna. "Five feet west of the marker, right?" she asked.

"That's what the field notes said," he confirmed.

She aligned her body with the above-ground marker that announced the pipeline's presence. She stood on the upstream side;

an identical plastic post, across the road and in the other barrow pit, rose up and marked the downstream flow. She faced west, and holding the pipe finder in a way that the antenna stuck out directly in front of her, she took inching steps in the direction she faced. Sure enough, after about five feet, the antenna arm swung gracefully toward the opposite marker.

"There she is," Alicia said, her voice joyous.

"Good job."

She used the heel of her boot to dig a mark into the ground at the angle of the line's flow. Max came over and set the boxes side by side on the mark. "Go get the geophone and the receiver," he told her, and she scurried back up the hill to her vehicle, rooted around in the backseat, and brought the items to him down in the pit.

"All right," he said, "set it up."

Alicia spiked the geophone off to the side of the boxes, its white fuselage pointing to the sky like an aroused PVC penis. She then set her receiver in front of them, at the same angle. Max knelt and inspected the alignment of equipment and found it agreeable.

"So what you do is, you set the boxes like so." He turned a dial on each a half-turn, and LED lights atop the boxes went through a series of colors until settling on green. "Now set your receiver." She reached over and depressed the power button.

"We're all set," Max said.

Little Bonk had called them both around eight that morning, told them not to make haste in coming out to the field, that the German technicians were way behind on getting the tool ready to slip into the line. (They weren't really German, a point Max had wearied of making to him; the tool was from Germany, and the analysts who interpreted its readings remotely were German, but the technicians accompanying it were from Houston—this was not a hard concept.)

"Nine-thirty will be fine," he had told Max. "I imagine you'll sit there with your thumb up your ass until noon and hand it off to the day guys. You know the drill."

"I do, at that," he had said.

He now drew the picture for Alicia as they stood outside her car. The

Toyota bumped with the percussion from its speakers, the Bluetooth geophone's blowback coming through them as the wind battered it. Max rubbed his hands together and blew into them for warmth; between Alicia's mobile office equipment and her luggage, there wasn't room for both of them in the car. He would relay this information and then go sit in his own rented Nissan, across the road and out of the wind.

"Dollars to doughnuts we don't track today," he said. "I've seen it too many times."

"So we just sit here and—"

"And at noon we hand off to Smithlin and Macartney and we go get some sleep."

She chuckled. "And for that we get twelve hours' pay? Doesn't seem fair to those guys."

"We stick to the shifts," he said. "Ours is midnight to noon. Theirs is noon to midnight. Fair isn't the point."

"I know."

"Besides," he said, a smile brimming, "you won't feel sorry for those guys in about twenty-four hours, when you're running on fumes of adrenaline. We've got five days of this coming. The hours have a way of balancing out."

"I understand," she said. "So at noon, we drive to where, again?"

"Marshall."

"Right. Because that's pretty much where the pig will be when we come back on."

"That's the hope, if all goes well." He choked back the rest of the thought: *If they take long enough to prep the tool, maybe we come right back here. Or maybe they kick it until tomorrow. Or maybe they miss their batch of oil and send us home.*

He went over it all with her again, how her receiver, picking up the ELF waves and the magnetic hit, and geophone, recording the aural passage of the tool, would dictate the time she would record on the tracking spreadsheet. She need only verify that the gray timer boxes, more precise backups, tripped upon passage. He peeked in her window and verified that the signals were already running from the receiver on the line back to her computer, which sat on a makeshift desk in her passenger seat. The tool itself, a monster twenty-eight footer that would come swimming down the line, would gather information from inside the pipe. Their job was to make sure passages occurred and that the whole works kept moving. "Every stop," he said, "you put out traffic cones, timer boxes, geophone, receiver. The pig goes by, you collect everything, load it up, move down the line, and do it again."

"Lather, rinse, repeat," Alicia said.

"Pretty much. I do a checklist, every time, because checklists work for me. Some guys—*people*—do it all in the same order every time, so it becomes muscle memory. Do what works for you, and keep your head in it. It's easy to get tired out here. It's easy to get careless. Everybody, I don't care who they are, has driven off and left something behind, or forgotten to set it out in the first place. It happens. If it does, let me know, and we'll figure out how to fix it."

"OK. I don't want to mess up."

He smiled again. Her earnestness became her. "Nobody does. You will. *I* will. That's why we work in teams out here. We back each other up. You're gonna do great. Don't worry about it."

She looked—just for a second, and then the second was gone—as if she might tear up. Max thought it best to move along.

"I'm cold," he said. "I'm getting in the car."

While they sat in their separate vehicles, waiting out Little Bonk and the technicians back at the launch valve, Max thumbed out and sent a delayed reply to Janine on his phone.

OK, let's proceed.

He semi-expected some grand psychological or physiological impact from the issuance of those words—shallow breathing, a heart attack, elation, melancholia, something—but near as he could tell, the wind whipping outside his window hadn't broken pace, and his mood and nervous system remained intact. It was Janine's contention that their marriage, or at least its efficacy, was in the final throes of an untended death. Maybe the last rites—the what's-mine-is-mine-and-hers-is-hers and the paperwork and the court filings—would pass through just as quietly.

Little Bonk broke in with a group message for the four trackers:

These sauerkraut eaters aren't gonna be ready to go until after lunch. You guys be ready to make the switch at noon.

One, two, three, four, the emojis sprang up in response: thumbs-up (Alicia), thumbs-up (Smithlin), fingers in the OK position (Max), flexed muscle (Macartney).

Now, a text from Alicia to him: *Sauerkraut eaters?*

He wrote back. *Little Bonk's colorful personality. Those guys are from frapping Texas. The tool is from Germany.*

Oh. LOL. That's funny.

I guess.

Can you tell me the Little Bonk story now?

What story?

You said his name was a long story.

Oh. Right. Not much to it: His dad, Mark Bonk, was my first boss out here. We all called him Bonk. When the kid came along, especially after he grew up and joined the crew, we all called him Bonk, too. You can't have two Bonks.

Nobody needs that, she replied. He guffawed.

What I mean is, one became Big Bonk and the other Little Bonk. That keeps them straight. When it was just the old man, we didn't need distinctions.

There's a word for that, she wrote.

Oh?

Retronym, she wrote. *It's a new name for an old thing. Like, there used to just be guitars. But then they invented electric guitars, so you had to call the old guitar something else, so they became acoustic guitars.*

You're pretty smart.

English major. Nothing smart about that.

Still.

She messaged a thumbs-up. Emojis, he had learned, were the off-ramps of text conversations. He dug back into his email, looking for... something. Nothing there.

Does he know we call him that? she wrote.

Max chuckled at the *we.* It was a good sign. She was one of them.

Hell no, he thumbed out. *I don't think he'd like it much. To his face, he's always Bonk.*

Got it.

Behind his back, call him what you like. I sometimes call him Debra.

The laughing-and-crying emoji came back at him. Max was proud of himself for pulling that one out of his ass.

M ax left her around 11:30, scooting down the line to the next passage point, where he waited for Macartney to show up for the shift change. Max had already made arrangements at the Comfort Inn in Marshall, telling the clerk he would be coming in early and would appreciate a room, if one was available. By the time he drove the forty or so miles to town and scarfed down some lunch, the clock would be drawing up near two p.m. He would need to wake up by nine to have a bite, pack up his stuff, watch a little TV and head out into the field again. Once the job was rolling, the clock—more than the landscape, more than the monotony, more than anything—held sway.

Macartney rolled behind him about ten minutes before noon, his jacked-up Ford 350 belching noise and black exhaust, the bed carrying his four-wheeler, which showed up on every job and, as far as Max could tell, never got untethered from the truck. Macartney was a real hillbilly boy, which had nothing to do with where he was from and everything to do with how he lived. He was profoundly interested in cheap beer, outdoor recreation, and computer porn, and was doggedly incurious about the larger world. If it weren't for pigging, he probably never would have been compelled to leave his home county. He sure as shit didn't fly; was flat-out terrified of it was more directly the point. While everybody else mobilized out to jobs on planes and in rental cars, Macartney burbled in with his big truck, laying ninety thousand miles a year on it.

Max swung out of the car, popped the hatch, and began gathering timer boxes for transfer to Macartney's crew cab. As he passed his counterpart's open window, he handed through a memory stick containing the spreadsheet. He returned to his car and gathered a fire extinguisher and the hard copy of the spreadsheet—computers had a tendency to crash and die, and in the most remote of places, so everything got backed up old-school—and brought those back. Macartney, finding the electronic spreadsheet in good order, handed the memory stick to Max. They had done this ballet hundreds of times before.

"How's the chick working out?" Macartney asked.

"She's doing fine."

"Well, she ain't really done anything yet."

"She was great in Buffalo."

"One site," Macartney said, dismissive.

"Yeah."

"There's, like, three hundred on this one."

Two-hundred sixteen, but whatever. "OK, Steve. I'll text you around nine, see where you are."

"Hey, wait a second." Macartney got out of his truck, looking a little like a man fashioned out of string beans. Max flashed on what he had told Danforth, that everybody on the line was a fat ass. *Exception to the rule here*, he thought.

"Yeah?"

"Why are you training her? Why not me or Tommy?"

"How the hell should I know?" Max was irritated on any number of levels, but most of all, he could feel the encroaching clock now, just a hair past noon. They were into the time that belonged to him, not to the company.

"I just don't understand why Dex hired her."

"Well, it's simple, Steve," Max said. "He got tired of Hanley fucking up every day of the goddamn year, just like you did."

"Yeah."

"OK, then."

"I think she's stuck up," Macartney said. "Wouldn't have a beer with me and Tommy last night."

Smart, Max thought. "Well, maybe she doesn't drink," he said. "You ever think of that?"

Macartney plainly hadn't thought of that, nor, Max figured, had he ever thought of anything that deviated from his own desires or experiences. Macartney gave a little smirk—one that said, *well, you got me that time, Mr. Max*—and climbed back into his truck.

The drive to Marshall gave Max the time to chew on a few things, to unsatisfactory conclusions all around. The exchange back on the line settled into his stomach like a bad lunch. He saw now that Dex had little choice—*no choice*—in who drew the duty of getting Alicia up to speed. Little Bonk was out for reasons pragmatic (he didn't spend much time in the field once things got rolling) and obvious (his libido and the intracompany trouble it might induce). But neither Smithlin nor Macartney would have been any better, and now Max thought they might have been even worse. Steve's attitude, in particular, had surprised him. Max had never known the guy to be edgy about much of anything, and yet what he had seen at the change of shift was latent hostility looking for an ignition source. *Why?* The answer came easily enough when Max turned the question toward the familiar: Would he have supported Alexandra if she had bopped up to him and said, "Hey, listen, Dad, I'd like to chase the pig around"?

Hell to the no. Not because she lacked the capability—anybody with a decent brain and the ability to run a computer could do it. But if she had done it well, some of the guys out in the field would have felt their balls shrink. Simple as that. This woman frightened Steve. For all Max knew, she frightened Tommy, too. And that shifted everything in a way he hadn't prepared himself to absorb.

Max decided he would start pulling away from Alicia, small bit by small bit, not because he didn't like her (he did) or didn't think she could handle the work (she could), but because he wasn't willing to be redefined as some sort of overseer or protector by her presence on the job. He hadn't signed up for that. For the good of the crew, and as a personal favor to Dex, he would hang in until she could handle all the functions on her own, then that would be that. Some jobs, they might be on the same shift. Others, they wouldn't. So it had gone with every other pig tracker on the crew for more than three decades now. Once she could stand on her own, she would stick with the crew, or not, on her own merits. Max would be out of it.

He had purposely told Alicia to book herself a place in Marshall, not tipping his hand as to where he was staying. She had a few choices; not many. The only real dictate was to keep the nightly rate somewhere in the low one-hundred-dollar range and to get a Mantooth rate if one was available. Tomorrow, he would have her project out where they would be on their third shift. He wouldn't give her the answer. And once she figured out how to do her nightly hotel reservation—project the pig's eventual location, find the nearest place to stay, call and book a room—another rope binding her to Max would be cut.

Sure enough, that's how he preferred to go. The job had a pleasing solitude to it, one he aimed to preserve. The whole crew congregated in a single place to start, and after that, they were solo ships in a loosely confederated fleet. You worked the line with your partner, and when shift change came, you went your own way and your partner went his. Or *hers*.

That was the deal for more than just the trackers on the line. From here until they trapped the tool in Cushing, Little Bonk would mostly be a ghost, flitting from hotel room to hotel room, somewhere in between where the pig was and where it was going that day. Most traces of him would be in the emailed updates and the every-four-hours calls to the shift leaders, making sure all was well. Little Bonk would show up at a shift change or two, just to get an updated spreadsheet and to shoot the shit with his guys, but that was it, unless some unforeseen problem emerged mid-run. He didn't want the extended face-time any more than anybody else did. The job ran on solitude and self-reliance. To an outsider, that might have been viewed as a drawback, but it was Max's favorite part.

He counted on it.

PIZZA HUT

Monday, March 25 | 1:13 p.m.
Forty-seven minutes before targeted bedtime

Max used the right angle of a slice of pepperoni pizza as a fork, picking up the last of his pasta primavera and shoveling it into his mouth, followed by the pizza in four quick bites. He stacked the plate on the three others at the table's edge. Loaded with the requisite carbohydrates, he could feel his eyelids growing heavy.

The young man who had seated him for the lunch buffet—a gangly kid in an ill-fitting black shirt and baggy black trousers—swung by and wrangled the plastic plates. "Ready for the check?" he asked.

Max glanced up and caught the nametag pinned to the shirt. MARC, ASSISTANT MANAGER. "Yeah, I guess so," Max said. "Appreciate it."

Marc started to slip away, and Max, hearing his own voice as if he were a bystander, asked, "Hey, can I ask you a question? You got a minute?"

The young man cast his gaze about. It was the two of them, plus the woman cooking pizzas in the back, plus another kid Max figured to be the dishwasher, although he hadn't seen much evidence of industry there. Max had steadily depleted the wares during lunch.

"Sure," Marc said.

Max's sense of dignity had, finally, caught up to his impulse. He wished there were a way to just let this go, but if he did that, he would look even dumber than he did now.

"OK, this'll sound weird, but just bear with me, it's for a...a project, I guess you could say."

"OK."

"Do you live here in Marshall?"

A direct enough question, and one that brought up the kid's defenses. "What's this for?"

"For?" Max was puzzled. A good question, one he wished he had asked of Danforth. "It's not really for anything, just my curiosity. If you're from here, I'd like to ask you what your favorite thing about the place is."

"About Marshall?"

"Yeah."

"Well, I grew up here, so I guess the best thing I can say is that I know it pretty well." Max nodded at this, unsure if he wanted the kid to keep going or to be let off the hook. "Listen, mister," Marc said, "I'll get your check, OK?"

"That's fine."

However long this takes, Max thought, *it's going to be the longest however-long-this-takes of my life. It might be easy for Charles Foster Danforth to bop up to strangers in airport concourses, the over-learned freak, but it's a little harder out here in cold-ass Missouri.*

He looked out the window to his left, across the parking lot to the Comfort Inn, up to the third floor, where his room awaited. Better to get back to the mundane and the reliable. Shower, have a little tug, let sleep come on. Already, a headache was gathering strength, an insurrection he had tried to put down with a few ibuprofen.

What had he gone and done that for, putting the kid on the spot like that, looking the fool? He couldn't eat here again, that was for sure.

Rhetorical though it was, his internal questioning had an obvious answer: The kid's response, if he had been inclined to offer one, would have been an offering he could take back to Charles. It would have pleased him, and Max noted, with some astonishment, that he enjoyed pleasing the odd old man. Further astonishment came when Max also noted that he had kind of looked forward to hearing what Marc had to say. Imagine that.

"Here's your check," Marc said, slipping it onto the table. "You can pay up front."

Max felt his face go flush. "Thanks."

"Listen," the kid said, "sorry I was defensive and stuff. The truth is, my favorite thing about Marshall is that I can still see my way out of it."

"What do you mean?"

"I mean, I'm just doing a job. But next fall, I'm moving to Kansas City. Gonna go to school. I've been living with my folks, saving my money."

Max gestured to the empty bench. "You want to sit down?"

Marc creased himself at the middle and slipped in. "Thanks."

"I'm not keeping you from anything?" Max asked.

"Just cashing you out."

"OK, Marc. Good enough. What are you going to study?"

"I haven't decided. Something business-related. I'm kind of getting a late start."

"How old are you?"

"Twenty-two."

"You're a kid," Max said.

"I guess. Anyway, I should have gone four years ago. Wanted to. I'd been running track, was pretty good at it, and then I busted my knee—"

"No kidding," Max said. "I ran track."

"Yeah? Which event?"

"I was a quarter-miler."

"I did the distance events," Marc said. "Sixteen-hundred and thirty-two-hundred meters."

"You've got that big pumping heart."

"I guess. But my knee's for shit now."

"So—"

"So anyway," Marc continued. "I was gonna go run track up at Truman State, but I got hurt, and I kind of..." He gazed off, contemplating. Max waited. "I guess I kind of got depressed. Didn't go to my classes. Just hung out and drank and stuff."

"And stuff," Max repeated, smiling. He knew about stuff.

"Anyway," Marc said, "I'm ready now. Better late than never, right?"

"That's what they say, yes."

For all its other wonders, the chat with the ambitious kid at Pizza Hut had put Max behind the clock. It was nearly two-thirty when he finally disengaged, wished the kid luck, said he would come by and see him if the crew was out this way again before fall. He tamped down the urge he had to file a report to Danforth now, lest he give more time away. It was two-thirty-five when Max breached the hotel room. Two-forty-one by the time he unpacked his clothes for the next shift, shimmied out of the ones he was wearing, got the geophone and the gas monitor charging in a wall socket, and had his computer plugged in, ready for consultation when he awoke. Two-forty-four when his full nakedness slipped under the hot stream of the showerhead. Two-fifty-one when he stepped out again and began drying himself. Two-fifty-three when he closed the blinds tight, fastening them with a clothespin to keep out the daylight. Two-fifty-four when he turned back the covers and climbed into bed. Two-fifty-eight when he fell asleep with his flaccid dick in his hand, the porn still playing on his phone screen, having never brought Max to the heights he hoped to reach.

8.3 MILES OUT OF MARSHALL

Monday, March 25 | 11:41 p.m.
Forty-three minutes before the anticipated pig passage

Alicia had her equipment positioned properly and up and running before Max got to her. He had come from the previous site, where Macartney still waited for the pig that would be arriving any second now. Max had gathered a copy of the electronic spreadsheet and all but two of the timer boxes. Macartney would swing the rest of the items by after he got his last pass of the night.

"Damn well done," Max told Alicia now. "You don't need me to stick around. You've got this."

She laughed, reached for his wrist, and said, "Really, I'd prefer you stayed. A site or two. Just to be sure."

"No worries."

They had spoken briefly back at the hotel, a little after nine p.m., Alicia coming through the sliding doors with a bag from Subway, Max

headed out for Taco Bell. Intentionally, Max had held it to chitchat—
Did you sleep well? Looks like we're on target. See you out there. She was
fledgling as a pig tracker, but she was also fully capable. Time to let her
fly. Gallop. Walk. Whatever a pig tracker did. Waddle.

Macartney's text pinged both of their phones.

MP33.79
10:44:43
2.99 mph
Boxes 1789,1668

Max sent back a thumbs-up; seconds later, Alicia did, too. The time,
for many newbies, was the hardest part of the learning curve. They
worked across several time zones—Central on this run, Eastern when
they were in New York, Mountain, even Pacific on the odd California
job. But pipeline time was always, ceaselessly, relentlessly Mountain
Standard. Complicating matters was that they were conversant in
the time wherever they happened to be standing for matters of shifts,
flights, and eating schedules, but it was pipeline time for the pig.

"You got that recorded?" Max asked her.

"Yep, just now."

"Pipeline time?"

"Yep."

"What's the ETA at this milepost?"

Alicia, now seated in her car with the door open, peered at the
computer spreadsheet. "Eleven-twenty-five, twelve-point-three-nine
seconds. It went up."

"A few seconds, yeah," Max said. "It was a little slower to him than
anticipated. So be ready. It could balance out."

"How does that happen? How come it's sometimes fast and
sometimes slow?" she asked.

"Well, it's only a few seconds. But different reasons. Maybe a slight
variance in the pressure. Maybe a minor surveying mistake. Maybe
some oil bypass on the tool. That's why we watch and we listen."

"Got it."

"You got your reservation for after shift?" Max asked her.

"Yeah," she said. "Comfort Inn in Harrisonville."

Damn. She is good. That's where he had put in, too.

"Sounds good."

"I figure I might as well reel in those loyalty points," she said.

"Abso-damn-lutely. Might as well get some reward for being out here."

"I hear that."

"You doing OK?" Max asked. "Everything making sense?"

"Sure."

"Good."

They waited, with Max standing outside her open door, Alicia inside the car. He called the line operator in Calgary and let the engineer on duty know that he and Alicia would be on shift for the next twelve hours. He confirmed his phone number, promised to call back with an update in a couple of hours, said his goodbyes, and hung up.

A few seconds later, his phone pinged again, the group message with Little Bonk and all the trackers.

Hammond, 2/24
12 hours
61 miles
$94.48 hotel

"Good job, remembering that," Max said. He felt a bit sheepish that she had beaten him to giving Little Bonk the daily report for the timesheet and client billing. He had told her, what, the day before that midnight shift change was the best time to report in, since all daily hours and billable expenses were encompassed from midnight to midnight.

In quick succession, Smithlin and Macartney and Max followed with their stats, and then Little Bonk rounded it out: *Thx, all.*

"You cold?" Alicia asked.

"Naw," Max said. "I'm fine." The gusts had died down, which made all the difference. They probably wouldn't see the thermometer above thirty-five, but that was tolerable enough if the wind weren't cutting into them.

Several minutes on, Macartney arrived, rolling black smoke in his wake. He got out of his truck and pulled the last two timer boxes from the cab.

"Just throw them in the back of mine, if you don't mind," Max said.

Macartney tossed him a dorky salute and slow-walked to the hatch of Max's Nissan. He ambled back to them with his thumbs hooked in his belt loops.

"How y'all doing?"

"Hanging in," Max said.

"Hi, Steve," Alicia said.

He peered in at her. "First pass of the job coming, huh?"

"Yep."

"Poppin' your cherry."

"OK," Max said.

Macartney gave them a grin. "I'm just joshing around. You know that."

"I know," Max said.

"All right, kids, don't do nothing I wouldn't do." He wheeled back to his truck, climbed in, and blew past.

"Hillbilly fuck," Max muttered.

"What does he want us to do?" Alicia asked, a half-smirk crossing her face. "Double negatives are hard."

Sixteen minutes out from the ETA, they heard the first thumping through Alicia's geophone, the sound of the big pig's cups striking the welds inside the pipe, amplified through her car speakers. *Kachunk-a-chunk-a-chunk-a-chunk.* A few seconds' pause. *Kachunk-a-chunk-a-chunk-a-chunk.*

"She's coming," Max said.

"It's louder than it was in Buffalo."

"A bigger tool. A bigger pipe."

"Ah, OK."

They listened longer, and the sound drew nearer, straining through the speakers with rising urgency. Max showed her again how she could use the cab control unit to dial in the purest possible sound, filtering out such variables as wind and rain and power line frequencies.

"Sometimes, if it's really late and I'm close to a house, I'll switch from the speakers to headphones so I'm not disturbing anyone nearby," he said.

"It does sound like we ought to jack this sucker up and go cruising," she said, giggling, over the concussive thump that spilled from the car.

At about three minutes out, the sounds from the insistent flow of liquid could be heard through the speakers.

"That's the product," Max said. "It's pushing down the line. We're getting close now."

He watched the computer display from her wireless receiver, which sat out at the pipeline marker with the timer boxes. Over and over, the fractions of a second sped by, pushing the numbers ever higher.

"Here it comes," he said.

The sound that came wasn't the old Midwestern tornado chestnut— *it sounded like a freight train*—so much as feedback and a long whoosh, almost euphoric in its cascade. The receiver posted the ELF hit and the time of passage, and the mag hit showed on the screen as if a rope had been expertly whipped. Max peeked over the car roof into the barrow pit. Blinking red LEDs flashed back at him.

"Timer boxes picked it up," he said.

"OK, cool." Alicia recorded the time, first by hand onto her hard copy and then by punching it into the electronic spreadsheet, along with the timer box numbers. The algorithm chewed on the new information and spat out a new set of ETAs, right down the line.

She started out of the car to grab her equipment, and Max issued a gentle reminder: "Text me the data so I can update my spreadsheet," he said.

"Right. Sorry."

"No big. It's your first pass."

"Yay!" she said. "What do I get?"

"You get to do another one."

After Max took his pass at the next site, they made a show of hanging out together until Alicia's next one came, but there was no reason to anymore. She had it down. She studied her field notes, put the equipment in the right place, got a crisp, no-doubt-about-it pass. Max imparted a few basic words of advice about how to position the car on blind hills, what to do if she couldn't get the equipment exactly where it needed to be, to skip any site where she wasn't certain of safety, and other such hypotheticals, but otherwise it was her show now.

A memory came to him of teaching Alexandra how to ride a bicycle—his thick hands there for her as guardrails on the first few wobbly attempts, but no longer needed just as soon as she figured out the proportions of balance and propulsion. By sundown that day, she was whipping up and down the sidewalk on Parkhill Drive. He could close his eyes and see it there in the past, in high resolution, as if it had happened just a whisper ago.

"OK, I'm gonna scoot," Max said. "For the rest of the night, let's just make sure we drive past each other when we're moving between sites. That way, we know we're moving along, OK?"

"Sounds good," Alicia said. "I'm going to kind of miss the company."

"You won't for long. The solitude is my favorite part of the job." He scrambled to the next bit, seeing her eyes flicker. "No offense to you. It's been fun. I'm just saying, in general, you learn to enjoy being alone."

"I guess."

"OK, then," he said.

Max moseyed on to the next site, 1.47 miles in line flow from where Alicia had just taken a pass, 1.52 miles from where she was headed. The pipeline marker stood on the high side of the barrow pit on a lonely stretch of dirt road. He positioned the car to where the Bluetooth antenna could make a line-of-sight connection with where the marker lay, then he put the car in park and climbed out, his senses locking in, a whistle on his lips. Over the years, he had stopped being surprised by what he sometimes encountered in these desolate places in the pitch-black of night. Dogs running loose, unconcerned with him. Old men on four-wheelers, wailing into the gaping nowhere. Raccoon hunters slipping out of the woods. If anyone was lurking, he wanted to make sure they knew he was around.

He set his headlamp—his "dickhead light," as Big Bonk used to call it, for reasons Max had never quite corralled—and he craned his neck, casting the beam over the route he would have to walk to get his equipment in place. The crusted snow from some weeks-ago storm stubbornly clung to the wall of the pit, in a place the sun didn't reach. He would be careful through there. He had turned ankles in stuff like that.

A wind kicked up, filling his senses with the scent of cow dung from some adjacent, unseen pasture. He twitched his nose, sniffling, and he set to work. Traffic cones got dropped at the front and back of his vehicle on the roadside. He walked out the timer boxes first, setting them down at the marker, then extracting his pipe finder to establish the line and the angle of travel. He positioned the boxes.

Back to the car. He gathered the geophone and the receiver, toting them in one hand across the expanse. He lined the receiver up perpendicular to the timer boxes, and he spiked the geophone to the side. An amazing instrument it was, as sensitive as a virgin's clitoris. He could set it in six feet of crusted snow and pick up the sound of a passing pig twelve feet farther below that.

He reached down, turned the dials on the timer boxes, engaged the receiver, then trudged back to the car. As he sank into his seat, the readouts—mag and ELF—started sliding across his screen.

The phone rang. Little Bonk.

"Hey, Bonk."

"How's it going out there?"

"Steady Eddie."

"Good to hear. And Alicia?"

"All good."

"That's great. Tommy had good things to say."

"Oh?"

"Yeah. Said she was on time, knew the drill. You're a teacher, man. A molder of minds."

"Well, that's good to know."

"Anyway," Little Bonk said, "I'm just checking in. Gonna get some sleep. I'll call you around six, as usual."

"Sounds good."

"Stay safe out there."

How's your son?

They were eight miles down the line from where they had started, three a.m., the darkest of night upon them, the passes coming right on schedule, the handoffs clean, the exchange of information seamless. A couple of stops at each other's car door just to check in. Minor chitchat.

He's good. I get to see him next week. How's your daughter?

The question caught him crosswise. He wasn't sure he knew how to answer. For the longest time, Alexandra had been on a glide path through her own life and her own priorities. They talked often, but aside from recent Janine-driven events, he couldn't for the life of him remember the last time they'd gone deep enough for him to be able to tell another human being how she was in the dark depths of her private thoughts. Alexandra tended to keep things circumspect, which was fine, and he tended to ramble on, which had been fine until it wasn't. What's more, the question from Alicia wasn't congruent. An inquiry about a little boy caught in some unexplained domestic dispute was different from one about a grown, sovereign woman.

All right, I guess. Busy, busy.

I hear that.

There wasn't anywhere to go from there. And then Max Wendt went.

I'm in the middle of a divorce. We haven't had time to talk much.

The message hung there in the maw between them. It was alone and untouched an aching, protracted time, long enough for Max to wonder what in the hell had possessed him to share it. But it was out, gone, not a draft email that he could reconsider and shit-can. He had written it. She had received it.

I'm so sorry, Max. That must be hard.

Yeah.

Do you want to talk about it?

Later.

OK.

He waited, thumbs over the touchscreen, the arrangement of words not yet catching up to what he wished to convey.

I appreciate it, though. Really.

You bet.

T he sun began muscling into the sky just before seven, twenty-one miles into their segment of the run, and the nighttime ceded the stage to pinks and oranges smeared across the horizon. It was the part of the night shift Max most looked forward to, how the world could seemingly be at a dead stop under the cover of black, only to emerge once the spin of the earth flipped on the lights. At once, songbirds began putting notes on the air, tractors plied the nearby fields, school buses took to the roads, and life went on. Max and Alicia went on, too, interlopers in a place that belonged to others.

I'm tired, she wrote. *Eyes heavy.*

First full shift on nights is always the worst. You'll sleep like a baby, though.

Can't wait.

He began to write out a cautionary note, about how it became harder to stay awake once the sun rose, as counterintuitive as that might seem, and how she should take extra care now that her synapses probably weren't firing the way they had earlier. They were sharing the roads now, and that heightened the risks. He then reconsidered. These things were hers to discover, just as he had once discovered them for himself. Just as everybody had to on the first big job.

It helps to walk a little bit, he wrote. *If you've got time before a pass.*

That's OK?

Of course.

OK. I didn't know if I needed to always be in the car.

It's fine. That thing is humping so hard, you'd hear it through the speakers even if you were 100 yards away.

Thanks, she wrote. *P.S. You said "humping."*

A chuckle rumbled through his throat. *See, this is what happens when you get loopy.*

LOL

At nine, a shade over twenty-seven miles into their shift, Max reminded her to text Tommy and tell him where to meet up at shift change.

Already done it.

OK, good, he wrote. *We're on the downhill now. Three passes left for you, four for me, and we're done. Piece of cake.*

It hasn't been so bad. I'm hungry, though.

Me, too. There's a good Mexican joint close to the hotel in Harrisonville.

Ooooh. I like Mexican.

Want to go?

Yesssss.

He sent her a thumbs-up.

The *kachunk-a-chunk-a-chunk-a-chunk* picked up intensity. He had put the earphones on, sitting as he did in front of a tidy farmhouse with a small yard of brown grass out front and chicken coops in back. Max took seriously these many hours he spent idling in places that weren't his, making efforts to leave no trace that he had been there and to not be disruptive while he lingered. As the pig came ever closer, he mimicked the beat by squeezing air and saliva through his back teeth, making a scrunchy accompaniment. This had all gone so much better than he'd had any standing to hope. A full shift—so far—of perfectly captured passes, no equipment failures, no timer boxes left back in a ditch somewhere, just a smooth cruise toward a handoff to Smithlin and Macartney.

The sound of flowing oil now joined the ensemble. What's more, Max realized, he wasn't just getting a capable co-worker, someone the whole crew needed in Hanley's regrettable wake. He might also have a friend here, too, maybe someday. A friend his daughter's age. *Imagine that.* She was a good egg, Alicia, and given a moment to ponder it, Max realized that she and stuck-up Charles Danforth were the best prospects as friends he had cultivated in a good long time. *Not bad, considering the losses in between.*

And then, in the next moment, the time for reflection was gone. The pig barreled through, a *whoooosh* piercing Max's ears, a ping on the receiver, lights up on the timer boxes that he could see through the passenger window. He sent the data along to her.

MP60.42

9:03.71

3.01 mph

Boxes 1552,1553

Alicia, less than a mile ahead, came right back at him: *Thx. I can hear him coming.*

COMFORT INN, HARRISONVILLE, MISSOURI

Tuesday, March 26 | 5:03 p.m.
Three hours, fifty-seven minutes before wake-up time

Max couldn't sleep. Hadn't slept. Wasn't going to sleep. The TV cut a fuzzy beam of gray light into the room, as Chucklehead Panelist No. 1 and Chucklehead Panelist No. 2 heatedly debated matters in D.C. that had never seemed farther from Max's self or his cares.

Lunch with Alicia had been a bad idea. Or, maybe, it had been the best idea ever, because it had left them neatly cleaved from one another. Max wasn't sure. He was so far from being sure, in fact, that he had just let the question go, desperate in his hope that what was sitting on his head would release and move on and sleep would take him, as it surely intended to do once he gave it enough space to maneuver.

And back it all came on him, the heavy thoughts and his lazy-tongued way around them, and his wishing he could have another go and withdraw from the questions—*the perfectly natural questions*—that had brought her to a breaking point, right there in the back booth at Best Burrito.

"Have you thought about how you can balance this job and your kid?"

"Did you?" she asked.

"It was different for me. I had a wife."

"Well, maybe I should just go and get me one of those."

"I'm sorry. I didn't mean anything by it."

"You should be sorry. One, it's sexist as hell. Two, it's not any of your business."

She was right about all of that. He should have left it alone. And yet, hadn't she been just as intrusive when they talked about Janine and the pre-packaged divorce waiting for him at home? Hadn't she asked how he was feeling, what he was going to do, was he hurting? Hadn't he said it was all right when he was out here, a respite even, that he didn't know yet, that, yeah, sometimes it did dig at him below the skin?

Damn right he had.

So they had sat there, each of them cursing the misfortune of having not yet gotten their food before the squabble flared, and they ate in silence, pretty much. He had said he was sorry again, and she had said it was OK, just a tender area for her. But it wasn't OK. The pain flaring from the inside of her was obvious enough. He didn't even have to look for it. He didn't want to look for it. He wanted to go his own way and make it stick this time.

Max found his phone and engaged it. The field updates populated his email queue. The day crew had cleared another pumping station while Max lay there alone with his speeding thoughts. This thing was moving right down the numbers. In less than seven hours, he would be on the clock again, working down the line, exhausted.

He called Alexandra, who picked up on the first ring.

"Dad, aren't you working nights?" Her voice stretched out in the concern, amplified and stressed. She had remembered. The good daughter.

"Yeah. Couldn't sleep."

"You don't sound good."

"I'm fine."

"What's up?"

"Just wanted to hear your voice, kid."

"Dad, you're sweet. Listen, it's not a good—"

"Go," he said.

"Get some sleep, OK?"

"I will."

"I love you."

"I love you, too, Pookie Nose."

"We'll talk soon, OK?"

"Bye now."

He hung up. What had he hoped for with the call? Maybe calm, maybe perspective. Then again, maybe that cocaine-rush feeling only she had ever inspired in him, that sure knowledge that no matter how long he did or didn't live, no matter where she was or he was, he would love her with every particle, that nothing would ever be reduced or given back. On Alexandra, he was all-in, from the first moment he saw her.

For a whisper, it worked. The bleakness in his heart and his head pulled back, like a wave receding from the shore, and then the respite was over and the blues washed back in.

Max swung himself out of bed and plodded to the bathroom, sitting on the pot in the darkness. He covered his nose and mouth with his hand, trying to block the smell, belabored breathing through the cracks between his fingers.

This was no fucking good, right here, this exhaustion and this lack of addressing it. He knew little tricks for stealing bits of sleep out in the field. On a steady run like this, maybe he would have a thirty-, thirty-five-minute wait for the pig. Set the alarm on the phone and bag twenty-seven minutes of hard sleep, rocked back in the car seat as far as it would go. He would need every scrap of that he could get.

He stood up and flushed. Light still off. TV now off. He felt along the wall, back to the bed, and he climbed in again. He checked the time: 5:37. His chances at shuteye were dwindling fast. He would give it an hour, then he would go get dinner, because what the hell difference did it make whether he was up and moving or in bed when he couldn't sleep?

Max closed his eyes.

A rap at the door. *Jesus Christ.*

He thrashed, flicked on the bedside lamp, found his terrycloth robe hanging off the rolling chair. He slipped into it.

Another knock.

"Hold on." *Fucking-ay. Was the do-not-disturb sign not on the handle?*

He opened the door. Alicia, red-faced, stood there, by turns the biggest surprise ever and not surprising at all.

"I couldn't sleep," she said.

"Me, either."

"I'm sorry."

"Me, too."

"Can I come in?"

He stepped aside, opened the door wide for her. She headed for the chair. "No," he said, and he motioned for her to take the edge of the bed. He sat.

"What's up?" he asked.

"I'm scared," she said. "Your questions scared me. I'm sorry."

"No, I'm sorry. Don't be scared. It's none of my business."

"I miss him so bad. I'm trying, you know? I am."

"I know."

"I was hard on you."

"You weren't. I deserved to be shut down."

Everything spilled now. Whatever she was holding, for however long she had held it, it was coming up and out. She wept. Max sat. He leaned forward. He made soothing sounds. He lacked words to accompany them. She wept more. He went to her. He leaned in. He stroked a strand of hair back. He reached for her, and she pitched forward, into his hug, and he sat next to her, and he held on.

"Do you want to talk?"

She shook her head into his shoulder, the tears still coming. He grasped her again, holding on, quiet murmurs, gentle words, until at last she was gassed and sleep took her. He cradled her and lay her back, until she was fully on the bed, and then he pushed himself up. He turned off the lamp. He felt his way to the couch. He lowered himself into it, drawing up his legs so he would fit, and he turned his body until he faced the back cushions, and he closed his eyes and sleep took him, too.

To: Wendt, Max
From: Janine Garwood, Garwood and Associates
CC: Alexandra Wendt-Keisling
Re: Re: Re: the plan

Thank you, Max. Once the paperwork is drawn, the lawyer said you can sign online. When it's filed, you'll get your money. Thank you for not making this harder than it has to be.

To: Wendt, Max
From: Charles Foster Danforth
Re: Re: Let's start anew

Maxwell, old chum, you gave me a badly needed comeuppance, and I thank you for your forbearance and your good humor in doing so. I sensed something about you that night we spent stranded in Minneapolis—that, perhaps, under that shambolic presentation of yourself there was an interesting man I'd like to get to know better. I have a sense about these things sometimes, you see, and you certainly haven't let me down.

Speaking of Minneapolis...

I seem to recall your mentioning, in our first conversation, that you tended to travel on Sundays and Saturdays for weeklong jobs. As you so jovially threatened to have one of your cohorts kick my "skinny ass" just this past Sunday, I'm wondering if that means you'll be passing through the Land of 10,000 Lakes on Saturday. If that is, indeed, the case, I further wonder if your pass-through might align with my own layover there, from about 1 to 3 p.m. (I'll be in the Dallas area before that—technically, a town in the great in-between of Dallas and Fort Worth that is called Grand Prairie. I've seen pictures. I think it oversells itself by half.) At any rate, should serendipity smile upon us, it's not a long layover, but it would be time enough for us to have that beer that's dreadfully overdue. I should regret it if we miss the opportunity.

I know it's a longshot. But longshots are the ones most worth taking. Please let me know.

P.S. I hope you haven't forgotten about the errand I sent you on. Don't let me down, Maxwell. I'm counting on you.

COMFORT INN, HARRISONVILLE, MISSOURI

Tuesday, March 26 | 8:58 p.m.
Two minutes before the alarm

Max's phone buzzed across the nightstand to the far-too-loud tune of "Authority Song." He fell from his tenuous hold on the couch, catching the floor with his hip. Alicia, startled into awareness like a cat, bounced up, bewildered. She flipped on the light and looked at him, uncertainty apparent on her face about the hows or whys of her presence in the room, until remembrance flooded back in.

"Is that Mellencamp?" she asked.

"Simmer down," he said as he rose, rickety, to his feet, his voice froggy and too harsh. He had meant to be funny, because, really, how else was he supposed to approach this situation—the awkwardness, the inexplicable shame, the what-the-hell-happened—except with humor? He gave her that hand-down wave that said *no big deal*.

He made his way to the phone. "It's Dex," he said. The ringtone gave it away. He slipped an index finger over his lips for her benefit, then put the boss on speaker.

"Dex."

"Hey, Max. You up?"

"Sure."

"Listen, I was trying to get hold of Alicia about some paperwork, but she's not picking up. You seen her?"

Max looked to her, and she mouthed a terse *fuck*.

"Yeah, we had lunch after the shift. I know she's staying at the hotel here. Maybe she just didn't turn up the ringer on her phone. It happens, you know?"

"Sure. Where you guys staying?"

"Harrisonville."

"Comfort Inn?"

"Yeah," Max said. "The usual."

"I'll just call the front desk, have them ring her room."

Max flicked his hand at Alicia. *Go.*

"You want me to go check on her?" Max asked. He watched her lace up her shoes, feel around in her back pocket for her key card. Thumbs-up from her. He returned it.

"Nah, no need," Dex said. "I guess I just got a little concerned, maybe she got lost or something. She wouldn't be the first."

"Hanley," Max said.

"Yeah. Jesus Christ, that guy."

"I'm sure she's here. She was as beat as I was when we got back from lunch. You know. Nights."

"Man, I know. You had your shot at the office, buddy boy. You chose this."

"Man, I know."

Dex hung up. Max set his phone down, still out of sorts. He set his hands on his hips and rolled them forward, his back screaming. The couch was not a good idea.

He slipped into the bathroom and peed. His alarm went off. He dashed out to quiet it. He got his stuff in order. He shook his head, trying to clear it.

After a few minutes, his phone pinged. *That was a close one.*

Heh, he wrote back.

I'm hungry, she wrote.

Me, too.

They sat opposite each other in a booth at the pizza joint, splitting a medium pepperoni. They were the only ones in the place, nearly ten o'clock. The manager had been none too pleased to see them come in, and as he lurked nearby, making a show of closing up the place while they talked, his mood gathered no improvement.

"That was dumb," she said.

"It wasn't. You didn't know you were going to stay." Max regretted the word choice as soon as it cleared his lips, the lasciviousness that tinged the syllables even when he had meant nothing of the sort. "I mean...I know. It's no biggie."

"I feel like I almost got caught, like I did something wrong. But I didn't. *We* didn't."

"You needed a friend," Max said. "I was glad I could be that."

"But you're not." She said it matter-of-factly, as if she had described the color of a car. The words still stopped him short.

"What I mean," she said, "is you don't really know me."

"You don't know me, either."

She sat back, pushing her plate away. The manager swooped in for it. "Are you done as well, sir?"

Max was mid-chomp. "I am not," he said, mouth full, and the manager whisked off.

"You're a good guy, Max. Thanks for letting me stay. Thanks for not taking advantage."

"You're welcome." *Did she think I would?*

"I'm sorry you had to sleep on the couch," she said.

"It's OK."

She cast her eyes downward, her hands clasped in her lap. Max drained his iced tea and ate two more slices, leaving the crusted ends like crescent moons on his plate.

"I'd like to tell you about my son. About my...situation," she said. "If you're OK with that."

"I am."

"I didn't mean to be unkind," she said. "When I said you're not my friend, I meant...I don't know. I think anyone who *knows* me has to know this. And I'd like you to know me, Max. I'd like to know you, too."

Now Max pushed back from his own plate, and again the manager appeared, as if answering a buzzer.

"Check?" he asked.

"In a minute," Max said, sending him off again.

"Pushy," Alicia said.

"The hell with him. You OK with this? We can wait, if you want."

"No," she said. "No, I'm ready to talk about it."

"OK. I'm all ears."

"When I got pregnant," she said, out of the blocks fast, maybe so she wouldn't change her mind and take that out he had offered her, "I was about a year away from being done with college. I was a little older, because I'd taken a year off when my mom got sick before she died, and then I took another year, just, you know, grief, I guess. But I was finishing up school, I was on my way—"

"And you got pregnant."

"Right."

Max knew this story. Not *this* story, but the story of how a pregnancy you don't see coming—*but you should have, you dumbass, you should have seen it coming*—shows up, and it's like shaking an Etch-a-Sketch of your designs on how life is going to play out. Time to start over, only with no blank slate. Alexandra had been a gift from the universe, but Janine standing there in their new house, crying, telling him, "I'm pregnant," that had been no gift. That was sheer pressure, crashing down on their heads, biology and the vagaries of the ovulation calendar not caring one whit how they wanted the procession of their Big Life Events to go. A mortgage that extended them, and a coming baby, all in short order. It had been more than they felt ready to contemplate.

"So, anyway," Alicia said, "I go through my options. Terminate it? No. I can't. I mean, it's an option, but it's not an option for me. Carry to term, keep the baby? I didn't see how. Not then." She welled up. "I mean, I see a million ways now how I could have done it, how I could have figured it out, but then? Dead ends, all around. I had allies, but I didn't know I could lean on any of them. And I didn't have any confidence in me."

"I understand. Assets aren't much use if you don't know you have them."

"Exactly. So, I'm thinking adoption, that's the answer, right? I'll carry the baby, adoption, baby gets a family that loves him, I get to move on with my life. But this is a big decision, right, so I reach out to the guy—it didn't mean anything, which is so weird to say because my life is now wound up with his, you can't even begin to separate them out, I mean, Jesus, I had to remind him that we'd even been together—and I say, 'This is what I want to do.'"

She paused now, the gravity of the replay pulling on her. Max looked up, annoyed, at the manager who kept hovering.

Alicia pushed on. "He tells his family—wealthy family, they own this auto parts manufacturing company up in Lansing—and they're all, 'We'll take the baby.' Like they're picking out some clothes or something. 'We'll take that one.' And, of course, in the moment, I'm, like, great, this will work out great. I can get on with things. I agree to a closed adoption, because, you know, I have plans. And they want it, because then I'm out of the picture, and they don't have to think too much about the fact that their son lay down with the likes of me."

"No." Reassurance that those sentiments couldn't be true, and all because Max knew they probably were. He wanted to punch people in the mouth. Who? Didn't much matter.

"Regrets. Oh, god." She wiped an escaping tear with the cuff of her shirt. "I had regrets. Almost instantly. It took me years to work up the gumption to try to undo it, or change it, at least," she said. "I have a wonderful lawyer. An advocate. And we've won some rounds against a family that can bury me in court costs. *Bury* me. So where we're at is, Rexford is old enough to be told who I am. He knows. I get to see him once a month, for a couple of hours, supervised. We're making bonds with each other. I don't want to change his life. He has a good one, with people who love him, and he's not going to have to worry about a lot of the shit I've spent my life worrying about. I just want to be in his life, and I want him to be in mine. I want to spend time with him where we don't have a goddamn chaperone. You know?"

Max nodded.

"It's worth the fight," she said. "I have to keep a job, and this is a good one. I have to keep on this, for him and for me. I can't slip up."

"Jesus." It was all Max had.

She dug into her satchel, brought up a wallet, and opened it. She slipped a nail into a pocket of it, and she pulled out a photo. She pushed it across the table. A wildly grinning little kid in a baseball cap, with a freckled nose and prodigious front choppers, greeted him. "That's Rexford."

"I can see you," he said. "The nose freckles." She pulled the photo back and stashed it.

"Your questions scared me," she said, an echo of the earlier evening. "I can't be scared."

Max offered the softest smile he had. He waved the manager over, gave him his card, asked him to run the bill. "I won't scare you ever again," he said. "We gotta go to work."

On the way out, Max stopped at the register. Alicia gave him a curious look.

"Can I ask you a question?" he said to the manager.

"I guess."

"What do you like best about living in Harrisonville, Missouri?" Max grinned at him, gave it a little extra smartass-ness for good measure.

"Well," the manager said, "it's always nice here when people don't overstay their welcome."

Max answered him with a tug of his cap. "Good night, then."

In the parking lot, where rain beat sideways across the blacktop, Alicia said, "Why'd you ask him that?"

"I have no idea." She gave him a look that he might have seen Alexandra in had he not seen someone else. *You goof.*

"It was kind of fun, though, wasn't it?" he said.

COUNTY ROAD 98

Wednesday, March 27 | 3:52 a.m.
Eight miles from the Kansas line

Max's phone went off—"New Kid in Town," the Eagles. He had never much cared for the song, but given that Alexandra had taken the time to teach him how to assign different ringtones to different callers, he had gleefully matched people and tunes. Dex had his. "Butterfly Kisses" for Alexandra. "Dueling Banjos" for Macartney. Ben Folds Five's "Song for the Dumped" for Janine, just this week.

The Eagles for Alicia. It fit.

Max put her on speaker. "Hey, what's up?"

Garbled feedback came at him. Pieces of sentences flew. A male voice: "What're you—" Alicia: "Please, I'm just—" Rustling, smothering, the sound of movement, a metallic hiss, a tumbling thump. Chaos.

Max popped his Nissan into drive and lit out of there, striking the lead traffic cone and spinning it into the middle of the road, his equipment left in the barrow pit, recording nothing as he drove out of range. He glanced right at his computer, in the passenger seat, and he thumbed the touchpad to bring up the map, which expelled an electronic trail in his wake. One intersection south, one intersection west.

He mashed the accelerator to the floor, and the Nissan hunkered down and responded, bolting down the wet pavement into the enveloping night, two beams of light slicing through the canopy of darkness and fog.

Blindly, he rooted in the console for the phone, brought it up to his face as he swung right onto a muddy dirt road, a wide turn at high speed, tires spinning through the muck. The connection was dead. "Shit." He hit the callback, eyes shooting rapid-fire between the road and the screen. Dead zone. "Fuck."

Finally, interminably, he was upon the site, faintly visible ahead. The strobe on the roof of Alicia's car threw its continual patterns into the wet, heavy air, and beyond her, on her side of the road, the hulking shape of a pickup truck, its headlight beams swallowing her car and finding his.

Max parked behind her, maybe fifteen feet of clearance. He unbuckled. He got out. His knee ached, his heart hammered away, his breath came up short, and then he found it again. From her door, a man—Max sized him up, maybe six feet, maybe two-hundred, two-fifteen—stepped back.

"Is there a problem?" Max couldn't make out the tenor of his own voice. He wasn't sure it was even his.

The man stepped toward him. "You her boss?"

"Co-worker." Max held his ground but dared not show aggression. *Shit, why'd this come up now, when things were going so well?*

"I don't want y'all out here."

"We're just doing a job."

The guy swept left with a massive arm. "You're scaring my kids. That strobe light woke 'em up."

Max followed the line of gesture. A farmhouse loomed off the road, ghostly, a wraith. She probably didn't even see it. "Didn't mean to do that," he said.

Alicia got out of her car now, a tremor through her. "I'm sorry I disturbed you, sir."

The guy spun on her. Max tensed, ready to get physical. It had never come to that. Angry landowners? Sure. Hazard of the job. They usually just wanted some grievance to be heard and acknowledged. He had learned how to judge their demeanor, how to say the words that let the tension out like a pinprick in a balloon. This guy, Max didn't know, except that his anger was out of proportion, and that was worrisome.

"Shut up," he spat at her.

"OK, we're just going to go, all right?" Max said. He nodded at Alicia, who stood, stiff, fearful. "Go get your stuff." She scurried.

"I'm gonna call the sheriff," the guy said.

"You know what?" Max said. "Let me call for you. I think we'd be interested in talking to him. We're out here doing a job, in a public right of way, I think he might be interested in hearing about that, and about how you're harassing us." *Well, Max, you called the bluff. Let's see if you're a genius or a fool.*

Alicia dashed up from the barrow pit, her legs under her now, and deposited the timer boxes in the car. She went back for the rest of it. Max glanced at her, then held gaze with the guy. Misty rain came down on all of them.

"You scared my kids."

"We didn't mean to. I told you that. We're trying to make it good."

She was back now, receiver and geophone tucked away, the two traffic cones to follow.

"You don't have to call nobody," the man said. "I'm going back inside."

"We'll just go, too." To Alicia, Max tossed: "Come on."

When she was safely in the car and on her way, Max and the man turned from each other, headed their own directions. Max walked partway to the vehicle with eyes closed, his heart in palpitations, the falls of his feet landing in the little pockmarked puddles, relief sweeping in but terror not far gone. This guy ended up being something approaching reasonable, or at least willing to let it be once they had signaled departure. What would the next one do? There would be a next one. Maybe less reasonable. Maybe angrier, not just about the intrusion but also about something more, something behind the walls of the houses they don't always see, or something out in the wider world that finds the fuse of men's anger. Maybe the next one comes with a gun. If Max were to hear a shot, could he take off running, arching his back and making himself concave, cartoon-style, staying just out of reach of the bullet?

Hell, no. He would be a goner before he hit the ground.

He found her at the next site, her equipment set up, processes running on her computer, as if nothing had happened. He knelt, peeking in the window she had opened for him.

"You OK?" he asked.

"I think so." A brave face, but the tremors were still there, underneath. "Did I do something wrong?"

"What, besides not being able to predict the behavior of every other human being?"

"Did I mess up?" she asked.

"No." He spoke softly. "No. You did it exactly right."

"OK." She sounded dubious.

"Listen, last year, I'm in downstate Illinois, these two guys rolled up on me at an intersection. They're drunk, being stupid. We talked through open windows, I'm being calm, they're escalating. I did the same thing you did. I called up Smithlin and he came over and evened things up."

"What'd they do?"

"Left. That's the way it goes. Two-on-one, maybe they have more gumption than sense. Two-on-two, it's time to go home."

She nodded. "I was frightened," she allowed.

"It's frightening. Always. I don't care who you are."

"But I was also thinking, well, look, I'll just try to talk to him, let him see I'm no threat and—"

"Precisely the right thing."

"But I lost control of it."

"No, you didn't. He lost control of himself. That's not on you. You follow?"

"Yeah."

"OK."

She looked at him. "We missed your site."

"And yours, in just a second. It's OK. We'll catch it here."

"Are we going to be in trouble for missing them?"

"No. I'll explain it in my notes." He eschewed telling her just what that entailed, a long email to Little Bonk to describe the scene, a robust bit of paperwork Little Bonk, in turn, had to fill out for Dex called a "near-miss report," which Dex would then turn into a fairly laborious memorandum for the client and the crew about being safe on the job.

Max boiled it down for her now.

"Listen," he said, "there are various levels of response to something like that, OK, and you basically just have to assess the situation. Some people come out and just want to talk. Some…" He held the memory from all those years ago, the sound of the pistol rapping against the window glass while he slept, the sheer terror of waking up to the barrel on a line with his nose. *No fucking need to tell her about that now.*

"You called his bluff," she said.

"Yeah. A gamble. Sometimes that works."

"I bet it wouldn't have for me," she said. "Guy like that, I bet he'd get angrier if a woman called him."

Max kicked the dirt. "Probably."

"That's why I tried to talk to him. I figured if I was just even-keeled, he'd come around. When he didn't—"

"Look," Max said, "you did everything right, OK? Everything. The main thing is, *be safe.* You can always drive away, just leave your shit right there in the ditch. You will never get in trouble for that. OK?"

"OK."

"I gotta go back and get my gear, and then I'll go to the next spot," he said. "You OK?"

She nodded. "Yeah. Thank you."

"You bet. I'll see you down the line."

Just after nine a.m., the text was off to Macartney: *Shift change at MP138.62. Pig due at 12:12 local/11:12 MST.* Max had gotten back the muscle-flex emoji, so they were right down the numbers, the whole way, the little schism in the shift dispensed with if not forgotten.

A message from Alicia moved across, the phone buzzing in his hand.

Iola?

Yeah, he typed. *That's where I'm headed.*

Super 8?

Yeah.

That looked best to me.

Not a lot of choice, he wrote. *Welcome to southeast Kansas.*

Lol.

Aside from exchanging pass information, there hadn't been much chatter after the night had been interrupted—at one spot, she had messaged that she couldn't set up on the downstream side, as the notes instructed, so she measured off from the upstream marker. He filled the information into the spreadsheet so the analysts could make sense of the incongruent passage time there later. He had been tempted a few times to throw a line to her—something banal like *hanging in there?*— but he held back. He didn't know this for a fact, it was just spitballing, but he thought maybe she would be sensitive to anything that wasn't completely sincere after the incident outside the farmhouse. Maybe the best response, for her, to what had happened was to put it away and keep doing the job. If he sounded her out in a tentative way, she might glom onto that and be defensive. He went back and forth. Maybe he was projecting how he would have handled it when he put those thoughts on her, he wondered. Maybe so. Maybe no. Do or don't. He didn't.

The pig chugged through, and Max, stiff and rundown, drew himself up out of the car and walked out to the timer boxes in a ghostly morning fog to make sure they had tripped. Up close, they flashed red at him, confirmation. He turned the boxes off, gathered everything in one swoop, and plodded it back to the car. He settled into the driver's seat, recorded the information, sent it off to her by text, and moved on.

On he went to his next site, two and a half miles beyond her—an hour-plus wait for the tool he wished had come earlier, before the mess, when sleep was tugging insistently at him. Max set up his equipment, then tucked into an adjacent section of woods, slipping in among the gnarled trees. He found a spot well off the road, where he could still see the car but nobody passing could see him. He tugged the zipper on his FR jeans and relieved himself on a rotted-out tree stump. He thought of a line he had told Alexandra when she was a little girl, about why Daddy liked working outdoors. *I can pee wherever I want.* Oh, Janine had raised hell about that later, a gripe far bigger than the transgression demanded. "Great, Max," she said when it was just the two of them in bed. "You going to take the call when she drops her drawers and pees in the middle of recess?" And, of course, he'd snapped back at her: "Oh, leave me alone. She laughed." He had nursed that hurt over the years, and a thousand others like it, and he had carried them around as an amulet against being rigid and no fun, the way Janine was.

Now, he took a cockeyed look back at that particular exchange. How many times had he shown up and dumped out the contents of his work life into a home that necessarily chugged on without him? How many times had he given little thought to how Janine, Alexandra, the neighbors, the guinea pig (*what the fuck did Alexandra name that thing?*), the folks at church, anybody, everybody had to adjust to his arrivals and his inevitable departures? What if Janine had been upset or concerned about any one of a hundred things—all of which he had either missed or hadn't been alert enough to see—except the one thing she lost her shit about? Wouldn't that be something? Nice time to figure it out, if true, some years past her point of give-a-damn.

Puck! That's what Alexandra had named that hairy little freak show. Max was pretty sure she had been thinking of some kid on those MTV shows she loved to watch, not Billy Shakes' jester, but whatever the case, the misadventure of having that particular family pet had ended ignominiously enough. The guinea pig had escaped her grasp one day and, in the throes of freedom, had impaled himself on a pest-defender spike in the backyard.

Should have called him Mercutio.

I *see what you mean. Day 3, and I'm dragging.*
Upon the phone's ping, Max looked up from his notes at the clock on the receiver transmission. 11:03 a.m. A pass due in sixteen minutes, and then he would be off to shift out with Macartney. Hunger dug at him.

Yep, he wrote back. *Three more shifts to go, knock wood.*
I'll sleep a week after I get home.

Can't, Max wrote. *We're doing the Toledo line pretty quick after this one.*

Dammit! But...Michigan. I can drive to that one. Yay, me!

I'll send you notes from my two flights from hell.

LOL...What are you going to do on your off days?

As little as possible. Maybe look at some furniture for my rental.

A long break in the repartee. Ellipsis-in-a-box. Then nothing. Ellipsis-in-a-box. Nothing.

I'm sorry, Max.

It's OK.

How long have you been married?

Max verged on embarrassment at punching in the number, less over the loss than over how unspeakably old he now felt. *Almost 35 years.*

Wow. Long time.

Doesn't seem like it until I do the math. Sort of like how I feel 18 until I look in the mirror. A lie, that pithy line.

Well, I'm just sorry.

I appreciate it.

If you ever want to talk...

Thanks. Maybe at some point.

OK.

It was the second time she had dropped the offer out there for him. Everybody makes the gesture or some other variation of generosity (*call if you need anything!*) once, Max figured. It's what humans do so they can maintain a thin veneer between actually doing something genuine and engaging in the apathy to which they're more accustomed. If she offered again, Max thought he might have to take her up on it, if he had much of anything to say.

It's hardest at night, he wrote. He wasn't sure how to put the next part. Lacking the words, he sent the simple thought on.

Loneliness, she wrote back.

No, it's more than that, he thought. It wasn't just what you went to bed with; it's what you were conditioned to expect when you woke up. Every other hour of the day had been a relative cinch. Freed from the ennui of life with Janine, he could fill his days with what he wanted to do. But the nights were different. The going down and the coming back up and all the hours in between...in those strung-together moments, he was a broken man.

Yeah, I guess, he wrote.

I understand.

In Iola, a couple of hours later, Max sat at a window seat at McDonald's and finished off two Big Macs, a medium fries, a Coke and an apple pie. There was a Mexican joint downtown he liked; if he got to sleep quickly enough, he thought, maybe he could scoot out around eight and take his time at dinner before rejoining the line.

He was glad Alicia hadn't tossed a lunch invitation his way. He would have gone—he liked hanging with her, much to his surprise—but the late-morning thoughts about Janine had worn on him a bit.

He had started thinking he needed some help sorting this out, and he had also started thinking about who that sounding board could be. Danforth was a possibility, if Max could stand the pontifications and bizarro errands. (Max had resisted asking the counter kid at McDonald's if he liked living in Iola. If there were an answer in the affirmative, it would be unspeakably sad. If there weren't, why ruin the kid's day? Give him a bus ticket and a pack of smokes and tell him to run.)

Big Bonk? The Bonker was out. Not that Max didn't appreciate him for who he was, but Bonk was a guy you go pheasant hunting with, not opening the long-closed doors of the mind and heart. Dex? No offense to him, a straight-up good guy, but talking to the boss blurred too many boundaries. Little Bonk, Smithlin, Macartney? Bags of nope.

Alexandra...

Max could never tell her this, would never tell her this. Alexandra wouldn't be a fair broker with his feelings. It killed him to acknowledge that to himself, but the truth is the truth regardless of whether it does you harm or disillusions you. Alexandra loved him. Alexandra was also partisan to her mother. The galaxies of what that meant soured his mood. Max gathered up his wrappers and tossed them in the garbage.

At the Super 8, he checked in, carried his gear up to the room, and went through the checklist, as ever.

Geophone and gas monitor, charging on the breakfast bar.

Computer plugged in and ready to go.

That night's clothes laid out on the ottoman.

The day's dirties bagged up and packed away.

Boots off and in the corner.

Phone plugged in and charging on the nightstand.

Shower, eight minutes, long enough to wash away the grime.

He came into the main room, toweling himself, at 1:56. He slipped into boxers and a T-shirt, the room cold from the March gloom outside.

He checked his messages one last time. Considered whether he wanted to lie down and have a pull, masturbation being the best sleep aid he knew.

"I'm good," he said aloud.

A knock at the door. He rerouted. Opened it.

She stood in stocking feet. Sweats cinched with a drawstring. Detroit Lions T-shirt. Max preferred the Packers, but who gives a shit? She clutched a pillow at her chest.

Max stepped back. Pulled the door wide for her.

Alicia came in, passed him, found the near side of the bed, turned down the covers, set her pillow on the stack, slipped in.

Max walked to the foot of the bed. He stood there and looked at her. "I saw you drive up," she said.

"What are we doing?" he asked.

"Sleeping better than we would otherwise," she said.

"OK."

"It can't be anything else," she said.

"I don't want it to be anything else," he said.

She turned down his side. He moved on, over to the window, and he pulled the blinds tight, securing them with the clothespin. The room went black. He approached the edge of the bed, feet tentative, heart hopeful, mind moving double speed. He let himself in, sandpaper feet sparking against the sheet. He turned away from her. She turned away from him. He closed his eyes, counting silently backward.

Ninety-nine...ninety-eight...ninety-seven...

"Good night," she said.

"Good night."

The darkness gathered them up.

SUPER 8, IOLA, KANSAS

Wednesday, March 27 | 6:33 p.m.
Two hours, twenty-seven minutes from the scheduled alarm

Max's eyes popped open, as if on a time lock. Darkness poured into his retinas, and the pupils went wide, hungry for any light that could be found. Slowly, parts of the room took shape, like terrain shifts. A valley there along the thermal unit. The office table and chairs a high steppe.

Awareness—where he was, whom he was with, the time on the clock—came to him in small pieces, and then it came all at once.

Well, he thought. *Isn't this something?*

The sleep had been the best he'd had in weeks. He and Alicia had subdivided the bed, and property lines had been respected.

And still...

Her presence wasn't a pass-through. She had changed the room, the hours, the bed upon her arrival. Though they never touched—*they didn't touch, did they?*—he could feel her move. He could smell her now, everywhere. He could hear her murmur in her sleep. And all of it, every electric moment, had sent him into contented slumber.

Awareness heightened all of that now. It also brought the what-ifs that would project out from here. What if Little Bonk, the only one who could stumble into this, found out? Well, so, what if? They had done nothing wrong. And even if it hadn't been entirely innocent, Max wasn't her boss, held no position of authority over her, so what was Little Bonk going to do even if he did find out?

Well, at a minimum, he would tell everybody else. And the chemistry on the crew would be transformed, probably for the worse and probably forever.

There was a lot to lose here.

What would Alexandra think? Dumb question, of course. She would stand four-square opposed, and even if she could be brought around to the rational notion of two people chastely getting through the night—or the day—she would fixate upon the age difference, maybe try to picture her daddy lying down with one of her friends, only to blanch at that image.

Janine? Well, hell, given the current prevailing attitude, Janine might wonder why it didn't happen before, or whether maybe it had, which would give her a whole new peg on which to hang the ideas of how she and Max had drifted to different harbors.

The sheets rustled, and the mattress rolled gently as Alicia sat up. Max closed his eyes, breathing deep, in and out, through his nose and mouth. She rose, soft feet treading the floor, into the bathroom, door closed behind her. A small handful of seconds, the sound of water falling, then the rush of the faucet, an open door, soft light through Max's eyelids and then off again, a trail back to the bed, and she was in.

"You awake?" Soft words, whispery and warm.

Max feigned sleep.

She drew up the covers on her shoulder and turned, and Max dropped a soft groan. He peeked an eye open. He waited. Soon, the deep breaths came, the muscle twitch of R.E.M. sleep, and she was adrift again.

He opened both eyes.

Maybe there was nothing to go worrying about just yet. Maybe this was just a one-off. Maybe tomorrow, they would be in Tulsa or in Pawnee, or maybe he would be in one and she would be in the other, and they would be in their own beds, and that would be the end of this, whatever it was. Max had a tendency to see the trouble before it arrived. Sometimes, it never did, but still he would be standing there, a half-dozen contingencies ready to be deployed for any occasion. It's the way he was wired. It's what made him good at the job. You can't be who you're not.

Who was Max Wendt?

He was a guy who hoped she would stay, again and again.

Max went back to sleep.

CORONADO MEXICAN RESTAURANT, IOLA, KANSAS

Wednesday, March 27 | 9:18 p.m.
Two hours, forty-two minutes before shift change

Max swam a triangular chip through the salsa and told Alicia how it would play out from here. The run had been entirely predictable—no delays and no shutdowns—and the pump orders for the next twenty-four hours showed no events that would knock them off stride. Something could still happen, but the window was shrinking. Sometime tonight, Little Bonk would give them the go-ahead to buy their tickets home.

"Twelve hours tonight, twelve more from the day crew, eight from us, and that's it," Max said.

"The trap?"

"Yep."

"And that's it?"

"That's it."

Alicia's brow creased, like she was working out a geometry proof.

"What's up?" Max asked.

"We're going to be, like, five hours from Kansas City."

"Right."

"So do we just turn around and go?" she asked.

The server dropped by, refilled his tea. He thanked her, tried to say her name. Asunción.

"*Gracias.*"

"*De nada.*"

"You speak the language?" Alicia asked.

Max held his hand aloft and wobbled it. "*Mas or menos.*"

"Do you know what that means?"

"Yeah. *Maybe I do and maybe I don't. You'll never know.*"

"It means all that, does it?"

"Yep," he said. He ate another chip.

Alicia raised her hand. "Asunción?"

"What are you doing?"

"Just hang on," she said.

The server, seventeen, if that, came back. "Asunción," Alicia said. "*¿Vives aquí en Iola?*"

"*Sí.*"

Max thought he could noodle out that exchange.

Alicia went on. "*De todas las cosas de este lugar, ¿qué es lo que más te gusta?*"

Even that, Max thought, or at least the spirit of it. Something on the order of what he had asked the guy at the pizza joint.

Asunción, though, left his rudimentary understanding buried under the sheer tonnage of her words, spraying rapid-fire from her mouth as if this were the first time she had ever been spoken to. Max took in the dizzying fusillade, looking from the girl to Alicia and back again. At one point, the young girl took her dress by the corners and spun gleefully, childlike, and Alicia clapped and said, "*Oh, eso es muy bueno. Muy bien.*"

The girl curtsied and then scurried off, back to the job. Max looked at his work partner in wonder.

"What the hell was that?"

"Asunción will be sixteen next month. Her uncle owns the restaurant. She loves living in Iola, and she has many friends, some from school, and some from her neighborhood. She already had her *fiesta de quinceañera*—"

"What's that?"

"Her fifteenth birthday party. It's a big deal in her culture. But this year, she gets to have her Sweet Sixteen party and invite all of her friends, just like girls do in America. Her mother made her a beautiful dress, she said, and she can't wait to wear it."

"She said all that?"

"She did."

"And you understood it?"

"I did."

Max bobbed his head down and peered at her. "Who are you?"

"I'm the woman who slept with you last night." She flushed crimson. "This afternoon. Today."

She had gone there. All through dinner, they had made a cordial yet concentrated show of not going there.

Max rocked back. "Hell of a situation we've got here, huh?"

Alicia shrugged. "We're getting through the night. Question is, how do we get back to Kansas City, remember?"

Dinner arrived, and they went through all of it quietly and what was left of the job and what needed to be in their plan from here on out. Max recommended that they stay in Pawnee—it was smaller, quaint, closer to the line but less likely to be where Little Bonk would choose. He would no doubt stay in Tulsa, where the pickings among the hook-up crowd would be more plentiful. After the tool trapped, they could finish out their regular twelve hours and get closer to the airport for an early flight out Saturday.

"You want to keep staying with each other?" she asked.

"I've been clear on that, yes. But you should get your own room, just so the expense report balances out."

"I understand," she said. "We're not sneaking around."

"Well, yeah, we really kind of are—"

"What I mean is—"

"I know what you mean," Max said. "I'm just avoiding unnecessary situations, you know?"

"It's not about sex," she said, a little loudly for his liking. "Not for me."

"For me, either."

"But even if it were—"

"You're making an intellectual argument," Max said. "One I agree with, by the way, but one that's also beside the point. On some of these jobs, you're going to have to work with Tommy or Steve. Pretty regularly, in fact. So..."

"I know. So it's best not to let this be a thing for everybody else."

"That's all I'm saying."

"OK. I get it."

They picked at their food. Max checked his watch. Opened his phone and let the email stash grow. The day crew had cleared another pumping station.

"What did you think?" she asked.

"When?"

"You know when."

"I knew you'd be there."

She tossed her fork into her rice. "You did *not*."

"OK, no, I didn't know you'd be there. But when you knocked, I knew it was you, and I thought you might be coming to stay."

She leaned in. "Why'd you think that?"

"Because I almost climbed in bed with you the other night," he said. "I had a sense that it would have been OK—"

"A good sense."

"But I didn't, for a lot of reasons you can probably imagine," he said.

"I can."

"So why'd you take the initiative?" he asked.

"Same reason, pretty much."

"Pretty much." He clenched his lips and nodded.

"You're a good guy. You've been a good friend to me. I want to be your friend. We can lean on each other, right?"

"Two days ago, I wasn't your friend."

"Things changed," she said.

"For me, too." He drummed his seat with his fingers. "Too much is changing. I'm not talking about you. It's just—well, things have to be—I mean—"

"We're just getting through the night, Max."

"The day," he said.

"The afternoon," she said.

"Whatever," he said.

The laughter busted them up.

CUSHING LINE, MILEPOST 271.26

Thursday, March 28 | 11:42 a.m.
58.86 miles from the end of the run

Little Bonk leaned against the grille of his Dodge, ballcap pulled low on his forehead, wraparound sunglasses glinting, a toothy smile. They had left the gloom behind in Kansas. Oklahoma greeted them like peak springtime. It had made for a pleasant working morning.

Max gave a wave as he pulled up. On Little Bonk's left index finger, aloft, a tethered thumb drive spun in circles. Max maneuvered parallel to the downstream marker, getting his car aligned perpendicular to Little Bonk, who walked toward him now. Max lowered the window.

"Mind slipping me the spreadsheet?" Little Bonk asked, catching the drive midflight and handing it through.

Max took the drive and slipped it into an open USB port. He brought up the navigation window, then grabbed the Excel file and copied it over. He ejected the drive and handed it back.

"Everything going OK?"

"By the numbers," Max said. "You'd have heard from me otherwise."

"Damn right." The drive was back on Little Bonk's finger, resuming its rotations. He ambled off to the pickup to download the document. Max got out and set his geophone so he could keep contact with the line while waiting for Macartney. If things got too tight, he would walk out the timer boxes and his receiver, get prepared for one more pass. He'd had to do that often enough when he was shifting out with Hanley—another reason to be glad that guy was gone, with all his shrugging and saying, "Sorry, man," and creating more work for everybody else—but Steve tended to be considerably more reliable than that.

Sure enough, along the horizon, a sandy cloud spread out against the azure backdrop, no doubt Macartney's belching hot rod of a truck bearing down. A few seconds more brought the low-gut growl of the engine and the rolling smoke left in its wake.

"That guy's a one-man Superfund site," Max said. Little Bonk, back with him at the Nissan, chortled.

Max trotted out to the fenceline to gather his geophone, and he moved the Nissan up behind Little Bonk's truck, giving Macartney the spot at the above-ground marker.

"Gentlemen," Steve said when he climbed down from his perch.

"Hey, Mac," Little Bonk acknowledged. Max simply handed across the goods—the hard copy spreadsheet and his own thumb drive—and went back to the Nissan for the timer boxes while Macartney made the electronic transfer.

"You want to grab some dinner tonight?" Little Bonk asked Max after his tasks were through and Macartney had tossed back the memory stick. "We could hit that steakhouse again."

"Can't tonight."

"Oh. OK."

"He's gonna be busy," Macartney said, rocking his hips forward and back, scrunching up his face. "Know what I mean?"

"Are you fucking stupid?" Max said.

"Whoa, now," Little Bonk said.

"Fucking imbecile."

"Who pissed in your garden?" Macartney asked. He seemed half taken aback by Max's response to him and half ready to escalate the situation.

"We're not doing this," Little Bonk said.

"Fucking-ay right," Max said. Now, to Macartney, he said, "You're gonna have to work with her, you know. You gonna say that shit to her?"

"What's your deal, man?" Macartney came back. "I didn't mean nothin' by it. I've talked junk about you and your old lady a million times. *You've* talked junk about me and my old lady just as much. Chill the fuck out."

"Yeah, well, she ain't my old lady, or yours," Max said. "She's part of this crew. Just don't be a dumbass, hard as that might be."

Macartney stepped to Max, who put two hands on his chest and shoved him back. The wild left hand Macartney let go, as he stumbled backward and without a center of gravity behind it, would have been harmless enough had it not clipped the fattest part of Max's nose, which now spilled blood.

"Jesus Christ!" Max yelled, his hands coming up to catch the flow.

"Enough." Little Bonk, the shit-talkingest member of the crew sometimes, got himself between them, an unnecessary intercession. Macartney looked stricken and left small by what he had done. Max, tending to the damage, wasn't about to re-engage.

"Jesus, Steve," Little Bonk said now. "Jesus, guys. Max, are you OK?"

"Whatever."

"Fuck," Little Bonk said. "Fuck! I gotta report this."

"You're not reporting anything," Max said.

"Shit," Macartney said.

"Not another goddamn word," Little Bonk said. "New rule: We don't talk sexual shit about Alicia."

"Damn right," Max said.

"Other new rule: We don't call each other dumb."

Good luck making that stick with these morons, Max thought. "Yeah, OK."

"OK," Macartney said.

"And no fucking hitting, ever again. What if a Mantooth rep had seen that? You'd both be on suspension, minimum. Maybe worse."

Max and Macartney nodded.

"Now shake hands," Little Bonk said.

Max looked at him. "What are we, twelve?"

"I'm not sure I'd give you that much credit right now."

"My hands are bloody," Max said, holding them out. "I'll pass."

"I'm sorry, man," Macartney said.

"Yeah, whatever." Max brushed past them and shuffled off to his car.

While Little Bonk headed off to the next site to talk to Alicia and Tommy as they shifted out, Max pointed the Nissan toward Pawnee—44.6 miles on, per his GPS program—and a pending assignation that now sat in his gut like yesterday's cheese.

He had flat-out lost it with Macartney, and that wasn't good. And over what? A stupid, immature bit of innuendo that had no basis in fact. He was lucky to come out of it with a bloody nose, now stanched by a wadded-up tissue jammed into his right nostril. The truth of the matter was, anyone who ended up getting Alicia as a work partner would have gotten some ball-busting from the other guys, to one extent or another, because they'd pounded on each other so freely in that realm for so many years now that nobody was just going to up and stop. Yeah, maybe Max would have been less a party to it than the others, but that was mostly a function of his being a generation older and having the perspective of fatherhood—he could always put Alexandra into a hypothetical and use his responses to guide his own behavior. He sure as hell wouldn't have countenanced anyone speaking of her the way Macartney had bagged on Alicia. But could Max say, for a fact, that he wouldn't have laughed along if, say, Macartney had been ripping on Tommy for being paired off with her? He could not.

The phone rang. Alicia. He put it on hands-free.

"Hey."

"Just made shift change," she said. "Bonk was there."

"I know."

"He asked where I was staying."

"So you told him."

"Well, yeah. Of course. He seemed—I don't know—perturbed when I told him I was going to Pawnee."

"Perturbed, how?"

"You know, worked up. 'There's nothing there. What for?' You know what I mean?"

"It's closer to the line."

"That's what I said. That's what I said you said."

"Shit."

"What?"

"Nothing. Did he say anything else?"

"Wait a second. Did I say the wrong thing?"

"No."

"I don't get it," she said.

"It's a long story." In all the times he and Little Bonk had done this line together, they had bunked in at Pawnee exactly once—when there was an eleven-hour line shutdown and it made sense to stay close, in case of an unexpected startup. He had guided them to Pawnee because he knew Little Bonk would be miles away in Tulsa, because there'd be no chance of discovery of their doing something they were entirely free to do, so why all the damned skulking around and secrecy, and why was Max now feeling gun-shy about the whole thing? It was like the *Wizard of Oz* song: because, because, because, because, because. Because it felt right as far as it went. Because it didn't feel right in the larger, pulled-back context of the crew and their families and their kids and society and the world. Because Little Bonk was intuitive enough to wonder just what the hell was going on in Pawnee, and just stubborn enough to try to find out. Because Max was scared—for reasons he knew and for reasons that evaded him. Because Macartney had gone and done his thing, entirely predictable and entirely stupid. Max had escalated it by losing his temper, and now, the whole notion was looking worse by the minute.

"So, tell me," she said.

"I will. Later."

"See you in Pawnee?"

Max bit down, hard enough to slice his tongue. The tinny taste spread out in his mouth and mingled with the blood backing up from his nose. "I don't think we should."

"OK."

"It's not that I don't want to." *Jesus, Max, what are you doing? Take the off-ramp and put this thing in the rear view.* "I just don't think we should."

"I didn't think we were doing anything wrong."

"We're not."

"But we still shouldn't do it, this not-wrong thing," she said.

"Yeah. No. I mean, we shouldn't. Not tonight."

"I don't understand."

"I'm just trying to be...I don't know...prudent."

"OK." She drew the letters out, as if her own definition of prudence were vastly different than whatever he was peddling. "Dinner later?"

"Yeah, maybe."

"Maybe?"

"Maybe," he said. "Let's see how things shake out."

"OK."

Alicia hung up.

Max drove on. Somewhere behind him, she followed. *Does she feel as shitty as I do?*

The phone pinged. He looked at it. Little Bonk. *See you at the trap in the morning. Get some sleep.*

Yeah, Max thought. *Unlikely.*

To: Charles Foster Danforth
From: Wendt, Max
Subject: Re: Re: Re: Let's start anew

Chuck...

I'll be traveling Saturday, as you expected. Good memory.

Glad you wrote when you did. I was able to work it where I'll have a long layover in MSP. Don't want to miss this opportunity to catch up. I'll get into Billings kind of late, but that's no trouble.

I'm getting divorced.

Hate to drop it on you like that, but I'm remembering what you said about how sometimes just saying it straight out helps. This didn't, by the way, but maybe I'll get used to it, and maybe later it will. Anyway, I'm looking forward to talking. We have some topics backed up, seems like.

I've got about eight hours of work left on this job, plus a long drive back to Kansas City to turn in my rental car and start flying back. I always get antsy around this time, on edge, not because I want it to end, but because it's over and I've got to go back home. I'd rather be here—and believe me, you don't want to know where here is—than there. Is that weird? Don't answer, Chuck. Save it for MSP. I'm serious. No more messages, no more criticizing my grammar, no more chores, OK? I'm looking forward to seeing you. Don't mess that up for me by being you.

There's a joint on the C concourse called Twins Grill. It's got good burgers. I'll just camp out there when I arrive. Come over when you make it, whenever that is. Like I said, I arranged a long layover. I'll work with your schedule.

And also, one last thing, don't you ever, ever, ever again question whether I'll complete an assignment. Try this on for size:

Marc in Marshall, Missouri, says the best thing about his hometown is that he knows it and the people, and that they've all been supportive as he's tried to figure out what he wants to do. He manages a Pizza Hut now, but he's dreaming bigger than that. Nice kid. I'm rooting for him.

The guy at a pizza place in Harrisonville, Missouri—I didn't catch his name, because he didn't toss it—thinks I'm an asshole. He's probably not far wrong.

Asunción in Iola, Kansas, says, and this is a direct quote that I had a friend write down for me: "Soy feliz aquí porque tengo una gran familia a la que le gusta estar juntos todo el tiempo. Tener una familia hace que los buenos tiempos sean mejores y que los malos sean más fáciles de tomar."

I'll see if you can figure that one out. You probably can. You'll probably tell me everything that's wrong with the sentences because, in addition to stuck-up English, you also speak Spanish, Latvian, German, and Esperanto. Well, you can take it up with Asunción, pal. I'm just the messenger.

Max

P.S. You know I'm kidding about "don't mess that up for me by being you," right? I feel like we've got this patter down, but I'd feel like shit if that upset you. I'm trying to be mindful of what I say and how it's taken. It's hard. I feel like I'm not saying what I mean sometimes. And sometimes I'm saying exactly what I mean and it isn't getting through. What's the right balance?

DON'T ANSWER. Save it.

See you Saturday.

PECAN GROVE MOTEL, PAWNEE, OKLAHOMA

Thursday, March 28 | 1:22 p.m.
Thirteen minutes after arrival

Max hustled inside with his gear and some microwavable meals he had grabbed at the mini-mart. He had moved with alacrity—a Danforth word—because he hadn't wanted to see Alicia out in the confines of Pawnee, where he would have to face her, where he would have to tell her something real about how he was feeling and why he had pulled away, where he would have to make some larger account of the delicate dynamic of the crew. Better she should go her entire tenure with these guys never knowing what they were saying or thinking about her. She could suspect it, certainly. Any self-aware woman would. But he would just as soon never put words to it. Back away, be done, leave it alone, maybe someday be able to say to her, "Hey, remember that time..." No matter what she might now think of him. No matter how much he might miss her tonight and any other nights they might have had.

And he would miss her, that was for damn sure. He was losing human contact. She had given him some. His gratitude abounded. His longing for it went further still.

He and Big Bonk had talked about that on the night Max crashed there, proving that two over-the-hill-and-down-in-the-valley guys could yammer on about women to a degree rivaling any shoes-and-shopping-oriented women's show could engage the banter about men. Big Bonk had sworn himself off the women, claiming without shame or consternation that the wedding tackle wasn't as reliable as it used to be, and with the decrease in usage had gone a sharp decline in want-to. "Be nice to have somebody around to smooch," he had said, and then he had just as quickly dismissed it on account of the aggravation involved during times when the kissy-face stuff wasn't prominent.

Max had seen things another way. Sex with Janine had never abated to the point that either of them was dissatisfied with the frequency. If anything, he suspected she would have been up for even less if he had shown a fading interest in it. What Max had long before begun to notice, and found himself unable to reverse, was the rote quality to it all. Touch here. Suck there. Three minutes of stimulation. Four minutes of digitation. The windup. The finish. *See you next time, folks.* The reason he so enthusiastically bopped his bologna—aside from the old mountain-climbing rationale of "it was there"—was simple: The only delimiter was his own imagination. It was far superior to real life in that sense.

But as he told Big Bonk that night, and as he reminded himself now, his deepest pining lay not in sexual matters at all. He was fifty-five, for chrissakes; the swinging-dick days he'd never really had in the first place were far behind him now. He wanted to be wanted. He wanted to be of use. He wanted to be of comfort and companionship. Into that massive crevasse of self-doubt had walked someone who simply didn't want to be alone in the sleeping hours, someone who caused him to realize he didn't want to be alone, either. They had made a faithfully chaste move toward each other. It was goddamn beautiful, in its way.

And now it was goddamn over.

After showering, Max sat on the edge of the bed in his underwear, lights off, and churned through his meal. First, a pepperoni Hot

Pocket. Next, instant mac 'n' cheese. Two bottles of Diet Coke, one after the other, down the gullet. A burp, a shit, shut out the lights, crawl under the covers, a short session of self-stimulation, eyes closed, *faster pussycat, faster*, climax.

When it was done, Max fell asleep.

Night hung in full bloom when the alarm went off at nine, rousing him. He blinked on the table lamp, a cringe following as the light hit him at once. He drew up the email on his phone, checking the progress of the flow. Little Bonk's dutiful updates at four and eight p.m. had them set for the final push into Cushing. If Max had done the math right, the handoff would happen not five miles away.

He texted Macartney: *How we looking?*

The answer came back, all business: *306.29. 12:08 local/11:08 mst*

Thx, Max texted back. He suspected he had some repair work to do with Macartney. Steve's attitude out in the field would no doubt reveal just how large the job would have to be. Max resolved to do it, however heavy the lifting. Macartney wasn't the kind of guy he could go to and say, "Hey, let's work together on repairing our relationship." Hell, no. If Max were to say something like that, Macartney would look at him like his tongue had a ponytail; it just wouldn't make any damn sense. Macartney was many things, but caring and sharing and liberated weren't among them. This would be a solo patch job, a series of kind words and jovialities that would slowly move the man back to his usual, genial, backslapping place. If Max could swing that, he would feel better about what went down out on the line. He couldn't do anything now about how things had slid sideways with Alicia— he hoped time would be the universal salve of any fractured feelings there—but at least he had a chance to set things back where they'd been with everybody else. What had he said the previous night to her, back in Iola? *Too much is changing.* "Damn right," he said now to himself. "Let's throttle it back a hair."

He gathered up the night's clothes and wriggled into them. Wouldn't be much to eat in town this time of night. Even Subway, close to a last resort for Max, would be closed. It looked like a night for an overcooked hamburger from the hot box at the truck stop. He grabbed his car key, the real-thing room key with the oblong plastic tag from the seventies, and his wallet, and he scooted out the door, straight to the parking lot, where the Nissan waited.

As he opened the door to it, Alicia's car rolled into the parking lot at the other end of the building. He sank into the seat and shut the door, gunned the engine, backed out, then took off, looping wide around the low-slung motel as she picked out her parking spot.

Once he was on the main drag, he let go his breath.

RECEIVE VALVE, CUSHING, OKLAHOMA

Friday, March 29 | 8:07 a.m.
A minute from the pig's expected arrival

L ittle Bonk had them set up in formation, with Alicia parked at the fenceline with her receiver, ready to signal when it picked up the pig's transmitter about fifty yards from the trap. Max stood where the pipe rose out of the ground, his hand on the steel, feeling the slight shimmy as the pig drew near and struck welds. He would get the wave from Alicia, then give the good word to Little Bonk, another thirty feet down the line, so he and the station tech could try to ease the tool past the nominal.

Max hadn't wanted to be anywhere near the finish of this job. He had texted Little Bonk about an hour earlier, suggested that he hand off his timer boxes to Alicia after his final field pass, let her come in alone, and he would get moving down the road. *Be a good learning opportunity for her*, he said.

No, Bonk had written back. *Want you both at the trap.*

So here the two of them were, the air between them thickening rather than clearing. The passes all morning had been perfunctory— straight-up data, no joking exchanges on text, no stops on drive-bys to ask how things were going or to ruminate on the weather. The easy give and take was gone. The warmth, too. Could Max have expected anything more or less? Probably not. But he had hoped there might be a place or a time where one of them could say, *look, we've got a good thing going here at work, let's not let whatever happened between us be a big deal.* Each moment they *didn't* speak of it or allude to it only made it more ominous. Max wanted an out, a release point for the pressure, a reset of time and distance.

"Anything yet?" Little Bonk shouted.

"I can feel it," Max said. He looked to Alicia and shrugged, questioning. She shook her head.

"Not yet," Max said.

"Ought to be here by now," Little Bonk said.

Just then, a honk from Alicia, and then the unmistakable sound, the pig pushing pressure, a hiss and then a little pop as it came into the above-ground part.

"Here we go," Max said.

The tool moved down the line, stopping near where Little Bonk stood. He, in turn, flipped on his trusty old-school handheld receiver— kind of the R2D2 of pig tracking; not the most technologically up-to-date machine available, but user-friendly and quirky in an agreeable way. He swiftly zeroed in on the null, the blank spot on the pig where the transmitter signal didn't come through. He marked it with his hand.

"Needs to move up a little bit, Jim," he told the tech. The Mantooth guy bumped the pressure just enough to push the tool the rest of the way in, and then it was over. Five days, three-hundred-thirty-plus miles, the end of the line. Little Bonk called in the arrival time to the line operator in Calgary. Within seconds, the remotely controlled valves kicked in, isolating the pig in the trap. In a few hours, the rest of the Mantooth crew would muster here and the pig would be pulled. Max hoped to be sleeping by then.

Alicia by now had joined them. "That's how we do that shit, right there," Little Bonk said. "Well done, you two."

Thanks and handshakes all around. Max held on just a bit with Alicia and hoped she could sense what he couldn't find words to say. She withdrew, kept her eyes averted. Max looked to Little Bonk, hoping he didn't pick up on it.

"Just leave the timer boxes at my truck, if you would," Little Bonk said. "You guys all set for tomorrow?"

"Yeah," Max said. "I'm gonna go ahead and get close to KC, since there's still time in the shift."

"I'm going to go back to the motel and get some sleep," Alicia said.

"Good enough," Little Bonk said. "Listen, you know we've got the Toledo line coming up. Alicia, you feel like you're up to speed on all this?"

"Yes, absolutely."

"It's a piece of cake, comparison-wise," Little Bonk said. "Forty-two-hour run. Nothing to it."

"She's ready," Max said.

"I'll bet." Little Bonk chuckled. "Well, look, I think we can switch it up, then. Maybe you and Macartney, Max? You guys haven't been on the same shift in a while. Days?"

"Fine."

"Cool. So you and Tommy on nights, Alicia."

"Sounds good."

Little Bonk clasped his hands. "Great. Excellent work. I'll see you next week in Michigan."

M ax drove hard into the morning sun, up the gut of Oklahoma, back into Kansas, angling against the line they had just followed as he veered toward the Missouri border and Kansas City. The relief he had hoped for by gaining his release had arrived, but with it a whole new set of worrying points.

How had this thing gone so sideways? Yeah, OK, he hadn't been particularly communicative to Alicia after the fracas with Macartney, but he might have hoped she would be able to see between the lines of the thing and just let it be. Now, he was at odds with Steve, barely on speaking terms with her, and dealing with at least some measure of suspicion from Little Bonk. (*I'll bet*, he had said. *What the hell was that?*)

Being so wrong-footed at work rattled Max. More than that, it scared him in a bone-deep way. The way Max figured it, everybody had at least one place where they weren't dumb, weren't out of step, weren't wracked with trauma or foreboding. The field had always been that place for Max. Every outbound flight, every drive into the North Dakota oil patch, was a trip to reunite with the best version of himself. For the first time, he felt unwelcome and off-kilter at work. And that simply would not do.

His mind turned against him now. *Something eating at you, Max? Good. This is an excellent time to queue up a half-dozen of the dumbest things you've ever done, the most embarrassing things you've ever said, the most humbling failures. And you know what they are, right, because you've got them cataloged and cross-referenced, and the edges of the impressions never blur no matter how many times you replay them. Let's do this.*

Here's one, for starters: Remember that time Janine and Alexandra and Kara caught you nekkid dancing in the kitchen, your dick flailing like a baby's arm? Let's ruminate on that, shall we? How many people do you think Kara's told by now? It's gotta be twenty or thirty, at least, right? She's young, single, knows a lot of people, maybe she told a whole bunch of them at the bar one night. Max Wendt flashed his dick at me. And you know what, chances are good she has friends whose parents are friends with you. It's probably gotten around to them. Idiot.

Wait, here's another one: Next week, Alicia and Tommy are going to have a couple of long nights on the line. Maybe he'll say something like, "Hey, how'd you like working with Max?" And she'll tell him that it was fine, right up until you turned out to be an asshole at the end. "Do you know why?" Tommy'll ask, and she'll say, "Nope. Just turned into an asshole." And Tommy, who doesn't like you that much anyway because you always get first dibs on every job, will say, "Yeah, Max is a prick, sure enough." You'll never look at either of them the same way. Should have stuck to the plan, Max. Should've gone your own way, trained her for the job and stayed out of the rest. You didn't, and here you are, buddy boy.

Oh, hey, remember...

Max cut himself off with a thunderclap of a thought: Why the hell was he going to Billings anyway? For three days—two, really, once he figured in laundry and packing time—alone in Alexandra's little house under the Rimrocks. It was pointless.

He picked up the phone, found the main Delta reservations number in his contacts, and placed the call on hands-free. After a few miles with the strained Muzak backtrack, the agent came on the call, and Max detailed his request.

It took a bit of explaining for Max to push across his notion. Yes, he still wanted to go to MSP. Yes, he still wanted the long layover. No, he didn't want the Billings flight. Yes, Detroit. Detroit is where he wanted to go. It took some undoing, too, because he had already checked in for the MSP and Billings flights that morning. "Well, you can fix that, right?" he asked.

"Sure," the agent said. "There will be a cost." There always was.

For the first time, the road opened up to Max. A few days alone in the Motor City, or wherever the hell he decided to go. Maybe he would go out to Midland and see his old friends the Rayners at their new place on the lake. Maybe he would hunker down with room service and sleep his interlude away. Damn, it was good to have options.

Three hours in, a good two and a half hours short of the city, the sugar high from Max's snap decision drained out of him. Squinting into the relentless sun had creased his forehead and stoked a reverberating ache inside his cranium. Manufactured whimsy was no match for that.

He found a Super 8 off the highway, a lonely outpost on an exit with a gas station and a hamburger stand. He pulled into a parking lot empty save one car, presumably belonging to the desk clerk. Max got out, opened the hatch on the Nissan, pulled one of his clamshell suitcases from the cargo hold, set it on the ground, and went through his routine, the sun bearing down like a trig exam.

First, the car-top strobe. Pulled it down. Wrapped the cord tightly around it. Slipped it into its protective sleeve. Set it just so into the top compartment of the suitcase.

The geophone next, wrapped in its vinyl covering like some giant black eggroll. Stashed in the bottom compartment, between the individual carrying cases.

Now the receiver, also wrapped in vinyl and stuffed into a mini-cooler, into the bottom compartment.

Now the individual items, into the three open carrying cases lining the bottom compartment of the suitcase. Dickhead lamp. Check. Pipe finder. Check. Safety glasses. Check. Gas monitor. Check. GPS drive. Safety ribbon. Three-way converter. Tape measure. Door sign magnets. Check. Check. Check. Check. Check.

Finally, the various Bluetooth cords and the cab control unit went into the cooler with the receiver. Max consulted his checklist one last time; tired as he was, he didn't trust himself to get it right on one sweep. But he had done it. Muscle memory for the win.

Max zipped everything up and hucked the clamshell back into the cargo area, then closed the hatch. He slipped the backpack strap over his shoulder and brought it to heel against his ribs. He yanked out the other suitcase from the backseat of the Nissan, stood it up, jerked up the handle, kicked the door closed with his foot, reached into his pocket for the key fob and set the lock.

His phone pinged with a message.

Lawyer said she just emailed you the document.

OK, he thumbed back. *I'll look later.*

When her reply drew out, Max knew Janine wasn't happy with that answer. Sure enough.

It's Friday. Can you look now? Maybe we can get this on the docket and be done.

Max leaned against the car. He moved over to the email program on his phone, and there was the message with an attachment. He brought it up and didn't bother to read it, just looked for the little yellow boxes denoting where his electronic initials and signature went. Two of the former, one of the latter, and it was done. *Congratulations, bubba. Only a judge stands between you and full-metal singlehood now. Go celebrate with a tug and some fast food, you fuck.*

Out on his feet, he wandered toward the hotel door.

MINNEAPOLIS/ST. PAUL INTERNATIONAL AIRPORT, C CONCOURSE

Saturday, March 30 | 12:22 p.m.
341 air miles from Kansas City
459 air miles from Detroit

M ax had to give it to the old boy. Unlike Max's own clothing
choices—fire-resistant jeans and shirts winter, spring, summer,
and fall, as if he might have to stop, drop, and roll his way through
America's airports—Charles Foster Danforth's sparked with creativity.
Gone was the satin running suit. In its place, impossible to be unseen
as Danforth strode toward him with a relentless smile, were a paisley
western shirt with rhinestone buttons, skinny blue jeans tucked into
turquoise cowboy boots, a ten-gallon hat with silver buckles on the
band, and a leather duster with a ruffed-fur collar.

Max inched out of the booth, laughing, and though he was
surprised that his long-distance friend greeted him with an embrace,
Max returned it with full enthusiasm.

"Well, how you doin', Tex?" Max said, pulling back and admiring the get-up. "I think the dude ranch is on the F concourse. F for what-the-fucking-fuck."

"You like this?" Danforth stepped back to offer more of an eyeful, giving a little curtsy. "A few whiskeys with friends, and all of a sudden, I'm at Tony Lama's, buying out the store."

Max retreated to the booth and bid him sit. "You look good, bud. Probably cost quite a bit to get that hat its own ticket, though."

Charles giggled as he sat down. He lifted the hat from his noggin with both hands and gave it a seat of honor. "My friend, it's good to see you."

"Likewise. How long do you have?"

Danforth checked his watch. "An hour and fifteen minutes," he said. "Long enough to break bread. Not long enough to catch up. We shall have to do this again."

"We will."

"I'm sure."

The server came around, bringing the menus Max had declined two hours earlier, saying he would wait for his friend. Charles requested a mimosa, Max his fifth coffee.

When she was gone, Charles clasped his hands at the center of the table. "So, Max," he said, "you left me in the lurch on quite a bit. It was difficult to honor your request to not write back, but honor it I did."

"Appreciate that."

"Now, then," Charles said, "all bets are off. Where shall we start?"

Where, indeed? Max could have pushed that question in any number of directions, starting with the situation weighing on his head with the greatest insistence. But, he supposed, he would probably do better to explain how he had managed to get himself almost divorced before he bothered with explaining how he had slept with a woman his daughter's age—not to mention clarifying that it was nothing *more* than sleep—and somehow managed to make his time at work as uncomfortable as every other hour in the day. Wanting to address none of that, Max took another alternative.

"Your son," he said. "You said you wanted to tell me about Chas." Max pronounced the name like *bras*.

"Chas, with a long 'a,'" Charles corrected him gently. "How did you come to divorce, Max? Did it surprise you? Or is it a mutual decision? Has it been in the works for a while?"

"My divorce? It doesn't have anything to do—"

"It does," Charles said. "Trust me."

OK, Max thought. *How do I explain this?* Could a divorce simultaneously be a surprise and a foregone conclusion? Could it be by turns mutual and unilateral? And when did the clock start on the expiration of this marriage? Initially, Max had drawn a direct line between his day-late arrival and Janine's decision to broach divorce, that she had wanted an opening and he—or, more directly, the unreliability of commercial air travel—had given her one. But left to his own thoughts and remembrances during twelve-hour stretches in the field, he had come to other ideas that had just as much merit, and perhaps more. Maybe they were put on this trajectory when Janine went into business and Max declined her subsequent offer for him to leave the field and join her. Maybe it had been even earlier than that, after Alexandra went off to college and their shared responsibilities began to scatter, too. They were always good about rallying around their daughter, and they were less so about coalescing on anything else. Or maybe a marriage was like any other living thing, and the day it first draws breath is also the moment when it begins sliding toward a place where it gets extinguished.

"Janine wanted out," Max said at last. "I mean, she was the first to bring it up."

"So maybe you wanted out, too, but hadn't said anything? Is that what you mean?"

"I don't know. I don't think so."

"You don't know, or you don't want to say, Max?"

Goddamn this guy and his questions. What does it matter? "Janine said she wanted out, so we're ending it."

"And that's what you want, too?"

"I don't know. It doesn't make any difference."

"But it does," Charles said. "It makes all the difference there is."

"Janine said it. If she hadn't said it, we wouldn't be getting divorced. That's the whole thing, right there."

"But how do you *feel* about that?"

Frustration fed hostility in Max like oxygen bolsters a flame. His fist hit the tabletop like a hammer, bouncing the drinks and the sugar packets, the sudden violence bringing the chatter at adjacent tables to a screech-stop. Max, shocked to awareness, picked up his napkin from his lap and sopped up the overflow.

Quietly now, so only Charles could hear, he said, "I'm living in a rental house my daughter owns because she thinks I should. My wife thinks a big check will send me away happy. Everything is shit. How do you think I feel?"

"You're angry."

"Goddamn right."

"Good."

"Good?"

"You can work with that."

"Well, lucky me."

Max thought something more might be coming, some cosmic through-line that would pull together the whats and the hows of this work Charles had in mind, but his friend skittered off from there.

"Do you remember 9/11?" Charles asked.

"Your son."

"Yes, the day Chas died, but what I'm asking is, do you remember it?"

"Sure. Of course." Max had been in Detroit, watching TV like everybody in America eventually was, utterly dumbstruck by what he saw. It was the stuff of nightmares, low-flying jets hitting buildings, the technicolor reality of his most common death dream, where he would be in a plane that couldn't gain altitude, skimming the curve of the earth at top speed until...And then, in the aftermath, every flight in the country blinking off for two days, not a single jet stream cutting the sky, Max and Dex and the crew holed up in their hotel rooms, wondering how they were going to get home. Janine, little Alexandra, alone and scared in the Parkhill house, *please, Max, please, Daddy, just please, please come home...*

He remembered.

"Everybody old enough to understand what was happening

remembers that day," Charles said. "I don't. That is, I don't remember the events of it, not as they were happening. We'd been on Cape Cod, Mary and I and Chas and Remmy."

"Mary's your wife?"

"Yes, that's right."

Max nodded.

"We'd asked the boys to come to the Cape for the weekend. We had something important we had to tell them, and that house had been a place where we'd had so much happiness as a family. We wanted to do it there."

Max's words left his mouth and made for the wind before he could even give a thought to stopping them. "You told them you were gay. *Are* gay."

Charles broke into a wide-mouthed smile. "Well, Max, aren't you perspicacious? What was your first hint, the blue boots?" Max frowned. Charles modified his tone from mocking to unadorned gentleness. "I'm kidding. Yes, that's what we told them. It was time. I thought, perhaps, they already knew. I was hopeful they did, just to make it easier, but it was a surprise for them. Mary and I had covered the topic long before and made our peace with it. I was the one growing tired of not fully acknowledging the truth."

"What did your kids say?"

"Remmy was hilarious, as he tends to be. He said, 'Congratulations or condolences, whichever applies,' and we had a laugh." Yesteryear's storm clouds slid across his eyes now. "It was different with Chas. Many things were. He left that night, said he had to get back to the city for work. We asked him to stay. I practically begged him. I thought if he did, if he just stayed and we did some of the things we always did as a family, we could work through the discomfort of it all. He said he had to go. I knew he was struggling, and he tended to struggle alone. That was his way. He said he would call in a week or so. That was Sunday night. Monday came and went. Tuesday..."

"I'm so sorry, Charles."

He went on. "Mary decided to go back to Biddeford. She left Monday, as did Remmy, back to school in Boston. I stayed on at the Cape. End of the season, you know. I was gone all that morning, out on the water.

Chas made the call he promised me. Left a message on our machine. He was in the South Tower. He said, 'Well, Pop, I should have stayed. Goodbye.'"

"Jesus."

"Indeed."

Charles dabbed at his eyes with the cloth napkin. He pushed his half-eaten sandwich away. Max sat silent and still, and he ached for his friend. He couldn't imagine such crushing finality, and he hoped it never came for anyone he loved. He had been lucky with both of his parents—long fades into good night, plenty of time to say what demanded to be said and plenty of time to figure out how to leave the rest out. Even so, when Gustav moved through his mind, all these years later, Max would pine for all the time he had been robbed of with his old man. Same with Belle, although that was a different pain and one mitigated somewhat by her longer stay.

"Here's the thing I try to remember," Charles finally said. "I think of this especially when it's just me and the night and my thoughts, and I know I can't always trust what my mind is pulling up and putting in front of me. I remember that everybody that weekend had a shared truth and a choice to make in response to it. Mary and I chose to tell our boys something difficult, something we felt they had a right to know. Chas chose to go back to New York. I chose to go sailing. Yes, certainly, I've had moments these many years when I've fervently wished I'd been there to get that call, to say goodbye, to tell my son the joy he brought to my life. But I went sailing. And that, with the information I had, was a valid choice. I can't change it just because I don't like what the circumstances turned out to be. Do you understand what I'm saying?"

"I do," Max said. "It's—well, I guess it's an evolved point of view."

"Oh, yes, if it's evolution you're after, come see me." Charles chuckled.

"You know," Max said. "This will seem pretty trivial—"

"No such thing."

"—but I made a choice yesterday. I'm not going home to Billings. I'm headed to Detroit, gonna spend a few days doing whatever I want to do, or maybe even nothing."

"Which is also a choice," Charles said.

"Exactly."

"Why Detroit?"

"Well, the next job is near there, just a few days from now."

"Yes," Charles said, "but you could have gone anywhere. Why Detroit?"

Max chewed on that a bit. There really hadn't been any grand plan. A job was coming up quickly, so he went where the job would be. The point had been it wasn't Billings.

"Just going to the job," he said again.

"But Max, when you decided to change your plans, how did you *feel*? You brought this up. There must be something there."

"I'm relieved, I guess."

"Oh?"

"Yeah. It's definitely relief."

"I'm proud of you, Max," Charles said. "If you feel relief, maybe that's exactly what you need."

They finished with coffee, Charles' first, Max's seventh. Max found himself wishing even more than usual for a first-class upgrade. He would need easy access to the lavatory.

"Do you mind my making an observation?" Charles asked.

"Oh, you're going to start asking permission now?"

"Max, you're a rascal."

"That's the observation?"

"No," Charles said, "that's a bonus. Here it is: You're sad."

"Is that a mindreader's cowboy hat?"

"Max."

"Because that's fucking genius, right there."

Charles, flummoxed, tugged at the ring on his left hand. Max followed the line of action. "Wedding band?" Max asked.

"Yes."

"You stayed married?"

"Yes."

"Impressive. I'm straight as an arrow and can't keep a wife. You joined the other team and still have one."

"Are you finished being a smartass?" Charles asked.

"For now. Maybe."

"May I go on?"

"Please do."

"I don't have much time left with you, Max," Charles said. "I'd like to get us squared away on this."

"Go. Say your piece."

"I have a question."

"Shoot," Max said.

"Have you thought of talking to someone about what's going on with you?"

"You mean besides you?"

"*Max.*"

"Yeah, OK—"

"I'm talking about a dispassionate third party. A counselor. A headshrinker, in the parlance of the more crude among us."

"Like me," Max said.

"Max, my friend, your problem isn't that you're crude. It's your utter fear that you might *not* be crude."

Max ignored this and proceeded to his answer to the question. "I've thought about it."

"And those thoughts have led you where?"

"Here."

"This is a hopeless conversation."

"No," Max said. "I mean it. I've thought about it, sure, but I just don't have the time—"

"I'd daresay nothing in your life could be more worth your time than this," Charles said.

"—and anyway, I don't want to. So I'm here. I'm talking to you. I'll keep talking to you, if you want to keep talking to me."

"I'm anything but dispassionate on the subject of you," Charles said.

"I kind of thought so," Max said. "I wondered, back in Billings, if you were trying to pick me up when you asked me to have a beer."

"Oh!" Charles chortled. And then he snorted. He snortled. And then he laughed, a gut-ripper, a machine-gun blast of giggles that prompted Max to look around, embarrassed. The laughter morphed into a coughing fit, and Max steamed.

"You know, it's not the most outrageous thought in the world," Max said, his teeth half-clenched. "Especially now that I know your spurs jingle-jangle-jingle, cowboy."

"Oh, Max," Charles said, finally getting the better of his fit. "I'm sorry. That tickled me. No offense, old chap, but that was never my interest."

"No?"

"No," Charles said. "I'm flattered, of course, that you thought so, but I like a man who's a little..."

Thinner? Richer? Smarter? More urbane? Max lined up the possibilities.

"A little *shorter* than you," Charles finished.

"Letting me down easy, huh?"

"I'm sorry."

"Hey, what are you sorry for?" Max said. "I'm the one who wasn't interested. You wouldn't happen to have Mary's number, would you?"

That uncorked another round of laughter from Charles, self-renewing guffaws that had tears breaking trail on his face. The wave pulled Max in. Bemused glances from other tables fell on them. The server came by with the check, and Charles paid it with a flourish, then gathered up his rancher's finery.

"I must go," he said. "Thank you, my friend, for a most delightful lunch. Let's keep in touch."

Max rose for the goodbye. "You can count on it."

He reached for Charles, pulling him into the kind of bear hug he would give to Alexandra when she was a girl and the thunderstorms gathered, chasing her into closets and dark spaces. *I love you. It's OK. It will pass.*

Charles disengaged, patted Max on the cheek, and moseyed off.

Max wandered down the concourse in search of a restroom. He found it, and in close proximity he found the art gallery Charles had prattled on about the night they met. After discharging his caffeinated load, Max moved in for a closer look.

The Cuban art remained on display, a small selection of portraits and pop art. Max felt drawn to one photo in particular, of an old Cuban woman with a dark face, almost black, lines folded into it like the markings of a topographical map. She wore a purple blossom tucked into her hair, a breezy moment in what was otherwise an unspeakably harsh life. Most striking was a huge, lit stogie she sucked on, her top lip curved conspiratorially over the rolled tobacco. Her oblong eyes tilted downward in sadness and weariness. Her bulbous nose, like that of a boxer who had taken too many punches, dominated her wizened face. Max found her by turns fascinating and pitiable. This was no fat cat chomping a cigar. In her, Max saw endless years, unspoken pain, the hopelessness of now. He wanted to make her laugh. He also wanted to get as far away from her as he could. These competing impulses lived together, uneasily, inside him.

Had Charles seen something like this in him? *You're sad.* Damn right, he was, but not like this picture. Was he wrong about that? Could it be possible that he presented to the world a face that futilely masked what was behind it? Out of all the people in the terminal that night, why had Charles chosen him to approach, to chide for drinking diet pop, to strike up a conversation?

What did Charles see in him?

Amid the quiet interlude and unspoken thoughts, Max's phone went on a violent tear, playing back Ben Folds' funny, furious reaction to a woman who kicked him to the curb.

Janine.

Max stepped away from the art display and into the ceaseless flow of foot traffic and took the call as the rivulets of shuffling travelers enveloped him like a swollen waterway steals land after a spring storm.

"Hi, Janine."

"Are you coming home today?"

"You made me leave home. Remember?"

"Jesus, Max, are you on your way to Billings? It was the Cushing line, right? It's Saturday. So you're traveling, right?"

"I'm in Minneapolis. I'm not coming."

"Why?"

"Janine—"

"Never mind. It's not my business."

"OK."

"Look, Max," she said. "Whatever you're doing, you might want to come back."

"To Billings?"

"Yes."

"Why?"

"Alex got some news. They can't have a baby."

Max felt his knees go. He backed up to the wall for support.

"Max?"

"I heard you."

"OK."

"I'm coming."

"OK."

He hung up. Before him, airport life spun on, people going and coming, making connections, finding their way home, or, perhaps, finding their way somewhere else. In any case, they knew where they were headed.

Max, suddenly, did not.

The in-between swallowed him. On the G concourse, there was a gate and an eventual flight still four hours away, and in the wrong direction. His baggage, already marked, waited somewhere in the bowels of the airport for that connection. On the F concourse sat another gate and another eventual flight bearing a seat he had given up, headed to the place he now desperately needed to go.

Max oriented himself, then he began to run.

To: Wendt, Max
From: Charles Foster Danforth
Subject: We begin again

Hello, Max...

I've been thinking of you since we parted. I wish I had the time to say all the things I wanted to say, and to hear the things you wanted to say. But isn't that how it goes in the moment? Time and words run away from you, and you're left to sort them out later, when you can reimagine the interaction.

I owe you an apology and a proposition (oh, Max, behave!). Let's take these in order:

I'm sorry for declaring you "sad" without giving you some greater context on why I observed that, and why I felt it was important to say it. I recognize the dynamic we're in, and that I really have no standing at all to say some of the things I do. (Similarly, you have no standing to say some of the things you do, which I'll get to in the proposition.) We have been remarkably patient with each other, which is one of the hallmarks of a worthwhile friendship. I feel like we're building one. I hope you do, too.

When I was a boy, my mother told me that I was an uncommonly perceptive child, and as she was an uncommonly perceptive woman, I was inclined to believe her. My father thought less charitably of me—I sense he knew who and what I am before I did—and so some portion of my life has been spent learning how to embrace my mother's vision and forget my father's. That's no easy task, for anyone. Even today, long after both are gone, I would be sorely tempted to exchange a hundred of my mother's kind words for one loving interaction with him. What a terrible bargain that would be. Thankfully, I am not permitted to make it.

I will admit that the perception my mother saw in me, such as it is, has not entirely been a blessing. It's easy to get lazy, to assume that others see things the way you do, for feelings to get trampled. That has happened far more than I'd care to tell you. I regret every instance I know about, and it pains me to think there are surely some I don't remember, people I've hurt without even realizing it. Oh, to have time and clarity enough to make amends to everyone. But I don't. We don't. We simply must do better today than we did yesterday and hope that for however many tomorrows we have to do better still.

I believe I told you I was a pediatrician. I found children a delight to treat, because they did not hide their symptoms or engage in false bravado. If they hurt, they told you where. They told you for how long. If you asked the right questions, you could be sure you were getting accurate answers, so far as the child was able to supply them. Usually, his or her parent (mother, most of the time) could fill in the blanks. If they cared for the child enough to bring him/her in, they cared enough to pay attention to what was going on before the visit with the doctor.

In any case, with adults you don't always get that kind of honesty. It's not because they're fundamentally dishonest—most people aren't. Rather, it's that they build calluses and armor around the places that hurt, so they can deny the pain and avoid having to deal with it. They do this knowing, in their hearts, that the crash is going to come at some point—you can ignore trauma only so long before it comes out sideways, and usually with a spectacular display of collateral damage. But they accept this risk if it means they don't have to deal with their hurts today.

This was you in the airport restaurant: "I don't know." "I'm not sure." "I don't think so." Everything you said was couched in a negative.

You're covering up some profound hurts, Max. I could see it in you that first night in the airport. I could see it in you at lunch.

This is human nature, by the way. You're not defective. Indeed, you are fully what you are and what you were coded to be. I just happen to believe that we can move beyond our programming.

So now we come to the proposition:

I would like to continue our dialogue—not with me as the stuffy old overly pedantic guy, and not with you as the smart-aleck tough guy who puts me in my place. I would like to talk about real things, a true give and take, and I would like to react to one another in genuine ways. If it's anger, be angry. If it's sadness, be sad. But, please, Max, don't cover up, don't deflect, and don't blow me off. What I'm saying is this: If you have something to say, say it. And if you're not sure you want to say it, don't say it until you are sure. In return, I will be fully present and fully genuine with you. This should be important to both of us. We must make the most of our time, not only in consultation with each other but also here in this existence.

What do you say?

As a gesture of good faith, I will tell you something about my marriage to Mary: We were kids—and, goodness, yes, really just children—who were supposed to be together. Our families demanded it, we acceded to that demand, and it was only by virtue of a friendship that we found on mutual terms that we held it together. She must have known a year into things, if not sooner, the truth about me, and she bore it until I could no longer, and then we pledged ourselves in partnership, if not in romantic love. She was free to do as she pleased, with a healthy amount of discretion. (My grandfather had a wonderfully vivid expression for what I'm talking about: "There are eyes in the potato patch.") I was similarly free to pursue my own desires, and similarly responsible for ensuring that my business remained no one else's. That's what we told the boys that day on the Cape: This is the situation as far as sexual orientation goes, but our family is an altogether different situation, and one that shall continue.

I felt like I could make that promise on September 8, 2001. Three days later, everything changed. If we hadn't lost Chas, we might well have made that pledge stand up. The pain, alas, was too crushing, too fierce, too all-encompassing, and our family blew apart. Mary remains my wife, only because neither of us had the will or the reason to end the legalities of it. Our lives play out separately. That's when I retired—I was fairly young, you know—and began doing what I do now. I had a need to be on the move, not so fixed in my little Maine town, and to be of service. And it has been a great gift in my life. I've made so many friends. You're one of them.

Imagine that, Max. You are part of the light that cuts through my darkness. I am grateful.

PRINCETON AVENUE, BILLINGS, MONTANA

Sunday, March 31 | 1:23 a.m.
Seventy-six hours, seven minutes before departure

Max lay propped up by pillows in the darkness, phlegm congregating just under his throat. On top of everything else, a cold. This was the work of the sniffling older guy in 2C, no doubt, his snorts and sucks and hacks setting down the most unsatisfactory of syncopated jazz notes. Just over two hours of flight, listening to that specimen of mortuary fodder hack up the same ball of snot, rinse it around in his mouth, then swallow it again. Christ Almighty. Max had all but run for the parking lot once in Billings.

He leaned over the side of the bed now, hacked until he loosed his own gob, then spat it into a tissue.

Everything had slowed down once Max had finally heard from Alexandra, after a half-dozen calls got banished to voicemail and two texts languished on his phone, delivered but not acknowledged.

Finally, she had written back: *Sorry. I was asleep. I'm OK. Come home. I miss you.*

He was coming home—that part was non-negotiable. The circumstances by which he had done it had been unusual, though. It had started with a lengthy explanation to the counter agent that he really did want to go to Billings—yes, yes, his luggage was bound for Detroit, so, please, just hold it there for a couple of days, but get me to Billings and then get me a one-way back to Detroit a few days later. She had been skeptical. The computers had balked, having been programmed, in an age of color-coded travel, to home in on booking shenanigans. Finally, a supervisor had taken pity—or, at least, had found Max credible—and rebooked the Detroit one-way (at a $437 markup for change fees and fare difference, an amount Max would almost certainly have to eat when it came to his expense report) and offered him the last seat, first class, on that evening's flight to Billings. Full fare. Max would have paid at twice the price.

Max rolled again to the edge of the mattress and expelled another dollop of sickness into the tissues that grew like little white mushrooms on the floor of his room.

Much kept him awake, beyond the clockwork spasms of his diaphragm. His gear, for one thing. He was out of sorts with his routine now, unable to assess what had survived transit and what had not. In a couple of days, he would receive (if he was fortunate) a suitcase full of soiled clothes, underwear with pee tracks in it (*hello, fifty-five!*), socks gone crunchy with grit, muddy jeans and shirts. He would spend mobilization night doing laundry. Not his goddamn routine.

Then there was Alexandra, both the overarching issue of infertility and whatever role he was to play in her dealing with the unwanted circumstance. The plan, at this hour, was a family meeting at Alexandra and Tyler's later in the morning. Fine as far as it went; Max would have done whatever was asked of him, and Janine would, too, he was sure. Max's problem was one of concept. The family, in case nobody else was aware, wasn't doing too hot these days, and the pain Alexandra and Tyler were now in—fantastic galaxies of pain, Max was sure—was the kind that got eased only by time. Max felt utterly inadequate to the task of saying anything about this; he had contorted himself intellectually the entire way home, trying to get close to what he might have felt, years earlier, if he and Janine had found out they couldn't have a child. Try as he might, he couldn't access the concept. Janine *had* gotten pregnant, surprisingly so (though Max knew it was stupid to be surprised by that), and they'd never had to confront even the theoretical of a barren womb. Max could take a cruder whack at it and imagine Alexandra being plucked out of their lives. Even the hypothetical of that would crater him in sadness. But it wasn't the same, was it? He hadn't loved his child when she was conceptual and still in stardust. He had loved her with everything he had after he knew she was coming. He had loved her with everything he would ever have upon her arrival, and he had held that love every subsequent day since.

The considerable difference in the scenarios—beyond the obvious one—was that he and Janine had never hatched anything so ambitious as The Plan, not the way the kids had, with Alexandra even giving it the post-ironic capital letters in the note she wrote to him and Janine. *The Plan: Make a substantial amount of money before I am 35 and Tyler is 45, have a child or two, and give those children the kind of upbringing that comes only with limitless horizons and no want of anything material or emotional.* Alexandra, and Max observed this with all the love in his heart for her, had probably seen it as humility that she had written "a child or two" and not dominated the details. Which, of course, is when the universe sweeps in and says, *Hey, how about none?* The first time Alexandra had ever been told she couldn't do something had been a doozy.

Max considered this, and fear settled over him. Had he diminished Alexandra with these thoughts? The room pulled away from him in the darkness. He was alone and isolated, cold, untethered, floating away from the moorings he had known.

He spat into another tissue and let it fall away. He rolled onto his back and wriggled until his head and neck were again elevated. He closed his eyes, and he waited for a cracked egg across the eastern horizon. Sunlight would bring order where there was none. It would sustain hopeful things. It would bring clarity. He just had to get there.

He tilted his head and looked to the window. He closed his eyes.

The night was resilient. Max was not.

SANDALWOOD DRIVE, BILLINGS, MONTANA

Sunday, March 31 | 9:04 a.m.
8.2 miles driven in sixteen minutes, five seconds

As ever, indigestion set up camp in Max's gut as he pulled up to Alexandra and Tyler's place on the far West End. Out here, nestled under the Rimrocks, the mini-mansion-dwelling denizens had their own enclave, close enough to town to do their business and far enough away to not be blighted by the neon casino signs and halfway houses that sat in Billings like pockmarks. The rich here, like anywhere, were self-selecting. You needed a portfolio to play. Max knew he was out of his element; what perpetually boggled him was how Alexandra had managed to migrate from working stock, as she had been raised, to this. It wasn't that she had been welcomed that bothered Max. He had met some of her friends, liked them, was glad she had them. She would show up from time to time in the Business Achievers column of the *Herald-Gleaner*, and he would be proud, just as any father would. He just didn't get it, how this kid straight out of central Billings—house on a busy street, middle class (sometimes low, sometimes high, subject to the vagaries of crude oil), public schools, Lutheran church—had ended up out here among the 4,000-square-feet set. He had raised her on Darrell Waltrip and Brett Favre, on Kraft mac 'n' cheese and Dr. Pepper; she had found salvation in Warren Buffett, sushi, and bottled water.

He was getting out of his pickup, his jacket pockets filled with the tissues he was going to need, when Janine pulled up behind in a sleek, zippy new Cadillac—not the money-boat Cadillac of old, but something more whimsical and fun, a splashy blue. She waved, and he returned it before he considered whether he wanted to.

Max ambled up as Janine climbed out. "New wheels?" He coughed, hurried a tissue to his mouth, and surreptitiously spat.

She smiled. She stepped back. "You like?"

"Pretty nice. Don't spend everything before I get my cut."

"Max."

"I'm just saying."

"Do you suppose," Janine said, "we could set our business aside and focus on Alex?"

"I suppose."

Tyler was out on the porch or the veranda or the portico or whatever the hell the HGTV generation called it now, beckoning them. They headed in, Janine in the lead, Max covering the rear, with Tyler getting a hug from her and a grim declination of a handshake from him ("Got a cold." "You get a flu shot?" "Yes, doc."). Inside, Alexandra came with a brave face, a kiss on the cheek for her mother, an extended embrace that Max couldn't evade, the same as the one she always gave him when he came off the road and yet also different and new, a grasping and a holding on now that the stakes had changed for her.

"I've missed you, Pookie Nose," he whispered in Alexandra's ear, and she giggled, and for a singular moment that was enough.

"Max," Tyler said, "do you want me to take your hat?"

Max doffed it and handed it with a long arm, struggling not to cough. "Here's my hat, what's your hurry?"

"A good joke never grows stale, Max."

They all got settled in the living room, Alexandra in a love seat,

Tyler standing behind her, Max in the farthest chair he could find, and Janine holding down the edge of a three-seat sofa.

"So," Alexandra said, "Mom knows this. The bottom line is three awful words: premature ovarian failure. I can't produce viable eggs. So..."

"So," Max said. "So that's—"

"Yeah."

"Sweetie, I'm sorry." He coughed and covered.

"Dad, are you OK?"

"Just a cold. Don't worry."

"OK," she said. "Thank you. We're all sorry."

"What causes this?" Janine asked.

"Genetics, maybe," Tyler said. "I mean, you guys obviously managed—"

"Just the one," Max said. He smiled at his daughter.

"One was all we needed," Janine said.

"Right," Tyler said. "It could be autoimmune. Sometimes it follows chemotherapy, which obviously wasn't the case here."

"It's just bad fucking luck," Alexandra broke in. "Sorry, Dad. That's all it is."

"No fucking problem." That broke her between giggles and whimpers. "Oh, Daddy," she said. She put the little-girl second syllable on it only when she was at her most vulnerable.

"Max," Janine said.

"What? It sucks. That's what I'm saying."

Tyler again. "Trenchant as that is, I think our time here is better spent on what we might do now."

"Adopt," Janine said.

"We've talked about that," he said.

"It's a good option," she said. "So many children in the world who need love."

"Sure," he said. "It's just that this has been quite a blow, as you know, and—"

Max watched Alexandra. She wasn't in the moment anymore. She had floated to the periphery of things, her eyes on the French doors leading to the backyard, her mind maybe there, too, or maybe somewhere else. He couldn't know. He was certain, though, that it wasn't in what was becoming an exclusive exchange between Tyler and Janine.

"Honey," Max said, "what do you want?"

Alexandra came back into the now. "You know what I want. I've been clear about what I want."

"Right," he said. "What do you want that you can have?"

"Seriously, Max?" Janine looked at him, alarmed. He threw his gaze back to Alexandra. *Come on now*, he thought. *Talk to me.*

"I don't know," she said.

"It's just that we have a plan," Tyler said.

"I know about the plan," Max said.

"It's a good plan," Janine said.

Alexandra stood up. "It *was* a good plan. There is no plan now. Got it?"

That's the answer, right there, Max thought. While Alexandra, Janine, and Tyler pivoted to the notion of making a new plan in the absence of the old plan, Max stood, a coughing fit upon him, and he slipped into the backyard, closing the door on Janine's "Max, what are you—" and stepping into the sun. First day of April, no fooling, the warmth on his cheeks. He smothered the cough and spat out the residue and then, eyes closed, he stretched out his arms and let the sky fall on him.

"You just left," Janine said, behind him.

Max turned. "For a second, yeah. You guys seemed to have it well in hand."

She sat at the breakfast nook on the patio. "Our daughter is hurting."

"I know."

"And you left."

"Jesus, Janine," he said. "I was coming right back."

"Like you always do?"

He walked toward her, finger pointed. "That is not fair. I didn't cause this, and I can't fix it. I'm here for her. She knows that. And you know it, too." The vocal burst taxed him again, and here came the coughs again, a whole line of them. He set his hands on his knees and bent over, forcing them out.

"You should see a doctor," Janine said.

"I'm fine. Don't worry about me."

They stared each other down. Max queued up his responses for every way she might decide to push it now. Talk about spreading your defenses thin. Should he cover for his itinerant ways in general, or for Alexandra's specific issue today, or for the hundred thousand shattered shards of a marriage, each of which could be weaponized if one of them chose? How many past unkindnesses from Janine could he sharpen and stab her with today? How many instances of neglect by him could she pull up as evidence of his aloofness? Could they even be counted?

Janine sat. "I'm sorry for what I said."

"Thank you."

"It's just...so many times you were gone. So many times," she said. "Even when you were here."

"I know," he said. "But please don't you ever tell me I don't love her completely. Because you're wrong. And more than that, you're unfair."

"I know."

He sat down opposite her. *If I look as hurt as she does, we're in a hell of a mess.* Max thought now of the times, sparingly few, when pain had to be left to run rampant or it wouldn't leave otherwise. So you lie down and you take it. This was such a time.

"How'd we come to this?" he asked.

"Little by little. It only seems like a lot at the end."

"Janine," he said, "I'm trying. I really am. I don't have it figured out as well as you do—"

"I don't have it so figured out," she said. "I just got a head start. Nothing can be done about that."

"Can we just, I don't know, assume that we've both got the best intentions? We have Alexandra. She's always going to be yours and mine. Ours. Can we not let our stuff spill into that, please?"

She reached for his hand, gripping his middle and ring fingers and rubbing them, playing with the wedding band that was still there. He set his free hand atop both of hers.

"Thank you," he said.

Alexandra came out now and caught the tenderness between them, and she sat next to her mother and set her head on Janine's shoulder. "Look at the two of you," she said.

"We have our moments," Max said.

"So, listen." Alexandra sat up straight. "Tyler and I have been talking for a while—you know, we didn't just find out Thursday or whatever that this was the situation. It's been a drawn-out thing, so we've kind of known but had tried to stay hopeful..." She made tiny bites on her lower lip. "You know, we've kind of suspected."

"Sure," Max said. He marveled silently that she had held it close this long, then he shifted away from that in full understanding. The circumspect ways she'd had, even as a little girl, were Janine's influence on her coming through. They had served her well more often than not.

"Anyway, we're going to let it sink in, take our time with the biggest decisions," Alexandra said. "But I do want to start divesting. I think, regardless of what we might decide, we're going to want to wind down a little bit and give ourselves some freedom, you know?"

"A wise decision," Janine said.

"We're thinking a trip to start. Just the two of us."

"Sounds good," Max said.

"So, Mom, if you want any of these properties—"

"I'll send over a list."

"Dad?" Alexandra asked. "I could give you a real nice price on that Princeton place."

Max shoved his hands deep in his pockets as he leaned back in the chair. "Sorry, honey. I was going to wait to say anything, since I have to leave so soon and all this other stuff was happening, but I'm not going to be staying there much longer."

"Why?" Alexandra asked.

Janine: "Where are you going?"

Max grinned at them, big as anything. Wasn't it something, when a half-baked idea just popped out? A fleeting thought at breakfast, as he scrambled his eggs with sausage and peppers—*Why come back here between jobs? Why not just stay out there?*—gets tucked away as quickly as it came, only to pop out again to the astonishment of dear old erstwhile wife and darling daughter. It was worth it, Max thought now, to see their faces twist at his unplanned revelation.

"That's the thing," he said, drawing a fresh tissue near to catch the next coughs gathering in his throat. "I have no idea."

THE HOUSE ON PRINCETON AVENUE

Monday, April 1 | 10:13 a.m.
Time needed to empty it: One hour, sixteen minutes

Max could scarcely believe the ease of modern living, so long as you didn't have to consider the parts that involved nurturing interpersonal relationships, negotiating the tricky terrain of job politics, and mitigating the vagaries of unknown interlopers. Strictly from the standpoint of *what do you need* and *when do you need it*, what a time it was to be alive. Almost everything you could want or need or pine for was yours, on demand.

So it was that Max, on a whim that became a mandate, had gotten up, had driven to the U-Haul franchise on Grand Avenue, had ordered up yet another moving truck (a smaller one this time, the hindsight of recent experience saving him all of ten bucks), had learned that he could, with a few quick keystrokes on an app, arrange for labor to help him load it, and had headed back to Princeton Avenue to close up.

"You want to double your money?" Max asked the broad-shouldered kid who had shown up at Alexandra's little rental and had hucked his boxes and belongings and bed onto the truck as if they were nothing.

"Who wouldn't?"

"Good answer," Max said. "Follow me."

The unloading went quicker than the loading, with Max's worldly possessions, such as they were, deposited into the largest storage unit he could get in the Heights. Max paid the kid and added a generous tip, then bid him so long. Alone, he took in where he had landed. The space was filled maybe thirty percent, the rest cavernous and clean, rather like a loft apartment, Max thought, if you were willing to look past the absence of windows and the fact that it would become a tomb if the rollaway door were pulled down and latched.

Still, Max thought, possibilities abounded here. On his necessary swings back through town, he could open the place up, let the breeze in, relax in his recliner, run a TV and DVD player off the generator, and almost be home. Somewhere in the boxes was a blender. A cooler filled with ice, a mini-fridge, some lime juice and tequila and triple sec, and it could be margaritas till closing time. Draw down the door, lock it up tight, head to a hotel room. A right fine plan, all of it.

Max fished loose his phone and called Alexandra, who picked up on the first ring.

"How are you feeling, Dad?"

"Better."

"Yeah? You still don't sound good."

"Better," he said again.

"I'm glad."

"Listen," he said, "I'm done over at Princeton. Place is locked up. Keys are on the kitchen counter. You'll have to bill me for the cleanup."

"Dad, what—"

"Listen, Alexandra, just listen, OK?"

"OK."

"I really appreciate what you've done for me. I do. You're the good daughter."

"I'm the only daughter."

"Right, but you're also the best daughter. The thing is, I'm a little—it's just—"

"Untethered?" she offered. "Unmoored? At loose ends?"

"All of the above."

"I get it," she said. "Me, too."

"But it's weird. I'm kind of OK with it."

"I'm glad." Max thought he heard a crack in her cadence.

"I'm just going to ramble for a little while, I think," he said.

"OK."

"Like you're thinking of doing." He tossed it out with a lilt in his voice, an opening if she would like to step into it.

"Tyler and I think that's the prescription right now. Cut ourselves loose and travel."

"If you're going to Toledo," Max said, "maybe we could—"

She laughed at that, his very intention. "Not many beaches there."

"No, I guess not."

"You take care of yourself, Dad."

"You, too, Pookie Nose. The phone is always open."

"Same."

"OK."

"Bye."

"Alexandra, wait."

"Yes?"

He looped out of the storage unit, around the long line of stacked-up boxes he would have to rearrange sometime, whenever that might be. "Just a sec," he said. "I'm formulating."

"OK."

He bent at the middle, the phone pressed hard between his shoulder and his ear, and he used his right hand to twist and wrench the wedding ring from his left. In its vacated space, Max's lower finger narrowed like an hourglass, and a patch of white skin marked where the metal had stayed, mostly, for the preponderance of his life. He set the wedding band on the desk his helper had jammed into a corner, and he lifted his finger for a sniff. A mistake, that was.

He now went to the door, pulled it down, flipped the latch, engaged the lock.

"I'm sorry for the things I missed," he said. "I tried to be there, but..."

"I know. You did your best."

"I hope so. Wish I had some do-overs, though. Been thinking about that some."

"Dad," she said. "I love you. Besides, life is full of second chances. At some things, anyway."

"Yeah." He was sure now that he heard the break in his own bearing.

"I have to go," she said.

"Me, too."

"Bye."

The transactions played out to their inevitable conclusions, with the return of the rental truck, Max's reunion with his own vehicle, and the recession to a first-floor room at the Country Inn & Suites in the Heights and Max's short stay before he began flying east.

He sequestered himself with cough drops and a roll of Vitamin C bombs and mucous-suppressants, a cavalcade of potential cures. He had two nights to get himself right. Every aloft jet cutting lines in the sky doubled as a test tube of communicable illness, and Max had always been thankful he had generally stayed relatively healthy, a fact he ascribed to good habits, serendipity, and, perhaps, a business traveler's herd immunity. But he had been nicked this time.

The television blared into the blankness of Max's darkened room, and he felt the turning of his mental machinery, right on time, lifting him out of where he was and into where he was going and what he would be doing when he got there. It was a run he did often, a forty-two-hour affair that almost always came off without a hitch, a straight shot south out of Michigan and into Toledo.

But the variables had changed. These past couple of days had unfurled without the usual text banter from Little Bonk, without a phone call from Dex, which wasn't necessarily unusual and yet carried a tint of inexplicable worry for Max. And Alicia—oh, what a looming mess that was, perhaps, depending on how her own processing of their long, strange week together had gone. He hadn't considered that until now, preoccupied as he was with matters of flesh and blood. It would have to keep waiting.

Max wished for the routine, perhaps the presence of his equipment so he could inventory and supplement it, but that lay in a storage hold in Detroit, if he was lucky.

He clicked off the TV, and darkness crowded in, and he lay back into the propped-up pillows and tried to find a quiet landing spot. It was of no use. His thoughts overran their gutters and flowed off into every empty space.

To: *Charles Foster Danforth*
From: *Wendt, Max*
Subject: *Re: We begin again*

Charles...

Your last email was my favorite yet. You cuffed me about pretty good, but you did so with care, too, and I appreciate that. I really do. No sarcasm here at all. I can't promise you there won't be some in the future— maybe even in this note!— but there's none here.

I used to tell Janine—my wife, I told you her name before, I think— anyway, I used to tell her that she could slap me around, verbally or otherwise, that I probably had it coming, but if she didn't end it on a note that we could use going forward—I think in the corporate world they call that a "growth opportunity"—it wouldn't do much good, because I'd probably just repeat whatever I'd done to tick her off in the first place.

You know, I thought I was being wise when I said that, but now that literally everything is hindsight, maybe I was just being a wiseass. Maybe I was giving her too much responsibility and me not enough. I don't know.

Remember I told you about my daughter, Alexandra, and her plan? The Plan. It's all been blown to hell. She's infertile. Just found out. (Why did I just flash on Holly Hunter, in Raising Arizona, saying, "Ah'm barrrrren"? I love that movie, but what the fuck? Max Wendt and had another dumb thought.) So that's what we've been dealing with the past few days. Oh, wait! Right. So after you went moseying down to your flight in Minneapolis, cowboy, I found out about Alex and flew back to Montana instead of Michigan. No luxurious days in a hotel for me, bubba. I went to my daughter and unpacked my house and put everything in storage and nuked a bad cold with pharmaceuticals (I thought for a bit that I was just having an allergic reaction to your hat, but no dice), and now I'm about to get on those flights to DTW. The Wicked Witch of the West: What a world, what a world! At least she got out of it.

Max Wendt on a tangent...

Sorry about that, Charles. The mind flies around. Too many fires to put out and not enough quiet places to let the thoughts settle. To respond to you directly, I like your idea about how we're to talk to each other, selfishly, if only for a place to set down the load. I'll do my best.

Anyway, back to it: I'm frustrated by the stuff I can't change. Alexandra lost The Plan. She's so self-possessed, Charles, so in control of herself, but she's hurting so bad and it seems like the only thing I have to offer her are my arms and the collection of Dad Jokes I've been building up without even realizing it. Seems to me that the fix is time, which we've all got even if we don't know how much, and whatever she's got inside of her. I've loved that girl since she drew breath. That's a long time, a big chunk of my life. But I have nothing for her now. It's not right.

Anyway, she and her husband (Dr. Tyler Keisling, M.D., PDQ, BFD, WTF) are about to engage the second part of The Plan in the absence of the first. They're pulling all their money together and getting out of Billings for a while. It's hard to imagine the place without her, just as it's hard to remember what it was before she arrived.

I guess I'm getting out, too, only I didn't make it any farther than a storage unit for my stuff. When we're done with this job in Toledo, I'm going to just drive around a bit and see some things—maybe Nashville, maybe Louisville, maybe Cleveland, maybe Chicago—and then head to the next job, the Upper Peninsula. No reason to go back to Montana. Nothing there for me. Can't change that, either.

Janine's racing off to D-I-V-O-R-C-E in a new Cadillac. Nothing can be done about that. Not sure I'd want it done anyway. We had a moment at Alexandra's, something really nice, but then it was gone again. She's relieved. She's out from under. I'm out from under, too, but what I'm feeling ain't relief.

And I know I probably should be thankful that it's gone as smoothly as it has. I've got a friend, Big Bonk, a mentor, really, the guy who put me in this line of work, and he's busted up three marriages, each one of them a trauma. Janine's made sure this is more like outpatient surgery. I mean, I signed our divorce petition in a parking lot in Missouri, for Christ's sake. I haven't had to do anything except respond to her messages. Credit to her, I guess, for efficiently managing this thing she wants into being, but I can't shake the feeling that I don't have a role here outside of being a chess piece somebody else is playing.

I mean, Janine could be Missy in this C.J. Box mystery series I love, this elderly sociopath who's always trading up husbands and breaking the old ones and getting more and more influence, but I don't see that. I don't think Janine's interested in trading up or trading in. She wants to be done. And that hurts.

And, look, I feel like a chump for woe-is-me-ing through all of this. My burden is no heavier than anyone else's, and much lighter than many. Yours, for example. I want you to know I've taken your words to heart, all of them. Never mistake my sarcastic armor for disregard, OK? You're a good friend. I don't know how or why a couple of guys like you and me became that, but I'm thankful just the same.

Max Wendt on the plane

P.S. One more thing. On the last job, I was sleeping with a woman who just joined our crew. Don't get your rhinestone undies in a wad. Take the literal meaning of "sleeping with" and apply it. No mingling of compatible body parts. No bumping uglies. No hiding the sausage. No making the beast with two backs. Should I keep going? I got a million of them.

Why do I have the feeling that this last bit is going to be the only thing you process?

COMFORT INN, CHELSEA, MICHIGAN

Wednesday, April 3 | 5:52 p.m.
17.29 miles from the start of the job

The night-before job meeting was management theater, where Little Bonk (like Big Bonk and Dex before him) would fill out the paperwork in triplicate—scope of work, expected window of work, safety considerations, whatever else was sitting on his head. Only occasionally did Little Bonk deviate from the script, on those rare occasions when he really had some news to impart to the group.

Maybe protesters were marching down the right of way, worked into a pique by this or that perception of the evil Mantooth Energy had wrought. "Stay in your car, don't engage—shit, drive away if you have to." That had happened a time or two, and Max *had* engaged. "Hell, I hate Mantooth, too," he would tell them. "I'm just a contractor. Just a guy slugging it out for a paycheck." That usually shut them down, disarmed them. *A fine diplomat I could have been*, Max thought.

Or maybe there had been some bears spotted along the route, an uncommon but also not-unheard-of occurrence in the Minnesota North Woods or the upper reaches of Wisconsin when members of the *ursus* genus were either burrowing in for winter or emerging in the springtime. Years ago, those considerations had led to a bit of impromptu songwriting by Max, the formulation of a little ditty he would sing at full volume as he stepped from the car on lonely nights in the timber, just to signal his presence and not surprise any animal that could triple his size and quadruple his ferocity:

> *Hey, bear*
> *Hey there*
> *Don't eat me*
> *I'm all gristle*
> *Don't scare me*
> *Or I'll bristle*
> *Just run off*
> *In the thistle*
> *I need space*
> *You're an ace*
> *Hey there*
> *Hey, bear*

Max sat now with his hands wrapped around a cardboard cup of coffee, at the right elbow of Little Bonk, who was lost in his safety-report scribbles. He glanced at his watch and noted the hour. "Early is on time, on time is late" had been Big Bonk's admonition when he brought Max aboard, and damned if Max hadn't made that gospel not only in his own job performance but also in what he expected of others, particularly his daughter, who'd taken to it winningly.

That his fluttering thoughts landed on Alexandra drew out the pangs again, the ones he had been eating all day as he flew to Minneapolis and then Detroit and then had a surprisingly easy time of it with his early-arriving luggage before the short drive to Chelsea. First time in forever he felt bad about charging out to a job in some faraway state while there was hurt back home. He had done so only because he wasn't impotent here the way he was back in Billings, while Alexandra and Tyler tended to themselves and Janine stretched her newfound wings. He flashed on Alexandra now as a little girl, not a recent loser in the biological lottery, and at once he was back to the song, which had so amused and perplexed the long-ago version of her.

"There's no bear," she had once told him.

"Well, no, not *here*."

"Why do you sing that, then?"

"So he doesn't show up."

"I don't want a bear coming around me."

"I won't let him."

"But what if you're not here?"

"Well, sing it until I come back."

Alicia was next to join them. She took the chair at the other end of the breakfast-room table, to Little Bonk's left. Max offered a tightlipped smile. She nodded. Against intention, his mind reeled off into the extrapolated interpretations of what she might have meant by that. Silently, he tried to fight himself back to level as she and Little Bonk got it going.

"Easy drive for you," Little Bonk said, nudging her knowingly. "Must be nice, not cooling your heels in airports."

"Yeah, right," she said, a ready laugh on her lips. "The hundred-mile drive down from Saginaw was nothing. The disengaging from my kid and having to listen to his father, that I could do without."

That pulled Max's attention down the table. She glanced away when she noticed.

"My kids know the score," Little Bonk said. "Dad leaves, so don't hassle him. Mom runs things and—"

Max double-tapped his watch face. "Where are those guys?"

Bonk redirected his attentions. "Same old, you know. Tommy probably fell asleep four minutes ago. Steve's watching hillbilly porn."

Alicia twanged the opening bars to "Dueling Banjos."

"That's it," Bonk said. "Alicia gets it."

"Every single job, it's wait around on those two," Max groused, much to Bonk's bemusement.

"Well, you can go, man," Bonk said. "Nothing I'm gonna say that you haven't heard before."

"I'll wait."

As if on cue, Macartney shambled in and unloaded himself into one of the two chairs opposite Little Bonk.

"Fellas," he said. "Alicia."

"Hi, Steve," she said.

"Where's your twin?" Bonk asked.

"Shit if I know. I ain't responsible for him."

"Call him. Wake him up."

"Yeah, OK."

"I'm here." Smithlin's voice filled in the space his body hadn't yet penetrated. Around the corner he came and took the last chair at the table.

"Hope we aren't keeping you from anything more important than your job," Bonk said.

"All right, all right."

Bonk settled his shoulders and clutched his paperwork, the tabletop all his. "OK, knuckleheads. And Alicia. Let's do this thing."

And so it went.

Little Bonk divvied the crews the way he had said he would back in Oklahoma. Smithlin and Alicia on nights, midnight to noon, with Smithlin leading the shift and filling any remaining holes in her training. He would have no duties there; Max had made sure of that. They would put down a couple of hours of tracking in the morning if the tool launched by the 10 a.m. target, and Macartney and Max would swoop in on the day shift, noon to midnight.

"Which one of you guys wants shift lead?" Bonk asked.

"I don't care," Max said.

"Me neither," Macartney tossed in.

"Extra two bucks an hour," Bonk said. "Surely somebody cares."

Max: "Not me."

Macartney: "Nuh uh."

The thing was, Max *did* care, and the money was scarcely a factor. There was no glory in being the guy who made the every-two-hours call to the control center in Calgary, who made the pumping-station calls, who sent the every-four-hours emailed updates to everybody who had even a glancing interest in the job. No glory and, to get right to it, a hell of a lot of potential headache, especially if some tracker started following a ghost pig down the line, as Hanley had done more than once.

Max cared because he was good at it, seasoned by as many years of doing as Steve Macartney had spent breathing through his country-ass mouth. Macartney, on the other hand, was a hot mess who flaked out on the calculations. If Bonk tabbed him, he would get the money on payday and Max, somehow or some way, would end up doing the work.

"OK, Steve, you've got it," Bonk said. "Executive decision."

Max let the air out of himself.

"All right, kittens," Bonk went on. "Forty-two hours. No planned shutdowns. We'll see. This one usually goes off without a hitch. That means, if the numbers hold, we'll be landing in Toledo around four in the morning, local time. That's—"

"Two a.m. pipeline time," Alicia said. "Night shift." She looked to Tommy. "Our shift."

"Exactamundo," Bonk said. "Check out the brain on the newbie. You're leaving these guys in the dust."

Max dropped his head back, eyes parallel with the patterned ceiling tiles. Then he pitched forward and collected his backpack, his silent signal that it was time to break up the meeting lest Bonk ramble into a detailed menu of his coming nighttime shenanigans.

The five of them moved like cattle from the breakfast nook toward the lobby, then herd integrity broke down. Bonk headed for the parking lot, probably to outfit his car, as he would be the earliest out in the morning. Smithlin and Macartney diverted for the elevator.

"All set?" Max asked Alicia.

"Of course."

"Good." He gestured toward the elevator. "Going up?"

"Prefer the stairs."

She, too, peeled off and was gone. Max sidled up to the front desk and scooped a cookie out of the jar.

COMFORT INN, CHELSEA, MICHIGAN

Wednesday, April 3 | 7:48 p.m.
Seventeen minutes after dinner

Gluttonously full of Smokehouse 52 barbecue, Max sauntered across the parking lot toward the sliding glass doors fronting the lobby.

Yes, he had said to the aptly named The Enthusiast—a platter of pulled pork, beef brisket, smoked chicken, and ribs. *How could I not,* he had said to the sides of collard greens and mac 'n' cheese. *I'd be a fool not to,* he had said to the third and fourth and fifth glasses of sweet tea. *I'm no amateur,* he had said when his server asked if he had saved room for some banana pudding.

Now, what he had wolfed down fairly sloshed at his stepping aside as Alicia emerged from the other side of the glass.

"Hey," she said.

"Hey."

"Getting some dinner," she said.

"Just got some. Interested in barbecue? Good place here."

"No, I'm—" She cut it off and pointed at the fast-food place across the road. "Just something quick."

Max followed the line of her indication, and he offered an agreeable smile. On a four-day job like this—mobilize, two days of tracking, demobilize back home—a tracker could pad the bottom line of the paycheck with some unused per diem. More of Big Bonk's timeless wisdom hung out there in quick-cueing memory: "If you can't eat your fill on sixty bucks a day out there, you ought to grant serious contemplation to the condition of your digestive tract." Less colorfully put, the sixty bucks was yours no matter what; it was up to you how much of it you wanted to shove down your throat. Max, of course, savored every morsel and penny. Alicia, younger and less voracious and with worries on her head, was probably salting it away.

"I'll walk with you," he said. He had laundry still to do, but it could wait.

She shrugged. "Suit yourself."

The place was slammed, the destination of choice for a squad of sportos and their hangers-on, and the overwhelmed counter staff bid them find a seat and be patient and we'll get to it just as soon as we can, OK? *OK.*

Max was happy for the interlude, if not for the reckless teenage clamor around them, but that, too, granted some cover as he looked for a way in.

"I should apologize to you," he said.

"For what?"

"For...you know."

"Yeah, I do."

"I'm sorry," he said.

"For what?"

She tossed the responses back at him tersely, the syllables clipped and neat, the pitch of her voice as she tried to deny emotion betraying the presence of it.

"You know," he said.

"Right. I do. Want to take a third spin?"

"I'm just sorry."

"So you said."

"You're mad."

She leaned back, away from him, creating distance. He looked to the counter—*now would be a good time for that food*—and then back to her. "I'm not," she said. "I was. But I'm not. I don't have time to be mad. I don't have the *privilege* to be mad. I've got shit to do, and I've got to make it work out here somehow. If you'd been listening to me, you'd know that."

"I listened."

"Well, thank you for that."

"I'm trying here."

She bobbed her head low, eyes intent, words sharpened. "But you cannot say what it is that you did that now requires an apology. I wish you could. If you could name it, I could forgive it."

"I'm sorry," he said again.

"All right. Fine."

"I am."

Lower now her voice went, and fiercer. "I felt *shame*. I felt shame for something that I had no reason to be ashamed of, according to you. According to us. That's the deal. And I didn't deserve to feel that. And you damn sure didn't deserve to put that on me."

The kid from the register called a number. "That's mine," she said.

Max stood with her. "I'm sorry," he said.

"So you keep saying. Thank you."

"No," he said, "I really am. I want to make it right."

"You can't. It doesn't matter, OK? I accept that you're sorry. Let's leave it be. On the list of things I care about, you don't even rate."

"Ouch."

"Don't take it personally," she said evenly. "How can it be personal? We don't even know each other, remember? We're just colleagues."

Little Bonk was slipping into his rental as they came back around, Alicia's stride direct and scarfing landscape, Max's overloaded and trailing.

"See you out there tomorrow," Bonk tossed to them, doffing an imaginary hat.

"Sounds good," Alicia said. She slipped past and through the opening lobby door.

"Purposeful, that one," Bonk said. "Have yourself a night, Max."

"Have yourself two, Bonk."

"Oh, I will."

Max watched him rev up and go, a whiparound to the main drag and wherever the Chelsea recipient of Bonk's whimsies happened to be. The server at the strip-mall Mexican joint? The haircutter? Max had his own balls in the air—a bad idiom, now that he considered it in the context of Bonk's lascivious ways—and had long since lost interest in tracking the kid's peccadilloes, yet he admired the energy, if not the attendant betrayals to the Missus Bonk back home. For Max, an easing out of the day's clothes and into bed, with maybe a late movie thrown in and some self-amusement, was more the speed of things at this time of life. Maybe he could disappear into the monotony of the way things used to be. Some things, anyway.

He swept through the lobby, another cookie for his trouble, then he got to it.

To: Wendt, Max
From: Janine Garwood, Garwood and Associates
Subject: Your payment

Max...

    I have wired $295,388 into your checking account. It should show up by tomorrow morning. If it does not, let me know and I'll investigate.

    As you know from the dissolution agreement you signed—and I thank you for doing that promptly—our divorce will not be final until one last hearing, which you do not have to attend, and a waiting period. I have gone ahead and fulfilled my portion of the terms so there are no lingering issues.

    I appreciate what you said at Alex's about setting us aside and focusing on her. Consider it done. I expect that I will receive the same consideration. You're a good man. That's never been at issue.

    Take care of yourself. – J

COMFORT INN, CHELSEA, MICHIGAN

Thursday, April 4 | 12:49 a.m.
Seventy-two minutes after sleep came;
three hours and six minutes before it will return

The heavy thump on the door came first, the infernal Ben Folds ringtone next, a bang-bang one-two. The attendant effect was to send Max crashing out of the peaceful slumber induced by the old Fredric March film that had long since played out on the still-running TV. Max flopped out of bed, flailing, and barked a gruff "be right there" at the door, which got him two more half-a-beat thumps in return. Meantime, Ben Folds kept at his percussive piano and his black T-shirt recriminations and Max wriggled into his own shirt (backward) and leaned, unbalanced, into his wadded jeans (fly down) and grabbed for the damn phone and found the remote and quieted Teresa Wright as she spoke from the TV about Hitch and here came the thumps again and would Ben Folds ever just get over it? *All our hearts are broken, OK?*

Max flung open the door and found a standing, slurring, surly Bonk on the other side of it. As he stepped back and let his soused boss in, he engaged the phone and shut down the concert.

"Janine, what?"

"Good evening to you."

"Evening? It's goddamn morning."

Bonk listed left and right and back again in the middle of the room.

"Sit down," Max said.

"I am sitting," Janine said.

"Not you. Bonk."

"At this hour?"

Bonk righted himself and found the overstuffed chair in the corner, a hard tumble.

"Finally coming around to how late it is, huh?"

"Max, don't be ugly."

"I'm not ugly," he said. "I'm half-asleep."

"I'm sorry."

Max stared down Bonk, who was unaware, having developed a quick and absorbing interest in the crotch of his pants. He dabbed at the patch of flame-resistant denim with a fingertip, as if brushing away whatever illicit knowledge it might harbor. Then he belched, long and loud, expelling a fast-moving cloud of alcoholic stink that crashed into Max, who all but retched at the Jack-and-nachos infusion.

"I emailed you about your money," Janine said. "I didn't hear back."

"I was asleep."

"I know. I'm sorry. It's just that you usually answer so quickly, and it's a lot of money, and—"

"I was asleep."

"I know. Again, I'm sorry."

"So what do you want from me?"

The harsh, unintended pitch of the words pulled Bonk out of his fascination. He leaned forward now, elbows on thighs, chin in hands, intent, amused, maddening.

"Just make sure it's there in the morning," Janine said. "That's it."

"OK."

"I was worried, that's all."

"About me?"

"Well, yeah, I guess."

"Not your problem anymore."

"Don't be mean."

"I'm trying not to be."

Bonk let go with a string of high-pitched giggles, a machine-gun spray of uncontrolled and inexplicable personal indulgence.

Max tilted the phone away from his mouth. "What's your fucking problem?" Bonk popped a hand over his mouth, and the giggles slipped sideways from under his fingers in little pops.

"I assume that was for Bonk," Janine said.

"Correct."

"Alex told me you're leaving Billings."

"Funny. I never said that."

"But she said you emptied out—"

"Janine," he cut her off. "You don't have to pretend to be interested in me. You've cut your check. I'll go quietly."

"Harsh," Bonk said.

"Shut up."

"That for Bonk, too, or for me?"

"I gotta go," Max said.

"Good night."

Max cut off the call, freed from it and still trapped by everything else. Bonk certainly wasn't offering quarter. He sat there with that shit-happy dumb grin, staring. Max spun and hucked the phone sidearm at the bed he had vacated, and the pillows swallowed it.

"Trouble at home?" Bonk asked.

Max sank himself into the foot of the bed. "Do the other guys get the pleasure of your nocturnal visitations? It'd make me feel better if you spread that joy around a little."

"Just you, Max. I trust you."

"Grateful."

"Trusted," Bonk corrected.

Max tilted his gaze left. Sobriety had come on quickly. "Well, now."

"What's up with you and Alicia?"

"Up?"

"Something happened."

"You're drunk."

"That don't mean something didn't happen."

"I went with her over to Wendy's. You and I've done the same, many times."

Bonk shook his head. "Something's off."

"Everything's fine." Max tried to hold the tension there, but he couldn't do it. "She say anything?"

"Didn't have to."

Max brought his hands to his face, cupping his nose and mouth. *Here is the church, here is the steeple...* His palms smelled of smoke and sauce. "Bonk," he said, his words now tonal like a PA system. "Get some sleep, man."

"I know what Dex told you."

"Dex tells me a lot of things. Anything in particular on your head?"

"About Alicia. Told you to keep her away from me."

"Bonk—"

"He had no right."

"Where have you been tonight?" Max asked.

"None of your business."

"Right. It's never been my business. But Alicia's Dex's business, isn't she? This crew, also his business. If he knew you were here, drunk, four hours before you have to be at the launch valve, also—"

"Still ain't right. You should have backed me up."

Max stood without a glance at Bonk, who rose with him. Max went to the door. "If you'd go grab some sleep and take another look at this when you wake up, maybe you'll see that I *am* backing you up. Now go." He pulled the door open to the inside and stood sentry.

Bonk huffed past, his boots dragging the carpet. "We ain't through with this," he said as he stepped into the soda-light brightness of the hallway. Max closed up behind him.

Off came the shirt, into a fresh tangle went the pants, down came the lights, out blinked the swashbuckling Errol Flynn movie that had been spilling silently into the empty air. The bed was accepting enough of Max's offer of a reunion, but the attendant peace that had bonded them earlier had now lit out for other locales. Max couldn't find sleep again, only questions and worries that got eaten by the darkness.

We ain't through with this. Bonk's infrequent nighttime visits generally came with twenty parts preening horseshit to one part raw truth, and Max figured that line for the genuine kernel amid the manure. Now, he would just have to see how the kid played it. He had to think it would blow over, at some point. Bonk wasn't naturally adversarial, and besides, Max had known him since he came screaming into the world, with Big Bonk subsequently handing out cigars like he was Fidel Friggin' Castro to the land men, the guys at the pumping stations, the safety coordinators, the office staff. Max figured he had the advantage of time here, both from his investments in Little Bonk and from the reliable returns of exercising patience with him.

Ominously, he also knew that you could go broke and beaten by dismissing the aptitudes of another man when his blood was running high. The kid was stung but good from whatever he did or didn't know about Dex's warnings to Max. There was also the high probability of long-term problems kicking around at home, the simplest explanation for his recklessness away from it. Dealing with that was the kind of fix that came only from the inside. Big Bonk, a collector of his own extracurricular trophies, wasn't going to help with that. What could Max say, even if it were his place to say it? *Just stay gone and keep your own counsel, if you can follow my euphemism*? All he had to show for that was a marriage run up on the rocky outcroppings.

No, this thing bore watching. Patience. Preparation. *And sleep*, Max thought. *Some goddamn sleep.*

Some things a man can give himself. Some things withhold themselves against any level of desire.

When Max had finally expended want, slumber took him down.

COMFORT INN, CHELSEA, MICHIGAN

Thursday, April 4 | 6:57 a.m.
Three minutes before the alarm

Inside lane. Not outside, where Max would have to make those wide turns, not too far inside, where he felt squeezed by the infield and the others on the track. Dead middle, quarter-milers on both sides of him. A guy he could draft off if he needed. A guy who could draft off him. *Suit yourself, man. I have plans that don't include you.*

The gun went up. Max's tail end rose with it. A finger twitch on the track surface, always. Anticipation. A little fear, too, to be truthful. One you blocked. One you tried to sharpen for the moment. A good start was everything, as much as or more than a good finish.

Max's well-stretched hips locked and then loosened, all in a fractional second. He leaned ever so slightly forward, and he held himself there, and...

The gun.

Max launched forward, one big stride for separation, a couple of quick dig-ins for traction, and then fully upright, into the form he was endlessly refining, Coach Pryor's voice in his ears even now: *"Your natural speed's for shit, Wendt, but your technique is superb. Not perfect, but damn good. We can work with that."*

Elbows tucked in, fists rising and falling with his stride. *"No unnecessary movement, Wendt! Run it again!"*

Hip joints fluid, the strides reaching out in synchrony, machinelike in their precision. *"Rhythm, rhythm, rhythm. Come on, Wendt. You're better than this."*

At one hundred meters, he knew now who was in it and who was not. Gallagher, the Laurel kid on the far outside, he was a comer. Bradley, from Billings West, on his left, it was going to come down to the kick. Van Zandt, his teammate, on the right? No chance. Not today. Sorry, Elvin.

At two hundred and fifty, things started to loosen up, in a bad way. The labored breathing set in, for Max and for everyone else. He fought himself to contain his movement. *"No goddamn head torques, Wendt! Tighten it up!"* He leaned into the final turn with every piece of resolve he had.

"Now finish it!" Sure enough, the separation had come. Gallagher and Bradley. Max. Nobody else in it, not now.

"The kick! The kick! The kick!" Max dug as deep as he could. He strained. He picked up the beat. Here it came now, the tape. It's happening...

Max rose up, torso only, the rest of him pretzel-bent into a sleepy tangle under the sheet, and he gasped and gasped and gasped. His breath lay beyond his reach, and then it flooded back into his lungs and the morning light pierced the room and the first fuzzy notes of R.E.M.'s "Get Up" blared from his phone and it was over. Max fell back, his head denting his pillow, and he hit snooze.

From: Charles Foster Danforth
To: Wendt, Max
Subject: Re: We begin again

Dear Max,

Sorry, old chum, for the delayed response. I've been extraordinarily busy and have subsequently been away from my computer, a most enriching absence, I must say. I may try it again soon, and perhaps someday I'll just stay away for good.

Mary and Remmy and I gathered at our place on the Cape over the weekend. I must say, it's been far too long since we were together there. For reasons too complicated to go into here—yet also reasons you can probably deduce given what I've shared with you—the three of us have treated it almost like a time-share these many years since Chas died. We go separately, the boat gets the necessary workouts, the house gets lived in and thus avoids falling into disrepair, but the togetherness for which it was once purchased has left the scene.

It's sad in its own way, but it's also a validation that times and circumstances change and shift. We must change and shift with them.

I am, by nature, a sunny guy; I see the hope and the possibility in things. I hope that brightness has shone through in our dealings. If there's anything I wish to leave you with when we interact, it's the notion that we can choose a hopeful outlook. Even when events conspire against us, which they sometimes seem to do. (I shall spare you the rather long-winded treatise on events being completely unable to conspire. They just happen. The interpretation of them is a largely personal matter, and I suppose it gives us comfort to personify them with words like "conspire.")

Mary has met someone, a man who fills her with joy. It radiates off her. It sparks and it sparkles, and Max, I am quite happy for her. Of course, I have known about this man, in the abstract, for some time. But this weekend, she opened up to us—to me and to Remmy—and her overflowing happiness was the prompt for much rejoicing.

Mary wants to marry this man. (His name is Bob, a brown-paper-bag of a name if you ask me, but he didn't pick it and thus should be held blameless for it, and he's a liquor wholesaler. Quite the successful one, apparently. Cheers!) And I intend to honor this wish by granting her a divorce she probably should have had long ago. I even understand her compulsion to marry again, even if I said to her, "Mary, you are 68 years old. Why marriage at this stage of the game?" (Forgive the cliché.)

And here is what she said: "I've never known such love. It would feel incomplete if I didn't stand in front of everyone I love, and everyone he loves, and everyone we love, and consecrate it." Isn't that just the most wonderful thing? She has asked me to give her away, quite literally and in the wedding-ceremony function. It shall be my pleasure. I'm pleased to be here and to be able to give her this.

So, yes, Mary will get her divorce and her new marriage, perhaps both in the same week, depending on the pace of legality. Wouldn't that be a hoot? You usually see such things only in B movies. Wouldn't it be fun if it all became a great scandal? (Well, no, it probably wouldn't, now that I think of it.) In any case, we will do this quickly. Mary does not want to tarry. I understand. The older one gets, the more loudly the unceasing clock ticks.

I will honestly say, in the company of my own mind, that there have been moments of quiet distress for me. One does not let go of a long marriage—even one as profoundly malfunctioned as ours was—without some mourning of the loss. I've had my time alone, grappling with that. And, yes, on some level, hearing Mary proclaim this great love with a fervor she never had with me stings a bit, even as I fully acknowledge that I have not the capacity to feel that way about her, nor to give her an avenue to feel that way about me. If that were in me, Max, I'd surely have exercised it in these intervening years.

But the moments of melancholy and the feeling that a part of me is perishing are drops of water in a gentle tide of happiness and anticipation. When our family had four legs—me, Mary, the boys—we ran just fine for a time, and had our losing Chas not happened, I'm confident we would have found our pace again even after my revelation. But we did lose Chas, and it changed us. A three-legged family is still a family. We just had to learn to lope along without falling down.

Bob's presence will change us again. And it will be a beautiful life. Again. For however long it lasts.

It was ever thus.

P.S. What do you suppose it was or is within you, Max, that led you to the decision to sleep—just sleep, I know; I saw your words and believed them, my friend—with a woman young enough to be your daughter? Where is that headed, do you think? Why did you tell me? What would you expect I would say? And would my response, in your expectation, be any different from the response you can supply yourself to all of the above questions?

If I may use your common vernacular, do you grasp how much it sucks that the one thing you really wanted to talk about was a tack-on?

You're still not getting what I've asked of you. Moreover, you seem to be deliberately missing it.

Do better, Max. I know you can.

HIGHWAY 106, JUST SOUTH OF STOCKBRIDGE, MICHIGAN

Thursday, April 4 | 10:58 a.m.
7.3568 miles into the run; 80.6176 miles to go

Max could have predicted it. He did, in fact, just more than an hour earlier. He had assumed a launch time at ten a.m. local—actual launch: 9:52:15—and that a prescribed flow rate of 2.1 miles per hour would be a little less than that coming out of the chute, as the pumping systems came fully on line. Sure enough, 1.84 miles per hour to the first checkpoint, Smithlin's. So when he texted Alicia and said, *I guess we're meeting at MP7.3568*, she had written back, *Yeah, looks like. How'd you know?*

Simple: math. The one thing he could count on. The one thing he could trust. Max sat in the cab of his car and dialed everything in. The receiver and geophone were out by the downstream marker, sending back signals and sound already. The timer boxes would come later, brought by Alicia. It would be a bit yet before he could hear the pig thumping up the line, where it would pass her on its way to him, with another passage at Smithlin in between. But it was sure enough coming in due time. Big mother, too. Twenty-four-foot crack tool. Easy to track. Settle in for the trip.

He could also predict the rest, barring something unexpected. The smart play for Alicia and Tommy after shift change would be to head back to the hotel in Chelsea and try to bag some sleep. The midnight handoff would come just north of Interstate 94, a stone's throw from Chelsea proper, and Max and Macartney would bunk down there again, too, then make the drive south to repeat the shift change the next morning.

Max thought it odd after all these years, long since Big Bonk had last been in the field, that his was the voice animating so many guiding principles of the work. "You come off the job in the day, drive in the daylight to where you'll be coming back on. You come off at night, get your ass to a hotel like quick and drive when the sun comes up. Safer that way." Max pocketed the words like an article of faith. And on every job, he took that admonition out and and heeded it.

He missed Big Bonk, truth be told. He found comfort in the old man's presence when he was one of them and felt his absence at odd moments now that he had been subsumed by retirement. Without him, the work was the same but different. The sameness, Max clung to. The differences seemed to be flying at his face with an ever-increasing velocity.

He mentally went again to the note from Charles he had read that morning while he choked down some powdered eggs and a too-hard Danish. It had come in the night when Max was still at odds with himself over whether any more shuteye would be granted to him. *Glad I didn't see it then*, he thought now. *It would have been over for sure.*

Now, he was inclined to take Charles' pointed reply at face value. When was he going to stop playing games with the self-important old dandy, anyway? For the first time, Max sensed exasperation from a man he figured had made his bones by never letting anybody see him rattled. And what Max got for all his inveterate chain-yanking was a series of questions he could stack up with all the other ones to which he, as yet, could supply no good answers.

He's got you beat, Max. Play it his way or go home.

First, Max would go to Toledo. After that, maybe some determination about coming clean. Then again, maybe not. Max still pined for the freedom that would come from untethering himself from having to return to Billings. He wondered, though, whether that latitude would just lead to complications somewhere else.

He envied Charles' attitude toward his wife's new love, and he simultaneously wondered how much of it he could believe. After all, Charles controlled the telling of that particular narrative. Maybe Mary was a relentless shrew he was glad to be rid of (though he doubted any of that). Maybe she was the fluttering of his heart that he futilely denied. Maybe she was just a woman filling up blank space in his life for so long, and maybe Charles felt relief to be moved out of that stasis. How could Max ever know for sure? It was Charles' story to tell, in whatever way he wished to tell it.

Max chose to believe his friend. Mostly because he wanted to. Mostly because it was a manifestation of where he wished his own thoughts could land with regard to Janine. Of course, she wasn't running into the embrace of new love, as far as Max knew. Maybe he could be happy for that if she were. Maybe he would want to be happy for that. Maybe that would be easier than hearing that he just wasn't needed anymore. That he wasn't necessary or vital or a partner or even a friend. No. Maybe a hot new lover for Janine would be easier to take than being told all of the above, explicitly or implicitly, and not knowing when, exactly, his role in things had been lost. Which means you don't know, exactly, how you could have averted that outcome. That was the galling part.

Max looked to his phone, caught the time, locked in. Any moment now.

And there it was, in a message:

MP2.2780
9:07:52
1.79 mph

Alicia's message dinged out to the group, and back came the thumbs-ups from Little Bonk and Smithlin and Macartney, and now Max.

Another ding, just for him: *Heading your way.*

Max thumbed back his response: *Roger.*

He saved his halting start of a reply to Charles, one he had already decided to shelve until he could do some hard thinking of his own. What he had here was a zygote of a message, an embryonic cluster of word cells too undeveloped to even be called a thought. That wouldn't do.

Screen cleared, Max punched the update into his spreadsheet and watched the new numbers unfurl down the document. An hour and twenty minutes to Milepost 4.6689, where Tommy would right about now be switching out with Steve. Another hour and a half after that to get to Max. He was way early, but Alicia's part of this was done and she needed sleep. He never liked to keep a tracker waiting for him to show up. Better to switch early and catch up on his reading (or, more likely, start fielding Macartney's incessant questions about the job Little Bonk had saddled him with). He would be getting paid either way.

Here she came now, onto the long straightaway where he sat on the highway. As she approached, she crossed the centerline and brought her car nose to nose with his, as he had taught her to do when the sightlines allowed, the better not to roust the delicate sensibilities of the equipment. He gave a wave at the windshield, and a terse one came back, and any buoyancy on Max's part flattened out again. *This has gotta get better, right?*

She got out, easy as pie, a thumb drive and the paper spreadsheet in hand. He got out for the exchange and to help transfer the timer boxes to his car, with two of them bound for the marker next to the receiver and the geophone. It was all a well-choreographed ballet, done hundreds upon thousands of times before and yet somehow always new. *This*, Max thought. *This is what I love. Me and the line and the miles ahead.*

Max pushed his front door closed with his rump and stepped toward Alicia. The ground sat uneasy under Max's boots, giving way. He looked to her, and she stared back at him oddly, as she might if he had spoken to her in some inscrutable tongue. "What?" he said. "Max," she said.

And then the world went vertical, as if inverted by an unseen hand of the gods, and his yelled name came out and darkness followed and Max just didn't know what to make of that. Or of anything.

EIGHT SECONDS

"Max, Max, Max, Max, Max. Max!"
A flutter of the eyes, blurred images shooting past, like a View-Master disc on a turbo spin.

"Max, are you OK?"

Darkness.

FORTY-FOUR SECONDS

"He fell over, face-first. Yes, he's alive. I think he's alive. Oh, Jesus, his eyes just rolled back. Just get here. Get here."

Lucidity. Fadeout. Lucidity. Fadeout.

Lucidity.

"An elephant is sitting on my chest."

"He's awake."

"It hurts."

"He's in pain. Please hurry."

Darkness.

"He's gone. No, not *gone* gone. Hurry, please."

NINETY-SIX SECONDS

"Did you get those coordinates? Hurry, goddammit."

"Hurts so bad."

"I know. I know. They're coming."

"So bad."

"I know. Hang on. What? No, I won't. I'm not going to hang up. I'm right here. I won't hang up. Get here. Please."

ONE HUNDRED AND SIXTY-FIVE SECONDS

You don't forget the first time you sit down with death. You can't. And, oddly enough, you don't want to. Not after you've been there with it. Death isn't an idle companion. It's not just a face in the crowd. You're in its presence, and you know it. You feel it. You see it. Even when it makes its final move silently, you're aware, attenuated, the prickle on your arm or along your neck telling you it's beside you, and it's watching you just as surely as you're watching it. You will meet again. Death knows this. You? You don't think about that. You have other things on your mind.

Death took Gustav Wendt that way. Quietly in the end. Ruthlessly. Without quarter or relief. June 18, 1986, was the final call, the date that went into the newspaper, that got stenciled onto the little pamphlets they handed out with impatiens—Gustav's favorite—at Trinity Lutheran when they said goodbye and put him to rest.

And that damn day never passes again without the memory, the stink, of death. It can be the brightest day of the year, and often it is. Yet it reeks of death. Death remembered. Death emblazoned. Death that came and took everything it wanted.

The thing is, nobody who knew and loved Gustav needs a date of benediction to remember him; there was too much life in all the days leading up to it for him to be forgotten. June 18 was, simply and finally and without room for further argument, the day death took the last of what Gustav had to offer. Death had been draining him for days and weeks and months, clear back to the previous November if not earlier, a cough he couldn't shake, a hacking and a wheezing that his only child urged him to have checked.

"I will, Maxie, I will," he had said, but saying is one thing and doing is another, and it wasn't until January, when Gustav was coughing up blood and the chore couldn't be put off, that the doing was finally engaged. What you get for that, for waiting to feel worse when you still feel mostly all right, is the bad news: Death is circling you. We will try to fight it off. We'll have to burn you down, with no assurance that any life you'll want remains in the ash.

What could Gustav do? What can any of us do when there's a gamble that can come through, no matter how long the odds? What can any of us say when there's a wife and a son and a daughter-in-law and a grandbaby on the way? You take a flier on trying to show death to the door.

"I'll be fine, Maxie. I will beat this thing."

What played out from there was predictable enough. However sick Gustav was, he got sicker still. However diminished he had been from a year earlier, when the cellular takeover had surely started and yet had not announced itself and he had been feeling and looking just fine, he became ever more diminished. Why does death, that damnable bastard, always get a head start? Maybe because the call for death goes in at the moment of first life. Think about that one. What if we're not living; what if, instead, we're just dying at variable rates, from the get-go?

As coming death took a more powerful grip on things, however much those who loved Gustav wished he would stay, they all began to prepare for the possibility—no, the certainty—that he would be leaving. Death spent springtime in Gustav and Belle Wendt's living room, watching over him, waiting. Belle and Max watched Gustav, too, but they also watched death, and they felt simultaneously powerless and protective. It was the most helpless of stalemates, and a false one, at that. The battle had been lost but wasn't yet over.

The juxtaposition of life and death imprinted itself on Max that interminable spring, as he watched his father die and waited, every bit as anxiously if with more anticipation, for his own child to arrive. Alexandra left the womb on June 10. Max and Janine placed her in the crook of her grandfather's arm four days later, and she rolled toward him as if she belonged there and they cried over her and over him and Gustav slept with his mouth open through it all, his gaunt face drawn up like a knapsack. He didn't know. They hoped she might, somehow.

And four days after that, it was done and Gustav was headed to moondust.

"Maxie, do you want to come in?"

"Come in?"

"We are waiting for you. So many of us, Maxie."

"Mom?"

"Of course. Do you want to come in?"

Max considered the question. It was quite an offer, one imbued with more beauty and grace than Max could have ever imagined, had he ever dared to imagine such a thing. The peacefulness spread out before him, the chaos he had risen out of receding like the sound of a crying child whisked into her parents' arms and taken out of a store. Unbearable and then loud and then fading and then faint and then gone.

"Maxie? You coming?"

"No, Pop. I'm not done yet."

ST. JOSEPH MERCY CHELSEA HOSPITAL

Thursday, April 4 | 5:22 p.m.
Six hours and two minutes after the event

"Hey, Bright Eyes. Good to see you."

Max blinked.

"You've been out a while. Good."

He looked at her.

"Do you know what happened?"

"No." The single word came out hoarse and crinkled. His throat hurt, like it often did at the beginning of a cold.

"Do you know where you are?"

"St. Joseph Mercy Chelsea Hospital."

"But you—"

"It's on your nametag," he said. He stretched his neck like a turtle for a closer look. Bad idea. In time, his eyes focused on the words. "Jenn. I'm a reader, Jenn. Jenny, Jenn, Jenn, Jennifer."

She winked and stretched out a long index finger toward him, *faux*-accusatory. "You're a clever one, Bright Eyes."

"I am."

"What's your name?" she asked him.

"Bright Eyes."

"What's your real name?"

"Maximilian Heinrich Wendt."

"That's quite a name."

"My parents gave it to me. Blame them."

"What's your date of birth?"

"July 3rd, 1963."

"Did you graduate from high school in 1981 or '82?"

"Eighty-one. Years before you."

"I graduated in '83."

"You don't look it."

"Good genes. OK, Maximilian—"

"Please," he said. "Call me Max. Or Bright Eyes."

"OK, Bright Eyes. The surgeon will be coming up soon."

"Surgeon?"

"Yes. And I have a message for you from a Mister...Bonk." She peered in at her jotted notes. "Is that a real name?"

"Sadly."

"*Bright Eyes*," she said. "Aren't you just a wicked one? So, listen, Mr. Bonk wants you to know that Dex and Alexandra are on their way. They ended up on the same flight in Minneapolis, so that's good, right? Of course, they won't be seeing you tonight. Tomorrow, maybe. We'll see."

"We'll see."

"Also," she said, "Mr. Bonk said he's never seen anybody go to such lengths to get out of work." She harrumphed. "Well, that's not nice."

"It's fine once you get to know him," Max said. Damn, but the words hurt to push out. "Have you got five years?"

She laughed at that, big and booming and joyful. "*Briiiiiight Eyes*. You're funny. Welcome back. Surgeon'll be here soon."

M ax didn't like this surgeon business, not one little bit, and he liked not knowing the full range of details even less. He cast his eyes about the place. His name, written on a whiteboard on the far wall, the letters CCU under it. Cardiac care unit. He had figured as much, the elephantine squeeze on his chest now a memory that came back, along with others. Alicia's crumbling face as he walked toward her. The trips into and out of the darkness. Someone putting an aspirin under his tongue. *Pop?* Had he really seen Gustav there at the swinging gate, looking as he had in the late '70s, full head of black hair, the gray streaks just starting to make inroads. Max had wanted to reach out and touch that face, to feel the whiskers breaking the surface, the way he had touched them as a boy and later as a grown-ass grownup, shaving his father's face when the older man could no longer do it for himself. *Oh, Pop, I wish you could have stayed. I wish I could have stayed, but...*

Surgeon. Max had met just one in his whole life, the guy who'd re-inflated his lung after the motorcycle crash back in '08. That had been nothing, an in-and-out procedure, and still Janine had lost her shit, and that had been the end of the motorcycle but not the end of Max, which had been his entire point. "Jesus, Janine, the deer dashed out on me. Would have happened if I'd been on a bicycle. I'm going to be fine." And Janine's point had been, yeah, well, a bicycle doesn't go down at sixty miles per hour and break all the damn ribs on your left side and blow a hole through your lung, now does it? An unassailable point, that.

Anyway, that guy had been pretty cool. Stood bedside, post-op, and fed Max little paper cups full of water, which Max had lapped up with enthusiasm. "Lucky you had a helmet on," he had said. "Some guys' personalities improve when their brains are scattered on the highway. Would have done damage to you, my friend." A few weeks later, on the follow-up, Max had asked the guy what he should do with the unused painkillers he had been given. The surgeon had shrugged. "You can get thirty bucks a cap on the street." It had been a joke. (Surely it had been a joke.) Max had turned them in to the pharmacy. Six hundred and ninety bucks' worth, if the guy's numbers were right.

"LAD, Mr. Wendt."

"LAD?" This guy wasn't like the surgeon in Billings at all. Courtly. Older. Glasses. Looked a little like that guy on *Mister*

Rogers' Neighborhood. Who the hell was that? Max ran through the montage from all those times the TV had babysat Alexandra and he had been but a bystander. *Stuffed animals, mostly. Puppets. Margaret Hamilton, the Wicked Witch, she was on there one time, I'm pretty sure. Mister McFeely! Well, now it's going to be impossible to think of him as anyone else. Concentrate, Max. Dr. Bradshaw, he said. Like Terry the quarterback, only smarter. You better hope.*

"Your left anterior descending artery. It was blocked."

"And that's why—"

"That's why you collapsed, yes."

The man's matter-of-fact demeanor irritated Max. *Another day at work for him. The biggest damn deal ever for me.* "So I've got a plugged ticker?" Max asked.

McFeely—*Bradshaw!*—looked surprised by the question. "Well, no. Not now."

"No?"

"Don't you see?" he said. "You're here. You survived. We've dealt with it."

"You have?"

"A stent. You'll be taking Plavix for a while, or maybe forever. Who knows? Not much damage to the muscle."

"Plavix?"

"To prevent clotting."

"Ah."

"You see, Mr. Wendt," Bradshaw said now, drawing nearer the side of the bed, "the survival is the thing. Without that, the rest is... unnecessary."

"Sure."

"Do you understand what I'm saying to you?"

"I guess not," Max said.

The doctor knelt now, eye to eye with Max.

"The widowmaker. That's what we call what happened to you."

"Funny," Max said. "I'm almost divorced."

Bradshaw pushed on, unamused. "Survival odds were not in your favor. You were lucky your co-worker was there. You were lucky to be only twelve miles from us. Our EMTs were in the helicopter and to you in seven minutes. You were lucky to be back here in ten. You came straight to us. We had the stent in you not much more than fifteen minutes after you arrived. You were exceedingly lucky."

Max nodded.

"Won-the-lottery lucky," the doctor said.

"I understand."

"Rest now."

The doctor stood. Max reached for his hand.

"I'm grateful."

"I know," Bradshaw said.

"My kid, she's coming—"

"Tomorrow," Bradshaw said. "We'll all talk tomorrow. Rest tonight."

"How long will I be here?"

Bradshaw disengaged and slipped back toward the door. "Tonight and tomorrow, probably."

"Then I go home?"

"Sure."

"No shit?"

"No shit," Bradshaw said. "Like I told you, lucky."

ST. JOSEPH MERCY CHELSEA HOSPITAL

Thursday, April 4 | 11:57 p.m.
Chance of surviving a widowmaker
in a non-hospital environment: 12 percent
Chance of a second heart attack within five years: 18 percent
Chance of further sleep anytime soon: 0 percent

Max, awake, thought about shift change. It was coming, if it hadn't already occurred. Had his day gone as he had expected, he would be handing off the spreadsheet and the timer boxes to Alicia, telling her what he had been seeing and hearing from the tool ("Good mag hits, sound coming through perfect. You can't miss it."). He would be packing himself off to the Comfort Inn, where he already had a reservation, and he would be setting himself up for morning.

Boots by the door. FR gear, fresh from the suitcase, folded over the back of the desk chair. Gas monitor and geophone charging. Phone juicing up by the bed. *Good night, good people.*

They were fourteen-plus hours into the run. Twenty-eight to go, give or take. Tomorrow's another day.

Tomorrow's another lifetime.

Should he feel grateful to be here amid the beeping of medical electronics, the white light in the corridor spilling into his room from the crack in the door, the antiseptic neutral scent of cleaning supplies? Sure, yeah, OK, he did feel gratitude, in that the alternative—dying alone by the side of Highway 106—was worse. Not seeing Alexandra again was worse. Not responding to Charles, even that was worse. He had always assumed that near-death experiences come with transformational epiphanies. *I'm going to do that which I've denied myself for so long. I'm going to run that marathon, learn to play the guitar, visit the Far East, tutor a kid. Given another chance to be me, I'm going to be the best iteration there is. Yes!*

No.

Max wanted to be at the Comfort Inn, pawing at sleep. Not because that's where Alexandra was now—they had briefly let him chat with her on the phone after she got to town—but because that was where the next day started, with a drive straight south to shift change. Maybe Braun Road or Willow Road or Arkona Road—it could be any of the three, experience told him. Then he would hand it back to Alicia another twelve hours on, in the nighttime heart of the most neglected part of Toledo. "Watch yourself," he would tell her. "Almost there now."

The hospital staff had taken Max's damn phone from him. He could be tracking the job from his bed, monitoring, seeing the emailed updates from Bonk, picturing how it was playing out. *Can I have it back?* No, not tonight, they had said. Rest. *Tomorrow?* We'll see, he was told. A bunch of damn Zen masters, the whole lot of them.

Max supposed it was shallow, wanting nothing more from an unexpected gift of living than the same thing he had always pursued. Well, he never claimed to be deep. He would argue, if the debate were pushed, that life hadn't been a series of exit ramps from challenges and hard decisions and harder circumstances. He took the work because Big Bonk dangled it. He stayed in it because he liked it and it brought some dough into the household. And, well, because a pipeline man knows inertia is a powerful thing. You send a batch downstream and put a little pumping power behind it and...an object in motion and all of that. A fifth-grade science lesson playing out in his mid-fifties. Besides, it's not as if a lot of other opportunities had come his way. Once, in a time long past, he could run. He could shoot a little bull. He could crack wise—a market of diminishing returns, he was learning. He could whittle down a stack of commercial-grade novels. He could track a pig. That was it. Guess which one paid. Shallowness was one thing. Lack of depth, forged by circumstance, was another.

It wasn't lost on Max that the larger questions—what of Alex, of Janine, of this unresolved thing with Alicia, of Bonk—were the sort that got set aside when he was alone on the line, doing his thing. He would have to step to them eventually, he figured.

That would certainly start soon enough. Alexandra would be here come a more reasonable morning hour, and sure as she was his daughter, she would have her say. Dex would have his. Everybody would have a narrative, everybody would have an angle, everybody would have a desired outcome. Max included. He would have to hold tight to his while considering the others, lest he lose himself even more than he already had.

"Dad," Alexandra had said on the phone not four hours ago. "How'd this happen?"

It was the kind of question you don't answer because it was never asked in a way that really expected a response. Less rhetorical and more incredulous. He knew how. She knew how. Dr. Tyler Keisling knew how, too, and had been on Max's ass about it for a long while.

"Just lucky, I guess," he had said.

"Dad."

"Lucky to be here," he had corrected. *Nice save, Max.* Probably best to leave out the part about the LAD being clogged with Ding Dongs and beef jerky; she could take that to Tyler later, if she wanted, and let him crow about it. Bradshaw no doubt would have that covered soon enough, along with a shiny new be-the-best-possible-you plan.

"I will see you in the morning," Alexandra had said.

"OK, Pookie Nose."

"Mom sends her love."

"Oh? She got out of this just in time."

"*Dad!*"

"Tell her to keep her love. I'm just glad she sent her money."

"Dammit. Just stop."

"I'm sorry."

"I can't take the sarcasm."

"Really, I'm sorry."

"I was so scared," she said.

"I know. Me, too. I'm sorry."

"I'm glad you're OK."

"Never better."

She had laughed, despite herself, a snort blast muffled under the weight of her worry. "You're a piece of work. Good night."

Night, anyway. As with so many back-and-forths with his daughter, Max wished he could have parts of it back now, a wish of convenience that he had no way of bringing to life with the moment having moved on from him. He thought now of Charles and something he had said that night they met in the Minneapolis airport. *You're a still-waters-run-deep kind of guy, aren't you, Max?*

And here, all this time later, Max had the answer that should have been at the ready there on the concourse floor. *Nope. Gravity handles the running of the water at any depth. I'm just trying to keep the boat off the rocks.*

ST. JOSEPH MERCY CHELSEA HOSPITAL

Friday, April 5 | 9:21 a.m.
Twenty-one hours and fifty-nine minutes after the event

As outlined for Max in another playful visit from charming nurse Jenn, he was moved to a telemetry unit first thing, making him just another animal getting patched up before release back into his natural habitat. Jenn had suggested that he try walking to his new room, with the guardrail of an orderly, and Max had said, "Sure, I thought you'd never ask," and off he had gone to his new, temporary address. Rode the elevator. Walked at a normal gait, the only difference being the flap in his gown and the exposure of his knobby knees and the tube socks sliding down his calves. Hadn't been so bad, either. He felt a bit spent afterward, as if he had reeled off too many quarter-miles. Nothing unusual, though. He sometimes felt winded after a second trip through a buffet.

Now, he lay in bed, and Alexandra and Dex and Dr. Bradshaw

pinched into a gaggle around him, intent and deferential, right up to the particulars.

"So he can leave tomorrow?" Alex asked.

"Sure," Bradshaw said. "Barring some complication in the interim, which seems unlikely."

"How unlikely?"

"It's unlikely."

Dex now: "No work for you for a while."

"As I understand it—" Max began. *Damn, but it's good to see Dex.* You know a guy for—what?—thirty-five years, you think you really know him, but they hadn't seen each other since Big Bonk's retirement. Dex's ascension to the office job had kept him at home in Minneapolis, and what with phones and computers and next-day mail, there hadn't been much point in face-to-face encounters. He looked thicker now, older. *I guess not everyone ages as gracefully as me.*

"No restrictions on work, provided he's not unloading trucks or some sort of extreme exertion," Bradshaw cut in.

"What about heavy loads of metaphorical horseshit?" Max asked.

"We'll give you an extra pill."

"He's coming home and resting," Alexandra said.

"Sweetheart—"

"Tyler says—" she began.

"I already have a doctor, Pookie Nose." Max swept an arm toward Bradshaw. "You were saying?"

Bradshaw leaned forward from the counter he was planted on, hands clasped between his knees. "I have some rounds to make, so bottom line: You'll be tired for a bit, but it shouldn't be long. Fact is, you're in far better condition now than you were a minute before the attack. If it were me and I could afford to take some time off work, I would. But you're not me, are you? And I'm not you. You can get on a plane, if that's what you need to do"—at this, Alexandra nodded vigorously—"or you can go back to work. For some people, that's the answer. You're repaired, Mr. Wendt. You've lost some heart muscle, but the organ is strong. You can get thirty years out of it, maybe more, depending on a range of factors, including your own behavior going forward. That's the deal."

"The world is my oyster," Max said.

"I prefer snow crab, but I concede the point," Bradshaw replied. "Look, here's the thing: There's a part of this, a big part, that's physical. That's the part that put you in peril. That's the part we've mitigated. But there's also the unseen part that's inside you, that we can't reach with all our wonderful technology. What were the stresses in your life that increased your risk factor? Why did you choose what you ate? What was your attitude toward exercise and movement? What is your spirituality? How do you cope? Who are you? And I will tell you that many, many people grapple with what I'd call a survivor's guilt in the aftermath of these events. *Why am I here? Why did I beat the odds? Why me?*"

The room drew in on Max. It was silent, blurred at the edges, and neutralized of touch and scent.

"I cannot speak to any of that," Bradshaw continued. "My part of it is this: I can tell you that a vital piece of your interior plumbing was blocked—rather like a garbage disposal that you've fed too quickly, and now the dishwasher backs up the sink—and I fixed that. My piece is done. The rest is yours. Make sense?"

After the doctor left, they sorted it out, with Max's vote counting for less than the other two, the very scenario he had feared and yet also the one he was prepared to accept. For now. For the good of the order.

"You're coming home," Alexandra said. "We have lots of room. Or we can set you up back at the Princeton house, if you'd like to do that."

"We'll figure something out," Max said.

On the subject of work, Dex, a sensible guy, had a sensible plan. The current run was more than half-over, and they could limp to the finish line with Tommy and Alicia on nights and Macartney running solo in the daytime with some backup from Bonk. Three days after landing the pig in Toledo, they were headed to the top of the Port Huron line, way the hell out on the Upper Peninsula, damn near Wisconsin, and then across to the Mackinaw Straits. They could run as a three-legged crew on that one, too, and call someone out of the bullpen from a crew down in Tulsa, and Max could cool his heels at home. No work on the calendar for two weeks after that. Perfect timing for his return.

"Makes sense, Dex," Max said.

"It'll do you good," Dex said. "It'll do everybody good."

"I'm coming back," Max said. "Keep my spot open."

"Of course you are."

"When you're ready," Alexandra said. "You don't have to rush back out there."

"Nobody's rushing," Max said.

"Who are you and what have you done with my father?"

Later, Dex had gone, but Alexandra stayed awhile, sitting in the chair next to the bed, chuckling idly through the morning TV game shows, holding Max's hand when his short bursts of sleep came. They ate from the plastic trays of cafeteria food—broth and gelatin for Max, a purported cutlet for Alex—and they idled in each other's presence. Alexandra read the dispatches of the world on her phone, Max caught up to the job updates on his, finally granted its release back into his possession. He was simultaneously shaken and unsurprised to learn that he was incidental to the operation, the only suggestion that he had been part of it at all being his name on the duty roster Little Bonk had sent out at the start of the job and his absence from the subsequent memos. One little excising, one minor alteration to the regular lineup, churned his soup into stomach acid.

While Alexandra stepped out for a call, Max slow-texted an email to Charles.

> *Had a massive heart attack. I knew I shouldn't have had that third helping of brisket. In Chelsea, Michigan. Direct all inquiries to:*
> *666 Hell Suite*
> *St. Joseph Mercy Chelsea Hospital*

Alexandra returned, a heavy drop back into the chair. Her eyes were red and glistened with tears.

"How's your mother?"

"Fine. How'd you know?"

Max chuckled, a gentle gurgle. "Well, I've known you both a while—"

"Yeah, but—"

"—and you're a little more, I don't know, *fluttery* when you get off the phone with the good and endlessly wise doctor."

"Don't be mad at Tyler for being right."

"I'm not mad at anybody. Are you OK?"

"I'm fine. You're not even mad at Mom?"

"Not even your mother."

Alex gripped his hand. "She's fine. She's worried about you."

"Nothing to worry about."

"You should call her."

"Not a good idea."

"Why?"

Max drew her hand up and kissed it, between the first and second knuckles. "Because I love her."

Alexandra flinched. Really, truly, honest-to-godly flinched. "I don't get it."

"I love her, but I'm not in love with her," Max said. "And she's not in love with me. And I don't know when that stopped, for her or for me, but it did, and I have some—"

"Anger?"

"Yes. No," he corrected. "It's more intense than anger but also less destructive. It comes out as sarcasm—"

"*Everything* comes out as sarcasm with you."

"—but it rises up on me and catches me by surprise, and I haven't figured out how to moderate it or anticipate it, but I'm trying. I really am."

"Dad, you should talk to somebody."

"I am."

"For real?"

"Yes," he said. "I am. And for now, I've just sort of figured that your mother, you know, she came to peace about moving on without me, and that happened when I was unaware that I'd have to do the same thing. I'm not blaming her. Probably unavoidable. But she's figured out how to live apart from me. I'm not there yet. I've got to figure out how to live apart from her before I can just call her up and say, 'Hey, Janine, what's shakin'?' Understand?"

Alexandra sat quiet. She nodded. Max kissed her hand again.

"How to be a better galoot," he said.

Alexandra snort-laughed, sniffled, grabbed a tissue, and wiped her nose.

The phone rang on the table on the other side of Max, a clattery, clanging, *this-is-why-we-rid-the-world-of-landlines* alert.

"Who could that be?" Alexandra asked.

"My counselor, I imagine," Max said. "Sweetheart, could you ask the nurses if they have a manure spreader we can borrow?"

"You're such a pain in the ass."

"And?"

"And answer the phone, you big dummy."

Hi, Charles. What's new?

"How did you know I was calling?"

Who else?

"Max."

I mean, I just sent the email. I told you where I was. Elementary, my dear fussbudget.

"A heart attack? How severe?"

The big one. Big One. Capital-letters big.

"LAD?"

Well, yeah, if you insist on being clinical. Are you in the medical field?

"Max!"

Just messin' with you. Probably not too many eight-year-olds keeled over on your watch.

"Are you done?"

Maybe.

"Max. I wish I could say I'm surprised. But I'm not. I feared this."

Don't fear the reaper.

"*Max.*"

Blue Oyster Cult, 1976. *Agents of Fortune.* Good album. Good tune.

"*Are you done being silly?*"

More cowbell.

"*Max?*"

Yes. I'm done.

"*I was worried about you. Hadn't heard from you. I feared maybe I'd cuffed you around too much in that last note.*"

I'm fine. Was busy working. And dying.

"*Don't be flippant.*"

I'm not. Being factual.

"*You didn't die. Yes, you were fortunate to survive, but you didn't die.*"

I saw my old man. He was at a gate. Dusk. Summertime. The brightest light before dark. He asked me in.

"*You saw that?*"

I did.

"*During the event?*"

Why do all you doctor types call it an event? It wasn't a game or a concert. Why all the euphemisms?

"*I don't know.*"

Just talk straight to me.

"*OK. I'm sorry.*"

I think I died, yes. What do you think?

"*I don't know, Max. We're out of the realm of medicine here. This... this is spirituality.*"

I'm just telling you what I saw.

"*I believe you.*"

I appreciate that.

"*Is this something you want to talk through? These are weighty things.*"

I appreciate that, too. Soon. Not now.

"*Promise?*"

Yes.

"*Please don't delay. Best not to let such questions fester and discover you're out of time. They're not easy, and mortality has a way of sneaking up and tapping you on the shoulder, doesn't it?*"

Neither are the ones you've already asked me. You gotta let me catch up before you fling more at me. I'm a heart patient now. I get tired.

"*Oh, Max.*"

And they're questions I'm still pondering. But I am, and I will, and we'll talk. OK? But not today.

"*OK. But soon, right?*"

Yes, soon.

"*Good. I look forward to that.*"

How goes the big family transformation?

"*Oh! Swimmingly. We're doing it Saturday. The wedding, I mean.*"

Quick.

"*It all came together. And it's time. Sometimes, Max, everything syncs up.*"

Sometimes.

"*What about you? Is someone there with you?*"

A whole floor of nurses. We're talking about a harem.

"*Oh, Max.*"

Even the dudes.

"*You amuse me.*"

My daughter's here. We're busting out of this hoosegow in the morning.

"*Going home?*"

Back to Billings, yes. Alexandra insists. Want to say hi?

"*Not now, thank you. I'd rather talk to you, if you don't mind.*"

You sly dog.

"*Oh, Max, hush.*"

I'll let her know you and your ten-gallon hat say howdy, pardner.

"*I'm ignoring you.*"

Good luck with that.

"*You're right. Impossible. And despite it all, I should like to see you again. Soon, I hope.*"

Me, too.

"*Any decisions about work?*"

I should be back in the swing of it in a few weeks.

"*It's amazing, isn't it? An event—pardon me, an attack—like yours used to be a death sentence. Now, if you survive it, it's just a blip in your week.*"

I feel like the Six Million Dollar Man.

"You better hold tight to that money. You haven't been billed yet."

Charles? Did you just make a joke?

"I have my moments."

Indeed, you do.

"Write to me when you get a chance, Max. The coming week will be extraordinarily busy, but write if you're so compelled, and I'll get to it as I can."

You can count on it.

"Be well, Max."

Be good, Chuck.

"You're incorrigible."

I know.

Max rolled right and put the phone on its cradle. He dropped his head back on the pillow. *Exhausting.*

"Dad?"

He tilted left, toward Alexandra. Tears streaked her face, her eyes welling up again to send more down the tracks after them.

"Honey?"

"Dad, who was that?"

How to explain Charles? Where to start? What to do with the hows and whys and wherefores soon to follow?

"A friend I've met in my travels."

"A close friend?"

"Yeah, I guess."

She shook her head, her lips bound and cinched together.

"What?" he asked.

"It's like you have this whole other life."

"Oh, sweetie. It's nothing so dramatic as that."

"No?"

"Of course not. He's just a buddy."

She crossed her chest with her arms, locking them. *Here we go.*

"A buddy you tell things to that you don't tell anybody else."

"Alexandra..."

"You saw Grandpa?" The words were out of her like a cannon shot, incredulous, hurting from the implication of what the notion meant, and Max hurt right along with her. A hell of a way to find out. And that swinging gate. That had seemed real enough. The complexion of everything maybe changes had Max stepped through.

"Like I knew him. When I was a kid," Max said, his words gone to a whisper.

"Was it the afterlife?"

"I don't know. I don't even know if it happened."

"But you think it did?"

"Yes."

"Oh, Dad."

"He was beautiful." Max's voice broke on the words. His daughter rose, fell bedside, and embraced him.

"What did he say?"

"He asked me to come in." More breakage. More spilling.

"Why—"

"No, wait, he asked me if I wanted to come in."

She separated herself from him, unburying herself from his shoulder, just enough to get a clear view. "Why didn't you?"

Max broke now, into full-on weeping. He had never let her see him this way, not even after Belle had followed Gustav into the ground almost fifteen years later, when Alexandra was old enough to know the loss and empathetic enough to know what it was doing to him. Not even then. Now, though, he showed himself to her.

"I told him I wasn't done."

They clutched again, tight and hard-docked, flesh and blood finding its own, the distances closing.

"I'm scared," she said.

"Of what?"

"That I'm not going to see you again."

He gripped her arms and held her there. "Honey, no."

"Tyler and I are leaving in, like, five days," she said. "We have to get back, get you settled—who's going to take care of you?—and we're going to be gone, well, I don't know, it could be a long time and—"

"I will take care of me. That's my job. The doctor said I have another thirty—"

"He said you *might*. You don't know."

"No," he conceded.

"What if you don't?"

He kissed her, cheek and cheek and nose and forehead, the way he did when she was a little girl. She had come into the world seemingly with more maturity than he and Janine had built in their generational head start, a self-knowing, certain, open-minded, open-hearted girl, but even a girl as grounded in her own sense of self as Alexandra needed a father's reassurance sometimes. Not in a long while. Now, though. Right now.

"I know somebody's waiting for me." That, too, broke him. Broke her. Max could tell because that's when she assumed control of herself again and cut the bindings. She settled into her own being, settled back into the chair, offered a hand, and Max clasped it. They sniffled. They laughed. The TV flickered on. The life around them funneled back in.

Max squeezed her hand, and she looked at him with that tightened smile that said little and betrayed all.

"Dad?"

"Yes, Pookie Nose?"

"What questions?"

Hey.

Max!

Yep. Still here.

I'm so glad! Dex has been keeping us updated, but not the same as hearing from you.

You in Toledo? Going out soon?

Yep.

Won't be long now. You'll have another under your belt.

I know. I feel like I've really got the hang of it.

You do. You're a natural.

Aw. Are you coming back?

Couldn't stop me.

LOL

A few weeks, I think. I think we're doing the Vandalia line then. Good one. Fairly short.

It'll be good to see you.

You as well. Listen, I need to thank you.

It's OK.

No, this is important. I'm grateful.

I just called 911. Anybody would have.

But you did. I'm glad it was you. I mean, sorry you had to see that, but I'm glad you were there for me. Thank you.

I'm glad too.

And I'm sorry, again, for everything. For bailing out on you like I did and making it seem like it was your fault. That wasn't right.

Thank you.

I don't want to talk it to death.

Me, either.

But I needed to say that. I got nervous. I should have talked to you.

Thank you for acknowledging that. I appreciate it.

Maybe we can talk more about it when you're not getting ready to work.

Sure. I'd like that.

So what's up? Anything new?

OH! Hey, it looks like I might get one weekend a month with my kid. Just me and him. Unsupervised.

What? That's fantastic.

It's not for certain yet. There's still a hearing next week, right before we head up north. But my lawyer is hopeful. Been a while since anyone expressed hope about this.

This is in Saginaw?

Lansing. Where the father lives. Gotta win one on the road.

I'll hold a good thought.

I need it.

What happened? Feels like a big momentum shift.

A lot. So much. The job, for one thing. That's huge. Bonk said he's going to give me a shift lead next week.

Great!

And the supervised visits have gone really well. Rexford and I have a good rapport, and the social worker sees that. And I think he's going back and telling his dad he's having a good time with me, that I'm helping with his schoolwork and stuff, and that's making a difference. Always felt like I was fighting the family more than the guy, you know?

Totally get it.

And I don't want to fight. That's the thing. I've had to, but it's not good for R. He's the important consideration. I could let the rest of it go, but I feel like I have to hang in there for him.

Yep.

Cross your fingers for me, OK?

All 10 of them. Twice.

Thank you.

Good talking to you. Get to work.

Bye.

INTERSTATE 94, ANN ARBOR, MICHIGAN

Saturday, April 6 | 8:37 a.m.
Four hours, twenty-eight minutes before the first flight home

From the uncomfortable unfamiliarity of the passenger seat, Max threw his hand at a right angle toward the windshield.

"Hey, there's a Speedway over there. Take this exit."

"Are you OK?"

"I'm fine, Alex. Just need to pee."

She worked her way from the middle lanes to the right, a skillful parting of the rush-hour waters, and ran up the ramp to the corner store. Max snapped the seatbelt off and swung the door out. "Just keep it idling. I won't be long."

"Take your time. Want me to come?"

"No, I've been doing this a while now. Pretty good at it."

"Oh, jeez."

"Got a whole technique and everything," he said.

He got out of there before the eyerolls and complaints about his ceaseless sarcasm could gather speed. He knew Alexandra deserved better than pithiness. She had been aces, right down the line, even after he had begged off further chitchat the night before and sent her back to the hotel for some decent sleep. There'd been a minor complaint from her—"I can sleep just fine here"—and then acquiescence, which was good. The old man, the senior partner of the firm Wendt, Wendt & Gone, ought to win one occasionally.

Max entered the store, throwing a friendly yawp to break the ennui of the cashier, and he plodded to the back, just in case Alexandra was tracking his movement from the parking lot. Miracle of miracles, he didn't really have to go—that, no doubt, would be coming five minutes after they got back on the highway—but the matter upon him was no less urgent.

"I ain't going," he told the pinned-up weekly specials on the bulletin board outside the men's room. "No, now, sweetie, I've thought about this, and I think I'll hang out here a little while and—"

"Not going where?"

Max spun a half-turn. The cashier had pulled a sidle-up. Sneaky kid.

"Um."

"Somebody in there?" the kid asked.

"No. I mean, I don't know....I was just practicing my lines. Toastmasters."

"OK."

"Great Lakes Region champion, three years running. I don't mean to brag."

"Yeah, OK. Look, if you're not gonna use it..." The kid went to step around him.

"No, I am," Max said, boxing him out of the lane. "Sorry. Gotta go bad. Old man. Unpredictable bladder. I'll be out soon."

On the other side, Max turned the deadbolt. He leaned against the door, one hand propping him up, his heart—*now with twenty percent less functional muscle and a hundred percent less gunk!*—playing a drum fill.

What the hell has gotten into me?

Rhetorical though the question was, the answers fell in like a chorus line.

One, two, three, four...

I'm gonna make a damn decision about something here.

I'm not gonna burden Alex with this back in Billings. Or anybody else.

I'm not a child. I'm not helpless. Not yet.

Still, I need to rest.

Five, six, seven, eight...

I also need to do something.

I need to move.

I need to feel like I'm as free as I think I am.

And I need to show her this. Might be my last chance.

Max emerged. The kid stood, waiting his turn. Didn't he have a job? If the criminal element in this town were halfway decent, it would be taking apart the front of the store while this guy loitered in the back, clueless.

"Sorry," Max said.

"Whatever, man. You didn't even flush."

Back in the car and on the interstate, the words Max intended at first didn't come and then, finally, damn near to Ypsilanti, they didn't come out right. He had half an idea of what he wanted to do and where he aimed to do it, and the challenge now was to bring Alexandra into his conspiracy.

"Let's turn around."

"What?" Alexandra gave him a quarter-note double take. "Why?"

Good question. What he had in mind at once seemed impossibly big, a notion too audacious to scale even for him alone, much less to pull her into it. And he couldn't bail out now to something slight, like a suggestion that they go back so Max could get the number of nurse Jenn, who'd come down to see him off and had brought a card signed by the CCU staff. That had brought forth a round of teasing from Alex.

"Dad, she was totally flirting with you."

"Was not."

"Are you kidding me? Bright Eyes?"

"That's just what it says on my insurance card."

Now, in the absence of anything thought-out and persuasive, Max let it fly. "Let's go on a trip. You and me."

Another incredulous turn of the head from Alexandra. "What?"

"You heard me."

"We are. You and me. Home."

"*Driving* trip."

"Where?"

"Wherever," he said.

"You're out of your gourd."

"I'm not."

"Dad, we've got tickets. I've got plans. Don't be silly."

"Change your plans."

"What? No."

"Two days. There's nothing at home that can't wait for two days."

"My husband has been waiting for two days already. We're flying to Europe. I have to get home."

A fair point, that. She did have plans. She didn't have The Plan, not anymore. But Alexandra had constructed a life out of bottom lines and benchmarks, ratios and deadlines. He was pushing her far out of her wheelhouse by mere suggestion, with a fair piece yet for her to cover if acceptance was to be in the offing. If she couldn't do it, well, that's life. Her life. Not his.

"OK," he said, "let's go to the airport."

"Now you're talking."

"I'll see you off, and then I'll go."

"Dad, no."

"No?"

"That's what I said." Her grip set in, choking the life from the steering wheel.

"Honey, listen to me."

"No."

"Listen."

Max counted down silently. *Ten, nine, eight, seven, six...*

"What?"

"I'm not going back to Billings with you. I don't want to, and more than that, you can't make me. So if you need to go, which I totally respect, let's go to the airport and get you on a plane, and then I'll rent a car and go get a hotel room—"

"What is this? What's going on with you?"

"Alexandra, listen to me. Just listen to me, OK?"

"OK."

Well, now you've done it. You have her attention. Can you validate it? Max was near certain he could not. He knew what he wanted to do, and he knew the things he had been thinking about with regularity since Alicia had come aboard the crew, since Janine had drawn her line, since Alexandra's plans had changed without regard for what she wanted. But how to bring them all together seemed impossibly complicated outside the confines of his own thoughts.

"Now, you can try to stop me," he said, "but I must tell you that the city of Detroit takes a very dim view of healthy young women wrestling their weak-hearted fathers to the ground in public. I mean, if I were a kid, yeah, you could maybe do it. But the optics are bad like this. So unless you want a felony on your permanent record, I suggest—"

"Jesus, Dad. Give me a break."

Softer now, he said, "I want to spend some time with you. The two of us. You drive. I'll sleep. You drive. I'll sing show tunes. You drive. I'll buy the meals."

"Oh, sure, now that you'll be eating salad."

"I always buy," he said. "You know this."

"I know. Maybe you ought to let me do it sometime."

She eased off the interstate at the next exit and turned left at the intersection, back to the cloverleaf that would send them in the direction they had come.

"This way?"

"This way works."

"I have to call Tyler."

Max waved assent. She found another exit to take and guided the car to a supermarket parking lot. She left it running while she got out, taking the phone with her. Max could imagine the conversation. *What is there to say beyond he wants to do a road trip and I've agreed?* Not much. You either fight about it or you don't. Tyler wasn't the straight-ahead fighting type, Max didn't think. He was more the type who lobbed smart-aleck verbal precision shots from safe quarter. Funny that neither Max nor his son-in-law had seen that tendency as common ground.

As she neared the car on her way back, Max heard only her final words: "Oh, jeez, Tyler, you can pack your own suitcase for once." She ended the call, dumped herself back into the front seat, and slammed the door.

"He took it well," Max said.

Her scoff was outsized, almost a mock. "He took it as anyone would."

"Fair enough."

"You know," she said, directing the car back to the highway, "we're eating, like, eight hundred dollars in airline tickets."

"Well, you are," he said. "I'm having salad."

"You are such a dork."

Back they went on the general route of their morning drive, past Ann Arbor, past the Speedway of the Interminably Languid, and then, some miles later, past the Chelsea turnoff. Max threw a glance to the Comfort Inn riding the high ridge, a place he knew so well. *Will it seem different when I get back there?*

They rode silently for a long while, wrung out by the energy required just to get around on the idea of such an abrupt detour. Max would catch glances at his daughter, her eyes latched to the road ahead, and he would feel the renewal of his unspeakable good luck at calling her his own.

"Do you really think she was flirting with me?"

"The nurse?" Alexandra said. "God, yes. You didn't see it?"

"I think I'm blind."

"Out of practice, more likely."

"Permanently," he said.

"You never know."

"I guess."

"You never know."

He rotated his bulk in the bucket seat, redirecting his lean toward her. The breath was coming out of him better than before, the pumping system of his body having been purged and cleaned. He was tired, no doubt about that, but the weariness felt temporary and more a manifestation of what he had been through than what he was still to traverse. Daily Plavix and better choices and regular follow-ups, and he would be a golden boy again, Bradshaw had said. What a time to be alive.

"Would it be weird if something like that happened? Me getting together with someone new at some point?"

"Weird?" Alexandra asked. "For me, you mean?"

"Sure."

She darted a series of side-eye glances at him as she chewed on an answer. "Not weird," she said, finally. "Different, I guess. Depends on the woman. You interested?"

"No," he said. "No candidates, for one thing. No time, for another. No energy for it, for a third."

"You sure, Bright Eyes?"

He nudged her with an elbow, a shot she returned.

"Easy now," he said. "I'm decrepit here."

"Oh, stop."

Onward, they pushed west, until Max directed her to take Highway 127 north, which would bring Lansing and Saginaw into play, an interesting coincidence.

"Where are we going?" Alexandra asked as she veered off.

"Iron River."

"How much farther?"

Max squeezed his phone out of his front shirt pocket and brought up his GPS program, then fed the info into it.

"Five hundred and three miles."

"Are you serious?"

"As a heart att—"

"Don't say it."

"Sorry. Bad idiom."

"No," she said, a laugh coming up sharply inside. "That's a simile. And anyway, you're a good idiot."

A PARKING LOT ON THE NORTH END OF THE MACKINAC BRIDGE

Saturday, April 6 | 2:33 p.m.
Bridge length: 26,372 feet
Bridge clearance at the apex: 155 feet above Lake Michigan

The April wind, having turned predictably fierce on the Upper Peninsula, whipped the legs of their pants as Max and Alexandra stood on a strip of browned grass and took in the great marvel of human ingenuity. Max slipped his own heavy coat from his shoulders and enveloped her with it, his massiveness in outline swallowing her.

"You should keep it," she said.

"I'm fine."

"It's really cold."

"I'm OK."

"OK, thanks."

As they had approached from Mackinaw City, now faintly visible on the other side of the water, it had all come clear to Alexandra, the geography and what it would require of her to cover the distance between the land masses.

"Oh, I'm nervous," she had said, and for good reason. She had never seen a bridge like this one. Probably had never seen anything more impressive than the ordinary span across the Yellowstone River back home between Miles City and Glendive. Max forgot sometimes that his daughter, with a bearing that bespoke worldliness and the pocketbook to travel wherever she liked, had mostly stayed rooted to home earth in Montana, building her stake. He also knew that when the wind was up, as it was now, this could be a dodgy drive across the lake.

"Just keep it to 45, like the signs say," he had said. "Here, it's a limit, not a suggestion."

He had dared not tell her what his endlessly curious mind had packed away over the many years of crossing this span and the subsequent side reading it had inspired, especially in an age when the information he sought was as close as his phone. Five workers dead between the start of construction in 1954 and the opening of traffic across the bridge in late 1957. Two cars that plunged over the edge, one on purpose, a death sentence at that height regardless of intention. Maybe a dozen people with enough despair to go out there, where walkers weren't allowed, and launch themselves toward the water. Lake Michigan, of course, was indiscriminate about accepting the sacrifices. In defiance of any notion of seemliness, Max enjoyed collecting the tidbits of the macabre. That didn't mean he was inclined to share them. "Just keep your eyes forward and drive," he had said.

Now, safely on the other side, Alexandra beheld the view with a requisite level of awe. The day had graced them with clarity, at least, amid the biting cold. Clouds like the stuffing Barney the Beagle used to pull from his bed, distressed and stringy, blew across the sky. A nearly perfect day for the view, especially if you could squirrel yourself away in a warm car afterward.

"I never knew it looked like this," she said. "If I couldn't see land, I'd think it was the ocean."

He huddled into her, and she slipped an arm across his shoulders.

"There's more of it to look at," he said. "We should get going. Still a bit of a drive yet."

He had the advantage of knowing what was coming, a route mostly west along Highway 2, mostly hugging the shoreline, each emerging vista prettier than the one preceding it. There were places to get out and walk in Naubinway and Manistique and Gladstone and Escanaba before they turned north and went into the forested interior of the peninsula. But there were reasons to push on, too, a good meal and a good sleep in Iron River central to getting them ready for what he wanted her to see on the next spin of the globe. He had already hustled her through lunch. *No sitting down. We've got places to be.* She'd had a hamburger, the rarest of indulgences for a woman who ordinarily dined with the fastidious Dr. Keisling. He'd had a garden salad, an affront to every mealtime sensibility he possessed.

He pointed back across the highway, toward the toll booth that had greeted them after the crossing. "The receive valve is over there on the other side. Or the launch valve, if we're crossing over and headed to Bay City or Port Huron."

"So you see this all the time."

"All the time."

What he regretted now is that he had never lingered, never taken this place in beyond the requirements of the job. In St. Ignace, just ahead, he'd had plenty of time, over the years, to hop a ferry and ride out to Mackinac Island, to see the Grand Hotel, to follow the footfalls of Christopher Reeve and Jane Seymour in that movie Janine loved. "Would you travel back in time for your one true love?" she had asked him years earlier after they had seen the film on the VCR in their first apartment together. "Why?" he had replied. "You're right here." The memory, or perhaps it was the regret, stung him now.

Alexandra doffed his coat. "Here," she said.

He took it, gladly. The wind cut into him with every gust.

"Race you to the car?" she offered.

"Decline."

"I'm kidding. I'm sorry, that was mean."

"No," he said, "it's fine. When you come back from Europe, I'll whip your ass at any distance you care to go."

"Promise?"

"Absolutely."

IRON RIVER, MICHIGAN

August 6, 1984 | 12,661 days earlier
4:46 p.m.

It was near impossible for Max to square the Mark Bonk sitting in the hotel lobby with the one who often planted himself on the porch next door, draining cans of Old Milwaukee. This guy was outfitted in safety wear, Oakley sunglasses wrapped around his eyes even indoors, all business. The other guy, the one Max had gotten to know a bit, prattled around in muscle shirts and cutoff jeans and flip-flops as he fiddled with a souped-up Oldsmobile in the driveway or chased Missus Bonk around the yard.

"Max," Bonk said, rising to meet him. "You made it."

"Yes, sir."

Bonk drew the Oakleys down his nose. "You can knock it off with the *sir* stuff."

"Sorry."

"No, it's fine. You're a respectful guy. Appreciate that." Max nodded. "But you're writing checks these other guys won't cash."

"Understand."

"Any trouble on the trip?"

None whatsoever, Max was happy to say. It had all been fairly surreal, the flight from Billings to Minneapolis and then the 300-plus miles straight out to Wausau and then up, every inch of the glaciated plains representing terra nova to a kid who'd barely left Montana in his twenty-one years. Max couldn't say he had ever pictured a job looking like this, requiring this kind of travel or these kinds of logistics. Max also couldn't say he had granted much time to pondering a job of any sort, so when Mark Bonk, neighbor, had proposed becoming Mark Bonk, boss, Max had figured, well, why not? He could always quit if he wasn't suited for it. He had taken it to his folks, and they had landed in the same place. "Sure, Maxie, sounds like a good opportunity."

"Wouldn't Milwaukee have been closer?" Max asked now.

"Moderately. Not enough to make a difference." That drew a smile out of Bonk. "But see, you're picking it up already. Tactical thinking about time and distance, man. That's the way to do it."

Bonk clapped him on the shoulder. "The thing is, you're looking at a long drive either way. Once we're done, it's five hundred miles in the car back to the airport in Minneapolis, buddy. But Minneapolis is one flight from Billings. Milwaukee is two. Time and money."

"Makes sense."

"Let's get you checked in," Bonk said. "Got some stuff for you up in the room. You'll meet the other guys at dinner."

Max paid for his room with the credit card his folks had co-signed. It held a three-thousand-dollar limit, a sum he had a hard time even imagining, much less racking up. The clerk ran the dupes through the imprinter, then called the number on the back of the card to verify the purchase. Back to Max came a room key affixed to a plastic blue oval.

"Do you need your receipt?" the desk clerk asked.

"Damn right," Bonk answered her. "Remember, kid. You gotta prove up every dollar you spend, or you won't see it on the back side."

"I understand."

"Good enough. Come on. Let's make you a true-blue pig tracker."

IRON RIVER, MICHIGAN

Saturday, April 6, 2019 | 7:13 p.m.
Dinnertime

The collision of then and now plowed into Max as he took in the details of the supper club, his usual first-night-in-Iron River destination. Sarah, the owner, had greeted him with a hug, a "so good to see you again, Max," astonishment as he introduced his daughter, befuddlement when he told her, no, he wasn't here on a job, not this time, just a leisurely trip. If you're not a fisherman and not a recreational type in the prime winter or summer season—and Max surely was not and the calendar surely wasn't yet there—you had to work awfully hard to get yourself to a place like this. Or you were lost.

Max couldn't be certain, even now, which of those hewed closest to the truth.

"It's like you're a celebrity," Alexandra said after they sat down and Sarah pushed off to her duties.

"Oh, it's much simpler than that," he said. "Thirty-some years of handing them my wallet."

Alexandra spread the menu and took it in. "I can see why. Look at this: spaghetti and meatballs. Lasagna. Manicotti. God, pasta carbonara."

"Best Italian place in Michigan," he asserted. He had no way of backing up that contention, but why let evidentiary technicalities infringe on a perfectly good case of surety? The best place anyplace was the place he knew there. He had dozens of them.

"You can't have any of this, of course," she said.

"I can," he said. "I'm going to."

Before Alexandra could let loose the one syllable—"Dad"—that led to all the others he wasn't willing to hear, he cut her off.

"Did I not go for a walk with you?"

"You did," she conceded.

"Did I not drink water all day?"

"You did."

"Did I not eat a small, respectable lunch?"

"Yes."

"OK, then."

"It's just—" she started.

"I know. But you and me, we've got to get something straight, OK? I didn't get myself into this mess in a day, and I'm not going to land back there in a day, either. And you're not my keeper—not yet." He thought now of his mother's last days, how she had insisted on dying in the house on Wyoming Avenue, and the way her needs pulled him back to her in a way that nothing else could, how seeing her off the mortal coil had superseded everything else. He hadn't resented it, exactly. He just hadn't been prepared for how easily he could push vital things to the margins once her needs swamped his. It had left him shaken. And if Charles Foster Danforth wanted to know what drove Max, there it was: an abiding fear of making Alexandra hold the bag for him at the end the way he and Janine had held it for Belle.

"I'm not trying to be your keeper," she said.

"I know you're not. I'm just saying, my bell has been sufficiently rung, OK? I get it. And even though I get it, I'm occasionally going to have some pasta, as reckless as that may be."

"OK," Alexandra said. "Just not the carbonara, please."

The parallels fell back on Max again as he murmured noncommittedly. Sarah, quite without realizing it, had brought them to the side of the room where he had dined with Bonk and the crew that long-ago August night, the eve of the first job, when Max had been trying to dial in the names of the guys he had just met and to draw a bead on their mannerisms, their senses of humor, their flashpoints. There'd been Davey Lawrence (now eighteen years in the ground) and Rick Baw (retired) and the guy Max had formed a fast friendship with, the one closest to his age and his absence of experience, Dexter Strongley ("call me Dex, everybody does").

Try as he might now, Max couldn't draw in the finer details of time and location. Sarah's restaurant, her parents' place back then, had surely changed, but for the life of him, he couldn't see how or plot the alterations on a timeline. Hadn't the red velvet walls in the ·bar always been there? Weren't these the same Samsonite chairs? The same industrial carpet? More than three decades of sitting down to chow here—sometimes two or three times a year—had blurred the discrete images into a whorl. What was from 1984 or 1991 or 2007 was indistinguishable from everything else.

Max did remember the spirit of the interplay from that night, if not the actual strings of dialogue. Lawrence, the veteran among the trackers, felt duty-bound to bust the balls of the newbie, mostly in ways that Max, even then, understood as a rite of passage he would just have to endure. When Lawrence cut too close to the bone, Bonk was quick to break it up and reset the room. Baw was mostly quiet and agreeable, an attitude good for the mix. It was Dex who summoned Max into quiet huddles when the other three were off on a line of chatter, and the two of them talked up the job and the opportunities it might unearth.

Sarah came back around for their orders.

"Has to be the spaghetti and meatballs," Alexandra said, and Sarah praised her good instincts for the menu.

"The usual, Max?"

"Of course."

"It'll be right up."

Alexandra tipped her glass of house red against Max's. He would have preferred a beer, but the wine got approval from his daughter and there were only so many battles he was willing to engage at once.

"What's the usual?" she asked.

He grinned. It was going to come known eventually anyway.

"The carbonara," he said.

They walked back in the full darkness, the hotel just a block down the hill. Max, held to a single glass of wine, walked a steady line. Alexandra, tipsy after three, gripped his arm. The downtown buildings—blighted and far beyond their mineral-driven heydays of the '20s, '30s, '40s and '50s, when the town's population was half again its current size—cast hulking streetlight shadows on the ground at their feet.

"So the next job starts here?"

"In a couple of days, yeah," Max said.

"I heard you talking to Sarah about it."

"She'll be glad for the business, I'm sure."

Alexandra pulled him closer. "Why are we here?"

"I told you in the car."

"No, no, no, you didn't," she said, and she laughed at her half-drunken bellicosity. "You said you wanted me to see it. That's not a *why*. That's a brush-off."

"Yes, I want you to see it. And some other stuff, too. But it's time I'm after. That's why I asked you to come."

"Yay!" She sputtered laughter toward the sidewalk. Max had never seen her even this moderately disengaged from self-control. A cup of coffee back at the room would bring her around, no doubt.

"So when do we see more stuff?" she asked.

"Tomorrow. I think we've both had enough of today."

She stopped on the sidewalk, concern setting in quickly. "Are you OK?"

"I'm fine. Come on." He tugged her by the hand, but she didn't move along with the prompt.

"You're sure?"

"Positive," he said.

"OK, then, let's go."

Max toweled off in the closet-like bathroom, closed off from the rest of the suite. He applied deodorant, brushed his teeth, patted down a few intransigent hairs that were still wet from the shower. He maneuvered his bulk in the compromised space, shimmying into a Mantooth Energy T-shirt, a handout from how many years ago, and pajama bottoms. His feet left moist prints on the tiled floor. When he went for the door and heard Alexandra weeping on the other side of it, he retreated, sat down on the toilet, and waited her out. He judged from her occasional walkaways with the phone, when they stopped for gas or a bathroom break, that she was taking this trouble to her mother. And while he would have given anything to alleviate the burden of grief—always offered to when she came back, red-eyed, and she always deflected, as was her right—he figured Janine for the better choice. Perhaps that's why Alexandra had made it.

He had been surprised that she hadn't accepted his offer of her own room—"Sweetheart, I have Choice points that'll last until next decade"—and had insisted on bunking with him. He had left her sitting on the queen bed nearest the window, waiting for her own bathroom time, caffeinated back into sobriety, and Max couldn't remember the last time they'd shared such intimate quarters. Middle school, if not earlier than that; the high-school-age version of Alexandra had insisted on her own fully functional wing of the house, and she rarely presented herself to them as anything less than scrubbed and made up and clothed. Now, he wondered if she was hanging close to him out of concern for his health or because of something more, something ancient and renewed.

The weeping, he knew what that was about, and he decided the only thing he could offer her now was the space to do it without his hovering around, trying to make better something that would not improve with his intercession. It wasn't long before she gathered herself and blew her nose. He gave it a few more moments, then emerged.

"All yours," he said.

"OK, thanks, Dad."

Max sat at the foot of his own bed, scrubbing at his head with a small towel, creating a need for a whole new round of taming the fast-thinning hair atop it. When he was done, he tossed the towel bedside and rubbed his noggin with both hands, Curly Howard-style.

"You want to watch some TV?" he asked.

"If you do."

He found the remote and flicked the flat-screen unit to life. The program guide began its vertical crawl, and Max pulled up ESPN by memory with three quick clicks. He then shushed the excitable sports desk anchor.

"You OK?" he asked.

"I'm fine."

"Run out of steam?"

"Sort of, I guess."

"I understand. It's getting late."

It wasn't late, of course—not even ten o'clock. But time, as Max had well learned, is kinetic and constant but also malleable, something that took up the empty space in whatever circumstances you jammed it in. Max had known nights of interminable stillness out on the job, when the hours between the start of his shift and his release had peeled off stubbornly, like the skin on an avocado short of ripeness. And he had known days that had sped by him, uncountable in their swiftness and sameness. And he now knew that the aftermath of a heart attack combined with a long drive could bring "it's late" to him before the nightly news had been delivered.

Alexandra unfolded herself and reset in a sitting position, facing her father.

"I'm scared," she said.

"Of this thing with me?"

"No," she said, and she expelled a breath she had been holding for days. "No, finally, not that. I think you're well in hand. I'm going to stop hectoring you."

"I'm glad."

"I'm scared of this trip Tyler and I are about to make," she said. "I'm scared of what's going to happen."

"Don't be."

"But I am."

"OK," he said.

"How did everything so right get so bad?" she asked, and that's when he went to her, and that's when she made room, and he held her hand and he leaned to her and he made himself available to whatever needed to come out. "We had a plan. And now it's gone. And now we're going to Europe. And I don't know what we're going to find there."

He took the other hand. He stroked her fingers with his.

"You're tending to you," he said. "You're tending to each other. That's smart. That's responsible. You guys, you can make another plan. Together."

"Do you think so?"

"Of course. I know you. You always have something you're striving toward."

Alexandra kept her head down, and Max let go of her hands, giving her some space. When she looked up again, he knew she had brought herself back from wherever faint hope and loss of control had threatened to push her.

"Do you think I'd have been a good mom?" she asked him, and his heart picked up the pace, filling with gratitude for a moment's vulnerability from his daughter.

"The best," he said.

"Really?"

"Absolutely. And you don't know what's coming, right, any more than anyone does. Nobody's had the last word yet."

"I guess."

"No, it's true," he said. "Time is with you on this thing. Time for the science to get better. Time for other options, other choices."

"I wanted this so bad," she said. The beaten-back grief had hold of her again. "I don't think I've ever wanted anything so much."

"I know." He took her hands again.

"I'm pissed off. I'm sad. I'm scared."

"I know."

"All at the same time," she said.

"I know. I'm sorry. I don't have any wisdom about it. I wish I did."

"I'll take what you've got."

Her looked at her, his heart brimming. "Hang on. Hold tight. Keep hope."

She nodded.

"Best I can do," he said. "Best anyone can do."

"Thanks, Dad."

"You bet, Pookie Nose."

She crinkled up her face at that. "Dad?"

"Yeah?"

"Do you suppose we could retire the whole 'Pookie Nose' thing?"

The entreaty was kind enough and soft enough, and still it got to Max—not that she had made the request but that he had ignored it for so long. She had never much cared for the name, even when she was a relentlessly sensible little girl and he had been unable to summon a sufficient definition of a "pookie." *Well, if you don't know what a pookie is, then I don't want its nose*, she had said. Still, he persisted. And, eventually, she gave up.

"I'm sorry," he said now.

"No," she said, "don't be. Let's just leave it back where it belongs. We're on a new thing now, right?"

"Deal," he said.

AUGUST 8, 1984

4:07 a.m.
53.9558 miles into the run

Max stirred. He surfaced near consciousness, then plunged back into the folds of sleep. All quiet. The night was a sunk cost. The dawn was still pulling itself up, still out of sight. And beyond him, eight feet below, the tool annexed fresh territory at 4.796 feet per second.

Clink, the sound of molested glass.

Again, Max's senses rose and fell.

Clink. Louder now.

His eyes came open. He sat still in the bucket seat of his pickup, hanging off the seat belt. He looked at the time.

Fuck.

Clink. Louder still. Insistent.

Max rotated his head left, toward the sound. His eyes found the source, the snub nose of a pistol that had rapped the glass, the long, bare arms behind it, the shirtless man, wraithlike in the spillover light from the truck's high-beams and the interior brightness Max had brought forth, and behind those, the face drawn up in its own inexplicable fear.

"Roll down your fucking window." The voice was muffled by the barrier between them.

Max held up both hands. *Here. I'm not armed.*

"Roll it."

Hand quivering, Max gripped the handle and cranked, and slowly, slowly, the glass withdrew and the pistol moved forward and into his space.

"Don't," Max said.

"Shut up. What are you doing here?"

Max closed his eyes. "Pipeline crew." He opened them again.

"What are you doing here on my property?"

"Pipeline crew," he said again, this time as forcefully as he could get the words out, the falter still evident.

The man withdrew the gun but kept it on a level with Max's face. God help him, Max couldn't look away from it.

"Nobody told me."

"I'm sorry," Max said. "I'm in the right of way. Just doing my job."

The guy waggled the gun at him. "I'll tell you where you are."

"I mean no disrespect."

"I'm calling the law," the guy said. "They'll sort it out. Get out."

Max considered his options. Meager and stupid, all the way around. Bonk had said nothing about this sort of thing, had given him no set of ways to play out such a scenario. *Keep aware of your surroundings* had been all he had said, and, well, Max had scotched that by falling asleep, hadn't he? The pig was on the fly, four minutes past him, on its way to Lawrence, and that would be that, wouldn't it? First full night on the run, and he would be out of a job before noon.

"I'm going to open the door," Max said.

The guy moved back, the pistol leveled. Max pushed the door open and swung his feet out to meet the earth. When he stood, he got his first decent, clarified look at the terrain. The headlights shone a path up the guy's driveway. The house was set back a piece, the windows downstairs burning, the ones upstairs dark. Max's feet straddled the hard-packed dirt of the country road and the matted grass where he had pulled off.

"I'm in the barrow pit," Max said.

"You're on my property."

"I'm in the right of way."

The guy swung the pistol in the direction of the house with a let's move it along motion. "Stop lipping. Phone's up at the house. Let's go."

"Nope," Max said. "No way."

"What?"

"I'm not going up there. You know what I'm here for. I've already missed my tool. I'm gonna collect my shit and leave."

"The hell you say."

"I'm gonna collect my shit and go. Fuck you, man. I'm not the first guy who's ever sat here."

"This ain't your call. Now let's go."

"No?" Max said. "Well, shoot me, then. I'm getting my stuff."

Max turned, went the other way around the truck, headed for the marker and his gear, fully expecting a bullet in the back or in the head with every step. He knelt to collect his material, hands shaking, his skin a prickle, every sense opened and alert.

His arms full, he went back to the bed of the truck and lifted his load into it. His accoster stood there, arms at his sides, a hand holding the gun by the butt.

Max climbed back into the cab.

"All you gotta do is call a guy and let him know you'll be out here."

"I know," Max said. "I'll tell my bosses."

He put the truck in gear and got the hell out of there.

Max tore through the grid pattern of dirt roads, the alignment sheets that showed the route between his spot and Lawrence's scattering across the passenger seat. He grabbed fleeting glances at the clock, doing the math out loud. He was eleven minutes out from the expected passage he had slept through, leaving the tool about fourteen minutes shy of passing Lawrence. He would be able to beat it there and try to cover his tracks. *If I'm right. If I'm right. God, I hope I'm right.*

Up ahead, the road pitched to a rise, and an amber haze hung higher behind it. *That's him, other side of the hill, downstream marker.*

Max rolled to a stop in the middle of the road, opposite Lawrence, who was pointed the other way. Lawrence cranked his window. Max did the same.

"Expected to see you before now," Lawrence said.

"Sorry."

"You get a pass?"

"No."

"Huh."

And here came the lie. "I just never heard it. I waited it out, thought maybe it'd show, but nothing."

"That's odd. Never had trouble at that site before. Some of them on this line are a little deep. Hard to hear it going by. Not that one."

"I'm sorry."

Lawrence pulled off his cap and drew it across his brow. "You know this is going to fuck everything up, right?"

Max had nothing for him. Lawrence stared him down.

"I'm gonna have to get to a pay phone, call Bonk, tell him it's not working out. Sorry, kid. That's how it goes sometimes."

Below the window, out of sight, Max's hands fidgeted into overdrive. "Don't wake him up. I'll just go back and tell him."

"You'd do that?"

"Yeah."

"That's right sporting, kid. Of course, I'm just fucking with you."

"OK," Max said. He all but wet himself. It was relief, yes, but it was also rage that he had no capacity to show. He could take a goodly amount of teasing and be OK with it, but this Lawrence guy was going to get his ass kicked if he kept pushing it. Job or no job.

"I'll get it here," Lawrence said. "Unless it doesn't show for me. Then maybe we're up against something."

"I'll go to the next site," Max said. Now pure relief flooded into him. "It won't happen again."

Lawrence put his cap on, straightened it, flattened the bill. "Yeah, it will, kid. Happens to everybody. Part of the job."

"OK."

"Just don't let it happen again tonight."

BETWEEN IRON RIVER AND ESCANABA, MICHIGAN

Sunday, April 7 | 10:06 a.m.
The upstream pipeline marker at Milepost 53.9558

Max waited until Alexandra had rolled up next to the marker to tell her exactly why this singular spot, just shy of fifty-four miles into a 204-mile run, was the lone pipeline-related matter he intended to show her, why they could leave here and start making the long drive back toward Detroit, why this small piece of ground, on a narrow dirt road and next to a fetid pond, was so all-fired important that he had to pull her away for two days and give her little margin before she would be on another jet, this one taking her much farther from him.

And, frankly, once they were there, with the boxy little two-story farmhouse he had come to know so well emerging like a ghost from the morning marine layer, Max wasn't sure he could put words to it. But he had made the bid and she had accepted, and so he plunged in. And as the telling expanded into the meat of the thing—the night with the gun, the night everything almost unraveled, the night he managed to hold it together—Alexandra grew increasingly horrified and Max became increasingly uncertain he could stitch things together even close to the way they lined up in his head.

"You did *not* FU him," she said when he got to the bit about disarming another man without touching him.

"I did."

"Jesus, Dad."

"I know."

"And you were how old?" she asked.

"Twenty-one." She was more than half again as old now. How in the world had time compressed like this? Being here, in different circumstances, brought that night hurtling out of the past, more than half of the life he had expended instantly pulled up, fresh in the memories and fragrant in the senses.

"And you never told Mom?"

"No," he said. "And you're not going to, either."

"No, I am *not*." That's the good daughter. Didn't have to think about it long to realize it would serve nothing but retroactive misery to bring this to her mother now, almost thirty-five years down the road from it.

Oh, Janine, what a role in absentia you've played in this thing then and now. They had been dating four, maybe five months—long enough to be something a good bit more than mildly serious, short enough to make other choices if so compelled. And the simple truth of the matter, one Max recognized even as the callow young man he had been, was that if he had come bounding back to Billings off his first run and said, "Hey, it was great, all of it, except almost being shot in the face," Janine, or anyone, would have pushed those other choices onto his plate: *You can have the job or you can have me, but it's not going to be both. I'm not going to bury you young just because you've got a hard-on for plane rides and hotel rooms.*

So Max had presented to her a sanitized version of reality upon his arrival at the Billings airport a few days later: *This job has a good future, and I'm good at it, and we'll be getting some more regular income. You know that West End apartment we looked at but didn't think we could swing? We can swing it now. You can move out of your folks' place. I can move out of mine. Hell, Janine, we can get married, if you're thinking in that direction. I know I am.*

Heady, irresistible stuff when you're barely old enough to drink legally and don't shave your upper lip but once a week. He told Alexandra this now, and he made sure to include the connection that he, swear to god, had put together only that morning, the one that transferred power to any other number of injuries the marriage incurred in the ensuing years.

"It was the first lie I ever told her," he said.

"You didn't lie, exactly."

"I omitted," he said, disdain imprinted on the second syllable of the word. "That's worse sometimes."

"You were just a kid," she said. "God, twenty-one."

"I was old enough. Old enough to know what I was pulling her into."

"It's done, Dad."

"I guess."

"I just can't believe that wasn't it that night," Alexandra said. "I'd have gone home. Somebody pulls a gun on me in my workplace and I'm, like, hey, no thanks. I'll deliver pizzas."

So Max went into it again, coloring in the rest of the canvas for her. The hell of it was, the gun wasn't the issue that lingered through the decades. That was just a work hazard, when he got right down to it, like five-foot snow drifts in a North Dakota barrow pit or the margins of a springtime flooded field between him and the above-ground marker. The part that haunted him was the original sin of falling asleep and letting the pig get beyond him. How many nights had he been roused from his own slumber and his own bed, Janine unconsciously unaware, by a dream where he was late or hopelessly behind? He couldn't begin to number them.

The part that filled him with pride wasn't dealing with the gun. It was recovering from an error and making it right, and making his boss proud of the work he had done. It was finding a future where one couldn't previously be seen. And it was one other benefit, the unlikeliest of all.

"So, the guy who had the gun on me—" Max started.

"You should have let him call the cops."

"No, listen."

Alexandra torqued herself to give him full attention. "Sorry. Go."

"Guy's name was Jacky Hamby."

"Funny name."

"Yeah," he said. "So, we came back a few months later, November, I think, before the snow flew, and Bonk—Big Bonk—puts me on the night crew again, and he says to me, he says, 'So this guy, just out of Northland, he called the pipeline company and wants to be alerted when we're going to be out there.' And I know it's him. I know it's that guy. And I know I'm probably going to be sitting there, middle of the night, just like before. I mean, I didn't say anything to Bonk, but the guy called the company, so now we're on the hook for making sure he's taken care of. So Bonk says, 'Why don't you call him? It's your shift.' He hands me a slip of paper with the number."

She popped a hand over her mouth. "Oh, no."

"Yeah. So, I called him. I mean, orders, right?"

"Awk*ward*."

"So here I am: 'Hi, Mr. Hamby, this is Max Wendt with the pipeline crew and we'll be outside your place in a night or two, probably really late, and it'll probably be me, and oh, by the way, I'm the guy you pulled a gun on and who FU'd you.' I mean, not like that, exactly, but close enough. I covered the bases."

"What did he say?"

"'Thanks for letting me know.'"

"No apology?"

"None given," Max said. "None asked for. But I'll tell you this: The night I showed up, I was nervous as hell. I turned off the strobe on my car. Put the headlights on dim even though I couldn't see for anything. Just didn't want to disturb him. But here he came again, right down the driveway, only I saw him because this time I wasn't asleep."

"He did not!"

"He did. And he's carrying a beer and a cup of coffee. Says to me, 'I'd give you some suds, but you're working.' Gives me the coffee. And he stayed out there, chatting with me, and after my pass came, he took my cup and said, 'See you next time.'"

Alexandra fell back in the seat. "Unbelievable."

"So," Max continued, "every time we came through, I'd call him before the job started. Sometimes three times a year. Sometimes we'd go a few years without coming out. But I'd call him, and I'd try to get on the night shift—usually did, because nobody but me likes it—and every time, he'd show up with a beer and a cup of coffee. Every time."

"Did he ever say anything about...you know?"

"Not a word. Here's the thing: He just wanted to be heard. Was it extreme? Yeah. That's fair. Definitely extreme, borderline criminal. But he wasn't a bad guy. I've thought about it. Would I get unnerved if someone was always parking outside our house on Parkhill—your mom's house? In the dead of night? Damn right, I would. If you were in the house, especially so. I mean, I'm not going to pull a gun. But I'm going to be on guard. No doubt."

Alexandra pointed at the house. "So he's up there now?"

"No." Max curled his bottom lip over the top. "He died a few years ago." Max remembered it. The usual call. The bad news. He frowned.

"Oh, Dad."

Max shook his head, as if he could that easily brush away the sadness that had pounced on him again. "Jesus. I think this heart thing has messed with my emotions."

She reached out, squeezed his hand. "Dad, he was your friend."

"I guess. He knew all about you, let me tell you. Saw pictures. Always asked after you. We talked about a lot of stuff, but I guess you were a pretty common topic. Makes sense, right?"

"Yes," she said, the single word faint.

"Anyway," he said, "let's go. Maybe we can get across the bridge today. Maybe even get to Gaylord. Make it a shorter trip to the airport tomorrow."

"Maybe."

The marine fog had lifted now, brightness muscling into the gaps left behind. Max engaged the window control and opened it a sliver. Morning air slid in, the smell of dewy grass and stilled water and pine. Spring, so long awaited, was asserting itself. Max saw it as the best kind of day, a hopeful one—the kind that comes as a counterbalance to all those days a guy slogs through, trying to get to the end with some tenuous hope that it leads to another beginning.

LAKE MICHIGAN CAMPGROUND, HIGHWAY 2

Sunday, April 7 | 3:18 p.m.
11.7 miles from the Mackinac Bridge

They parked the car well off the highway, got out, stepped over the sagging chain-link barrier across the driveway that was less a hard no than a declaration that camping season hadn't yet arrived. A night around the fire wasn't what they were after. Alexandra wanted to be next to the water, to feel the sand wedged between her toes, and no amount of "aw, honey, it's going to be awfully cold" from Max had managed to dissuade her. "Just a little on my feetsies," she had said, playful as all get out. "It'd be a shame to get this close and not do that." So there they were, conscientious trespassers.

They picked through the empty silence of the campsites to a sandy knoll along a path that led to the water's edge.

"Far enough for me," Max said. The windedness had stealthily come up on him. "I'll watch."

"You're OK?"

"I'll be fine. Just want to make sure I can get back." The breathing, labored as it was, came out better than it had the night before, and surely better than the night before that, on his final few laps around the telemetry floor back in Chelsea. What struck him now was how little he had noticed his air being slowly choked out of him before the heart attack. How he would gulp for it sometimes after walking a set of stairs, or when he was made to hoof it from terminal to terminal in some sprawling airport like the one in Minneapolis. Did he feel better now? No, not yet. He had just had a damn cardiac event. But he sensed he was going to feel better soon. He had been cleaned out.

"All right," she said. "I'll only be a few minutes."

"Take your time."

Max planted himself in the sand and drew up his knees, and he watched Alexandra make her way down to the water's edge. The gloom of the day before had blown out, leaving in its wake the clarity of a perfect calm, the water lighting up in the daytime like a shimmering turquoise. Alexandra leaned into a rock and became a one-legged bird, reaching low for the left foot and removing first the sneaker and then the sock, which she stuffed into the shoe. Left leg down, right leg up, sinking into the sand, she repeated the maneuver. Sock-filled shoes set atop the rock, she bent over and rolled her jeans legs up, one at a time.

"Here goes nothing!" she called to him, and he waved back.

She began a tentative-footed, dotted-line walk toward the water. On the ground beside Max, his phone pinged.

Divorce hearing tomorrow, and that's it except the waiting period.

He picked the phone up and stared at the words. They were direct enough and clear enough, and yet they somehow disappointed him. Not in the messaging or in the intent, but just in their being. Max had imagined the moment and had filled it in with profundity. Now that the time was upon him, it wasn't that at all. It was, he realized, anticlimactic. *Well, what do you know about that?*

Hearing a shriek, he looked up again, and Alexandra had entered the water to the tops of her ankles. Feet planted in the sublayer of sand, she wrenched her body around. "It's freakin' cold!"

"I told you!"

She was undeterred. She was staying in.

Max went back to the phone and looked again at the message and its options for reply. He chose the call icon. Janine intercepted it before he heard a ring.

"Hi, Max."

"You doing OK?"

"I'm fine." She expelled a heavy breath. "You got my message?"

"I did."

"Are *you* doing OK?" Max recognized it as both a parry of his question to her and a more direct query, given recent events, that she hadn't yet had a chance to register.

"I was lucky."

"I'm glad. How scary."

"I appreciate the concern," he said. "Truly."

"How are things with you and Alex?"

He wondered what report, if any, Janine had been given. He hoped they weren't going to become *that* broken family, the kind that was forever parsing what wasn't said out of what was. How prosaic.

"I am watching your daughter frolic in Lake Michigan in April," he said. And, indeed, that's exactly what Alexandra was doing, splashing through the shallow water as if she were wearing clown shoes.

"*Our* daughter."

"No, I don't think *my* daughter would do anything quite so out of character and reckless."

He intended it as a laugh line, but Janine took it sideways, and the regret came to him. He had long ago cashed out his opportunities to poke gentle fun with her and not have it end up as a wound. To compensate, he came now with the softer words that had queued up right behind: "It's no problem. I have a massive St. Bernard here with a cask of elixir if she has any trouble."

"Oh, Max."

"You did such a good job with her, Janine."

"I didn't do it alone," she said, and if Max had infinite days left to live and infinite opportunities to explain what those words meant to him, he was certain he wouldn't be able to meet the occasion. He tucked them away for safekeeping.

"Maybe not," he said. "But the best stuff is you."

"Thank you for saying that."

"You take care out there, Janine."

"You do the same."

"Bye now," he said.

His unflagging daughter had downshifted herself into stillness, her back to him, arms outstretched, palms up, cradling the sky. He set the phone down in the sand, and he rose to quietly wend his way to where she was. As long as it had taken him to get there, he didn't want to miss the chance while it was still in front of him, beckoning.

HAMPTON INN, GAYLORD, MICHIGAN

Sunday, April 7 | 8:42 p.m.
241 miles from the Detroit airport
Eighteen hours, twenty-three minutes before Alexandra's flight

While Alexandra was in the shower shedding the leavings of the Upper Peninsula—her stopping to shake the sand from her shoes at every rest stop had become the stuff of hilarity—Max whiled away on his laptop. Wasn't it funny how quickly the obligations had come back to him, either because he had let them in or because they had insisted on intruding? In two days, the crew would be headed to Iron River, where he had just left, and two weeks after that, he would rejoin them down in Pontiac, Illinois.

Already, he was making the turn from whatever he had been before what Dr. Bradshaw called "the event" to whatever he was now to whatever he would be once he was back on the job. It was his most fervent hope that, after the preliminary pomp of being welcomed back, he would be a plain old pig tracker. He had already resigned himself to the idea that whoever he was paired with first would make a point of swinging by his car and pretending to be interested in conversation between passages, all as a ruse to baby him through it. Max didn't like that, but he had never seen much point in trying to divert human impulse. He just hoped it wouldn't be too painful and wouldn't drag on too long.

And then there was the ever more urgent matter of Alexandra's departure, just hours away, and the uncertainty of when he might see her again. Though Max was trying his best not to impose his own sensibility on things, he wondered how different life might look, for both of them, once they arrived at that assumed but as yet unplanned reunion. He had already told her he wasn't going back to Billings with her, that whatever he would be doing, for now, was going to happen in places where memory and the specter of past obligations didn't have such a hold on him.

The clock had become like an otherwise well-regarded friend who had no sense of conversational proportion, telling them what they wanted to know and, in reminders increasingly stark, the impending eventuality they didn't want. It had made for an oddly bittersweet final dinner together, which Alexandra had insisted on paying for, and their mutual promise to make the most of their draining time.

While he waited for her to emerge clean and renewed, he had some business of his own.

On the first item, he had done some passenger-seat Internet surfing to gather the information he needed, as well as placed a surreptitious phone call while Alexandra had been away from the car at a rest stop.

He rapped the email out in just a few minutes.

From: Wendt, Max
To: Ingham County Clerk of Court
Subject: Docket 406794

To whom it may concern:
I'm not sure where to direct this, but I'm hoping it can be passed on to whoever the hearing officer is in

the above-referenced case. Any help would be most appreciated.

I don't have a stake in this case, and I'm not going to suggest I know the issues involved with any kind of depth. I do know Alicia Hammond, though, and that's why I'm writing. I'd like to make a character reference, if I could. I don't know if that's something that matters or not, but here it is just the same.

I'm a co-worker of Alicia's. She's a bright, forthright person. She's responsible. She's caring. She gets it. That's probably the best way to put it. She gets it, and, well, a lot of people don't. She's got a future in this job. We're lucky to have her.

Beyond that, and most importantly, she's all about doing right by her son. She's trying to build a life for herself, and making room for who he is and what he needs is the central part of what she's doing. As a parent, I can tell you I recognize that and I see it, and I respect it. I'm envious of it, truth be told. She seems to deeply understand the stakes at an age when, in my own life, I couldn't—and didn't—even see them. That's impressive.

I have no way of knowing what all must be balanced here in whatever decision is going to be made. But I have to think that if one of those factors is whether Alicia's son's life would be made better by her presence in it... well, that's an easy call, right?

Thanks for considering this.

Max Wendt

The matter of the second email, even with its sinewy connections to the first, had been slower in coming to him, and he wondered if he could even corral the disparate and flailing thoughts. They had been hitting him all afternoon, eventually driving him into a distracted silence that Alexandra had noticed quickly.

"You OK over there?" she had asked him as they made their way down the giant closed fist of the Lower Peninsula.

"Me? Fine."

"You're quiet."

"Quiet is underrated."

"Guess so."

He had noticed too late that she had taken it as a jab with a pointed message, as opposed to the off-kilter and humorous pokes he usually took at her. He had patted her shoulder, a ready smile to smooth any rough edges.

"Just thinking."

"You keep thinking, Butch—that's what you're good at," she said, invoking his favorite movie.

"You stole my line!"

"You gave it to me," she had said. Point to Alexandra.

Now, Max cracked his knuckles and got to it.

> *To: Charles Foster Danforth*
> *From: Wendt, Max*
> *Subject: You had questions. I have answers. I think.*
>
> *Dear Charles:*
> *Greetings from Gaylord, Michigan, home of Claude Shannon, the so-called father of "information theory." I got that from Wikipedia, which I know isn't an unimpeachable source, so please spare me that lecture, if in fact you have it warming up in the bullpen. (That's a baseball term, Chuck. Did you ever play baseball? Hard to be an American kid if you don't play baseball. As no less an authority than Foghorn Leghorn put it: "There's something a little ewwwww about a boy who don't like baseball.")*
> *Am I stalling? It feels like I'm stalling.*
> *Let me get to it.*
> *You asked me a series of questions some time back, and then I went and had a heart attack, but I can't duck you forever. I'm prepared to answer them now.*
> *1. What do I suppose it was or is within me that led*

to my decision to sleep with a woman young enough to be my daughter? I've thought a lot about that, especially while I've been spending the past couple of days with a woman who actually is my daughter, and what I've realized is that I don't have a very good answer in terms of my ability to defend the choice, but my answer is quite good in strictly emotional terms: The woman, my co-worker (she has a name, and it's Alicia), has some troubling issues in her life, and I do, too, and when we shared those things, we formed a sort of bond that was like quick-dry cement; the emotions we both let out solidified into a kind of intimacy faster than either of us realized. Now, I need to point out here: I never saw her as a potential lover. I mean, I'm not blind; she's an attractive woman. But I know she's not for me, generationally, temperamentally, in any way that's sustaining. Similarly, football jerseys look pretty good on slender 25-year-olds; they look stupid on a 45-year-old fatass at the end of the bar. That's a blunt comparison, but there you go. What I thought I could offer her was support, someone to lean on, someone who could help her shoulder a load. And here's where we get to revelation, Chuck: I couldn't. I can't carry her load any more than I can carry my daughter's inability to become a mother. It's her road to walk. I interfered with that.

2. Where is that headed, do I think? Nowhere good. I bailed out on her when I started to think about the pitfalls and perils at work, with not a single word of explanation. How do you think she took that? (And who's asking the questions now, bucko?)

3. Why did I tell you? Clearly, I wanted you to ask me the questions you did. It was somehow easier than asking them of myself. I'm sorry for that manipulation.

4. What did I expect you'd say? Come on, man. I know you well enough now to know I have no idea what you're going to say. So let's go with this: I get it, all right?

I can be a better parent and a better friend. Better man, in the whole of it. Working on it. That's going to have to be good enough.

5. Would your response, in my expectation, be any different from the response I can supply to myself to all of the above questions? No, I don't think so. You'd probably quote more poets and artists and philosophers than I did, because that's your bag, but I think I'm on the money.

I imagine you'll tell me soon enough if I'm not.

Until that time,

Max Wendt Beddy-bye

P.S. I'm still wrestling with your observation about how I'm sad. I can't dispute that I've been sad, but let me tell you something extraordinary: In a few hours, I will be pretty much a divorced man like you—the difference being that I'm not likely to start wearing gold lamé–and when the news came to me, I wasn't sad at all. It was something else, something unexpected. Not joy or relief, because it's hard to be joyous about cutting loose from someone you've loved for most of your life. (Again, we have common ground, my friend.)

It was a feeling of "all right, here we go," but I don't know where that is, or when I'll undertake the journey, or anything. But everything I don't know is also an opportunity, even if all I do with it is spend a long couple of weeks alone in a hotel, which is my plan at the moment.

And what is happiness or sadness, anyway, but a fleeting feeling that has too much to do with how events in your immediate vicinity are playing out? I'd take a gallon of contentment over an ocean of happiness, and then I'd store that contentment in your big ol' cowboy hat so no one stole it from me.

Be well, brother. I hope it was a beautiful wedding.

When Alexandra emerged, clad in flannel pajamas and with her hair blown dry, he closed the laptop and they retired to their side-by-side beds, and he wanted to try to remember these evenings most of all, when he had listened to her gentle snores as he awaited his own sleep and had reeled through the years that had brought them from there to here.

Wacky juxtapositions being Max's thing, he had also given fleeting thought to the twin beds of *The Dick Van Dyke Show*, then quickly bailed out on it when he realized the memory was miscast. He wasn't Rob Petrie, and she certainly wasn't Laura Petrie, beloved daughters and boyhood crushes being woefully incongruent categories of humanity.

"Do you want to watch a movie?" he asked.

"You can," she said. "I'm beat. Just keep it down, OK?"

"OK."

"Dad?"

"Yes?"

She sat up now, tossing the covers she had just pulled over herself. She swung her legs out of bed and faced him. He mirrored her.

"Can we say goodbye now?"

"Sure," he said. "If you want."

"I want. I want to say goodbye now and be glad when I wake up and you're still here with me. And we can talk all the way to Detroit, and then I can just get out at the rental car place and get on the shuttle bus to the terminal, and I can just go and you can just go. Because we will have already said goodbye, and it doesn't have to be sad or prolonged or awkward or stupid. Could we do that?"

And before he could say yes, to all of it, she was up and on his shoulder and he slipped his arms around her back and he clenched his hands together and he squeezed her, and she turned her head away so her right ear rested on his clavicle and she said, "Goodbye, Dad."

"Goodbye, Alexandra."

To: Wendt, Max
From: Charles Foster Danforth
Subject: Re: You had questions. I have answers. I think.

Max, old chum, I'd say you've graduated with honors.
   What ever will we talk of next?
   I look forward to finding out.
   With deepest regards,
   Chuck

HOW TO SPEND THREE DAYS IN DETROIT
IF YOU'RE MAXIMILIAN HEINRICH WENDT

Day 1 | April 8: You procure a rental car from one of the shuttle lots at DTW. You drive a couple of miles to the Romulus Big Boy and request something from the heart-healthy menu, which heretofore you have scarcely realized even exists. The grilled chicken breast with a small side salad and broccoli is palatable, even delicious in its way. Water, not iced tea. Not every meal, but this one. You can do this.

After the meal—late lunch, or early dinner, however you choose to define it—you hit the Comfort Inn, less than a mile away, and start spending some of those sweet, sweet Choice Hotel points you've been socking away for who-knows-how-many years now. The desk clerk— Johnny—will tell you he can't schedule the days for you right there, that you'll have to use the computer in the lobby and sign up for the free room nights online. "Come on, man," you will say. "I'm right here. You have my points right there on your computer." And Johnny will say, yeah, he does, and you will get 200 more just for checking in, but you've gotta do this part yourself. Regulations. And you figure it's because while the hotel company is happy to give you perks for all your business over the years—*we appreciate your loyalty!*—it's not inclined to be overly helpful about allowing you to access them. And, hey, man, Johnny just works here, so don't give him a hard time, OK?

You will take a suite, by the way. With the in-room Jacuzzi. You're here to live it up. Or sleep it off. *Tomayto/tomahto.* The room is right. The room is good. You're tempted to lie down, but you know where that leads, and this day—already full of laughter with your daughter, whom you've already said goodbye to once, who pressed a hand against the shuttle bus window as it was pulling away from you, who will be on a beach in France before the week is out—has one more chore before you can release it.

So you snare the binoculars from your work case and you head down to the rental car—a Toyota RAV4, and you love those—and you drive just a short way to a lonely pullout along a chain link fence, a vantage point from which you can see Interstate 94 and, beyond it, the runway grid of the airport. When the time is nigh, you scan the field. It will be a Delta jet headed toward Minneapolis, not that you will be able to recognize it from the ground, amid all the traffic down there at DTW, a Delta hub. But, indeed, a Delta bird does take wing within a reasonable window of time, and it does indeed bank around and head west, and that might indeed be Alexandra up there. And so you watch until all you can see is the jet stream tailings, and then you leave, because that's what she's done, and you remember that the flights go both ways, always, and you *will* see her again. Of this, you have no doubt.

You go back to the room. The bed calls your name. You settle in. You strip down. You climb in. Nothing is on TV, because nothing is ever on TV these days, it seems, so you choose a go-to: Turner Classic Movies. Even the cruddy movies are worth seeing, even if it's just to say later, *holy crap, I watched that steaming pile one time. Two hours I'll never get back.* The travel shorts from decades back are a pleasant enough diversion. Quebec City. You should totally go, man. What's stopping you?

Now, get this: Your usual in-room entertainment is an option. The flesh is willing, first time since "the event." How about that? And yet, you decline. How about *that*?

Here comes Ben Mankiewicz. How does a guy even become Ben Mankiewicz? What a great job that is, being Ben Mankiewicz. Ben Mankiewicz falls into a category that gets replenished often—Guys You'd Probably Enjoy Having a Beer With. He's funny and urbane, but not obnoxiously so, and he loves old movies, and you love old movies, too, and that's a pretty good basis for a beer-having friendship, if you ask you. But who is he? He's related to a couple of screenwriter Mankiewiczs (what a plodding plural) and a producer/director Mankiewicz and perhaps that is all the explanation one needs. Of course he would end up in Hollywood—by way of Atlanta, where the Turner studios are—and doing what he does.

But you're the progeny of a custom upholsterer and an English teacher, and you're a pig tracker, so maybe there's more to your professional pathways than the generational coursing of your blood.

Anyway here comes Ben Mankiewicz, telling you this next film is, for his money, "the best buddy movie ever made" and a story of two outlaws "choosing to live outside the established system," and can you believe this?

Butch Cassidy and the Sundance Kid.

Well, you'll be damned.

Day 2 | April 9: Have you ever slept so well for so long? You think not.

Downstairs, just before they close things up at 10, you have a little breakfast—a cheese omelet won't kill you, assuming that's really cheese and really omelet—and you take a bowl of instant oatmeal upstairs, along with a banana and an apple you slip into the pockets of your plaid pajamas bottoms. A guy's gotta eat.

Back in the room, you strip down to the suit the man upstairs gave you, and you fill the jacuzzi tub with water—not so hot to be scalding, but warm enough for a long soak—and you lower yourself in, and your butt cheeks form a hard dock against the bottom of the tub, and the water rises to your chin, and you turn on the jets and you go. The motor hums in the middle of your consciousness, so you never fully lose touch with where you are and what you're doing, and yet it's still the closest thing to pure relaxation you've felt in a good long time. You wouldn't even care to hazard a guess at the last time anything came close.

Which is just one of the reasons it strikes you as odd that you think of Johnny Appleseed. Now? Here? Why?

It's a flashpoint of memory, a sliver unbound to any larger moment you can recall, and you think of your mother telling you the popular version of the story—one reinforced in film and cartoon and song—about a man who blithely flits about the countryside, randomly planting apple trees while little birdies alight on his shoulder and sing along with him. It delighted you, this story, as it was intended to do. It was only later, when you were beset by the twin devils of cynicism and access to information, that the fuller story eclipsed some of the legend. John Chapman planted protected orchards, not random trees, and he planted dogfennel, too, for which he is cursed to this day, 175 years after he took leave of this life. He was a kind man, yes, but also a complicated one in his way, and nobody wants to talk about human complexities when the subject is hero worship. He died alone, unmarried, and maintained that his soul mate would be waiting for him in heaven if not here on earth, and good luck with that, buddy.

You miss your mother. It happens sometimes, almost never with a warning signal of incoming grief. It's almost always some impressionistic trigger, some moment of something mundane that leads to something else that leads to a memory, and away you go.

Her absence doesn't ache inside you, the way your father's does. You were his boy, right from the start, and nothing blunted that even though it's your mother's love of reading and her sharp tongue and her sharper wit that imprinted themselves on you. In all your years with Janine, she never once accused you of being too much like your father—you guess she would have loved to say that about you, that you took after Gustav. But Belle? Oh, boy, did Janine see the parallels, even if you never did. Maybe she was right. Maybe consider the possibility.

You get out of the tub, towel off, comb your hair, put on your day's clothes.

You eat your apple.

You lie down and go back to sleep.

Later, you wake up, and you peel off your pants and you entertain yourself. It's good to be back in the game.

And you sleep again.

Day 3 | April 10: Your day starts at night, during the in-between hours, with a phone call from Alicia at 3:17 a.m.—you looked at the time upon the ringing—and a panicked voice on the other end.

"Alicia?"

"Max, we've lost the tool."

"What?"

"Me and Tommy, we've lost the tool."

"Call Bonk."

"I can't get him on the phone."

"Dex?"

"I thought it was better to call you first."

"OK."

"We've lost the tool. We're so screwed."

"You're not screwed. Settle down."

"I need help. Tommy's...shit, he's gone to pieces."

"Simmer down. Just breathe. You have to settle down."

You hear concentrated breathing. "OK," she says.

"Where was the last no-doubt-about-it pass?"

"Milepost 97.5533."

"Write that down."

"OK."

"Now write down the time and the speed at that point."

"OK."

"Where are you sitting now?"

"Milepost 103.2626."

"Write that down."

"OK."

"Where is Tommy?"

"Milepost 105.8255."

"Write that down."

"OK. I think the damn thing has gotten beyond us."

"Alicia," you say, "listen now, OK? I don't care what you think. Let's work this problem, and then you'll know."

"OK."

"What you think is no good. We need data, not conjecture."

"OK."

"Now," you ask, "what do you do first?"

"You're not going to tell me?"

"I am not."

"Shit."

"Concentrate."

"OK. Shit. I guess I better make sure the line is still moving. Call Calgary?"

"Correct. And if it is, what rate are they showing at the control center. Ask them that."

"OK."

"I'll wait for you to call me back."

"Tommy wants to know if he should move up."

"No. Tell him to stay put. Neither of you moves again till you know where you're going."

"OK, I'll call back in a second."

You wait. You resist the urge to get out your own computer, fire it up, pull the maps and data from the last time you did that run—last October, right?—and start zeroing in on the answer. She can find it. You just have to give her the space to noodle it out.

The wait seems interminable, but it's really not. She calls back and reports what you wanted to hear: "Still moving. Same rate."

"It's just a math problem now," you say. "Time, speed, distance."

"OK."

"Work the problem."

You listen as she murmurs the figures she's dropping into the spreadsheet calculator you gave her that first day in Buffalo, the one you built in your own office while Janine entertained her realty staff downstairs and outside at the swimming pool. It's a plug-and-play tool. If you know the numbers, the spreadsheet delivers actionable data.

"Holy crap," she says. "It should be about an eighth of a mile from Tommy. It'll be there in just a few minutes."

"Call him and let him know."

"OK."

"Then call me back. If you get a measurable pass there, you're golden."

She blinks out. Maybe half a minute later, she blinks back in.

"Why didn't Bonk pick up when I called?" she asks you.

"He sometimes turns his phone off. Or just sleeps too deeply. It happens."

"I really needed him."

"It's OK."

"Sorry I woke you."

"It's OK."

"We weren't getting hits, couldn't hear it, nothing. I freaked out, I guess."

"Some deep sites where you are right now," you say. "Is the wind blowing?"

"Something fierce."

"There you go. Audio is useless, too, when that's the case."

A happy lilt in her voice. "Tommy got the pass!"

"There you go."

"Oh, Max, you're a lifesaver."

"You figured it out, not me. How many sites did you miss?"

"Four."

"Be sure to put it in the field notes."

"OK. We in trouble?"

"Not even a little bit."

"Thank god."

"It's a big lesson. We all learn it. You'll know what to do next time, right?"

"Yes. God, my heart's still beating hard."

"It'll pass. Get to work."

"Thanks again."

"Good night."

20900 OAKWOOD BOULEVARD AT VILLAGE ROAD, DEARBORN, MICHIGAN

Wednesday, April 10 | 11:17 a.m.
11.2 miles from the hotel

The Henry Ford Museum of American Innovation, where Max went after awaking and finding himself with a yen for history, was everything he hoped it would be. He had to hand it to the great industrialist: He dreamed big. He spoke big. He said things like, "I am collecting the history of our people as written into things their hands made and used....When we are through, we shall have reproduced American life as lived, and that, I think, is the best way of preserving at least a part of our history and tradition." That's not a guy whose aspiration was to convert a 7-10 split during a league match and show those putzes from McConnell Roofing who's got game.

The sheer breadth of the museum offerings boggled Max. The limousine Kennedy was riding in when Oswald took him down. (Max was not the conspiracy type, and he had learned the hard way to take his beer to the other end of the bar when someone, usually a generation older, wanted to bang on about Jack Ruby and the Cubans and everybody else who was in on it.) There had also been an Oscar Mayer Wienermobile and George Washington's camp bed and the Rosa Parks bus and Thomas Edison's purported last breath (seriously, in a sealed tube!). And so much more he wasn't sure he had the time or the energy to get to.

Max walked from agriculture to airplanes, wondering if a natural progression through the exhibits was going to eventually lead him to antisemitism and a frank accounting of Mr. Ford's brutal views there. He rather doubted it. Ford was a complicated man, to say the absolute least, someone who hired blacks and handicapped workers long before anyone else. Yet he was also a profoundly horrible man, one wholly susceptible to the loathsome anti-Jewish tropes of the time, and of time ongoing. How can the man who said "A business that makes nothing but money is a poor kind of business" also be the man who wrote "If fans wish to know the trouble with American baseball they have it in three words—too much Jew"? Max didn't think them the kinds of thoughts that come together often in a single, sentient body. *We must truly contain multitudes.* But is that really an excuse? That Ford was a man of complexity? Max didn't think it was. *It shouldn't be, anyway.*

Max was walking, and that's when the phone rang, Mellencamp again.

"What's up, Dex?"

"Holy shit, man."

That's all Dex got out before a docent sidled up. "Please step outside with the call, sir."

Max rerouted to the parking lot, finding his rented Toyota among the rabble, and he called Dex back to find out what's going on—*Marvin Gaye! The Motown Museum! A must next trip!*—and the day took a hard veer to the left.

Holy shit, man.

What Dex described in the renewed phone call was, by turns, so spectacular and so strange and so the stuff of a cheap pulp novel and so predictable and yet also so surprising that Max simultaneously wondered how it had taken this long to occur and why he'd had the rotten luck to miss it.

"So Bonk's wife—"

"Melissa," Dex said.

"—she showed up—"

"In Escanaba, man. Escanaba! She let him get on a plane, fly to Minneapolis, drive to Iron River, have a night there, get the job started, and then she fucking flew by herself, drove by herself, and caught him in the act."

"In Escanaba," Max said.

"In a hotel. With another woman. Dead to rights."

"Holy shit, man."

"Did I not just say that?"

Max wondered if the stance he had taken with Little Bonk from the start—*his business is his business, and I've got nothing to say about it*—had ended up serving the young man poorly. Hard to say. Maybe he should have advised the kid from a perch of hard-won wisdom, or made some sort of overture to Big Bonk to do it. It wasn't Max's responsibility, not in the least, and yet when you've known a kid since he was in diapers, you want to think you're more than tangentially interested.

Had Max ever considered infidelity? Sure, in the abstract. *Show me a man who says he hasn't, and I'll show you a liar.* But he had made it through his years with Janine without experiencing a legitimate opportunity or, more important, the sufficient motivation to undertake the considerable effort of concealing such a deed. Little Bonk probably hadn't granted much thought to the latter, and the problem with any guy who so flagrantly exists in the fullness of his libido is that it's hard to cinch up all the lies and loose ends that come with the scams. Max didn't know how Melissa came to the knowledge that compelled her to haul herself to Michigan to dispense justice, but he didn't imagine it was too difficult to unearth once she decided she ought to start sniffing around.

That was the no-mercy assessment. And then Max imagined the humiliation, the anger, the crushing surprise of the gotcha moment, and he also felt bad for Little Bonk. That is a hell of a way to get your comeuppance.

"How did you find out?" Max asked.

"Big Bonk called me, gave me a heads-up that my crew is running around out there without a field supervisor. Which is fine. They're halfway through the run. I can guide them from here."

"Jesus. What did he say?"

"Well, you know Bonk. Chicken-fried wisdom." Dex effected Big Bonk's slow drawl. "'Well, my boy's done hung his pants on the last bedpost that ain't his own, if you catch my drift. If he's gonna save his family—as I've told him he damn well ought to do—he's gonna be workin' someplace where he comes home every night.'"

"So Little Bonk is out. For good?"

"Looks like it. Even if he wasn't, he probably was, you know?" Dex said. "I mean, come on. She went up there and plucked him right out of a job, put his ass on a plane, and flew him home. So now he's stranded four trackers up in Michigan on account of his own peccadilloes. How could I trust him again?"

"Holy shit, man."

"As we keep saying."

"So you need a new field supervisor."

"Nope," Dex said. "Got one. You."

Dex didn't even have the words out before Max knew what was coming. They had gone this route before. If Max had raised his hand when Big Bonk retired, he could have aced Dex out of the office job. He certainly could have been the field supervisor. He said now what he had said to both possibilities before: "No."

"Max, I need you, man. We have this two-week break, then four jobs in five weeks. I can't run the crew in the field and be on the road drumming up business. Can't be done. If you don't want it, fine, I've never understood it, but I don't question it, either. But I at least need you to handle it until I can hire somebody."

"That shouldn't take long."

"I hope not. Maybe Kornbrock. You heard anything? Is he still unhappy at Qwest?"

"No," Max said. "You don't need that guy."

"Good tracker."

"Yes," Max said. "He is that. If you really want him, hire to do that job."

"I've got four trackers. I'm all set there."

"You have three."

"Max, listen, I know this heart attack thing has probably got you—"

"Alicia. Hire Alicia for Bonk's job. Then hire Kornbrock for hers."

Max thought he could hear the whiparound over the phone. "Have you taken leave of your senses?" Dex finally kicked out. "She's on, like, her fourth run. What am I going to tell Tommy and Steve if I do that? They'll be pissed."

Frankly, Max didn't give a good goddamn what Dex might say to those guys. Good trackers, nothing special, kind of inattentively scattered sometimes, the kind of guys easily replaced if they decided they would rather unload trucks on the graveyard shift at Walmart back home. But Alicia...

Max flipped the phone to speaker mode and brought up his email. A few click-throughs and he had the most recent four-hour update she had filed from the run. The embedded spreadsheet was perfect, the data entry pristine, the targets for the coming pumping stations dead-on.

"Has she made a single mistake on her shift lead this week?" Max asked.

"She missed four sites last night."

"Oh, really?"

"Well, no," Dex said. "She didn't miss them, per se. You know those deep sites in the national forest? About ninety-some miles in? We've been hit-or-miss there forever. But they didn't get passes."

"Did she explain all that in her field notes?"

"She did."

"Enough to pass muster with Mantooth?" Max asked.

"Yes, absolutely."

"And that's her first time doing it?"

"Yes."

"How do her updates look?"

"Perfect."

"Do Macartney's still look like they were done on an Etch-a-Sketch?" Dex chortled. "Yeah."

"She's the smartest person on this crew, and it's not even close," Max said. "You've got two weeks to go over everything she needs to know before we're down in Pontiac. Anything that's new or unexpected, she'll experience it and she'll learn from it. And I'll be there in case something flares up, which it probably won't."

"Maybe." Dex said it softly, in that giveaway tone that told Max his mental wheels were already grinding away. Max decided to bag the rest of his speech. He had a humdinger lined up, much more to say on the topic, but Dex's fine sense of perception would take him there without a shove. It was better to play it out that way.

"All right, Dex. I'm out," Max said. "Big days ahead."

"Where are you?"

"Detroit. Thinking I might head down to Chicago for a bit. Always wanted to see Oak Park, go to the Hemingway House and the Frank Lloyd Wright House. Then I can ease over to Pontiac when the job comes up."

"Rambling man."

"Something like that," Max said.

"All right. Talk soon. Thanks for the notion. I'm going to give this some thought."

"Thanks for taking it."

"And Max?" Dex said. "Keep your pants on."

"You're telling the wrong guy, aren't you?"

719 WYOMING AVENUE, BILLINGS, MONTANA

March 15, 2001

"Maxie, is she gone?"

Yes, Mama. She's gone for the day. I'm here now.

"Good. I don't like her."

She's good to you. She takes good care, like we told her to.

"She steals."

No, Mama, she doesn't. You're imagining that.

"I am not."

OK. I'll look around and make sure.

"I'm so tired, all the time."

I know you are.

"When will I not be tired?"

I don't know, Mama. Soon, I hope.

"I hope so, too."

Do you need something to eat?

"No. She fed me."

Good.

"Grilled cheese. She burned it."

That's not like her.

"I didn't like it."

Well, if you want something else, just tell me.

"Where is Janine?"

She's busy in the afternoons. That's why we got the nurse. She'll come to see you in the morning.

"I miss her."

She misses you, too.

"Where is Alexandra?"

She's at home.

"She never comes."

She's fourteen, Mama. She just forgets sometimes.

"I miss her, too."

I'll bring her tomorrow. Promise.

"I miss everybody."

I know you do.

"I will see your father soon. I miss him."

He'll be waiting. Maybe he'll have a game of chess ready to go.

"Unless he found someone else. Sarah Blackburn, she's up there, you know. Maybe he's playing chess with her."

Pop never liked Sarah Blackburn.

"Yes, he did. He told me once."

That doesn't sound like something he'd say.

"He said, 'That Sarah Blackburn really fills out a swimsuit.'"

That wasn't Pop talking out of school. That was just a fact.

"Oh, shush. You don't know."

I have eyes, Mama.

"Well, you shouldn't have been putting them on her."

Mama, I can't teach you a biology lesson right now, OK?

"Oh, shush."

Just relax, Mama, and try to get some sleep.

"Maxie, why aren't you at work?"

We've talked about this.

"I remember now."

I'm not working for a while.

"I remember."

I'm spending some time with you.

"You're a good boy."

I try.

"Are you going back to that job?"

Eventually. But you don't need to worry about that.

"I thought you were going to be a writer. You were so good."

I like money, Mama.

"You could have made money writing."

Maybe.

"You won that school essay contest when you were just nine years old. Do you remember that?"

I remember.

"Best in the whole school."

There were a lot of dumb kids in that school, Mama.

"I just want you to do something that matters."

I am.

"Oil. Yuck."

No, Mama, it's oil safety. It's important work.

"Maybe."

Anyway, I like it.

"You liked writing."

I did, but I saw not much future in it.

"You should have been a writer, Maxie."

Have I done so bad? I have a wife, a house, a beautiful daughter. I have you. Life is good.

"Done so poorly, you mean."

Have I done so poorly?

"Those are good things. You won't have me long, though. I'm leaving soon."

I know. But I still have you. I always will.

"OK, Maxie."

What brought this on?

"I just think sometimes. That's about all I can do now, is think."

I understand.

"I loved my work. I wish I could go write 'Mrs. Wendt' across the blackboard one more time. Do you love your work?"

Sure.

"And here I am, keeping you from it."

You're not.

"I'm sorry."

I'm right where I want to be.

"You're a good son, Maxie."

I try.

"I'm going to go to sleep now."

Good. I'll be right here if you need me.

"Thank you."

Sleep well, Mama.

HOLIDAY INN EXPRESS, SCHERERVILLE, INDIANA

Friday, April 12
Eleven days from the anticipated job mobilization

Max tried it with Chicago that first day and got himself a room at the Viceroy with an expansive view of all those downtown buildings scratching at the spring-blue sky. He had his head filled with delusions of a Windy City romp through Wrigleyville and Navy Pier, the Gold Coast and the Magnificent Mile. And after one night and $369—not to mention the gratuities that he spread around like the scraps of bread he and Alexandra used to throw at the duck pond back in Billings—he'd had enough. It wasn't precisely the money; he could play rich for a while with the jackpot Janine had dropped on him before he had to give due consideration to such mundane matters as housing and a place to rest his bank accounts. It wasn't even the choking traffic or the teeming people or the feeling that he had invaded a place where he didn't belong with his Carhartt jeans amid so much fine silk.

It was, at last, just a greater comfortability with the humdrum of chain hotels and franchise restaurants and suburban neighborhoods with unoriginal names (Briarwood! Nob Hill! Whatever!) and a cineplex showing twelve superhero movies and one animated kids' flick.

After a night of sleeping little and pacing much in his two-room suite, with the option of watching TV from a bed with fifteen pillows or from a sectional couch, Max checked out of the Viceroy, gave minor offense to the bell captain by toting his own bags through the lobby, and fetched his rental car curbside. Forty-six minutes later, having traveled on a route straight south and then east, moving with relative ease against the inflow of Chicagoland commuters, he arrived at a place where they recognized him on sight, where they had a room he could take right then—"Lucky you," said Denise, his favorite desk clerk in Schererville. "We had one we didn't need last night."—and where they said, *oh, hey, Max, there's still some fresh fruit left over from breakfast if you want some.*

That suited Max just fine, thank you. He pocketed an orange, then slipped upstairs to chase sleep he couldn't catch at three times the price.

Midafternoon, the ping of Max's phone brought him back to the surface.

Dad, just sent you an email. <3

Max, left bleary from the interruption, found the digital clock and tried to do the calculation. *Two-nineteen here so, what, nine-nineteen there? And yet it's the same sun that rises over both of us. What a world.*

Not for the first time, he wondered what kind of trade it was to be ceaselessly in touch and whether anybody now would trade back, giving up modern convenience for old-style solitude. It used to not bother anybody to wait for a handwritten letter or for a phone call—or, in the case of long distance, to wait till after eight p.m. or the weekend so the cost wouldn't be a burden. Now, we have so many ways to reach each other, so many ways to pierce someone else's bubble with nary a care for what the cost on the other end might be, that we willingly use one means of communication to call attention to another.

When it came to Alexandra, of course, the trade was worth

everything to Max. For Janine, especially as the sands ran out on them even as Max was unaware until the very end, it was less so. For everyone else, even those at work when the situation wasn't dire, Max would have preferred to hang out a sign that read Do Not Disturb, something even the Holiday Inn offered. But, no. He was always around, always available.

Until I wasn't, almost.

He brought up the email on his phone.

> Dad –
>
> *Two days here, and we know some things.*
>
> *1. We're probably not coming back, not as full-time U.S. residents, anyway. We had a long time to talk on the plane, and that conversation has continued here, and we just don't see it anymore—the working and grinding and exhausting ourselves. We had The Plan, and it changed. That's life. But there were elements of it that can still be enacted. We're going to try and then see what happens. Mom's going to help us liquidate. You sure you don't want that house?*
>
> *2. Europe is played out. Maybe Portugal; I don't know. Citizenship, if that's what we decide we want, is easier there than other places. But, as lovely as Europe has been and will be, we're now thinking Indonesia, Thailand, maybe even Costa Rica. What we've built up can go a long way in those places. We'll see. For now, we're just going to be wanderers. Kind of like you, but with a better view and a more exotic drink menu. (Gosh, I hope that doesn't hurt your feelings. I was trying to be funny.)*
>
> *I know this must sound like a sacrilege to the Work Ethic King, but it's what feels right for now. If it's not right later, we can change course. Tyler was talking about his father and how he believed in replanting himself every few years—a new job, a new church, a new hobby, something that broke him away from what*

> *he was doing and expanded his world. That makes a lot*
> *of sense to us.*
>   *I've attached some photos. Enjoy!*

Max thumbed through the pictures, enchanted. Sweating cocktail glasses on a table, the city lights colorfully out of focus in the backdrop. Selfies with Tyler. Alexandra in a beret, seaside, the ocean view something he had seen just once in his life, when he peeled away during his off-hours on a pipeline run through L.A. and stood in the surf at Santa Monica. But this backdrop was something else, Old World and comparatively ancient. Some pictures he felt as though he could step into. Others beat him back with their unflagging beauty.

And sacrilege? Not by a long shot. In all her years, Alexandra had occasionally given him openings to step in with guidance or instruction—not many, though, and he suspected that Janine's own efforts in such things far exceeded his—but his daughter had been unerring when it came to what she wanted. Why would now be any different?

His phone pinged again.

You get the email?

Looking now. Beautiful place.

It doesn't suck.

LOL

What do you think?

What makes you happy makes me happy.

Thanks, Dad.

Will be weird not to see you in Billings. Assuming I go back.

You have to go back. Your stuff is there.

True.

I'll go back sometimes. Mom is there, even if you're not.

Also true.

Will you come and see me?

Absolutely. You tell me when and where.

I will. As soon as we find a place, I will. Where are you?

Outside Chicago. Back to work in a few days. Just hanging out.

You ready for that?

Ready as I'll ever be.
Good. You doing anything fun?
Maybe.
Don't be coy.
I'm not. But can I ask you something?
Sure. Anything.
What would you think if I called that nurse?
Nurse Bright Eyes?
Yeah.
What are you going to call her?
LOL
I mean, what do you have in mind? I wouldn't go swinging on a rope into her work area like the Scarlet Love Pumpernickel or whatever.
LOL. Nothing like that.
What?
I was thinking I'd send her a box of fruit.
Fruit?
You know. Thoughtful, but not as forward as flowers.
Flowers are pretty nice, though.
So is fruit. And fruit is healthy.
Yes. Yes, it is.
I know a fruit grower right there in Midland, Michigan.
Of course you do.
So what do you think?
I don't know. She sure liked you. Give it a go. Just make sure you're not overly interested. There's a fine line between interesting and creepy.
This is the genius of the fruit idea. I think fruit says, "Hey, you're nice. Maybe next time I'm in Chelsea, we can have a meal or something."
It says all that, does it?
The fruit speaks many languages. You just have to listen.
LOL
So?
Sure. Go for it.
I just might.
Love you.
I love you, too.

CHERRYWOOD LANE, SCHERERVILLE, INDIANA

Saturday, April 13 | 1:36 p.m.
Ten days from the anticipated job mobilization

Max funneled his gaze down the asphalt—nary a cherrywood in sight, nor much in the way of any other kind of tree—and he imagined how it would go. A nice straightaway here, two blocks at least, more than he would need. He had come out of the Holiday Inn in the best get-up he could put together on impulse—another ratty Mantooth Energy T-shirt, a pair of paint-splattered sweats, his feet stuffed into thermal socks, those stuffed into the Velcro-fastening sneakers he always brought along for ease of on and off. The walk down to the intersection and the left turn and then, eventually, the right turn into suburbia had been the warmup. He breathed in and out, short blasts followed by deep intakes, anticipating the main event.

And he was off.

He counted the steps, nine to cross five squares of inlaid concrete, then he lurched himself forward, not a run—he wasn't sure, at this stage, he even knew how—so much as a strange sort of hyper-walk, a sliding, bum-stumbling, erratic, bizarro-interpretative dance down the sidewalk. He counted the squares along with his blown-out breath, and when he reached ten, he tamed himself into a walk again. Five squares farther along, he tried again, and this time the muscle memory of decades past kicked in just a smidge, and his arms found an oily smooth synchronicity with his legs, which still bowed out too far for his liking. Something to work on.

He repeated the alternations, down one side of Cherrywood Lane until it ran headlong into Rosewood Lane, then crossing over and coming back on the other side. Each time he transitioned to what could only charitably be called a jog, he found a little more of his unearthed teenage form.

Max deemed one circuit enough, to start, and he stood in front of a set of perfectly identical twin homes and he pushed his hips forward, trying to moderate the ache, and he tried to catch his wind and he wondered what had gotten into him. The more pressing thought, though, was the one that surprised him most: *I bet I can do better next time.*

Across the street, a young fellow—maybe Alexandra's age, maybe a bit younger—emerged from one of the houses in the full regalia: cross-trainer shoes, compression pants, safety-grade moisture-wicking shirt, biorhythm monitor strapped to his upper arm. One hand held a leash, and a youthful black Lab strained at the end of it, eager to go. The guy took the street at a full gallop, his dog clearing the way ahead, and he waved to Max as he went by at speed. Max watched them until they made the turn at Rosewood and disappeared into the thicket of houses.

After catching his breath, Max wandered down between the housing rows to the promised lake of Lakewood Estates. He shouldn't have been surprised. By any lake standard he would care to use, it was nothing more than pond, and a manmade one at that. Indiana being one of those largely empty, northern-tier drive-through or fly-over states, largely without the benefits of natural landscape grandeur, it had to oversell its charms.

Modest as it was, the lake had overseers. A few came out onto their tidy patios and gawked at him as he sauntered along the bank. On the far side, he came across the sign, FOR RESIDENTS ONLY, which explained matters.

Max was looking for his out when the ringing of his phone—Men at Work's "Who Can It Be Now?" for unknown callers—bailed him out of neighborhood disdain. He put his head down and got out of there.

"Wendt."

"This is Mr. Max Wendt?"

"You've got him. Who's this?"

"Hello, Mr. Wendt. My name is Remington Danforth."

Max, now back on Cherrywood Lane, came to a dead stop. "Remmy."

"Yes."

"Is Chuck OK?"

"Chuck?"

"Your dad."

"Oh, yes. Yes. I mean, yes, Dad is OK."

"You gave me a start."

"I'm sorry."

In reverse, Max followed the route in, back to the street fronting the subdivision, the rising tower of the Holiday Inn Express to the southwest a beacon for his impending arrival.

"It's OK. What can I do for you?"

"Are you all right, Mr. Wendt? You're breathing heavily."

"Went on a run."

"Ah."

"What can I do for you?" Max asked again.

"Yes, sorry. My father turns seventy next week, and given such a round-number kind of a birthday, we've taken it upon ourselves to throw him a surprise party next weekend."

"He'll be positively glittery with glee."

"I should think so. And, well, it's like this, Mr. Wendt: You are a good friend to him. He speaks of you often and fondly. And though it might be a longshot, I—"

"I'd love to. There in Maine?"

"Oh, that's wonderful! Yes, here at the house in Biddeford. My mother is going to take him out for lunch, and while they're gone, we'll gather everyone and give him a great surprise."

"I've always wanted to see Maine."

"Now is your chance. Can I get you accommodations? I'm happy to cover the cost."

"No, not necessary. It'll be my pleasure."

"I'm sorry for the short notice," Remmy said. "It's a surprise party, and, well, the thing is, once the list of guests expands, the whole idea of its being a surprise starts to have a limited shelf life."

"I get it. Wouldn't miss the soiree."

"Wonderful! I must confess, I snooped through Dad's email to get your number. I hope I didn't violate anything solemn. It was important to find you."

"It's OK. I'm glad you called."

"Excellent," Remmy said. "I have your email address here. I'll send you the details, if that's OK."

"Looking forward." Max entered the hotel now and tossed a nod to Denise on his way to the elevator.

"Splendid. Thank you ever so much, Mr. Wendt."

"Hey, wait a minute," Max said.

"Yes?"

"Did your pop ever tell you why you were named after a bolt-action rifle?"

"What an odd question."

Max now wished he could have it back. "Sorry. I'm an odd guy."

"No, it amuses me," Remmy said. "He did not because I was not."

"No?"

"No, sir. I believe I was named for a middling '80s TV show starring Pierce Brosnan. Mom and Dad loved that show." He waited for the laugh Max was all too happy to supply. "Not a very good story, is it?"

Max let himself into the room and plopped assward onto the bed. "I remember that show," he said. "Congratulations or condolences, kid. Whichever applies."

"You're funny, Mr. Wendt. I can mitigate the worst of it by sticking with Remmy."

"I feel like kind of an ass."

"Nonsense. I look forward to meeting you."

Max fired up his laptop and waited for the email. Remmy didn't tarry. As the details populated, Max brought up a browser window and started building an itinerary. The rental car would have to go to Chicago Midway, where he would pay a hefty fee for not returning it to Detroit. The way it goes. Then, he would catch a flight east. Rent a car on the ground in Portland, then drive about twenty miles south to Biddeford. A Holiday Inn Express there, which stood ready to shorten his stack of IHG points. A few clicks and all was booked, the flight, the rental car, and the hotel—two nights, because he was going to see Saco Bay for himself, and much more than that if time allowed. Points paid for everything, including the flight back to Midway and Chicago, where he could wait out the job.

Max thought he had been hoarding those rewards of the road for a reason, but over time, he had forgotten what the reason might be. Every time he didn't burn off all his vacation hours before the year was out, didn't take a day trip, didn't suggest a week in Napa to Janine—*and, let's be fair, she might not have gone anyway after a time, absorbed as she was in her own doings*—he wondered if he was just carrying around digital fool's gold in his wallet. Who knew it was all waiting for this moment and this version of the man, this newly divorced, heart-compromised good man—not a perfect man, not even close, but one who was trying to stay on the positive side of the ledger.

And who's a perfect man, anyway? There is not a one.

To: Wendt, Max; Smithlin, Thomas; Macartney, Stephen; Kornbrock, Eric
From: Hammond, Alicia
Subject: Cleaner tool run, Vandalia line, Pontiac, Ill. 4/23/19

Hi, everybody:

We've had the pre-job meeting with Mantooth Energy and are cleared for the above run. Please mobilize into Pontiac on Tuesday, April 23rd, in preparation for a cleaner run scheduled to begin the morning of Wednesday, April 24th.

For most of you—Steve aside, who'll be driving from home in Missouri—the best bet is to fly into St. Louis, receive your rental car and drive up to Pontiac. We'll track two cleaners through the line to the terminal station in Vandalia, Ill. It's a 168.2-mile run that we'll be doing at 4.1 mph, so figure on 41 hours, barring shutdowns or unexpected events. For now, book a one-way flight. As we get closer to trapping the tool, I'll let you know when you can book flights home.

Info sheet, map, contact list and tracking sites are attached. We'll talk more at our own pre-job in Pontiac.

Let's plan on staying at the Super 8 in Pontiac, and once everybody arrives on the 23rd, we'll meet downstairs in the breakfast bar. I'll bring some goodies, because we have much to celebrate: Max Wendt is coming back to work, and we have a new tracker on the team. Eric Kornbrock is joining us from Qwest. You guys all know each other, right? This is going to be good.

As you all know, this is the start of a four-runs-in-five-weeks stretch, and we're looking to be busy straight through the summer. Let's all show up with all our equipment and ready to go.

If you would, please acknowledge receipt of this email, then give me a heads-up via text when you're on your way on the 23rd.

Alicia

To: Hammond, Alicia
From: Wendt, Max
Subject: Re: Cleaner tool run, Vandalia line, Pontiac, Ill. 4/23/19

Got it. Just FYI, I'll be flying into and out of Chicago because that's where I've been hanging out. But I'll definitely be there on the 23rd.

Meet the new boss, much different from the old boss. You're going to be great at this. I mean it.

To: Wendt, Max
From: Hammond, Alicia
Subject: Re: Re: Cleaner tool run, Vandalia line, Pontiac, Ill. 4/23/19

Aw, thanks, Max. You feeling OK? Looking forward to seeing you.

I can't believe how quickly this all came about. Grateful. Sorry for Little Bonk. Eager to see what happens next.

P.S. I hear you did a good deed.

To: Hammond, Alicia
From: Wendt, Max
Subject: Re: Re: Re: Cleaner tool run, Vandalia line, Pontiac, Ill. 4/23/19

I'm not sure what you're talking about. (Did it do any good?)

To: Wendt, Max
From: Hammond, Alicia
Subject: Re: Re: Re: Re: Cleaner tool run, Vandalia line, Pontiac, Ill. 4/23/19

One weekend a month, for starters. Maybe more. We'll see.

The last note prompted him to make a phone call that had been put off long enough.

"Hi, Max."

"You busy?"

"Not at all. What's up?"

Max tugged at the shirt collar he'd been chewing in his nervousness and felt the clammy cold of it snap back against the skin of his neck.

"I'd like to chat about Oklahoma, if you're willing."

"You sure?"

"Yeah. Feels like we need to."

"OK."

"OK." Max cleared his throat. He had a good idea of what he wanted to say but an abiding fear of the barriers that might spring up between him and the actual expulsion of the words. "I messed up by just shutting you down and not saying anything, and you had every right to be hurt or angry or whatever it was—"

"I was hurt and angry," she said. "Was. I'm not now."

"I'm glad of that. And I understand. I do."

"I'm sorry. I interrupted you."

"Anyway," he said, off again lest he lose his nerve, "you were vulnerable with me, and I think maybe I thought I could protect you from something while also...I don't know..."

"I wasn't asking for protection."

"I know you weren't. I put that on you. Plus, I was damn lonely," he said. "And feeling damn useless. And I think I thought it could work for both of us, you know? You wouldn't have to be scared and I wouldn't have to be lonely and then—"

"And then the work circumstances intervened."

"Right."

"Bonk," she said.

"Jesus, yeah. Bonk, especially. But everything."

"I knew something was up when you got worried about him and the whole Pawnee thing."

"Yeah," he said. "My mind kind of took off on me. And I sort of—"

"Ghosted me."

"Yeah. Shit. I'm sorry."

"OK. I get it. I won't lie: I wish you'd said something at the time. It would have been easier than filling in the details with my imagination, you know? I thought I'd done something wrong, and I had no idea what it was, and you were just gone. It hurt. It really hurt."

"I'm so sorry for doing that."

"I know you are. I appreciate you for owning up."

"I just need to finish this, OK? Kind of had a whole speech planned." She laughed. "Go. Please."

"Spent some time this past week with my daughter. She's your age. You'd like her. She'd like you, I'm sure of it. She has some personal stuff kicking around that I can't protect her from, either. You get what I'm saying?"

"Sure."

"It kills me that I can't. But I'm learning, you know, that it's not my place. Had a great time with her, wished it wouldn't end, but it had to, because she's got to get back to her own thing."

"Yeah. We need our daddies. But it's easy to overstep, isn't it?"

"Damn sure is. You think you're understepping, though. That's the hard part."

"I get it. You know how many times my dad has wanted to punch Rexford's father in the face? One, it's comical to even picture it. Two, it would be no help at all. It's like, 'Sit down, Dad, and let me handle this.'"

"Yeah."

"I'm sorry. I interrupted again."

"You're fine," Max said. "Just one more thing. I think it's important."

"OK."

"What was good in Missouri and Kansas and Oklahoma wasn't going to keep being good, I don't think, if we'd gone on that way. That's not an excuse for how I made you feel. There is no excuse for that. And maybe if I'd talked to you instead of cutting out, we could have dealt with it, come to a decision together."

"Maybe," she said. "Or maybe I'd have gotten hurt in a different way. Or you'd have gotten hurt. Believe me, I've thought about that, for sure."

"I was scared," Max said. "Plain and simple. I should have let you into that so you had a say. I want you to know I'd be saying this now even if you hadn't saved my bacon. And thanks for that, again. I'm grateful."

"You're welcome, Max. Feel better now?"

"I do."

"So do I," she said. "Friends?"

"Well, to the extent that I can be friends with the new boss lady, yeah." He dribbled a chuckle behind it.

"I like the sound of that," Alicia said. "*Boss lady.*"

"You'll wear it well. And, yeah, we're friends. We can set that one in stone."

"I think you're very wise, Max."

"Well," he said, "I can't imagine you're going to get a lot of agreement on that, but I appreciate it."

BIDDEFORD, MAINE

Sunday, April 21
12:02 p.m. Eastern time

The seashore threw wide its sandy arms and beckoned Max into an embrace. He had been in southern Maine for twenty hours, and he had rigorously done what he could to avoid the water, wanting to see it the first time not at dusk after arduous travel but in the light of a day that hadn't yet been fully cast. The coast had validated his decision.

Max had eased east through the charming downtown and toward the sea, falling into the loose embroidery of narrow rural roads that led to clusters of houses close enough to be neighborly and spread out enough to suit the taciturn. As he would have done on any new job, he had taken the measure of the route from a zoomed-in satellite view and had noted the decreasing density and increasing estate size the nearer the water loomed.

At ground level, the view was so much more varied and vibrant than he had expected. Hills rose like hands to cradle the road. Once those were cleared and a wider panorama burst through, the Atlantic presented itself again. The eternal surf caught the light, with the seemingly calmer waters farther out rippling like a speckled blue bedsheet tossed and fluttered down to the mattress. Nearer, the inland tidal pools sparked orange glints of refracted light.

Max patted the box in the passenger seat. OAKHURST MILK, it read on the side panel. It was the best that the staff at the Holiday Inn Express could do for him. With a Sharpie, he had written CHARLES across the top of it. Not much of a presentation. Nothing to be done about that.

Ahead, the road terminated at Pool Street, and Max bore left, as instructed by memory and by the disembodied voice of his GPS program. The road made a gentle, faltering sweep for about a quarter-mile, and Max turned right on Granite Point Road and drove toward the sea again. When he got to the house, it was just as Remmy had described in his email: *Huge driveway. House, big windows, facing the water. You can't miss it. Drive on through to the dirt road beyond the house and park in the trees, if you would. You can walk back down and ring the bell. Looking forward to meeting you, Mr. Wendt.*

The instructions had been well followed. At least a dozen cars, all with Maine plates and all leaning hard toward luxury, had gathered in a clump. Max jammed his Hyundai with the Florida tags in there, a commoner's hedge against moneyed neighbors. Not a hundred paces back the way he had come was a house; he had seen it. But from here, he could gather no evidence of its existence. Even a small patch of Maine had swallowed him whole.

Max got out, shut the door, walked around to the passenger side, and retrieved his package. He closed the door and locked up. He sucked in a breath, the tailings of saltwater and pine filling his senses. He moved on.

At the front door, he set the package down, made a quick zipper check, sucked in his gut, checked once more, then gathered the box again. He could hear muffled laughter and conversation from the other side. He waited for a clear moment, and he engaged the bell.

When the door opened, Max found himself staring at Charles—

that is, the young man he could only presume was Remmy stood there like a younger facsimile of his father. Wind back the clock forty years, squeeze out the gray, thicken the hair atop his head, stretch back the wrinkles into nothingness, and it was the very man. His bearing and presentation—fine hands, collared shirt, pressed slacks, chinos—bespoke Exeter, or at least what Max thought Exeter might be given his middle-class bias against all things preppy.

"You must be Max Wendt."

"I must."

Remmy offered a handshake. Max met it.

"It's so nice to meet you," Remmy said. "Dad will be delighted." They regarded each other for a moment, as if reconciling what they saw with what they had heard about each other, and Max found himself at a disadvantage. He couldn't say he had expended much imagination on Remmy in his talks with Charles. Chas, yes, of course, you couldn't hear about Chas without imagining what he looked or sounded like. Remmy, for purposes of getting-to-know you, had been only a name. In the flesh, he became much more substantial than that.

"Oh," Remmy said now. "You brought a gift."

Remmy shepherded Max into the house, a well-appointed place that spoke to coastal living, family money, expensive schooling, and exquisite taste. "Everyone, this is Max Wendt, Dad's friend from Montana," Remmy said to the dozen and a half or so people gathered in the main room—the *great* room, as Max had seen such areas called in the blueprints for Alexandra's old neighborhood back home—and nods of acknowledgment and murmured hellos followed, and then they all returned to their gaggles, leaving Max to remain on the periphery. He wished now that he had stopped at the mall in Portland and bought a shirt befitting the occasion. His long-sleeve Carhartt wasn't getting it done with this crowd.

Max skirted along to a bookcase and made an inventory of things. Titles were arranged alphabetically by author, with hardcovers segregated from paperbacks (and there were damn few of the latter, more suited as they were to the hoi polloi of the reading world). Max was on to a second case before he found an author's name he recognized,

Updike, though he couldn't say he was familiar with the man's work. Not a Craig Johnson among them, not even *The Cold Dish*, for Max's money the best of the bunch. Maybe he would send one, a gift from his own preferred genre. Maybe he would just leave well enough alone. It would be a pity if Charles learned that Sheriff Longmire didn't wear turquoise boots.

Remmy came into the room again. "All right, everyone, they will be here in just a few minutes. Let's all quiet down and give him a big surprise."

Max followed the lead of the others, who found their way to the edges of the room and broke away from their larger groups into singles and doubles. Max wedged himself into a corner. The room went silent. Max breathed in and out, careful to maximize his intake and to release it slowly.

After a time, the front door opened and Charles' laughter came crashing down the hall, and the people waiting for him drew up into a more rigid silence and looked at each other in anticipation.

When Charles and Mary breached the room, the "surprise!" went up and Max found himself a quarter-beat behind in the yell. Charles— salmon long-sleeve shirt, blue trousers, deck sneakers—threw up his hands, delighted, and he did a half-pirouette toe-tap. "Oh, you did not!" he said, and his friends moved in on him, handshakes and hugs and kisses on the cheek. Max held back, out of the scrum, and as Charles' friends peeled off one by one, the birthday boy's casting eyes found him and he mouthed, "Oh, Max," and it wasn't until then, a singular moment that came and went in the same breath, that Max realized he was crying. Bawling, truthfully.

The party took place in the backyard natatorium, beside the heated swimming pool, with a hot bar and a bow-tied server cutting slices of roast and dishing up sides and salads, and a wet bar where the guests could have whatever libation they desired. Max sidled up and ordered a red wine.

"The cab, sir? Or would you prefer a pinot or the syrah?"

"Surprise me," Max said.

He took the glass and stuck to the pockets of emptiness among the gathered guests. He let himself out of the natatorium and into the backyard in full, and he angled toward a spindly tree at the back, one with new white blooms. He gathered an opening bud in his hand, and it was tender, almost like a piece of felt. He lifted it to his nose and drew in the scent of the coming life still in it.

"Plum tree. You should see it next month."

Max turned toward the voice he knew.

"Charles."

"Can I get that hug now, Max?"

Max embraced his friend, clutching tightly to hold back the resurfacing of the emotions he had finally beaten back. "It's so good to see you," Max said.

"And you."

They separated. "We had an apple tree when I was a kid," Max said now. "It produced good fruit every two years. That was nice. Always apple pie in the house during those seasons." He smiled and touched his belly. "In the off-years, it produced endless cleanup."

"This tree," Charles said, fingering a branch, "has been feeding the Danforths for a long, long time. As I said, next month it will be a wonder to behold."

"I'm sorry I won't be here to see that."

That drew a wan smile from Charles. "Nor will I," he said.

"What?" Max asked, and then realization was upon him, and then the bottom dropped out of him again, and then Charles was doing his impish twinkle and saying, "You didn't think I'd go without a party, did you?"

Max continued to reel. Little snippets of his interactions with Charles came to him, seemingly tossed-off lines that now held greater import. Charles, imploring him to stay on task and stop wasting time. Charles, talking about how the years run away. *Jesus, I thought he was just being philosophical.*

"So this wasn't a surprise party?" Max asked.

"*You*, my friend. You were the surprise. Remmy told me you couldn't come, the little scamp."

"Charles, I—" Max caught himself between the words. He began to brim again.

"It's all right, Max. It's fine. Everything is going to be fine. It's been a beautiful life."

"When did you find out, when did—"

"I've known for a while. Since before I met you. I'd hoped for longer, of course, and when that was no longer possible, some timetables got accelerated. The bucket is imminent, so I had to check off the list a bit more quickly than I'd hoped."

"Mary's wedding," Max said.

Charles nodded. "Yes. About that, I meant everything I said, of course, but I left some things out, too. I hope you understand."

What's not to understand? Mary's great new love had come even as her first love, or at least the man with whom she made common cause, was easing toward the exit. Max had thought Charles uncommonly graceful when, for all he knew, the man had substantial time in front of him. Now, he found Charles' attitude not of this world, and he began to break.

"I'm so sorry," he said.

"Don't be," Charles said. "I'm not. I've had a ball."

Later, everyone gathered in the main room, and Charles' longer-term friends piled into couches and chairs. Max, again, found space along the wall and watched as, armful by armful, Remmy and his mother brought the gifts out and set them on a glass table. Max's offering was conspicuous by its lack of formality.

Charles chose it first.

"I think I know whose this is," he said.

"You don't have to open that," Max called from the back of the room, drawing unwanted attention. His voice sounded outside his own body, as if it were not really his to use.

"Nonsense."

Charles worked a fingernail under the tape and pried up an edge. That done, it was just the simple matter of pulling it up and opening the box.

"Well," Charles said, hands on his hips, the item still in the box and out of sight to the others. "I simply don't know what to say. I'm not entirely sure what it is."

He reached in and drew the item out. Long, floppy, black felt arms dropped toward the floor. The hands, stuffed-animal fists, really, gripped rigid wires that hung loose.

"What is that?" someone asked.

"It's a hat," Max said.

"Oh!" Charles said, a chortle on his lips. "Oh, I see what it is now!"

He lifted the crown, from which the felt arms stretched out, and he set it on his head. The crown—a knit cap, really—was red and had a Chicago Bulls insignia stitched across the front. The arms dangled down Charles' cheeks, almost to the center of his chest. He grabbed the sturdy wires and manipulated the arms, making accusatory pointers of them and effecting a cartoonish voice as he directed them toward his guests.

"Well, what did you get me, Frank? And what about you, Julie? Don't hold out on me, Maurice." As Charles' gathered friends figured out what was going on, a rolling guffaw moved through the room.

"I found it in the Chicago airport," Max said. "Figured it would keep your cowboy hat company."

"I'm delighted, Max, thank you." Charles removed the hat, folded the arms and the wires underneath it, and set it aside. "You honor me."

With the gifts received and opened—it was generally accepted that Max's was the highlight of the bunch, if the reasons for it were a bit inscrutable to everyone but Charles—the party spread out. Charles had many admirers to see, many friends to embrace, and each time his social duties brought him near, he reached out and squeezed an elbow.

"He's quite fond of you," Mary said, when at last the conversational currents brought her and Max together.

"It's mutual."

Max was studying a collage of family photos in the hallway connecting the kitchen to the rest of the house. He pointed at one, a seaside shot of Charles and Mary and the boys from a more complete time. He could see the older Mary in the younger one, could see the fierceness of her love of the boys. With the benefit of inside knowledge, he could also see the distance between her and Charles—not animosity, but also not intimacy. She stood to Remmy's left, and Charles stood to

Chas' right. Charles touched the older boy who touched the younger boy who touched their mother, whose arms stretched across and took in both boys' shoulders. Only she and Charles were unbound.

"This is Chas?" he asked, his finger near the face of the taller boy.

"That is Chas, indeed. Nantucket. Nineteen ninety-two, I think."

"He has a nice face."

"He was a nice young man," she said. "Funny, in a sly way. He had an old soul, as they say."

Max marveled at her equanimity in speaking about him. He had noticed the same thing in Charles, the earnestness with which he discussed the son who had been ripped away from him. Max wondered how that worked, and how much they'd had to strive for whatever peace they had found with the loss.

A man who had been hanging back, obviously waiting for a chance to approach, came to them and slipped a hand across Mary's hips. With him, a few feet away, was another couple.

"Dear, these folks would like to meet Mr. Wendt," he said. "I would, too." He thrust a hand toward Max, who shook it. "Bob Gershon."

"Max Wendt. Pleasure."

"It was wonderful meeting you, Max," Mary said, and she and Bob made space for the others to move in. Max recognized them as Maurice and Julie from Charles' impromptu puppetry play.

"Mr. Wendt?" the man said.

"Max Wendt. Yes, sir."

Another handshake. "I'm Bub Hobus. This is my wife, Julie." Max also shook with her.

"Bub?"

"Well, Maurice. But nobody calls me that." He nodded toward the guest of honor, who stood a few feet away animatedly regaling someone with some fantastic tale. "Except Charles."

Max had to laugh. "Tell me about it. He calls me *Maxwell* sometimes. I didn't have the heart to tell him it's Maximilian. Good old Chuck."

That drew a flummoxed look. Max scrambled. "Nice to meet you."

Maurice—Bub—moved in a bit.

"Charles tells me you're a pipeline man," he said.

"I am."

"Julie and I own a pipeline system up in Bangor," Bub said. "You ever been up there?"

"No. Heard of it. Read some Stephen King."

"Ayuh," Bub said. "Nice place. Anyway, what we have is a one-way deal from down here in Portland to delivery up north, and then we truck it out to customers."

"So a gas line?" Max asked.

"Yes, that's right," Julie said.

"It's a family holding. It's legacy," Bub said now. "Inheritance dropped it on us, and we always figured we'd sell it when it came to that. But we're out of probate now, and—"

"My family," Julie said.

"I see."

"We want to keep it, but we need some help," Bub said. "Need somebody to manage it, keep us in compliance, that sort of thing. Run the operation, basically."

"I see."

"I'm an insurance man," Bub went on. "I'm a little out of my depth here. We both are, but we're dead set on doing this right."

Now Julie moved in. "Do you suppose we could talk for a few minutes?" she asked.

"Sure," Max said.

"Outside?" Bub asked.

"Of course. I think I could put you in touch with some people who can help you."

"Oh," Julie said.

"The thing is," Bub put in, "we'd like to talk to *you*. If you'd like to talk to us."

"Here?" Max said. "Now?"

"Just preliminaries," Bub said. "But, yeah. If you have a few minutes."

"Why me?"

Julie reached out, a glance against his cuff. "Charles thinks the world of you," she said. "And we think the world of what Charles thinks."

Max let them lead the way, into the natatorium again, out the door and into the backyard.

What is this world?

THE DANFORTH HOUSE

Sunday, April 21 | 3:27 p.m.
Seventeen hours and seven minutes before Max's flight

The party had staying power—no surprise when old and dear friends gather—but once Max came back inside, he felt that his own energy had been perilously subdivided, with much he still wanted to extract from the day.

When he sensed a clear shot at drawing Charles's attention, he took it, slipping in to say, "Chuck, much as I'd like to stay, I really should be going."

"So soon?"

"Just a little tuckered out. And I want to make it up to Portland for a look around before I go back."

"I understand. I'll walk you out."

On the porch, they stood in brief, silent appreciation of the afternoon's blessings. The sun was steadily winding toward its meeting with the western horizon, leaving the east and the ocean bathed in an amber half-light, and Max didn't think he had ever seen anything so magnificent.

"What's your pleasure, Max?"

"I'd like to see Saco Bay." At that, Max followed the line of Charles's arm, pointing toward the sea.

"It's right out there."

"I'll head down there for a closer look."

"That will be fine."

Max, not knowing where to take the words, went for a hug. Charles set a gentle hand against his chest, stopping him, then withdrew it.

"I should tell you that I'm not terribly fond of goodbyes," he said.

"I understand."

Max had wonderings. He had been stacking them up all afternoon, having to sit there and pretend he didn't know what he now knew about his friend. He'd reexamined every interaction, every word as he could best remember. The references to fleeting time loomed large in hindsight. Every cough and sniffle took on import in the backward glance. Did anyone else at the party know? Was Charles going to say anything more about it, like what it was or how long he might have? *He's talking about not being here next month, so are we talking days? Weeks? What is it? Is he in pain?* Max dared not let loose any of the questions on his tongue. It wasn't his business.

"What did you tell Maurice and Julie?" Charles asked.

"I told them I have a job waiting on me right now. Several, actually. They asked if maybe I'd come up and take a tour, talk about things more formally."

"What did you say?"

"Maybe."

Charles laughed, that boomer of a chortle that Max was going to have to try hard to remember once he could no longer hear it. "Oh, Max. Who knew you were so hard to get?"

"Heartbreaker, that's me." And then: "It's a real intriguing opportunity, my friend. I just need to spend some time with the idea and let it marinate."

"I understand," Charles said.

"Thanks for your faith in me."

"Thank you for justifying it."

Max could feel the breach coming again, as if everything he had buried deep was coming to the surface for an accounting. "No hugs?" he asked.

"Maybe just one," Charles said.

That was all the opening Max needed. When he finally let his friend go, Charles said, "But, please, not goodbye. It's better this way, isn't it? On some delightful day, you and I will be in the same place, in this world or in the next one, and we will pick it up at hello."

Max squeezed his lips together and nodded. Without another word passing between them, he stepped down from the porch, crossed the driveway, skirted the backyard fence, and let the woods take him in again.

THE ATLANTIC'S EDGE

Where every clock is ephemeral

Max sat in the chilled, wet sand and, for the first time, let go of time and speed and distance. Charles couldn't have known back on the carpeted floor of the Minneapolis airport that if he dropped something like Winslow Homer's *Saco Bay* out there, Max would hunt it down with web searches and by reading articles, no matter how obscure. Nothing special about the subject; the response would have been the same had Charles brought up space travel, the viciousness of certain dog breeds, or the peculiar mating habits of sage grouse. Mind fertilizer, all of it.

Max knew, for example, that Homer's inspiration wasn't where he sat but rather seventeen-some miles up the coast, on the southwestern side of his beloved Prouts Neck. He knew that the great painter had spent the better part of a decade on that particular piece, finishing but a few days before he had to ship it off for exhibition.

He further knew that all the Homer paintings he would care to see awaited him in Portland, at the Museum of Art, but only if he got a move on. *It's time to go, Max.*

He pushed himself up to a standing position. He brushed the clinging sand from the seat and the legs of his pants. He gave his attention once more to the water, now beset by smudges of purple and pink overhead, the markings of a final colorful passage into evening.

Men at Work and their paean to the unaware broke in on his parting solitude. He engaged the phone and held it against his ear.

"Max Wendt."

"Is that you, Bright Eyes?"

Max's body jerked into a concentrated rigidity. "Hello, Jenn."

"Hello, Max."

Max walked down from where he had been sitting to a spot nearer water. "I'm surprised—delighted—to hear from you."

"You sent me a box of apples."

"I did."

"You sent me a note that said you're not a creep."

"Well, I'm not."

"The note was an interesting choice. The apples were, too."

"Interesting bad or—"

God, I'm like a kid again. Like me or like me not? Wait, don't answer that. Give me time to grow on you.

"I'm on your phone, aren't I?"

Max drew up a hand to cover the wayward grin that had cracked across his face. "You are, indeed. Thank you."

"It was a good note, Bright Eyes."

"It was my daughter's idea," Max said. "Well, not her idea, exactly, just something she said about a fine line between interesting and creepy. I just thought I—" The words failed him now, but they hadn't when he had dictated his note to his friend Beth Rayner back in Michigan and asked her to get the bundle where it was going: *From Max Wendt, aka 'Bright Eyes,' 406-794-1978. I'm not a creep. I'm just out of practice. Hope you like apples.*

"I met your daughter at the hospital, didn't I?" Jenn asked.

"You did, yeah, briefly."

"Did she tell you I was flirting?" Jenn asked.

"Yes. Were you?"

"She sounds like a smart woman."

"She is." He could not strike the damn quaver from his voice.

"I don't ordinarily do that," Jenn said. "Flirting, I mean."

"Don't have a place to store all the apples, huh?"

She laughed, fulsome and unbound by volume. "You are funny. I remember now."

"That's not even my best stuff." *Dammit, I cannot get my voice to stop shimmying.*

"Are you nervous, Max?"

"Monstrously so."

"Don't be."

He swallowed down what had gathered in his throat. "OK."

"You should have my number now."

"I do."

"Don't lose it."

"I won't."

"When will you be back in Chelsea?" she asked.

"Three weeks by the calendar," he said. "But I'm resourceful."

"I bet you are. Let's see how it goes."

"I like that plan."

"Thank you for the apples."

"You're welcome."

"Will you call me in a few days? Mornings are better."

"You can count on it," he said.

"Are you taking care of yourself?"

"Better than ever," he said.

"That's good. Bye, Max."

"Bye."

The fullness of dusk had fallen on him. Max walked toward the bluff, where his car sat, waiting. He still had time for the rest of what he wanted to see, but it was a commodity growing ever more precious. The two-way flow of traffic on the highway had thickened as the last of the daylight faded. Headlights from the comings and goings made crosshatch patterns on everything they touched.

Max walked onto the switchback and made his way up, the imposition only a minor strain. He carried a fullness in his head and in his heart.

It was like Big Bonk had put it those many years ago in Michigan, the first time Max had ever set foot in a pumping station. *It's not hard or complicated*, he had said. *It's the easiest thing in the world, really. You throw open the valves, you give it a push, and you let gravity set the course.* Being barely sprung out of boyhood, Max hadn't grasped the simplicity of the lesson in a larger sense. It would be some time before the concept wrote itself as a simile across his dealings with himself and with other people. The stacking up of years had brought new complications to old relationships. It was often ceaseless and crushing complication, the kind that tended to obscure all but the most dogged moments of grace.

Now, though, he could see it, could see everything behind him arranged in a way he thought he could comprehend, with everything ahead waiting to be found out. Max was far beyond a boy but also, now, in view of being a better man. He wasn't ready to give up on those second chances Alexandra had once told him about. She was his heart, his aspiration, his gratitude, all bound up in one human package. He had to believe she had known what she was saying.

He slipped into the car, backed it out, and pointed it north. To Saco Bay. To Portland. Tomorrow, back to Chicago, and then on to destinations known and unknown.

Even without doing the math, Max could see so many ways all of this could flow.

ACKNOWLEDGMENTS

At the end of a book—as opposed to, say, the end of a pipeline run—it's customary to issue a public thank you to all those who participated in the gestation and the delivery. The recipients of these expressions of gratitude tend to be neatly cleaved into two distinct groups, those who are professional in nature and those who are personal.

My groups spill over, both ways. So...

To Lou Aronica at The Story Plant/Fiction Studio Books, who saw in this story something he wanted to become a part of, and thus let me become a part of what he's building. I'm deeply grateful.

To Nalini Akolekar, my agent, who stood by me patiently for three years as we tried to find the right story to bring to the right editor and publisher. We got there. I wouldn't travel with anyone else.

To Jim Thomsen, for his wise editorial counsel and for his abiding friendship, always.

To Dr. Jim Bentler, for taking time out of one of his rare days off and going over the ins and outs of modern cardiac care with someone he doesn't really know. I'm deeply appreciative. And thanks to Ceci Bentler, who does know me (sorry!), for hooking that up.

To my family—the Lancasters, the Clineses, the Lorellos, the Mottolas. You all have a permanent home in my heart.

To my friends, near and far, I thank you for your support. You've given me far more than I've given you, and all I can say in my defense is that I'm forever stumbling toward grace. I'll see you there.

To the steadfast readers, as well as to the ones my work has yet to meet. Every story starts out as mine. Every story ends up as yours. Thank you.

To the glorious beings who are independent bookstore owners and employees. You are the blood coursing through your communities. Special thanks to the indies in my home state of Montana. What blessings you are.

Most of all, to Elisa. The brightest light of all.

Craig Lancaster
Billings, Montana

CONNECT WITH CRAIG LANCASTER

Website: *www.craig-lancaster.com*
Twitter: *@AuthorLancaster*
Facebook: *www.facebook.com/authorcraiglancaster*
Instagram: *craiggler*